LIFE ON PLANET FUCKET

J. ROBERT BRANDTS

ISBN: 978-1-7347402-2-6 (paperback)
ISBN:978-1-7347402-3-3 (eBook)

Printed in the United States of America

Book Cover Design by ebooklaunch.com

Book Cover Photograph by Jennifer Reed

Visit the author at www.bobbrandtsbooks.com

This book is dedicated to my parents, John and Susan Brandts, who taught me to be tenacious and uncompromising in the pursuit of my dreams, and to never, <u>ever</u> settle for "just okay" with anything that I do.

CHAPTER ONE

My story begins in November of last year and, like most good stories, this one begins with a catastrophe. The catastrophe that initiated this story was a fire; a *house* fire, to be exact. To be even more precise, it was *my* house that I stood and watched burn to the ground last November.

Normally, a story such as this one would involve much wailing and pointing of fingers but, honestly, all I could feel on that night was relief; pure, head-to-toe, skin-to-marrow, sigh-from-the-gut, unfettered relief. Strange, I know, but that's how I felt. So, I stood there and watched as my house burned and all I kept thinking was: "I'm free...finally, I'm free."

The fire itself was also kind of beautiful in its own way. On more than one occasion I became somewhat mesmerized by the fingers of bright orange flames that clawed against the wall of black that was the night sky behind them. Awesome. Powerful. Out of control. Those were all words that crept into my head at one point or another as I watched the blaze devour my house. The hot air would then suddenly whoosh against my face, providing a stark contrast to the cold air that was biting at the backs of my bare legs, and it would break me from my trance.

It had been a particularly cold November in Maple Grove, and all New England for that matter, and all I had been wearing was my version of pajamas, which was a worn-out Red Sox t-shirt and a pair of old running shorts. It wasn't much protection against the elements, and I found myself wishing that I had remembered to grab my LL Bean coat as I was leaving the house. *Shit, I really liked that coat,* I remember thinking. A little voice then whispered in my ear, telling me that my coat wouldn't be the last thing that I would regret leaving behind in the soon-to-be graveyard of possessions that was my house.

I'd always had a funny relationship with things. My ex had always called me a pack rat and I used to drive her crazy with my closets and drawers filled with ever-growing piles of stuff. But tell me that I had to go out and buy a new this or a new that and I would freeze with indecision. "Too many choices," I would say about shopping for a new pair of pants or a new lawnmower. Truth be told, however, was that I'd always felt a certain loyalty to the *old* pair of pants or the *old* lawnmower. They'd given me years of good service and I couldn't stand the thought of just kicking them to the curb at the first signs of old age. What she also didn't understand was that I felt the same way about the people in my life; I prized loyalty above all else. She had obviously never embraced this quality of mine as *I* had ultimately become the old pair of pants that got tossed in the trash in favor of the new pair. But none of that mattered anymore. She was gone, my marriage was over, and now all that stuff that we'd accumulated together would soon be gone too; up in flames just like our relationship.

Looking back now, I realize that the experience of watching my house burn would have been an entirely different one had I not set the fire myself; a very small, yet very significant, detail to my story. I agonized for months over how to best accomplish my chosen goal of Freedom Through Fire and I ultimately decided on a lit cigar in the sofa cushions as the best method for torching my house; it would look accidental while still getting the job done. So, I'd moved my sofa over next to my curtains - because curtains, I remembered reading, made great kindling - lit a cigar, placed it carefully behind one of the sofa cushions and waited for the show to begin. And nothing happened. At first.

The cigar just laid there, its tip smoldering innocently, until I decided to take a more active role. I had to get down on my knees and blow on that cigar, until its tip glowed red, then I tapped it several times so some of the ashes fell to the cushion. Still, nothing happened. It was then that I decided to grab some pieces of newspaper to help the effort. I fanned and blew myself breathless and, just as I was getting ready to go grab some lighter fluid, the small flame popped to life. It had taken more of an effort to get a decent fire going than I had anticipated, and it made me wonder that if a guy as determined as I was to burn my house down had to struggle to get a fire started, how the hell does it ever happen by accident?

But once it got going, I have to say that it wasn't long before the house became an inferno. The flame climbed the curtains quickly - turns out they were right about their kindling-like nature - and it was lapping at the ceiling in no time. Once I was satisfied that the fire had reached the point of no return, I pulled out my cell phone and dialed 911. I did my best to sound anxious and desperate when I spoke with the dispatcher on the other end of the line; I didn't want anyone getting the wrong idea about what had happened. Or, in this case I guess, I didn't want them getting the *right* idea.

I played the role of distraught homeowner when the fire trucks arrived, yelling and screaming until my throat ached. They were absolutely convinced that I had been awoken from a sound sleep by the smell of smoke and I had come downstairs to see my house engulfed in flames. *Poor guy*, they were probably thinking. Typically, it would indeed be a sad story. In my case, it was akin to being paroled from prison.

At one point I closed my eyes and focused on the warm wind blowing on my face. I flashed on how ironic it was that this was the most warmth that I had felt from that house in years. A house that had seen so much happiness in its lifetime had become a joyless box filled with nothing but meaningless possessions. I had been feeling the weight of those possessions for a long time and had finally decided to do something about shedding some of that weight. Selling everything was certainly an idea that I had entertained but, ultimately, I decided that all of that would take too long; I needed to be out from under the weight as soon as possible. A fire, I decided, would be both quicker and more complete. There would be no temptation to keep the maple table from Vermont or the crystal serving dish from my mother; it would all just disappear at once, sparing me the thousands of angst-filled decisions that I would have had to make if I had taken the more conventional route. *It was better this way*, I had convinced myself.

Several times throughout the chaos I smiled inside as I watched the fire work its way through my house, being careful always to maintain my distraught exterior. The firemen worked hard to control the blaze, but their efforts would ultimately be in vain. The house and everything in it were destined to be ash. Just the way I wanted it.

It was on that chilly November night of last year that my life of homelessness began.

CHAPTER TWO

After giving my statement to the police, I spent the night in a local hotel. A neighbor had loaned me some clothes and I stopped at an all-night convenience store to pick up a toothbrush, deodorant, and a few other toiletries. It's kind of funny how even after a large life-changing moment like having my house burn down I still thought about seemingly trivial things like good dental hygiene and keeping body odor at bay.

I awoke the next morning feeling like I had felt the day after signing my divorce papers: I was now free, but it felt like someone had punched me in the gut on the way out of the door marked Freedom. It was all still a mixed bag and I was feeling very disoriented. I guess that was to be expected since it wasn't every day that you put a torch to your life.

I got out of bed and went to the bathroom to splash some water on my face and think about my situation. I was now homeless, that was a fact. Just about everything I owned had been reduced to a pile of smoldering ash. That was another fact. I'd had the presence of mind to take a few things out of the house the day before - things like my car title, some photos, and a baseball autographed by every member of the 1975 Red Sox team - and stash them in a storage locker at the bus station, but everything else was gone. That thought was both exhilarating and sobering at the same time.

After a couple of splashes of cold water, I heard my cell phone ringing and I went to answer it. I picked it up and recognized the number right away. I hit the send button. "Hello Linda," I said into the phone, probably sounding too casual given my past twenty-four hours. But I didn't care how I sounded to this caller.

"Ben?" the frantic voice screamed in my ear. "Is that you? Are you okay?"

"Yes, on all counts," I replied, still sounding casual, as if I didn't have a care in the world.

"What the hell happened last night?" she then asked. "I saw our house on fire on the news this morning!"

"You mean you saw *my* house on the news this morning," I corrected her, my casual tone now gone, replaced by the edgy, irritated tone that I had hoped would burn in last night's fire, along with my sofa and matching bedroom set. But the irritation at my ex-wife was still there, clinging to my gut like a large cancerous growth, and it was going to take more than a house fire to burn it out.

There was a pause on the phone, and I didn't have to see Linda to know that her head was now bowed, and she was gathering herself before speaking again. "Okay, *your* house was on fire," she finally said, her voice sounding less frantic than it had been earlier. It hadn't taken me long to deflect her concern and get her back to being pissed off at me again. I preferred her this way as it put us on equal footing. When she was being nice to me, or concerned about me, it made it very difficult for me to maintain my my-ex-wife-is-an-asshole mojo that I usually carried around with me. The two of us - my Linda-is-an-asshole mojo and I - had been pretty much inseparable for three years now and it had gotten to the point that I felt lost without it. "So, what happened last night?" she asked again.

I started pacing around the room. I was glad that we were going to have this conversation over the phone because, despite all our marital problems, I was never able to lie to Linda. If I ever tried, she always saw right through me. Over the phone I at least had a fighting chance to pull it off. "I don't know," I replied as my leadoff lie.

"Where did it start?" she asked.

"Downstairs somewhere," I replied, happy to be able to tell at least one truth.

"Did the smoke alarm wake you up?"

"Yeah," I said. Lie number two.

"Thank god for that," she said, sounding sincere. "Kylie was scared to death when she saw the house burning on the news."

Kylie. My ten-year-old daughter. The light of my eye. The one true love of my life. "I'm sorry she had to go through that," I replied, which was true. It was now a tie ballgame; two lies to two truths. This wasn't going to be as hard as I thought. "Is she okay now?"

"She will be once I tell her that you're okay."

"Isn't Willie there to give her a nice big reassuring hug?" I asked, not even trying to conceal my disgusted tone. William was Linda's live-in boyfriend, and he also happened to be a co-worker with her in the Journalism Department at the local college where she worked. It had always seemed awfully coincidental to me that within a few weeks of our break-up this guy's name suddenly started popping up.

"Why is it that you have to turn everything into a stupid game of gotcha?" she asked, sounding tired.

"Habit," I shot back.

"Well it's a fucking stupid habit and you ought to think about finding a way to get rid of it."

"Then I'd be fresh out of hobbies," I replied, feeling both satisfied by my cleverness and ashamed by my shitheadedness.

"Is this crap ever going to end?"

"Sure," I replied. "The day that a piano falls on Willie the Worm's head is the day that I drop the act."

There was a pause and then Linda fired an arrow right into my chest. "But I love him, Ben." There was another pause, giving me just enough time to wrestle with the arrow embedded in my chest. Then she fired a second arrow and this one found my heart. "And Kylie is starting to love him too."

Tears welled in my eyes, but I'd be damned if Linda was going to know that. "I gotta go," was all I said. And then I hung up.

I sat on the bed and bawled like a baby. Life fucking sucked.

CHAPTER THREE

Not knowing what else to do with myself, I showered, put on my neighbor's loaner clothes and went to work. I worked at the Valley Beacon, the local newspaper that touted itself as "The Voice of Western Massachusetts." Truth be told, its voice had been quieted to barely a whisper in recent years, thanks to people's shrinking appetites for local news. They wanted to read about war, death, disease and Angelina Jolie's baby, none of which were carried by the Beacon. We tended to focus on local politics, births, weddings, and feature pieces about Farmer Jim and his bumper crop of asparagus. The Beacon's readership had dwindled to the point that there was talk of making the switch from a daily format to a weekly format, which would cut expenses significantly. The great unknown was just how much that format switch would also cut the Beacon's readership. That was a question for Bob Collins - the owner, editor and publisher of the Beacon, as well as my boss - to wrestle with. Bob also happened to be my ex brother-in-law and we'd been friends since high school. You could say that our lives were intertwined in many ways.

When I walked in the front door of the Beacon's offices, I was greeted by a half dozen slack-jawed faces, each looking as if they'd just seen Elvis walk into the Beacon. "Morning everyone," I said as cheerfully as I could muster.

Bob was the first to step forward from the crowd of slack-jaws. "What the hell are you doing in here?" he asked, sounding more concerned than irritated.

"I'm here to work, just like I've done for the past fifteen years."

Bob shifted around on his feet, as if searching for just the right foot position that would allow him to say what he had to say. "We all saw what happened to your house last night, Ben," he said quietly, almost reverentially. "We all feel bad for what happened to you and, well, I'm just not so sure that your being here is a good idea."

"Why? Are you afraid that house-burning is a disease that one of you might catch?" I of course knew what he was saying but I had my reputation as a smart-ass to uphold.

Bob had known me too many years to take the bait. He ignored my sarcastic comment and said, "Why don't you take the day off Ben and go deal with the insurance company and everything else that you have to take care of in a situation like this."

In his own Bob, don't-talk-about-feelings-and-other-uncomfortable-shit way he was giving me permission to go off and grieve my loss - that suggestion was contained in his "and everything else" comment - but what he didn't realize was that I was in more of a celebratory mood than a grieving one. I had been set free. The shackles had been shattered and I was now a free man. No more being tethered to a box filled with a thousand tons of stuff. I could come and go as I pleased because the entirety of my life could now fit into a small bag. It was a time for rejoicing and yet I had to keep my impulse to dance on tabletops in check or risk raising suspicions. As I thought about it, I realized that perhaps Bob was right, and it would be best if I stayed away from people for a while. Dancing on tabletops would not be conducive to making my case as the grieving former homeowner. Besides, I'd forgotten about having to deal with the insurance company. "Okay," I agreed, "maybe you're right."

I tried to force a somber look onto my face, to give the gathered crowd what they expected, and wasn't sure how successful I'd been until they started coming up to me to offer their condolences. One by one they looked me in the eye, told me they were sorry, and then hugged me awkwardly. We had never been a hugging kind of office - a personality trait that started at the top with our editor-in-chief - and it was times like this that our lack of any real connections became apparent. But I dutifully nodded and hugged my way through the line of well-wishers and, after the last hugger had been dispatched, I waved and headed out the door. Bob followed me out and, when we were out of eyeshot of the others, he pulled me into an embrace and said, "I'm so sorry, Ben." It felt like a real hug, the first real hug of the morning as a matter of fact, and it caught me a little off guard. As always, Bob had been careful to make sure nobody saw him showing any displays of favoritism towards me, his friend and ex-relative. Bob had always been careful that way.

"No worries, Bob," I replied, surprised by the sound of a small crack in my voice and an accompanying tingling sensation in my cheeks. *Where did this sudden burst of emotion come from?* I wondered.

We broke the embrace and Bob said, "You sure are taking this better than I thought you would."

Oh oh, I thought. *Was I giving off a non-grieving vibe?* "I guess I'm still in shock," I replied, using the catch-all excuse for situations such as this in order to throw him off the scent.

"Yeah, well I know I'd be a basket case right now if my house had just burned to the ground."

"I guess you just never know how you'll react to something like this until it happens to you."

"Does Linda know?"

I stifled the *who-the-hell-cares?* response that was standing on my tongue, ready to make the leap out of my mouth, and instead said, "Yeah, she knows." Best to keep the response simple in those situations. More words inevitably lead to more trouble.

Bob must have sensed that I was struggling with the reins on some words that were anxious to bolt from the barn, as he quickly changed the subject and asked me, "So where are you going to stay?"

"I've got a hotel room for now."

"You know that you're always welcome to stay at my place." He seemed to sound sincere with his offer.

I thought about his wife, Gail, and their two young children, Jen and Amber, and was tempted for the briefest of moments to take him up on his offer. But then I thought about Linda and Kylie and how often Kylie liked to get together with her two cousins and I quickly realized that me staying in Bob's house would be a tremendously bad idea. "Thanks for the offer Bob," I replied, "but I think I'll just stay in the hotel for a while."

Bob shrugged. "Suit yourself. But remember that it's a standing offer."

"Thanks Bob. I appreciate that."

We both shuffled our feet for a while, feeling uncomfortable with the silence, and then Bob said, "Well, guess I'd better get back to work." He jerked his thumb over his shoulder and added, "Those guys are probably wondering what the hell happened to me."

"Yeah, they're certainly lost without you, Chief," I said, using my chosen work name for him. "And I have to get my butt over to my insurance company so I can see about getting some of that money back that I've been sending their way all these years."

Bob smiled. It was a warm smile. "Good luck with that. And let me know if I can do anything to help."

I nodded. "I will." Bob then gave me another hug - this one feeling more awkward than the first one, perhaps because he'd already put his "Bob the Boss" hat back on - and we said our goodbyes.

It had been less than twelve hours since The Fire but as I walked away from The Beacon, heading towards the Brown and Brown Insurance Company, I was already feeling strangely disconnected from my previous life.

CHAPTER FOUR

I walked into the Brown and Brown Insurance offices for perhaps the third time in my life. They'd been insuring me, my house, my family, and my car for over twenty years and yet I'd stepped foot in their offices less than a handful of times. Who says we live in a low-touch, disconnected world?

I told the polite, well-manicured receptionist who I was and why I was there, and she asked me to have a seat in one of their over-stuffed lobby chairs. There were no *I'm sorry* or *that must have been awful* types of comments. No reaction at all to the man in front of her who had just told her that his house had burned to the ground the day before. I guess she was used to hearing such things in her line of work.

As I sat down in the over-stuffed chair, I realized that I had a similar chair in my living room. Check that: I *used* to have a chair like it in my living room. Even more accurately, I *used* to have a chair like it when I *used* to have a living room. I could see that it was going to take a lot of practice before I fully embraced my state of both homelessness and chairlessness.

"Mr. Weaver?" I then heard a voice say from the direction of the receptionist's desk. I turned and I would have sworn I was looking at Rick Moranis from the movie "Honey, I Shrunk The Kids." He walked over to me with his hand extended and I stood up and shook Rick's hand. It was the first celebrity encounter of my life. "Austin T. Phelps, Mr. Weaver," Rick then said, thus snuffing my brief brush with fame. "It's a pleasure to meet you."

I nodded, still not quite believing that he'd given me his *real* name, and mumbled a "Nice to meet you."

"I'm the claims adjuster who's been assigned to your case, Mr. Weaver," Rick said. "Do you have time for a few questions?"

"Sure."

"Great. Shall we head back to my office?" he asked, holding his arm up as if ushering me through an invisible door. I headed in the direction of his extended arm and kept walking until he said, "It's that next office on your right." I turned into his office which was nothing more than a small gray cubicle in a large maze of cubicles. I'd always thought that an office was a room with a door, walls and a ceiling, but I didn't say a word; I didn't want to be the one to shatter Rick's I-work-in-an-office reality. Rick sat down in his desk chair and I sat down in the lone chair across the desk from him. "So, it sounds like you've had quite the twenty-four hours," he said.

I guess that was insurance agent-ese for, *"I'm so sorry about your loss,"* or *"How are you doing?"* It was better this way because I didn't have to tell any lies or put on false emotional masks. "Yes, I did," I replied with a wry smile.

"I know you have all kinds of concerns about what happens next and I'm here to hold your hand every step of the way, Mr. Weaver."

He sounded earnest but far from sincere. I got the sense that he was reading cue cards that were stapled to the portable wall behind me. "Ben," I said. "You can call me Ben."

Rick smiled a Jehovah's witness type smile - all teeth and no eyes - and that was when I decided that Mr. Austin T. Phelps and I could never be friends. "Ben it is then," he said cheerfully. "And you can call me Austin." *Will do, Rick,* I thought. I found myself feeling somewhat relieved that I wasn't truly in mourning for my recent loss because if I were, I would surely want to reach across the desk and throttle this guy. He reached into his desk, pulled out a file full of forms and said, "So let's get to these forms." He uttered the words with a barely repressed enthusiasm, as if he were a ten-year-old saying, "*So let's get to these birthday presents.*" He sorted the forms into several piles and then, pen now poised, asked me, "So tell me what exactly happened last night."

I went through my elaborate lie in detail, making sure to pause for dramatic effect at key parts, such as when I was shaken from my slumber by a screaming smoke alarm, and when I came down the stairs and saw my beautiful home engulfed in flames. Austin listened without interruption, scribbling notes as I spoke. When I was done with my sad tale, I sat back in my chair and threw out a deep, the-world-is-just-too-much-to-bear sigh.

"So, do you have any idea as to how this fire might have started, Ben?" Austin T. then asked without displaying so much as a flicker of emotion in response to my Oscar-worthy performance. This guy took the phrase "all business" to new heights of dispassion.

I shook my head slowly and stupidly in response to his question. "No, no idea," I said.

He scribbled in some more blanks. "Are you a smoker?" he then asked.

I shook my head. "Nope."

Austin T. smiled his game show host smile. "Good for you," he said. "In my line of work, we like to hear that from our clients."

I returned the smile. *Who gives a shit* what *you think?* I thought. "Filthy habit," I said with a tsk-tsk shake of my head.

"Were you cooking anything last night?" he then asked.

"Nope," I responded. "I ordered out some pizza last night."

"Any electrical problems that you know of in the house?" he asked.

Again, I shook my head. "Nope." I decided I would just keep my answers short and simple since Austin T. didn't seem to be swayed by my extra words and sentiments around the edges. Why waste my breath?

"Were you burning any candles last night?"

"Nope."

"Did you make a fire?"

Not in the fireplace, I thought. "Nope."

"Did you have a pile of old rags stored anywhere in the house?"

"Nope."

"Do you store any flammable liquids in the house?"

"Well, except for the fifty-gallon gas storage tank I keep in the living room, no I don't keep any flammable liquids in the house," I responded dead-pan. My inner smart-ass had a three-question limit for playing it straight and Austin T. had just gone over his limit.

I looked over and saw Austin T.'s eyebrow raise as he continued scribbling for a moment. He then looked up, eyes slightly wide, and his mouth hung open for a couple of beats, until he eventually realized that I was joking. Humor was definitely wasted on Mr. Austin T. Phelps. Once he realized I was kidding the Bob Barker smile returned to his face. "Very funny, Ben," he said. "Of course, we normally discourage joking about serious matters such as this, but I can imagine that you're still somewhat shaken by last night's events and humor may be your way of dealing with all of this." He nodded a few times and said, "I understand."

You don't understand diddly, I thought. "Thanks," I said. "I guess I am still feeling a bit shaken up."

Austin T. threw me one more nod of understanding and then wiped the smile from his face and returned to his forms. "So, where were we?" he asked. "Ah, yes. Do you store any flammable liquids in the house?" he asked again, with the exact same inflections he'd had the *first* time he asked the question.

"Nope," I replied, deciding to bite my tongue for the remainder of the interrogation.

And on it went for another hour, Austin T. asking questions and me uttering mono-syllabic, tell-as-few-lies-as-possible answers.

CHAPTER FIVE

I met my friend, Jim, for dinner that night. He had heard about The Fire and called me to arrange a get-together, but I think he was surprised when I told him "tonight would work fine for me." He was probably hoping for the arrangement of a Phantom Date, the let's-get-together-sometime-real-soon kind of date that materializes one time out of a hundred, maybe a thousand. But I certainly had nothing to do that night, and no place to go, so sitting in a restaurant talking with my good friend Jim seemed like a good way to go. I'm sure he had to do some fast-talking with his wife, Liz, as she wasn't the type who liked last-minute surprises like this. She'd probably had a nice dinner all planned for Jim and their two kids, Jack and Jennie, and above all else Liz liked to "stick to the plan." If I had to pick an antonym for the word "spontaneous" it would be Liz. She was a nice enough woman, but I sometimes had a hard time being around her; I always felt like there was some unspoken list of "do's and don'ts" hanging somewhere that I wasn't privy to and it made me nervous.

But Jim showed up at the restaurant, Old Hampton Tavern - known just as The Tavern to locals - at the appointed time with a smile on his face. I guess even Liz couldn't say no to a last-minute request from a friend whose house had just burned down. Tragedy has its privileges. I, more than anyone else, knew what Jim probably had to go through to keep our dinner date so I stood and gave him a big hug when he walked through the door. "Thanks for coming," I said into his ear.

I could tell that Jim went a little stiff when I hugged him - hugging hadn't ever been a big part of our friendship - but he endured it and said, "No problem," as he pulled away after the briefest of hugs.

"So was Liz okay with you coming tonight?" I asked without thinking. I regretted asking the question as soon as I'd asked it, because I knew it put Jim in an awkward position. The question itself assumed that there was some question as to who wore the pants in his family - though, truth be told, there was no question at all; it was Liz - but it also gave him no easy out in terms of an answer. He could either tell the truth, and come across as being your basic whipped husband, or lie to me and we would both know that he was lying. I wanted to reel the question back in as soon as I'd asked it, but it was too late.

Jim shuffled his feet a little, and then said, "Not at first, but she eventually saw how important this was." He then paused for a beat and added with an awkward smile, "She sends her best to you."

Bless his heart. He'd decided to go for the truth/lie combo; give me enough truth to pull me in and then finish up with a feel-good lie or two. Jim had gotten good at this maneuver, a way to save some face while simultaneously avoiding throwing Liz under the bus in front of his friends. Everyone knew how Liz was, it was hard to keep it a secret, but you'd never hear a bad word about her tumble from Jim's lips. In a strange way, I admired that quality in him. It spoke to his loyalty and I never had to wonder what Jim might have been saying behind *my* back when I wasn't around. The line about Liz sending her best to me was a bit over the top though and almost made me laugh out loud. About the only "best" that Liz probably wanted to send to me right now was her best glare. "Tell her I'm sorry for pulling you away from your family dinner tonight," I said. "I appreciate it."

Jim nodded and then, anxious to change the subject, said, "You wanna grab a seat?"

"Sure." We found a booth next to a window that overlooked the old mill and sat down. I glanced out the window and took note of all the people scurrying in and out of Cooper's Mill, probably doing their Christmas shopping. Like most New England towns, we had a large brick mill on the edge of town that spoke to our industrial past. Cooper's Mill had once been the number one producer of buggy whips in the world, but that market dried up quickly after Henry Ford started rolling out his automobiles, so the mill closed in the early twentieth century. It opened and closed several times through the years, as one manufacturer after another tried to make a go of it making broom handles, furniture, and assorted other things, but it was boarded up for good in the early fifties. Then, about fifteen years ago, someone in New England had the bright idea of turning all these abandoned old mills into retail shops, restaurants, and artisan's studios and Cooper's Mill came back to life. It was an improvement over the dark old mill that I had grown up fearing as a child; rumors had abounded about the various ghosts who patrolled Cooper's Mill and I had believed every one of them. It was still hard for me to step foot in the mill, even with all the brightly lit shops and holiday decorations adorning its exposed pipes and beams.

"So how are you doing, Ben?" I heard Jim ask, pulling my attention away from the shoppers going in and out of Cooper's Mill.

I swiveled my head to face him across the table. "I'm doing just fine," I replied. "All things considered."

Jim shook his head. "I don't know how you're even functioning. Man, I'd be sitting somewhere bawling my eyes out right now."

I flashed on my bawling session that morning in the hotel room. "Yeah, I've done my share of crying," I said, not bothering to tell him that not one of those tears was shed for my lost house. I would trade the love and affections of my daughter for a pile of wood and nails any day of the week.

"Were you fully insured?"

I nodded. "Yep. I just met with my insurance agent this afternoon as a matter of fact."

"So how soon before you get your check?"

"He didn't say. He just asked me a bunch of questions and then said we'd be in touch."

I saw Jim's brow crinkle slightly. "Does he suspect it wasn't an accident or something?"

I shrugged. "I don't know. There's no telling what this guy might be thinking. Austin T. Phelps is one strange duck and I think he lives for this kind of shit."

"That's his name?" Jim asked with a smile. "Austin T. Phelps?"

I returned his smile. "Yep. And the sad part is that the name suits the guy. Did you ever see the movie "Honey I Shrunk the Kids?"

"Are you kidding? Only about twenty times. It's one of Jack's favorite movies."

"Austin T. Phelps could be Rick Moranis's twin in that movie."

Jim laughed. "I'm not sure I would consider that to be a compliment if someone said that about me."

"Me neither. But it's true."

We shared another laugh and then Jim's smile disappeared, replaced by a somber look, as he said, "I just want to tell you that I'm really sorry about what happened to you Ben and that if you ever need a place to stay we have plenty of room for you in my house." He paused for a moment and then added, "I mean that."

I knew Jim was completely sincere with his offer. I also knew there would be no way in hell that I would ever take him up on his offer. Me and Liz under the same roof would not be a good thing. But more than anything else, I knew Jim was sticking his neck out even making an offer such as this. I would bet that he hadn't had a chance to discuss this with Liz yet - he'd barely had enough time to negotiate with her about this dinner date - and chances were good that when he *did* discuss the possibility of his good friend Ben living with them for a while, she would blow a gasket. All things considered, it was a very generous offer on Jim's part. I gave him a warm smile and said, "Thanks Jim. I appreciate the offer. I'll definitely keep it in mind."

Jim gave an emphatic nod and said, "Good."

The waitress then came over to our table and we gave her our drink orders; Jim ordered a beer and I decided on a margarita. I was in search of the warm, smooth buzz that only Rita could give me. Beer made me feel loggy, hard liquor made me loopy, but tequila had its own special way of making me feel like all was right with the world. I needed Rita right now.

"So, what are you going to do now?" Jim asked after the waitress had left.

I shrugged. "I'm not sure. I guess I'm just going to take it one day at a time for a while."

"Are you going to buy another house after the insurance money comes through?"

"I don't know," I lied. "I guess I just want to wait and see how I feel." I knew there was no way in hell I would place another millstone that size around my neck ever again, but it was too soon to say that to anyone, even Jim who I had always considered to be my best friend.

My best friend. I thought about that for a moment and all kinds of images flashed across my brain, most of them from when I was a kid. Back then the term "best friend" really meant something. Your best friend was the guy you could always count on to have your back. He was the guy who was up for anything, anytime, anywhere - all you had to do was call him and he was on your doorstep minutes later. He was the guy you could tell secrets to and trust that they would stay secret. Billy Harris had been my best friend growing up. We had been inseparable from the day we met in Mrs. Doleva's third grade classroom to the day he moved away during the summer before my freshman year in high school. I still missed Billy.

Adult friendships always seemed to leave me wanting more. I think I'd never really let go of the friend measuring stick that I'd used when I was a kid and it was hard, if not impossible, for adult men to measure up to that standard. There were too many responsibilities, commitments, insecurities, and other adult-type things that got in the way. I still longed for the fun, spontaneous, bare-your-soul friendships of my youth and they were nowhere to be found in the adult world. I tried many times over the years to call Jim, Bob or any number of other friends and arrange a fishing trip, or a poker night, or even just to go out for a beer, but they would inevitably have to beg off because they were driving kids to soccer practices or painting their living rooms that night. I eventually gave up trying to be spontaneous and just settled in to the more accepted routine of allowing the wives to book couples dinner parties months in advance, so everyone could plan around it, and savored the friendship scraps that could be gleaned from those infrequent occasions. But I still wanted more.

"So, are you going to rent a place?" I heard Jim ask.

The drinks came and it gave me some time to formulate my response. I took a long drink from my margarita before answering, savoring the warmth as it worked its way down my throat. I could tell right away that Rita had some muscle tonight, which is why I liked ordering margaritas at the Tavern. They never skimped on the tequila and, on this night, that was a very good thing. "I haven't decided yet," I finally replied. "I guess I want to just take some time to digest all of this before I make a decision."

Jim nodded as if he understood but I could see in his eyes that he didn't really understand. I knew without a doubt that if it was Jim's house that had burned down last night, he'd have been out looking at new houses all day today and he would have slapped down earnest money on a house before the sun went down. "So, what about clothes and stuff? Did you save *anything* from the fire?"

Funny, but the first thing I flashed on was my autographed baseball. "A few things," I said. "You know, pictures and stuff like that."

Jim flashed a wry smile. "I don't know what I'd grab first in a situation like that. I know the pat answer when someone asks you that question is that you'd grab your photo albums, because pictures are irreplaceable and all that, but when it came right down to it, I wonder what I'd try to save."

I saw a flash of the Old Jim - the one I'd met in college who was a free thinker and loved a good debate - and I tried to keep him out to play with me. "What if I told you I grabbed my autographed baseball from the 1975 Red Sox team?"

Jim smiled a broad smile. "I'd tell you that you were a very smart man and that I admired your priorities."

I threw him an exaggerated nod, as if nodding to royalty, and said, "Why thank you."

"And did you grab your baseball card collection too?" he then asked.

My heart sank. *Shit.* My baseball card collection was now on the regret-that-I-didn't-save-it list along with my LL Bean coat. "No, I didn't," I replied meekly. "The box was in the basement and I didn't have time to go down there." It was true that the box was in the basement, but it was a definite lie that I didn't have time to go down there. I'd had plenty of time to grab that box, but I had been in such a hurry to torch my house that I hadn't thought things through very well. I thought about my 1969 Mickey Mantle card - with the white lettering instead of the usual yellow, which made it much rarer and thus more valuable - and my Nolan Ryan, Johnny Bench and Reggie Jackson rookie cards, all worth thousands of dollars, and I nearly wept. More than the monetary value, those cards represented a piece of my youth, the piece that I strove every day to keep alive, and to lose them felt like I had lost a chunk of my insides.

"That's too bad," Jim said. "I know how much those cards meant to you, Ben."

Hearing Jim say those words suddenly made me feel silly. My entire house just burned down, and he was trying to console me over the loss of a box full of old baseball cards. "No worries," I said with a wave of my hand. "I probably should have gotten rid of those cards years ago anyway, when they had peaked in value. There are certainly bigger things to be worrying about." The words didn't ring true as I uttered them.

Jim looked at me for a second, as if assessing the veracity of my answer, and then asked, "Does Linda know about the fire?"

Why the hell is everyone so concerned about Linda?!?! I thought. I took another long pull from my margarita and simply said, "Yeah, she knows."

Jim had been around the block with me enough times on the Linda issue to know to keep his distance - if I brought it up it was fair game, otherwise keep your Linda questions and comments to yourself - so he did a quick change of topic. "You don't seem too broken up about the whole thing, Ben. Are you still just in shock?"

Jesus, what do people want from me? I thought. *Rending of clothes and uncontrolled sobbing 24/7?* I decided to go with a diversionary tactic, which was a personal strength. "In shock about what? About Linda?" I asked, knowing perfectly well that he wasn't asking about that at all. "Hey, that happened a long time ago and..."

Jim cut me off with a hand raised in a stop sign. "Stow it, bro," he said. "You know perfectly well that I wasn't talking about Linda. But if you don't want to talk about it, hey that's fine with me."

I stopped talking and finished the rest of my margarita in one large gulp. I could already feel Rita working her way into my head and everything started to soften around the edges. I don't know if it was the tequila or not, but I decided to wander a little way down the Truth Path with Jim. "To be honest," I began tentatively, "I'm feeling a little bit of relief right now and I'm trying to figure out why that is."

I looked over at Jim to try to gauge his reaction but saw nothing obvious. He considered my words for a moment and then said, "I guess I don't understand why you'd be feeling relieved at just having lost everything you own."

I'd give him a few more steps down the Truth Path. "Maybe it's because owning all that stuff had been weighing on me more heavily than I realized," I replied, feeling more emboldened by Rita's presence in my brain. "Maybe all that stuff has been holding me back and now I have a chance to explore new worlds of opportunity."

"You're starting to sound like you *wanted* this fire to happen," he said, sounding bewildered.

Oh, oh, I thought. *That's far enough. Time to change directions.* I decided to wander away from any discussion of the house fire on the Truth Path and instead head over to a different part of the same trail, one that spoke to the reasons *behind* my decision to torch the house. "Let me ask you a question, Jim," I said after ordering a second margarita from the waitress. "When was the last time you had fun?" I raised my hand, telling him to hold off on giving me his answer right away. "I'm not talking about garden variety fun here, where you and Liz go out to dinner and a movie or something like that." I leaned forward over the table and, with all the conviction I could muster in my voice and eyes, said, "I'm talking about balls-out, hold-nothing-back, laugh-until-your-gut-hurts, fun here. The kind where the smile is still on your face the following morning and no matter how much your head hurts the smile won't leave." I leaned back in my chair, satisfied that I'd asked the question exactly the way I wanted to, and raised my hand in a way that told him to go ahead and give me his answer.

Jim hesitated. I knew it would be a tough question to answer for a middle-aged man with a wife and kids. There are so many forces conspiring against having fun in a man like Jim's world - from work to home projects to the omnipresent honey-do lists -

and it's the unusual man who can allow true fun to sneak into the small cracks of his over-scheduled life. "Well," he began weakly, "there was the trip we took to Cape Cod last summer. *That* was a lot of fun."

"For who?" I asked. "For you? Or are you transposing the question onto your kids and simply telling me that *they* had fun? Because I seem to remember you coming back from that trip looking more tired than you did when you left."

"That's just because it had been a long drive back," he replied, not sounding at all convincing.

My second margarita arrived at the table and I took a long drink. Feeling more emboldened by Rita's soothing embrace, I started talking before considering my words. Sometimes that can be a bad thing, as words get shared that are often better staying locked away. But I felt like we were heading in a good direction and I didn't want to chicken out by veering to one side or the other just because I was afraid that I might make Jim uncomfortable. He needed to hear these words. Christ, *I* needed to hear these words. "It wasn't the long drive, Jim," I said with conviction. "You know that, and I know that. It was the fact that you spent a week of your life making sure everyone else was comfortable and having a good time and you forgot to ask yourself the all-important question: what do *I* want to do?"

"That's not true," he protested. "There was an afternoon where I went off to watch a Cape League game by myself over in Orleans. It was a beautiful day and I got to enjoy a good baseball game, complete with beer, hot dogs and Cracker Jack."

I noticed Jim's jaw set and he gave a barely perceptible triumphant nod of his head as he sipped his beer, as if he was thinking that he'd just put me in my place. He was in for a big surprise if that's what he was thinking. "I'm willing to bet that you spent that entire game feeling guilty because Liz had given you a hard time for leaving her and the kids alone for an afternoon." I saw Jim start to protest and I held my hand up in a stop sign. I knew he was going to try to defend Liz and I didn't want to hear it, so I decided to make a quick right turn on the conversational course. "Even if Liz *had* given you her heartfelt blessing," *which I know she didn't* I thought, "and you didn't feel guilty about going to the game, there's still the matter of deciding whether or not that particular experience would fall into the balls-out-fun category."

I could see that Jim's mind was scrambling for a response. On the one hand he probably wanted to try to put me in my place for my Liz comment. But he knew that if he did that, he would just be opening himself up to additional Liz comments and that would not be a good thing because, deep down, Jim knew I was dead on right about Liz. On the other hand, he was probably having a hard time coming up with a worthy response to my question about balls-out fun and that was making him feel uncomfortably exposed. Nobody liked to admit that their life was no fun. I'd put him in a tough spot. "Well Mr. High Adventure," he finally said with a mocking tone, "why don't you tell me about *your* last balls-out fun experience."

He had decided to go on the offensive. Good move, Jim. "I'm glad you asked," I replied. Just then the waitress came over and we both ordered some food. I also ordered another margarita. I noticed that Jim was still sipping on his first beer. It looked like I would be heading into The Jungle alone tonight.

I shifted in my seat and then jumped into my story. "I'm thinking that my last balls-out fun night was also yours," I began. Jim threw a confused look at me and I continued. "Do you remember that small apartment I lived in for a while after we'd graduated? Down there on lower Elm Street?"

An *aha* look came over his face. "Yeah, I remember that place," he said. "You had it set up like you were expecting a party to break out at any minute."

I smiled. "Yeah, I did. And the great part was that I was usually right." My mind quickly drifted back twenty years and I was once again standing in my place on 321 Elm Street. I had rented it from a friend's father immediately following graduation from UMass, knowing that my parents wanted no part of me returning to the family home, and it quickly became known as The Party House. The place started out simply enough - a couch, a bed, a few beanbag chairs - but over time friends started donating things to "the cause;" the cause being the creation of a place where they could come for kick-ass parties. And 321 Elm Street delivered. Within a few months I had a foosball table, a ping-pong table, a pinball machine, every kind of bong imaginable and two entire fridges dedicated to nothing but beer. It was a twenty-something's dream-come-true.

"And do you happen to remember the night that will go down in history as the last hurrah for 321 Elm Street?" I asked.

Jim started to look a little uncomfortable. "Actually, I wasn't there that night," he said sheepishly. "I was out with Liz that night. But I heard about it later from some guys. It sounded like quite the bash."

I was stunned. "What do you mean you weren't there that night? Of course you were there. We used to talk about that night and you always talked about it as if you were there."

Jim flashed an awkward smile. "I lied." He took a sip from his beer. "You'd always assumed that I was there that night and, well, I just never corrected you. It sounded like so much fun and I wanted everyone to think that I was there too, enjoying the fun." He let out a wry chuckle. "It had gotten to the point at one time that I actually started to believe that I had been there. It's funny how if you tell a lie often enough it can almost become truth, in your own mind at least."

I shook my head. "Damn. Your little lie must have gotten into my head too because I could have sworn that I have a picture in my head of you standing half-naked next to the ping-pong table, drunk as hell."

"Nope, not me," Jim said. "Must have been another good-looking friend of yours."

I waved it off. "Anyway, back to my point," I said. "That night was the last night that I remember having true, balls-out fun. It was wild, it was out of control, and, once my friend's father got wind of it, it was also the last party that house probably ever saw. He tossed me out of the apartment the following week and the whole place got turned into condos filled with old farts."

"Like us?" Jim asked.

I smiled and nodded. "Exactly like us," I replied. A brief silence then fell between us, perhaps to honor the memory of 321 Elm Street, or perhaps to mourn the fact that twenty years had passed so quickly. "Twenty years," I finally said, my voice trailing off. I looked over at Jim. "Can you believe that it's been twenty years since I lived in that place?"

"On one hand, yes I can," he replied. "It seems like a lot has happened between then and now. Marriage, kids, loss of hair," he said with a chuckle. "But on the other hand, I could close my eyes and put myself back there in a heartbeat. I can still see everyone's faces from back then and remember specific conversations we'd had."

This was the Jim I loved; the thoughtful, reflective one who too often stayed hidden away, afraid to come out and play. "Do you remember Derrick Lind?" I asked.

He laughed out loud. "Derrick Lind. Yeah, I remember Derrick Lind. He was the unofficial drug czar of UMass back then."

I nodded. "Yeah, that he was. He was also the guy who brought the magic mushrooms to The Last Hurrah Party and those little buggers are what helped to make that night so damned much fun."

"I'm sorry I missed that," he said, almost sounding sincere.

"Yeah, me too," I agreed. "I would have liked to have seen you on mushrooms. I'll bet you'd be a whole lot of fun."

31

"What? I'm not any fun now?" he asked half-jokingly.

I could tell that he was fishing for an affirmation from me, but I was in no mood to give him one that just plain wasn't true. "Actually, you can be a bit of a stick-in-the-mud sometimes." I saw his face drop and I quickly decided to back-pedal a little bit on my comment. "Don't get me wrong, you can have your moments." I quickly scanned my now-fuzzy brain for the right words. "I just think that all of us are so damned concerned with being responsible that we've forgotten how to have fun."

Jim's face perked up a little bit, but I could see that he was still feeling hurt. "And what's so wrong with being responsible?" I could tell by Jim's tone that the fun, playful Jim had run for cover and the good, responsible Jim was now back at the helm.

I took a deep drink from my margarita. "Nothing is wrong with being responsible. But if that's all you are, it can make for a pretty damned unsatisfying life." I leaned forward to add emphasis to what I was about to say. "Do you ever get the feeling that you're nothing more than a well-trained house pet?"

Jim's face scrunched up. "What the hell are you talking about?"

I leaned back again and sighed. "I just feel sometimes like I've been trained to do exactly what my master wants me to do and I never think about what *I* want to do, and I can't help but think that that's how the average Golden Retriever feels."

Jim chuckled. "So, you feel like a dog, eh?"

I nodded. "Sometimes, yeah I do. Don't you?"

"Can't say that I do," he replied quickly, almost *too* quickly.

"You don't feel like you're always thinking about what your master wants? And that you are always working to get that next little doggie treat tossed your way or maybe that next scratch behind the ears?"

Jim shook his head. "No, I don't." He paused for a beat, then asked, "And who the hell is the master in this little doggie fantasy of yours?"

"All the bosses I've ever had for one."

"Bob?" Jim said, sounding incredulous.

I nodded. "Yep. First and foremost, Bob is always my boss. He's the guy who signs my paycheck so that means he has the power to control my life and that means I always have to be aware of his temperature towards me." I paused for a moment to let Jim digest that thought and then added, "There are other masters too."

"Who?"

"My parents to some extent," I said, "though their influence seems to be lessening with each passing year." I saw Jim nod and then I stepped into the arena that I'd wanted to be in when I first picked up this thread of conversation. "And then there's the most influential master of them all," I said mysteriously.

"Who's that? God?"

He had a smirk on his face, as he knew full well my stance on God and religion, but I ignored his humorous guess and said, "Linda."

"Linda? Christ Ben, you guys aren't even married anymore."

I nodded. "I know that. But that doesn't mean she no longer has any influence over me. Same as my parents, it gets less with each passing year that we're apart but it's still there." I decided it was time to toss it all back into Jim's lap. "Don't you feel like Liz runs your life sometimes? Like she's the sole architect and interpreter of the Master Plan and she just tells you what to do, where to be, and who you spend your time with while you stumble along from one responsibility to the next?"

"If that were true," he replied, "I certainly wouldn't be here right now."

"So, you *did* have to fight for this dinner with me," I shot back. His silence told me everything I needed to know. "That just proves my point," I said, feeling like I was now on a roll. "Christ, you had to fight with Liz just to get some time alone with a friend who just lost his house in a fire, Jim. What if I had called you and said that I was just feeling a little down in the mouth? Would you have fought as hard to see me then? My guess is probably not. And how many small desires like that just get dismissed because you don't have the energy or inclination to go through all the hassle to get what you want, when you want it?"

He shrugged, looking a little defeated. "Hey, everything's a trade-off," he said. "When I got married and had kids, I knew that I'd be giving up some of the freedoms that I'd had when I was younger. That's just the way it is."

"But why does it have to be that way? Why can't we have the best of both worlds?"

"Because between work, the house, Liz and the kids there isn't a whole lot left over for other things," he replied, not sounding too convinced by his own words. "I vowed that I wouldn't be the kind of Dad who never spent time with his family and that requires a big commitment."

"But there's a huge spectrum of possibilities between the words never and always," I said, noticing that the "s" in always suddenly had an "h" added to it. Rita was starting to grab hold of my tongue. "What's wrong with just saying fuck it once in a while and turning your back on responsibility long enough to have a little fun?"

Jim looked side to side, scanning the restaurant to see if anybody was listening in on our conversation. I think the fuck it comment made him uncomfortable. "What the hell has gotten into you?"

"Besides a few Ritas," I replied, raising my now half-empty glass, "I guess what's gotten into me is a feeling that life is passing me by and I'm tired of being a spectator. I'm no longer satisfied with always riding the brake on my life. I want to punch the accelerator for once and see how it feels to speed off recklessly into an unknown future."

"Very poetic," he said sarcastically. "But not very practical for those of us who are still married and raising kids at home."

It was a low blow, and Jim knew it. But I was feeling no pain, so I steamed forward. "Just because you have kids in the house doesn't mean you can't say fuck it once in a while." I had intentionally added emphasis and volume to the words "fuck it" just to make him squirm a little more.

It worked. He did his sideways scan again and then said, "I think you've had too much to drink and…"

I didn't let him finish. "C'mon Jimbo," I said. "You can't do it if you can't say it." I leaned forward. "Repeat after me." I raised my finger as if it were a mini conductor's baton and said loudly and clearly, emphasizing each word as I spoke, "Fuck it…fuck it…fuck it." I felt a strange sensation surge through me after I finished saying the third fuck it and attributed it to Rita. She had the helm now and I was powerless to stop her.

Jim grabbed his coat and started to put it on. "That's it. I'm outta here."

"Oh, come on Jim," I pleaded. "We're just talking here. There's no need to get your undies in a bunch."

He finished putting on his coat, pulled it straight with added gusto, which told me that he was angry, and said, "You're drunk, and I have to get home now."

"Stay for one more drink," I begged. "I'll be good."

He looked at his watch. "I told Liz I'd be home by 8:30 and it's just about that time now."

I took another sip of Rita and then let out an involuntary "Woof!" I regretted it as soon as I said it, but Rita had put a gag in my internal editor's mouth which meant there was now zero delay between what I thought and what I said. Dangerous ground to be on for sure.

The woof comment pissed Jim off, I could see that immediately. He opened his mouth to say something but seemed to change his mind and just shook his head instead. I guessed that it was probably a good thing that *his* internal editor was still gag-free and on the job. "I'm sorry for what you've been through,

Ben," he said with surprising sincerity, given what I had just put him through. "And I want you to know that I'm willing to help in any way that I can." He didn't wait for a response as he then said, "Good night, Ben" and turned to go.

"Thanks Jim," I shouted after him. "And give some thought to those fuck its that we were talking about," I added, unable to prevent Rita from putting me in an even deeper hole with my friend.

After he was gone, I sat by myself for a few minutes, going over everything we had talked about as best I could with a brain that didn't want to sit still. I felt like I was soaring through the tavern and I just closed my eyes to enjoy the ride for a while. When I opened my eyes, I was surprised to see a woman seated across from me. She was smiling and I noticed a large tattoo on the top of her left breast. She wore a lot of make-up and her hair was all over the place, in a way that was popular back in the eighties. I couldn't take my eyes off her tattoo though. It was a coiled snake and its head was positioned in a way that made it look like it was looking down her cleavage. The small, clingy top she wore emphasized both the tattoo and her breasts and something told me that that was no accident. I wasn't complaining.

"Hi," the woman said. "My name's Marsha." She held her hand out above the table and I shook it. She held both my hand and my gaze a little longer than normal and it suddenly dawned on me that she was flirting with me.

"Ben," I replied. "Nice to meet you." I returned her smile in a way that I hoped would tell her that I was both intrigued and interested. I hadn't had much practice with women since my divorce; as a matter of fact, I hadn't had sex with a woman other than Linda for over twenty years. But Rita was in control and any inhibitions I would have normally felt in a situation like this had been snatched up by Rita and tucked in some internal closet. They would return later for sure, but for now I was a man without fear. I smiled to myself as I heard a small internal voice whisper, *"Fuck it."*

CHAPTER SIX

I awoke the next morning feeling like cotton balls had been stuffed in my mouth and large rocks had been stuffed in my head; rocks that wanted to move around a lot and pound incessantly against the inside of my skull. After getting my bearings, and seeing that I was in my hotel room bed, my head turned toward the sound of some not-so-gentle snoring to my right. I looked over and saw Marsha laying next to me, her mascara and lipstick-smeared face looking much different to me than it had the night before. I could see now, with a little more daylight and a little less influence from Rita, that she had to be on the downward slide to sixty. She was naked from the waist up and, without the help of her push-up bra, her breasts splayed sideways, obviously having succumbed to the laws of gravity long ago. I glanced at the snake tattoo above her left breast and I noticed that he was now looking a little stretched and faded; what had seemed exotic to me last night now looked sad and pathetic. As a matter of fact, now that Rita had loosened her grip on me, everything about Marsha seemed pathetic to me. She was obviously an older woman struggling to hold on to the last remaining scraps of her youth and I'm not sure there was anything sadder and more pathetic than that. Check that: the only thing sadder than that was a middle-aged man getting drunk on tequila and then *sleeping* with the sad, pathetic woman with the faded tattoo.

I got out of bed as quietly as I could, being careful not to awaken Marsha, and headed to the bathroom. I emptied my bladder and then went to the sink to splash some water on my face. The cold water felt good. I toweled off then looked in the mirror and mumbled to myself, *"Note to self: don't be so quick with the fuck-its when you're fucked up."* Rule #1 for my new life.

I popped a few Advil and then sat on the toilet to try to re-create the events from the night before. There were definitely a few blank spots in my memory. I certainly remembered Jim leaving in a huff. And I recalled mine and Marsha's initial flirtations. Then came several more margaritas and I could barely recall the stumble back to the hotel. I also couldn't pull up a whole lot of memory around mine and Marsha's Rita-inspired roll in the sack. Seeing her this morning, that was probably a good thing. I gave myself a small mental kick in the ass for having my first non-Linda screw in over twenty years with a woman who was probably almost twenty years older than me but who *thought* she was twenty years younger. *Was it any good?* I then wondered. I tried to remember something, *anything*, that would have given me a clue as to whether I enjoyed myself but there was nothing. A little kissing, a little groping, and then blackness. *Did we even do anything?* I wondered. Then I heard some moaning coming from the bedroom and I shot to my feet.

"Oohhh," I heard Marsha groan. "Where am I?"

I took a deep breath and reached for the doorknob; it was time to face the music. I strode into the room with a forced smile on my face and said, "Well good morning there, sleepyhead." *Sleepyhead?* Christ, I never even used that word with Kylie when she was growing up. *Keep it together,* I thought. *Just get her up and out and then we can all just go on with our lives.*

Marsha looked at me, blinked a couple of times, then smiled sleepily as she said, "Oh yeah, you."

"Ben's the name," I said with more indignation in my voice than I had intended to use. *What? She can't even remember my name?*

"Yeah, Ben," she said. "What time is it Ben?"

I glanced at the alarm clock next to the bed. "Eight thirty," I replied.

She sat up, threw off the covers, and stretched. I noticed the snake do a little dance as she stretched. "That's great," she said. "I promised my grandkids that I would pick them up at ten and take them to the park. I'd hate to be late."

Grandkids?!?! I thought. *Christ, I just slept with a fucking grandma!!!* "You're a grandmother?" I asked, unable to hold back the question that had shot from my brain.

She smiled broadly. "Three times over, with one more on the way." She must have seen my face drop as she added, "Don't worry there, Ben. There's no law against having a little fun with a grandmother."

Christ, a grandma! I repeated in my brain. *What's next? Sex with nuns?* "It's not that," I lied. "It's just that, well, I can't remember a whole lot from last night," I finally said. It wasn't what was truly on my mind, but at least it wasn't another lie.

She smiled a coquettish grin - well, as coquettish as she could muster under the lipstick and mascara-smeared circumstances - and purred, "So you're wondering if you were any good, is that it?"

Well yes, I was *wondering that,* I thought. "No, not really," was what I said. "I was more wondering how we got from the Tavern to here."

"We drove in my car," she replied. "And, for the record," she added with a small smile, "you were great."

Okay, I admit it, that made me feel good. I'd never been a very confident lover. I tended to assume that everyone else had more knowledge, experience, and techniques in bed than I did and that caused me to approach new sexual situations with much trepidation. One of the many advantages to my marriage to Linda was that she understood, and accepted, my less-than-Latin-lover-like approach to sex. We'd found that comfort zone together in bed and, while not take-you-to-the-moon thrilling, it had been satisfying. I'd hesitated to jump into that realm with anyone else since my divorce because of my internal doubts. Until last night. With Grammy Marsha. Rita had obviously taken care of any hesitations I might have had. "I wish I remembered more of it," I confessed while rubbing my temples.

"A few black spots, eh?" she asked as she climbed from the bed. She strode to the bathroom, naked, seemingly without a care. There was no self-consciousness as she walked in front of me and I thought back to how Linda, my wife of almost twenty years, would have never done that. She'd always hated her body and she worked hard to keep it covered as much as possible, even in front of me, her husband. "I don't even like to see *myself* naked," she would say. I looked Marsha up and down as she headed to the bathroom and saw that she was in decent shape for a grandmother of three, almost four. "Like what you see?" she suddenly asked, her back still to me.

The question caught me by surprise, and I felt a little embarrassed at having been caught checking her out. I decided to try to play it cool and quickly responded, "Yeah, you're in damn good shape for a grandma."

She turned to look at me. "Believe me honey, I work at it every single day." She then disappeared into the bathroom and closed the door behind her.

Honey?!? Now she was starting to *sound* like a grandma! I heard the shower go on, so I headed over to the nightstand and picked up my cellphone. I dialed the Beacon, got Bob's voice mail, and left a message telling him that I'd need another day to get things in order with the insurance company. That was a lie, but it was the shortest, most easily understood, way to say that I wasn't ready to go back to work just yet. It dawned on me as I hung up that I'd been doing a lot of lying in my new life. Or was it that I was telling just as many lies but I was just more aware of it now. Either way, if my name were Pinocchio, I would be hard-pressed to touch the end of my nose right about now.

I got dressed in my one and only set of clothes - borrowed clothes at that - and turned on the TV to kill some time while Marsha showered. I put it on some news show, sat down in my one chair, and didn't really listen to anything they were saying; I was focused on trying to formulate the best way to tell Marsha that our new relationship wasn't going to go beyond today. I knew that women didn't like to be viewed as nothing more than a one-night stand, but I didn't see a future in Ben and Marsha, and it would be best to just say that up front.

I heard the shower turn off and I started shifting uncomfortably in the chair. She came out of the bathroom and, still naked, was toweling her hair off. I felt a twinge of admiration for her, that she could feel so at ease in front of a man she'd just met the night before. "So, we have to talk," she said as she dropped the towel.

"Yes, we do," I agreed, thankful that she had gotten the ball rolling, though I doubted she was going to like the direction in which I eventually rolled that ball.

"I had a great time with you last night, Ben," she began. *Oh oh, here we go,* I thought. "You seem like a nice guy," she continued. *Poor old lonely girl has fallen for me.* "But I just want to make sure you're not thinking this is the start of a relationship or anything like that." *Huh?* "Truth is, I just needed a good fuck last night and after overhearing what you said to your friend at the Tavern, I figured that you might be a good bet." She smiled. "And it looks like I was right."

I'm sure my face betrayed every bit of shock that I was feeling, but I couldn't help it; I *was* shocked. *She's dumping* me! was all I could think. She must have interpreted my shock as hurt as she quickly added, "Now don't go getting all upset on me here." She continued to towel off her head. "We had a good time and all," the headless voice said from beneath the towel, "but I'm just not looking for anything permanent right now." She dropped the towel. "I like my life just the way it is, and I don't want a man coming into it and trying to rearrange my furniture, if you know what I mean." She smiled.

Her little speech had given me time to gather myself and my shock had morphed into curiosity. "How old are you Marsha?" I asked.

She didn't hesitate, didn't try to play the how-old-do-you-*think*-I-am? game, as she responded, "I'm fifty-eight years young."

"And where's your husband in this whole picture?" I asked, figuring that with all those grandkids there must have been a husband in the picture at one point.

"He's at home right now," she said as she reached for her clothes on a nearby chair and started to put on her bra.

Her casual tone surprised me, given what she had just said. Maybe I'd misinterpreted what she meant, so I asked, "Home as in his *own* home, or home as in the home that the two of you share?"

"The second one," she said, struggling to get her two breasts lined up the way she wanted them in the bra.

"You're still *married*?" I then blurted out, once again unable to conceal my shock.

She looked up, seemingly taken aback by my tone, and stopped adjusting her breasts for a moment. "What's the problem, Ben? This is a question that you're deciding to ask *now*, after the night we just had? I would think that if you had a strong moral feeling about the whole infidelity thing you might have asked a few more questions last night, before jumping in the sack with me." She then resumed her breast adjusting.

I felt confused and embarrassed. But in the great male tradition, rather than express any of those feelings to her I went with a smoke screen of anger. "If anyone should have a moral responsibility here it should be *you*," I said forcefully. "You're the one with a husband at home, not me. And you were the one who sought *me* out, remember?" I could feel my anger building and I did nothing to check it. "And where the hell is your wedding ring?" I asked, pointing at her hand. "If you're so damned married why aren't you wearing a ring?"

Marsha looked down at her left hand and played with her ring finger. "You got me there, Ben," she said softly. "You're right, it was all my fault." Her voice had taken on an entirely different tone; she sounded tired, almost defeated, as she said, "I absolve you of any blame for what happened last night." Then she reached for her shirt and started to put it on.

Now I felt like shit. "I'm sorry," I said. "You just surprised me with the whole husband thing, that's all."

Marsha looked up and I saw a wry smile on her face. "Wow, that's something different," she said. "A man who apologizes. Where'd you learn that little trick?"

I felt relieved to be on to a different topic, even it meant allowing her to throw my entire gender under the bus. I shrugged. "It came to me late in life," I replied.

She nodded her approval. "Good for you," she said. "That'll get you sex with a woman quicker than any roses or chocolate ever could."

I smiled. "Good to know," I said. "I'll keep that in mind."

Marsha hiked up her skirt, zipped it, and then said, "I know I said that I don't want a relationship right now, but that doesn't mean I've stopped making friends in my life." She stopped adjusting her clothes and stepped over to me, her hand extended. "How about you and I be friends, Ben?"

I took her hand in mine and shook it gently. Our eyes exchanged smiles. "That sounds good to me," I replied. "I can always use a new friend."

Marsha nodded and dropped my hand. "Me too," she said. "And Ben?" she then said, her look turning more serious.

"Yeah?"

"Our first rule of friendship is going to be that if you ever see my face looking like it did this morning, with mascara and lipstick smeared every which way, that you must alert me of this situation immediately." She looked me in the eye and arched her eyebrow. "Deal?"

I smiled. "Deal," I agreed.

"And Ben?" she added.

"Yeah?"

"Don't beat up on yourself about the whole husband thing." She smiled warmly and reached over to stroke my arm. "Trust me when I tell you that there are extenuating circumstances and you shouldn't be so quick to put yourself into the home-wrecker category."

I returned her smile, though I know it was a weak one. I was still having a hard time believing that I'd just slept with a married woman. "No worries," I said bravely. "I'm just glad the guy doesn't own a gun." It was my attempt at being funny and flip, but I could tell right away that the attempt had fallen flat on its face.

Marsha's eyes went to the ceiling and I could see tears forming in her eyes. "Yeah, lucky for us," was all she said, though I could tell that there were all kinds of words hidden behind those words. She then took a deep breath, let it out slowly, wiped her eyes, and said, "Look, I gotta get going or I'm going to be late meeting my grandkids."

I shuffled my feet uncomfortably. "It was a pleasure meeting you, Marsha," I said, deciding to keep it simple or risk saying something stupid again.

"Likewise," she said, the warm smile returning to her face. She headed to the door and opened it but paused for a second before stepping through. She turned towards me and, looking down at her front, said, "The only problem with these one-night stands is that I have to wear my whoring clothes out into the daylight the following morning." She rubbed her hands down her front. "Funny how my evening eyes love what my daytime eyes can't stand," she said more to herself than to me. She looked up at me, smiled and shrugged, and then headed out the door with a wave. "See ya, Ben," she said over her shoulder.

"See ya, Marsha," I replied.

And thus ended my first encounter with the inimitable Marsha Graves.

CHAPTER SEVEN

"Mister Weaver?" the voice on the phone asked. It was early afternoon and I'd just arisen from a much-needed nap. Rita was still in my system and she was having a hard time letting go of my brain.

"Yeah," I replied, trying not to sound as groggy as I felt.

"Austin T. Phelps here," the voice said.

"Yeah," I replied again, thinking that he was probably the last person in the world I wanted to be talking to at that moment. Check that: Willie the Worm would be the last person on that list and Austin T. would be a close second.

"I was just looking over some of the preliminary reports and I was wondering if I could ask you a few questions."

"Fire away," I said, not intending the pun.

Austin T. paused for a second on the other end. "I was actually hoping that you wouldn't mind coming in here to my office to talk."

Yes, I would mind very much, I thought. "Sure, no problem," I said. "When?"

He cleared his throat. "Would *now* be inconvenient?"

Now would be tremendously inconvenient. "I'll be there in twenty minutes."

After a quick shower and shave it was closer to a half-hour later that I strode into the Brown and Brown Insurance agency, but nobody seemed to mind. Austin T. led me back to his office cubicle and we sat down. He shuffled a few papers and I thought to myself just how happy he looked. This couldn't be good news for the home team. "I was wondering," he began "if you could walk me through the sequence of events the night of the fire once again for me."

"Why?" I asked, not liking the sound of this.

I didn't know Austin T. very well but I could tell that he was the type of guy who was a lousy liar. He was the kind of guy who would rather pound a nail into his big toe than utter something he knew to be false and I could see that he was struggling with what to say next. It was bound to be a lie. "I, uh, just want to be sure that I got everything right," he finally said, looking a lot like a kid who was swearing that he didn't know *how* that window got broken.

I decided to push him a little bit. "So why don't you just read back what I told you yesterday and I'll correct any mistakes that I hear," I said calmly.

That one threw him for a loop. He looked down at the papers on his desk, then looked up at me, obvious distress bouncing in his eyes. "I, uh, don't want to put any words in your mouth," he said uncomfortably.

"But they're all *my* words," I pointed out, "so what's the problem?"

Austin T. squirmed in his chair and then his face suddenly changed. The distress and discomfort disappeared, and it was replaced by the old Jehovah's Witness detached smile and eyes. He had his game face back on and I sensed that *our* little game was now over. "Let's just cut to the chase, shall we Mr. Weaver?"

"Please do Mr. Phelps," I replied, trying my best to sound like an English gentleman.

My impersonation was lost on Austin T. as he said, "It appears that there are some slight discrepancies between what you told me during our interview and what was found in your house."

My mind went into scramble mode, trying to get one step ahead of Austin T. and see where he was headed with this. *What could they have found that would implicate me as the arsonist?* "Oh?" I replied, trying to sound calm. "What was that?"

He looked down at his papers, as if he even needed them to remind him what he was about to say. He'd probably had a hard-on ever since he found out about whatever it was that didn't jibe with his notes. Guys like Austin T. lived for moments like this; they're tiny scraps of fame in an otherwise drab, boring existence. If he nailed me as an arsonist - and saved his company those thousands of dollars that wouldn't need to be doled out in a settlement - he wouldn't know what to do with himself. He'd probably do something rash like take his wife out for a round of *real* root beer at the local Tasty Top. *Was he married?* I wondered. I looked down at his left hand and saw a small gold ring on his finger. "I'd rather not say at this moment," he said, "because everything is still so preliminary. I'd prefer if you just walked me through that night one more time." He added a smile, trying to appear friendly and supportive, but I knew better.

Seeing no other way out, I obliged him and told my story one more time. I intentionally left out details that I had included before because I didn't want to give him any more rope for my future noose, if it came to that, than I absolutely had to. I was pretty sure that I had my story straight but with a bloodhound like Austin T sniffing around I knew I had to be extra cautious. After finishing my second telling of the story I nodded at him and said, "So there you have it. Again."

He returned my nod. "Thank you." He then looked down at his file and asked, "Is there anything else that you can think of that I would need to know regarding this investigation?"

Yeah, how about why you're such an asshole? "Nope, can't think of a thing."

"Hmm, hmmm," he mumbled, still not looking up from his file.

"Maybe there is one other thing," I then said before my internal editor could get a hold of my tongue.

Austin T looked up. "What's that?"

"I guess I wanted to let you know some of what's going on in my life as a way to explain some of my...er...behavior."

"Go on." He folded his hands on his desk and leaned forward. It was time to lay it on thick.

"My personal life is a bit of a mess and there's this guy, The Worm, who..."

"The Worm?" he repeated.

"My wife's boyfriend," I said. "His name is William, but I call him The Worm." I then threw Austin T. my best conspiratorial guy look, and added, "You understand, right?" I knew the answer to my question before I'd asked it - there was no way in hell that he would understand anything about what I felt - but I hadn't asked it looking for an answer; I was just trying to pull Austin T in a little closer somehow, perhaps turn him into an ally of sorts.

His look changed slightly and I though I detected just a small glimmer of Austin T.'s Inner Man trying to say something. But he put a sock in IM's mouth and replied, "No, I don't understand." He paused and then added, "But then I guess there's a *lot* that I don't understand about that night, Mr. Weaver."

We had apparently abandoned the "Ben" and "Austin" routine in favor of the more professional monikers. I guess I wasn't going to be able to finish my sob story, so I figured I'd play along with his newly adopted formal tone by adopting one of my own. "And what exactly is it that is so confusing to you, Mr. Phelps?"

He looked down at his sheets, oblivious to my own new butler-like tone. "I'll be honest with you," he said. "Everything about this case smells funny to me, Mr. Weaver."

Oh, oh. "How so?" I asked politely, quickly dropping my mock formal tone.

"From how it started to how you're reacting," he said while pointing toward me with his open hand, as if gesturing toward a museum exhibit that he was showing to a group of tourists, "I just can't shake the feeling that something isn't quite right with this case."

Time to do some damage control. "Look," I began. "If it's any help to you with all of this I can tell you that I'm a real smart-ass by nature and when I get into stressful situations that's the guy who comes out." I shrugged. "I just can't help myself." I looked at Austin T. and didn't see sympathy emanating from his eyes so I continued. "I've been going through a bit of a rough patch with my family situation lately and this whole house thing just feels like one thing too many for me to deal with right now, so I think I'm just tucking it away to deal with later. Does that make sense?"

Austin T. nodded but his eyes were still skeptical. *Maybe I underestimated Mr. Austin T. Phelps.* It was time to pull out my trump card. "Do you have any children?" I asked him.

He smiled, and it was his first true smile since I'd met him. "A baby girl."

I returned the smile, and it was also sincere; Austin T. and I finally had some common ground on which we could stand and talk. "How old?" I asked.

"She'll be a year-old next month," he replied, his fatherly pride absolutely gushing out of his eyes.

"What's her name?"

"Rachel."

Biblical name, I thought. *No big surprise there.* "You're going to love watching that little girl grow up, Austin," I said, bringing his first name back into play in hopes of further building our budding rapport. "There's no better feeling in the world than being a father to a little girl." I suddenly flashed on a time that Kylie and I were at the beach. She was probably around five years old at the time, and we were walking together along the shore, just the two of us. The waves were particularly big that day and she was a little frightened by them, but she hadn't wanted to admit her fear so all she did was reach up with her little hand and grab my fingers. I could tell she was frightened by how hard she gripped my fingers, but she never said a word. I remember feeling so whole, and so at peace with my place in the world at that moment. My purpose was to protect this little girl who was clinging to my hand and nothing would ever stand in the way of that purpose. Nothing. I then fast-forwarded to my present situation and flashed on the reality that it may be The Worm's hand that she reaches for now and I felt an unbelievably huge ball of anger, regret and sadness form in my belly, so big that it threatened to swell up and choke off my air.

I'm sure my face must have changed at that thought because I heard Austin T. ask me, "Are you okay, Mr. Weaver?"

Time to get back to work, I thought. "Yeah, I'm fine," I replied, shaking my head slightly in an effort at getting my bearings back. I wanted to get Austin T.'s sympathy but I didn't want to start bawling on his desk. "So how would you feel if another man came in, took your daughter away, and started to raise her?" I asked, surprised by how calmly those words came out of my mouth. Austin T. just shook his head and couldn't come up with an answer, so I decided to help him out. "Trust me, it would break your heart in ways that you could never imagine." I paused to let that thought sink in, then added, "And that's what I'm going through right now, Austin. Another man is raising my daughter and it's tearing me apart inside. And, quite honestly," I said, "even a house fire can't match the level of pain I feel inside at the thought of losing my daughter to another man." And that was actually the truth.

That was it, I was done. If he didn't feel any sympathy for my plight after that little speech, then he was made of ice and there was no hope for the man. "Thank you for sharing that with me, Mr. Weaver," he said, his tone betraying nothing. "That does help to lend some perspective to the situation, and I appreciate your candor." *Candor? What the hell kind of a word is that? That wasn't a word that a guy bursting with sympathy would use,* I thought. Austin T. then stood up and extended his hand to me. "I do appreciate your coming in here to talk to me and I'll let you know if and when anything else comes up."

I stood up and shook his hand. I wanted to say all kinds of things to Austin T. at that moment, but I held my tongue. The man still had his hands on the control panel to my future and I didn't want to say anything more that might piss him off or, worse yet, question my story about what happened the night of the fire. "Thanks Mr. Phelps," I replied. "And an early happy birthday to Rachel," I added with a forced smile. *And I hope she ends up running away with gypsies at the age of thirteen,* I thought; a thought that helped to add more sincerity to my smile.

I walked out of the Brown and Brown offices, onto Main Street, and was hit by a thought that I had a hunch might soon become my mantra: *What now?* I pulled my jacket tighter around the collar against the cold wind that had picked up then looked left, and then right, and, deciding that my fate lay to the left, started walking in that direction without any destination in mind.

CHAPTER EIGHT

Later that night I sat, having dinner by myself, in the Pioneer Diner. The Diner was an old rail car that had been converted to a restaurant sometime back in the thirties and hadn't changed much since the day it opened. It had the same tired booths with the same tired upholstery and the same tired food served by the same tired waitresses. Fancy dining it was not. It wasn't until a couple of years ago that they added an imported beer to their list of offerings - Molson, from Canada, and that was only because Bernie, the owner, had tasted it during a hunting trip to Quebec that year and liked it so much that he decided to start carrying it at The Diner - and if you wanted wine, it came in a box. But The Diner was like an old friend - you always knew what to expect from The Diner - and I needed that kind of reliability now.

I sat in my favorite booth – with a small window that overlooked the Sawmill River - and I scanned the menu absentmindedly, even though I knew exactly what I was going to order: meatloaf with mashed potatoes and gravy, rolls with lots of butter, and apple pie with a huge scoop of ice cream for dessert. Pure comfort food. Clogged arteries, fat, and heart attacks be damned. *Fuck it.*

Ruby came over to take my order. I think Ruby had been part of the original crew at The Diner and nobody I'd ever said that to could dispute it. She'd been a waitress at The Diner for as long as anyone in Maple Grove could remember; even Bernie the owner, who was now approaching sixty, remembered Ruby serving him tuna melts and malts when he was a kid. He inherited her when he bought the place over twenty years ago and, despite consistent customer complaints about Ruby's brusque manner - some would call it borderline rude - Bernie never considered letting her go. "It's just the damned tourists who complain," I'd heard him say one time, "and I ain't gonna run my place accordin' to what some damned leaf-peeping tourists want."

While it was true that it was mainly tourists who complained, Ruby was an equal opportunity abuser of customers. Locals and tourists alike were potential targets for her sharp tongue, it's just that the locals knew better than to complain. All a complaint would get you, locals knew, was even worse treatment from Ruby the next time you came into The Diner. Better to just take the abuse and keep your mouth shut or risk never seeing a piece of Bernie's meatloaf or Alice, his wife's, delicious pies ever again. That was too high a price to pay for most residents of Maple Grove.

Besides, it was entertaining to watch Ruby with unsuspecting newbies who happened to wander into her web. More times than I could remember I had witnessed Ruby crack her whip of caustic comments in the ears of tourists, or visiting parents of local college students who wanted to give their folks a taste of the local flavor, and then I would watch as they did a slow boil at their table after Ruby had taken their orders. It wasn't unusual for many of them to pack up and leave before their food arrived because they were so put off by Ruby's behavior. When I was in college, Jim and I used to pass the time while we were waiting for our food by picking out customers and placing bets on who would stick around long enough to finish their meal. We'd gotten pretty good at it by the time we graduated, and I still caught myself silently assessing a customer's resiliency when I sat in The Diner. On more than one occasion I thought I caught Ruby with a small smile on her face as she watched yet another customer storm out of The Diner.

"Hey there, Ruby," I said as she strode up to my booth. I hadn't expected a response from her, and she stayed true to form by saying nothing. I quickly got down to business and gave her my order, not daring to say anything stupid like, "Could you put the gravy on the side?" or "Could I get my salad without any onions?" Ruby didn't like exceptions or special orders. They were usually greeted with a comment along the lines of, "Why don't I just bring the potatoes, cream and butter on the side too and you can mash your own." Or, one of my personal favorites that I'd heard her use more than once, "I ain't your mother, and this ain't your kitchen, so I'll bring it how Bernie fixes it. How's that?" That one had been a catalyst for its share of customer storm-offs over the years and those who didn't choose to leave in a huff usually just nodded meekly in response. Ruby was a hoot.

After Ruby walked away with my order, I allowed my mind to wander for a while. The last couple of days had been rather eventful and I felt like I needed to try to get my arms around all of it. I thought about my house - or rather my *ex*-house - and realized that I already missed the feeling of sanctuary that a house provided. No matter how bad a day I had, I used to always be able to go home, close the door, and just shut the world out for a while. Not any more. A hotel room doesn't provide a very thick layer of insulation from the rest of the world, as I found out the previous night when I heard a couple in the next room arguing loudly deep into the night. I missed my castle.

But it was much too late in the game to dwell on those kinds of thoughts, given that my house was gone for good, so I shifted my mind's lens to a different topic. My recent life, prior to the fire, soon came into focus and I chewed on that for a while. Words like "boring" and "routine" popped into my head as I thought about a life that had been reduced to "work, eat, sleep, repeat" over the past couple of years. As I scanned the landscape of my life even further behind me, I couldn't see very much of interest that popped up there either. There was a trip Kylie and

I had taken to Disney World several years ago, soon after the divorce, but that was about it for worthwhile memories from the last few years. That was pathetic.

Tiring of the little pity party of one that I had inadvertently started, I tried to cast my eyes to the more positive side of my life's ledger. *I don't have mortgage payments, a lawn to mow, a driveway to shovel, or all those bills to pay anymore,*" I thought. Those were all plusses. I was freer than I'd been at any time since graduating from college and it was time to take advantage of that fact.

It then hit me that it was time for me to take a road trip.

When Kylie and I had gone to Disney World we had taken our tent trailer and we took our time getting down there, stopping along the way at various campgrounds. The tent trailer proved to be the perfect way to travel as the two of us got the small sense of adventure that comes with camping but without all the hassles of pitching a tent, sleeping on the ground, and worrying about the weather. We'd had a great time together on that trip and I'll probably always remember that time as being my last hurrah as The Man in Kylie's life. It was soon after we returned from that trip that The Worm entered the picture and I'd been forced to share her ever since.

I felt the pity start to seep in again.

I nudged my mind back to the logistics of my trip. I remembered parking the tent trailer over at my mother's house after the Disney trip and it hadn't been used since that time so, unless my mother had gone on one of her infamous cleaning rampages, it would still be there. Getting it would require a call to my mother, which had never been one of my favorite things to do but would be a small price to pay for my much-needed vacation.

Ruby arrived with my food and plopped it on the table with all the grace of a gorilla then strode off without a word. I scanned my steaming plate of meatloaf, mashed potatoes and gravy and smiled. This was going to be good, I knew it, and, better yet, I now had a plan for how to begin my New Life.

CHAPTER NINE

I awoke the next morning feeling anxious to get started on my New Life. I showered, choked down some free motel lobby coffee, and hopped in my car for the drive over to my mother's place.

My mother lived in the small town of Hampton, just a couple towns away from Maple Grove. She lived by herself in the same small farmhouse that she and Dad had bought soon after my younger sister, Debbie, moved out of the family home. They'd wanted to downsize their lives and it wasn't long after the move that they downsized their world more than either had anticipated when Dad suffered a fatal heart attack while mowing the lawn one afternoon. It had caught all of us by surprise but, true to her Yankee roots, my mother hadn't seemed to miss a single step following my father's death; there were, after all, gardens to be tended, barns to be painted, and a house to be cleaned. There was no time for self-pity or needless complaining in my mother's world; you just did what had to be done and you moved on. I'd seen countless women like my mother while growing up and living in New England over the years - women who were cut from the same cloth as their Yankee ancestors, ancestors who had made a life for themselves and their families through tough New England winters - and I knew from experience that nobody was going to change them. They were hard-wired to be industrious, unemotional and tough and I had accepted the fact long ago that my mother would never be the June Cleaver mother that I had longed for as a child. Things like hugs and goodnight kisses existed only in my imagination and I learned early in life to keep the messy workings of my internal world to myself. She just didn't have the time, or the inclination, to sit down and discuss things like feelings, dreams or the meaning of life. The few times that I had presented her with a personal problem I was given a short, practical answer - along the lines of "Just don't think about it so much" - and was then sent on my way to go finish a chore of some kind. June Cleaver she most definitely was not.

I pulled into her driveway and saw her dragging a fallen tree limb into the woods that bordered her property. The outside temperature hovered near freezing and while most seventy-year-old women would be huddled next to a warm fireplace on a day like this, knitting needles in hand, my mother was out dragging tree limbs. I shook my head and got out of the car.

I hurried over to my mother and, reaching for the limb, said, "Here Mom, let me finish this up for you."

She looked up at me through her glasses with the scratch-filled lenses - they were "still perfectly good glasses" according to my mother so she refused to buy another pair - and, seeing that it was me, handed me the limb without a word. If it had been anyone else offering the help my mother probably would have just continued what she was doing. With me, however, there was no shame in accepting the help because, in her mind, she was giving her son the gift of feeling productive. She never uttered those words to me before, but I had always gotten the sense that good, hard work was a gift from God to my mother and she loved nothing more than to hand that gift to her children as often as she could. "There's a few more over there," she then said, pointing to a far corner of her property. "Last storm blew 'em down." No hello, no hug, just a work assignment. Typical Mom greeting.

"So, how's it going, Mom?" I asked as I finished dragging the limb into the woods.

She shrugged. "Been better, been worse," she replied. It was the same reply I'd heard from her a thousand times before. Mom was as spare with her words as she was with her money and her time; waste of *anything* was the king of all sins to my mother.

"Why didn't you just call me about these tree limbs, Mom?" I asked. "You know I'd be happy to come over and help you out with things like this." I knew her answer before she opened her mouth. It would be the same answer she had given me hundreds of times.

"You've got your own life to live," she replied with a wave of her hand. "I manage just fine without you."

It was the same answer she always gave, and it hit me the same way it always did. I knew she said the words to be reassuring but they always inspired tremendous feelings of guilt within me. *Should I visit my mother more often?* I would wonder. *Am I being a neglectful son?* I tossed the limb with an extra bit of oomph in an attempt at channeling some of the guilt out of my body. It didn't work.

As we walked over to where the other limbs were laying on the ground, I found myself wondering if my mother had heard about my recent tragedy. If she had, I knew that she wouldn't necessarily mention it to me. Mom liked to give bad news a wide berth, letting the person who had been afflicted take the lead with the sharing of the story. She didn't like to pry into people's personal lives - her son's included - so she would just wait for the bad news to come to her. My own theory was that my mother was just plain uncomfortable with emotions like grief, anger, and sorrow so she tried to avoid them at all costs. I decided to plow through her discomfort and deliver the news. "Did you hear what happened to my house, Mom?" I asked.

She didn't break her stride as she replied, "Yep. Mrs. Hastings told me."

Mrs. Hastings was her seventy-five-year-old neighbor and, in direct contrast to Mom's don't-pry mantra, Mrs. Hastings was a snoop and a gossip. "What exactly did Mrs. Hastings tell you?" I asked, not even blinking at the fact that my own mother failed to find a house fire reason enough to push the pause button on her chores long enough to hug her son and say, "I'm sorry."

"That your house burned to the ground," she replied, no hint of emotion in her voice. "So, I suppose you're going to need a place to stay."

True to form, my mother headed right for the solution, choosing to bypass any messy discussions about the problem. Truth is, I hadn't even considered staying in my mother's house. "Nope," I replied. "I'm staying in a hotel downtown for now."

That got Mom to stop walking for a moment. "A hotel?" she said, her voice containing a small hint of incredulity. "Why would you want to waste your money on a hotel when you have a perfectly good bed right here?"

Forget about returning to the bosom of home and family after a tragedy, or getting some motherly TLC; my mother's main concern was the wasting of a resource, money, and she just couldn't allow that to happen if it was within her power to prevent it. To her credit, she didn't place the value of money over that of any other resource, like gasoline, or water, or even the tomatoes that she grew in her garden each year. She saw that each had value in their own way and that value must be fully realized or else...well, to be honest, I didn't know what the "or else" was. I just knew that it was really, really bad and was to be avoided at all costs. But not this time. "I'm fine there, Mom," I said. "It's close to work and I'm still dealing with stuff with the insurance company, which is right down the street from me at the hotel."

My mother looked at me skeptically. Then, satisfied that she wasn't going to win this battle, she withdrew her forces. For now. Mom had never been one to give up easily, but she knew how to pick her moments, so I felt certain that I hadn't heard the last of this argument. "So why did you come over today?" she then asked, turning to the pile of sticks and debris that was now in front of us after our stroll across her property.

I knew better than to bullshit my mother with anything less than the truth. If I said to her that I just wanted to check in on her, or that I needed some family time, she would have sniffed it out in a heartbeat and given me a verbal slap upside my head to let me know that she wasn't buying whatever it was that I was trying to sell to her. "I'm thinking about taking a trip in my tent trailer," I replied, "so I came over to pull it out of your barn and check it out."

I reached down and grabbed one of the broken limbs while my mother considered my words. I had managed to drag that limb to the woods and return to grab another one before my mother spoke again. "What do Linda and Kylie think of this idea?" she finally asked.

The question shouldn't have come as a surprise to me; my mother had always adored Linda and I think she still held out some poor, misguided hope that the two of us would eventually patch up our differences and retie the marital knot that had been untied several years earlier. And if she adored Linda then you would have to find a word many times stronger than adore to describe how she felt about her only granddaughter, Kylie. My mother was a different woman when Kylie was around; her stoic, Yankee woman persona would disappear and, in its place, would appear this smiling, doting, and loving woman who bore no resemblance to the mother that I knew. So, when she asks me what Linda and Kylie think about my tent trailer trip idea, I know what she's really asking is: *Do you think it's a good idea to leave your ex-wife and daughter behind? How are the three of you going to become reunited as a family if you're off in a tent trailer somewhere?* Deciding to simply take the question at face value, I responded, "Why would you ask me that? Linda and I are divorced Mom, so I no longer keep tabs on her, and she no longer keeps tabs on me." For some unknown reason I felt anger boiling up inside of me and I heaved the next limb with added gusto.

Seemingly ignoring my words, and the emotions behind them, my mother then asked, "So Linda doesn't know about this yet?"

I heaved a deep sigh of resignation, a small fog bank of breath streaming from my mouth into the cold air. "No, Mom, Linda doesn't know about this yet." I dropped the limb I had in my hands and added, "As a matter of fact, nobody knows about this particular idea yet except you and me." My voice had more of an edge to it than I had intended, and I silently hoped that my mother hadn't noticed.

My mother nodded, telling me that she understood. She then turned to the brush pile and said, "No need to get huffy. I'm just asking questions."

After finishing up the rest of the brush pile in silence, I headed over to the barn that housed my tent trailer. All my mother's barns - there were three of them on her property - looked like they were going to fall down at any minute, and the one that contained my tent trailer was the worst of the bunch. The entire barn sat at close to a forty-five-degree tilt, as if a strong north wind was constantly blowing on it, and I remember thinking when I first saw it many years earlier, when my parents first bought the place, that it wouldn't last through the next winter. But it did survive the winter, and many New England winters since, in this condition so I finally became a believer in my mothers' assertion that it wasn't going anywhere.

I opened the creaky barn door and propped a log in front of it so it wouldn't blow shut. I hit the light switch to my right and could practically hear the hallelujah chorus raining down on me from above as I looked at my tent trailer sitting by itself in the middle of the large barn, fully illuminated by the overhead lights. I had bought the tent trailer five years ago, to get Linda, Kylie and me out into the woods. I had enjoyed going off on backpacking and camping adventures with my buddies when I was younger and, knowing that tent camping wasn't Linda's thing -

which I'd found out the hard way during a nightmarish weekend in the Catskills early in our relationship - I wanted to find a way to introduce Kylie to The Great Outdoors. The tent trailer was the perfect answer. The first summer after I bought it, we took off on a two-week excursion through New Hampshire and Maine, stopping whenever and wherever our fancy took us, and everyone had a great time. It would prove to be both the first and last tent trailer adventure for all three of us. Marital problems started creeping in soon after that and Linda and I separated the following year.

I walked up to the tent trailer and heaved a sigh. It stirred both sadness and excitement in me. The sadness came from the memories of that blissful summer, when we were still a family and Kylie was still my daughter and my daughter alone. I remember showing her how to build a campfire during that trip and her looking at me with eyes that told me, "You're the smartest, bravest, most amazing father in the whole world." Those eyes believed in me so much that I couldn't help but believe in myself. I realized that I would probably never see those eyes again. I missed those eyes.

I could feel my heart aching so before the tears worked their way to my eyes, I shifted my mind's focus to the excitement that stirred inside me. The tent trailer represented the freedom and hope of the open road to me and I couldn't wait to answer the siren's call. Some men viewed sports cars in the same way but for me nothing compared to the feeling I got from carrying my entire life on my back. Whether it was with a backpack or a tent trailer, I knew that everything I needed in life was within my reach and that was both extremely liberating and comforting to me. I didn't need anyone or anything else to survive.

Another thought then occurred to me as I stood there looking at my tent trailer: this was now the number one remaining asset in my life. Rather than cause me despair, the thought inspired a smile to appear in the corner of my mouth. I wouldn't have had it any other way. I took off my jacket, tossed it on a nearby rail, and then started undoing the hasps that held the tent trailer closed. "Let's see what you look like," I whispered to the air as I prepared the trailer to be opened.

CHAPTER TEN

"How much would that cost?" I asked the man on the other end of the line. After hearing the large number, I let out an involuntary, "Really?!?" I thanked him for his time and hung up the phone. I sat on my motel bed feeling defeated.

I had opened my tent trailer that morning and was greeted by a blue-green colored canvas top that had at one time been white. It was covered with mold, to the point that there were now small holes in the canvas. I'd forgotten that I'd allowed Jim and his family to borrow the trailer a couple of summers ago and they must have put it away when it was still wet. I couldn't muster any anger at Jim, but the replacement cost was well beyond what my meager savings account could cover. My charge cards were also maxed out so the replacement canvas would have to wait until after I got my insurance check from Austin T. Phelps. Bummer.

I hadn't realized just how anxious I was to get out of town until I'd been told that I couldn't. Not yet anyway. After hanging up the phone I sat on the bed and mourned my state of stuckedness for several minutes. I would need to formulate a new plan, at least for the short term, and I didn't have any good ideas in the queue. Then the phone rang. "Hello?" I said flatly.

"Mr. Weaver?" the voice said. "This is Austin Phelps."

"Hi," I replied, perking up a little at the thought that perhaps he had my check ready to go.

"I was wondering if you could come down to my office some time today."

"Sure," I replied, my excitement gaining momentum. "What time?"

"I'm here until five o'clock, so anytime before that would be fine."

"I'll see you in a few minutes," I said and then hung up. I grabbed my coat and headed for the door, anxious to get Plan A back on-line.

Ten minutes later I was seated across from Austin T. Phelps. He hadn't yet told me why he wanted me to come down to his office, but I knew that it would just be a matter of minutes before he would be sliding a rather substantial check across his desk and wishing me luck with my new life. He shifted in his chair a couple of times while looking down at several pieces of paper laid out on his desk. I made a private bet that Austin T. probably brought forms home to read in bed at night, finding them infinitely more interesting than anything that could be concocted by Steinbeck or Hemingway. Eventually, he looked up from his forms and forced a smile. "Thank you for coming down here on such short notice, Mr. Weaver."

Oh, oh…we were back to using Mr. Weaver. Bad sign. "No problem," I replied. "I had to shift around a few appointments, but I figured that this was important."

My crack about the appointments flew right past him. "Yes, it is indeed important," he said solemnly. "If you don't mind, I have a few more questions for you."

*More questions?!?! Shit! This was **definitely** a bad sign!* "Questions about what?" I asked, trying my best to sound calm, cool and collected.

He looked back down at the forms on his desk. "It appears that we have a few discrepancies regarding your recent house fire."

Austin T. had paused before pulling the word discrepancies out of the air, which told me that he had wanted to use an entirely different word. Lies, perhaps? "Discrepancies?" I asked, plastering on my best innocent victim face.

"Yes," he said. He then picked up a sheet of paper and said, "Didn't you tell me that you were a non-smoker?" He then set the piece of paper down and looked at me. Hard. As if trying to divine my innermost truth.

I knew he was sniffing around the cigar ashes that started the fire, but I knew to play this one slow or risk appearing defensive. This would be an easy one to explain away so I just kept my air of calm. "Yes, I did," I replied.

Austin T. paused for a beat, as if reading something else off the piece of paper in his hands, but we both knew he was trying to make me stew a while before delivering what he thought would be a jaw-breaking blow to my story's chin. "Well, it appears that your fire began in your couch," he said slowly, "and the fire inspector determined that it all started with a smoldering cigar."

I threw him my best "Huh?" look and then I slowly morphed that into an "Aha!" look as I seemingly divined something of great importance right in front of Austin T.'s eyes. It was a great performance, the intricacies of which only I would ever get to fully appreciate. "I had been smoking a cigar when I got home that night," I replied, with the same "Aha" look of recent discovery on my face. "I must have been careless with some of the ashes." I shook my head, trying to appear disgusted with myself. "What a fucking idiot I am!" I then added for emphasis, hoping to throw Austin T. off his game a little bit by tossing a curse in there. Austin T. struck me as guy who rarely heard the word fucking in his life and I was willing to bet that he'd never even uttered it himself throughout his entire life. I also had my doubts if he'd ever *done* it in his lifetime.

I saw him blink hard at the sound of the curse, as if I'd just plinked him in the forehead with a peashooter, but he recovered quickly and asked the next question in his obviously pre-determined line-up of questions. Christ, he probably rehearsed this shit in a mirror at home the night before an interrogation. "But I thought you had said that you weren't a smoker, Mr. Weaver?"

"I guess I don't consider an occasional cigar to be smoking," I replied. Then I leaned forward and, in my best guy-to-guy conspiratorial tone, said, "Don't you light one up occasionally, Austin? You know, with the guys at a poker game or while watching a football game?" I knew perfectly well that Austin T. never, ever engaged in either one of those activities, but I was hoping he'd play along anyway. He didn't.

"Yes, I consider an occasional cigar to be smoking, Mr. Weaver," he replied in an irritatingly high-and-mighty tone. "And no, I *don't* ever light one up. As I said to you before, I consider it to be a filthy habit and I see no reason to ever use tobacco products."

I was beginning to dislike Austin T. Phelps. Intensely. But I pushed that dislike aside and tried to maintain my focus on the prize: I needed that insurance check to get on with my life and, like it or not, Austin T. was the gatekeeper to that new life. "Well, I just do it on special occasions," I said.

"And what was the special occasion that night, Mr. Weaver?"

Every time he said Mr. Weaver, I felt my blood pressure rise a notch, as if it was one more drop in a Chinese water torture. I wondered if he knew that and was doing it on purpose. Maybe I was underestimating Austin T. "It was Thanksgiving," I replied.

"And do you always smoke on Thanksgiving?"

"No, I don't."

"And why did you choose this particular Thanksgiving to smoke a cigar?"

"Because I was celebrating," I replied, smiling to myself in anticipation of my next line.

"Celebrating what, Mr. Weaver?" Drip, drip.

"The fact that I didn't bury the carving knife in the chest of my ex-wife's new boyfriend," I said without emotion. There was more truth to that than I cared to admit to myself, but that would have to wait for another day.

That one nudged Austin T. off his track for a minute. He didn't know what to say at first, unsure if he was dealing with a true-to-life homicidal maniac who could reach across the desk and bury his pen in his throat at any moment. He soon recovered, however, and muttered an, "I see," before finding his place in his connect-the-dots interrogation, choosing to completely ignore my knife-buried-in-The-Worm's-chest comment. "And how do you explain the presence of an entire cigar in the cushions of your sofa, Mr. Weaver?" Drip, drip.

I shrugged. "I must have dropped it there by mistake," I replied. "I was pretty drunk when I got home that night and I guess I might have dozed off on the couch while I was smoking the cigar."

"You don't think you would have smelled something burning?" Austin T. asked in his best incredulous tone.

I shrugged again. "I guess not. Like I said, I was pretty drunk that night."

He looked back down at his papers. "The policeman who filed the report didn't say anything about you being intoxicated that night, Mr. Weaver," he said, the doubt practically dripping off his words.

He was really starting to piss me off. "Must have been the adrenaline rush from watching my house burn to the ground," I replied with an intentional edge to my voice. "That would sober anyone up in a hurry."

Austin T. looked at me and seemed to be considering his next words carefully, which was very smart on his part because I was ready to reach across his desk and pop him in the nose. "Yes, well I suppose that could be the case," he finally said. "And please understand that these questions are not meant to be personal in nature Mr. Weaver," drip...drip...drip... "I am responsible for dispensing large sums of money and I just have to make sure that everything adds up, that's all." He paused for a moment and then added the line that's been uttered a million times throughout human history, to justify everything from the maiming of children to the gassing of Jews. "I'm just doing my job."

All kinds of possible responses ran through my head in an instant, but they were all quickly discarded as being too detrimental to my cause, and I eventually settled on the innocuous, "So are we done here?"

Austin T. nodded. "Yes, we are," he replied. He then added the ominous, "For now, Mr. Weaver." Drip, drip.

That last Mr. Weaver managed to sneak through my defenses and get under my skin, to the point that I blew right past my internal editor and all but shouted at Austin T., "What the hell do you want from me?" A little voice in my head was whispering to me to calm down and back off but I ignored the little bugger and continued my rant. "I've answered all of your questions and jumped through all of your hoops, so why are you holding up my settlement check? I'm living in a fucking hotel for crissakes and I don't even have a set of clothes to call my own anymore and you somehow feel the need to throw me on my back, stick your shoe on my throat and watch me squirm." I then leaned forward and asked with my head tilted to one side, "Why is that Rick?" I couldn't resist the last little Rick Moranis dig, maybe as payback for all the Mr. Weaver's he'd thrown at me.

I looked over and saw that Austin T. was both stunned and speechless. He recovered quickly, however, and, after straightening his back and shuffling some papers, replied, "The truth, Mr. Weaver."

"Yeah, the truth," I echoed, thinking he was asking me if that's what I wanted to hear.

"The truth is that it's the truth that I'm after, Mr. Weaver," he replied, a small self-satisfied smirk forming at the corner of his mouth, telling me that he was patting himself on the back for his little bit of wordplay. "And, quite frankly," he continued, "something smells fishy about this fire of yours and I want to be sure to sniff in all the corners before I approve any settlement checks."

He then leaned forward and, as if knowing that his words would be fingernails on a chalkboard to my ears, said, "It's my job." He then stood up and stuck his hand out. "Now, if you'll excuse me, I have other matters to attend to."

I stood up, looked down at his extended hand, and then just turned and walked out of his office without saying another word.

CHAPTER ELEVEN

The rest of that day was a blur to me. I walked, I watched TV in my hotel room, I walked some more; anything to take my mind off my new favorite fantasy: going back to the offices of Brown and Brown Insurance and squeezing the throat of Austin T. Phelps until his face turned blue and his eyes bulged from his head. I didn't want to kill the guy. I just wanted to get his attention and let him know that he'd pissed me off. And, well, maybe hurt him just a little. Okay, maybe hurt him a *lot.*

By mid-afternoon I decided that no amount of walking and no amount of Jerry Springer would be able to sweep the strangle-Austin-T. fantasy out of my brain. There was only one way to do that and it involved the consumption of copious quantities of alcohol. Having realized that, I muttered a silent "fuck it" in my head and made my last walk to the doors of The Tavern.

After my eyes adjusted to the low light of The Tavern, I saw that the place was pretty much empty except for a few older guys sitting at the bar. I'd always looked down my nose at men who sat on a barstool getting drunk in the middle of the day - thinking them to be pitiful losers with no self-control - but I suddenly felt a strange kinship to my fellow lost souls who were seeking a brief oasis from the ocean of pain and misery that was life. Okay, I still thought they were losers, but I had to find *some* way to justify the fact that I was about to get plowed at two o'clock in the afternoon.

I made my way to a table over by the window overlooking The Mill and sat down. It wasn't long before an older woman, probably in her sixties, came over and asked, "What can I do for you?"

71

I did an internal assessment of the various Weapons of Mental Destruction that were at my disposal and quickly decided on, "Tequila. With a bunch of lime." She nodded and walked away. Tequila would be perfect: smooth, fast-acting and able to hold a good steady state of numbness. Beer was too filling and other hard liquors too strong. I could sip my way up the feel-good ladder with tequila and then hang there for a long time. Perfect.

I looked out the window and saw the holiday shoppers scurrying in and out of Cooper's Mill. Thanksgiving was now over so the gun had sounded on The Great Christmas Derby. It would be wall-to-wall shopping from now until midnight on Christmas Eve. I'd always enjoyed this time of year but since separating from Linda I'd come to hate it. Christmas was about hearth and home, children, and family and I came up empty on all counts. I looked away from the shoppers and wondered what the hell was taking my tequila so long. I was surprised to see a rather large gentleman standing at my table.

"Mind if I join ya?" the man asked as he nodded at the chair across the table from me.

He was a big, bear of a man - maybe six foot four and easily two hundred and fifty pounds - and he looked like he wouldn't be posing for a GQ cover any day soon. He appeared as if he'd just stepped off the Grizzly Adams set, complete with a huge beard, unkempt hair and the token flannel shirt. I knew right away that this wasn't a man I'd be saying "no" to. "Not at all," I replied, nodding at the chair. "Have a seat."

Grizzly sat down with much effort, the chair being far too small for his large frame, and then said, "Drinkin' alone just ain't my thing. Makes me feel like a drunk instead of a drinker." He smiled at me and winked as he continued to get his bulk settled into a semi-comfortable position.

"Nobody likes to be a drunk," I concurred.

"Hell no!" he thundered and then started laughing. It was the kind of a laugh that shook the ground and turned heads, except I noticed that none of the handful of heads in The Tavern turned towards us at the sound of his laugh. "Don't worry about them," he said, noticing my quick scan. "Most of 'em are already halfway to comatose. It would take a hand grenade in the middle of the room to get most of them to move from their barstool, and even then, they'd move reluctantly."

"You a regular here?" I asked.

He nodded. "I am indeed." He stuck his hand out and I shook it, feeling much like a six-year-old holding his father's hand as the man's hand was beyond huge. "Grizzly's the name," he said, causing me to blink twice in disbelief. "My friend's call me Griz." Noticing my look, he added, "Most of us don't use our real names here." He looked over his shoulder conspiratorially and then leaned forward, pulling me in with him since he still had my hand, and whispered, "Most of us are here to forget about who we are and what we've done, and a different name helps with that." He then let go of my hand and leaned back, saying, "I was told I looked a lot like Grizzly Adams when I first started coming here and that name just sort of stuck." He shrugged. "Never heard of the guy until that day, but now I kinda like the name. It suits me."

I nodded and smiled. "It does suit you," I agreed.

"So, what should I be calling you, my friend?" he asked.

I nearly gave him my real name but caught myself and, in keeping with The Code, threw out the first name that popped into my head. "Luke," I said. I'd always dreamed of being Luke Skywalker as a kid and now this was my chance to at least have his name, if not his cool fighter plane and Jedi powers. I smiled to myself.

Griz nodded. "Luke it is,' he said. "Nice to meet'cha, Luke."

"Likewise, Griz," I replied. The waitress then delivered my tequila to the table and I asked, "What are you drinking, Griz?"

"I'm a whiskey drinker," he replied.

I turned to the waitress. "Bring a glass of your best whiskey for my new friend Griz here," I said. "And go ahead and bring me another tequila while you're at it. This one should be gone by the time you get back." The waitress nodded and, without saying a word, headed off.

"Thanks Luke," I heard Griz say.

It took a moment for it to register that he was talking to me, but I quickly recalled my new alias and turned back to him. "You're welcome, Griz," I replied with a smile.

"So, what is it that brings you into this fine establishment today?" Griz then asked.

I was momentarily taken aback that he would be asking such a probing, personal question so quickly but, after taking a large sip of tequila, I thought *fuck it* and decided to lay it all out there for Griz. "Do you really want to know?" I asked, sticking my toe into the conversational waters before taking the headfirst plunge.

Griz smiled broadly and spread his arms wide. "I got nothin' on my agenda today, Luke," he bellowed. "So, you tell me as much or as little as you want. I'm all ears."

I took the rest of my tequila in one shot and then sucked hard on a wedge of lime. The tequila tasted good. "Okay Griz, you asked for it," I said. "Sit back and let me tell you The Story of Luke." Our two drinks came to the table and we each ordered another one before taking the first sips from our glasses. I was already feeling my brain start to swim a little and I liked it.

Three tequilas later I had shared the complete Story of Ben, aka Luke, with Griz. Griz proved to be a good listener and didn't say a word the whole time, except for an occasional "Damn!" or "Shit!" It had dawned on me while I was telling my life story that I'd never done this before, shared the entirety of my adult life in one sitting with someone. I'd never been to counseling, or on a Man Retreat, where life stories are typically shared, and everyone else in my life already knew most of the sad, pathetic details so there was no need for a re-telling. I realized two things after I'd finished telling Griz about my life, including: my failed marriage; Willie the Worm; the slow, painful loss of my daughter; my boring, dead end job; and my recent house fire - my life sucked and I was drunk.

"Man, that sucks," was Griz's first response, basically agreeing with my own assessment.

"Which part?" I asked.

"All of it," he replied. "You're the fat guy everyone wants to stand next to," he said, accompanied by a look that nearly approached awe. He saw my "Huh?" look and added, "You know, the obese guy you want to be compared to so everyone will say how thin and in shape you look compared to him." Griz shook his head. "You sure made me feel whole lot thinner with that story, I can tell ya that."

"Glad I could help you out," I replied.

Griz patted his large belly. "And making *me* look thin ain't an easy thing to do!" He then laughed, loud and hard, and I couldn't help but smile. Griz's laugh had that effect on you.

"So, what's *your* story, Griz?" I asked, feeling ready to take my own life out of the spotlight. "What is it that brings you into this place in the middle of the afternoon?"

Griz stopped laughing and his look suddenly went serious. He took a large gulp of whiskey and then said, "I fucked up." He took another large gulp, emptying the glass. "I know what you're thinkin'," he said, "that we all fuck up, and that we gotta forgive ourselves, move on, and all that other bullshit."

I shook my head. "I wasn't thinking any of that," I said. "How did you fuck up?" My head was really swimming now, and I noticed that the d's in the word "did" had become a little soft and squishy in my mouth.

Griz motioned to the waitress for another whiskey, then said, "I won't burden you with the long story." I nearly interrupted to tell him that I had no place to go, and he could go ahead and give me the long story, but a voice in my head told me to shut up. Something told me that I wasn't the reason behind his not wanting to share the long story. "The short story,' he continued, "involves a wife and two little boys and a one-night stand that became a hand grenade in the middle of everything that I cared about." He paused, his eyes looking into his glass but obviously seeing much more than the glass. Griz's eyes were scanning the chamber of his brain marked "Dungeon"- the place where all of us go to re-live past hurts, taste guilt and regret, and beat the shit out of ourselves - and I wasn't sure if he was coming back anytime soon.

After waiting a few beats, and sipping some more tequila, I decided to try to pull Griz back out of his Dungeon. "So, what do you do for a living, Griz?" The question sounded stupid coming out of my mouth, coming as it did on the heels of his obviously painful confession, but it was the first question that popped into my tequila-coated brain.

Griz blinked a couple of times and I could picture his mind's eye backing up the steps of the Dungeon, old hurts grabbing at his ankles trying to keep him down there, and him kicking at the tenacious goblins as he tried to close the door. The tequila was inspiring some pretty creative thinking. Griz's eyes eventually came back to the here and now and he replied, "Huh?"

It was my opportunity to change my stupid question and I seized that opportunity. "I was just curious how you spent your time outside of this place," I said.

"I don't spend much time outside of this place," he replied somberly. "I eat and sleep at my place and I drink here, that's my life."

I found myself regretting having asked Griz about his life. I liked the jovial Griz much better. "Where's home?" I asked, not knowing where else to go with the conversational crumbs that had been handed to me. I also noticed that I'd added a subtle "h" sound to the end of "where's" which solidified my theory that I was now drunk.

Griz spread his arms wide and thundered, "*This* is my home." He then turned and waved his arm across the expanse of the bar. "And this is my family." Nobody turned around and nobody so much as raised their glass in salute to Griz, their brother-in-booze. I saw a flash of one my millions of possible futures - the one that put me in this bar with Griz for the rest of my life - and I suddenly felt a spurt of "oh no, what am I doing?!?" adrenaline cut through my tequila haze.

"Oh shit, what time ish it?" I then asked, finding it more difficult to utter that sentence than I could have ever imagined. My tongue was now officially not my own.

"Who the fuck knows and who the fuck cares?" Griz replied, sounding irritated to the point that I thought I might have just broken some Bar Hound's Code by asking what time it was.

Truth was, I didn't care what time it was either. I just knew at that instant that I had to get out of there or risk never leaving. Ever. "I have to go meet my shun and take him shopping," I lied.

"Your shun?" Griz teased. "I'm not sure you're in any kind of shape to be taking your shun anywhere right now."

He was right of course. If I ever showed up at Linda's doorstep with this much tequila in me, she'd probably call the cops and have a lifetime restraining order slapped on me. I decided to just bluff my way out the door. I stood up, grabbed my coat off the back of the chair, and said, "I jesh gotta go, Griz."

Griz dismissed me with a wave of his hand. "Fine, keep running," he said. "You'll be back here when you realize that you can't run fast enough or far enough to get away from it."

"Get away from what?" I asked, feeling more curious than desperate for a moment.

He smiled. "You know what," he replied cryptically. He then got up and raised his glass in my direction. "Good luck, Luke," he said and then he turned and headed back towards the bar. I watched him as he walked away and noticed that nobody even looked up from their drink as he sat down at the bar. I turned and headed out of the bar, trying like hell to keep the world from spinning out of control.

CHAPTER TWELVE

I woke up the next morning and found myself wishing that I could unscrew my head and stick it in a drawer somewhere. The pounding was unbearable. I got out of bed, slowly, and headed for the medicine cabinet. It was going to be a multiple aspirin day for sure.

I grabbed the aspirin bottle out of the cabinet, shook four tablets into my hand and tossed them into my mouth. I turned on the faucet and scooped a handful of water into my mouth to help wash down the tablets. I would have chewed a whole bottle of them at that point, anything to get rid of the pain, but I knew to stop at four. For now.

When I closed the door to the medicine cabinet something in the reflection from the small mirror on the door caught my eye. It was a flash of color coming from my right arm and I turned my body so I could get a better look in the mirror. It was a tattoo. *A tattoo?!?! Where the hell did I get a tattoo?!?!* Then a flash of memory shot through the fog and I remembered: I had stumbled into a tattoo parlor the night before, after leaving Griz, and had picked out a tattoo. Another in a string of fuckets. I looked more closely at the tattoo and saw that I had chosen a large bear, his teeth bared and claws out, and had the words "Fuck it!" emblazoned across the bear's chest. *What the hell was I thinking?!?!*

Thinking that perhaps I'd had the foresight, even in my drunken state, to get a temporary tattoo, I grabbed a washcloth, soaped it up, and tried scrubbing the bear from my arm. It hurt like hell because the entire area was still red and swollen. No luck. Me and the bear were now lifetime companions. Great. My head continued to pound as I turned away from the mirror. I also noticed that my entire arm was throbbing like hell too; probably still recovering from the trauma of the tattoo needles. It was going to be a good day.

I got dressed and headed to a nearby cafe for some coffee and breakfast. I was in the market for as many vasodilators as I could get my hands on and my stomach was grumbling like, well, like a bear. I chuckled to myself at my choice of tattoos. Had I viewed it as an homage to my new friend, Griz? Was I looking for something ferocious? Or was the bear just the first thing I stumbled on as I was flipping through the tattoo books last night? The brain cells that carried all that information were still lost in the fog bank inside my head and I was hoping that a few cups of strong coffee would help to blow some of that fog away.

Entering the cafe, I quickly scanned the small dining area and saw an available table near the kitchen door in the back. I made my way to the back of the cafe, stifling the urge to tell everyone to talk quieter, and sat heavy in the chair. The waitress, a young woman who was probably a student at the nearby university, came over quickly and asked, "Coffee?"

"Bring a whole pot if you can," I said, only half-jokingly.

She smiled. "One of those mornings, huh?"

I nodded.

"Tequila?" she asked.

I smiled. "Yeah, how'd you know that?"

She placed her hand on my shoulder. "It's the eyes," she said. "Tequila eyes are different than any other hangover eyes."

I found that I liked the feeling of her hand on my shoulder, probably attributable to the lack of physical companionship in my life. "I guess I should be wearing sunglasses, eh?"

She smiled what looked like a flirtatious smile and replied, "Nah, you wouldn't want to cover up nice eyes like those."

I didn't know what to say to that. It had probably been twenty years since someone had flirted with me - well, except for Marsha, but that didn't count because I was drunk - and I didn't know what to do with it. "Uh, thanks," I managed to mumble, though I was unsure what exactly I was thanking her for.

"My name's Angela," she then said, saving me from my tongue-tied state.

She stuck her hand out and I shook it. "Ben," I replied, managing a crooked smile.

"Nice to meet'cha, Ben," she said with a wide smile. "So, what can I get you today?"

I was momentarily thrown by the question, forgetting where I was and why I was there, but then the word "breakfast" zapped me between the eyes and I replied, "Hash and eggs would be great."

"Over medium?" she asked as she scrawled on her notepad.

"That would be great."

"Toast?"

"Wheat."

"Over medium?" she asked straight-faced.

It took me a second but then I smiled. "Sounds good."

She wagged her pencil at me. "Just seeing if you're paying attention there, Ben."

"That's a bad test for a morning like this," I replied, trying to put on my best wry grin. It almost hurt, my head was throbbing so much.

She shoved the pad and pencil into her apron pouch. "But you passed, so there's hope for you yet." She flashed one last smile and then jerked her thumb over her shoulder as she said, "I'll get your coffee."

I returned the smile. "Bless you," I said. As Angela walked away, I tried to assess what had just happened. *Was she just flirting with me?* I wondered. Or what she just simply bucking for a bigger tip? Since I was probably close to twice her age, I leaned more towards the tip theory, but my mind was still mush so it was hard to trust anything that it spit out. There was no mistaking that she had just taken a couple of steps beyond the normal customer-waitress border but there was no telling if that was what she did with every customer or if I had been singled out for some reason. I turned and watched her as she stopped at a couple of other tables and didn't notice any special attention being bestowed upon those tables' occupants. The fact that every table was occupied by a senior citizen may have had something to do with it.

Then another thought crackled through the fog in my brain and zapped me between the eyes: *You are pathetic!* I turned my attention away from Angela and let the voice in my head finish its finger-wagging lecture. *Christ, you get a little attention from some young, pretty waitress and you get thrown for a loop like some fifteen-year-old kid. Get it together!!!* It was a sane and well-deserved lecture as everything the voice was telling me was true. I *was* pathetic and I *was* probably twice her age. But then I felt the tingling of the Fucket Bear on my arm and I knew what I had to do.

CHAPTER THIRTEEN

It had been a day full of surprises.

The first surprise came when my headache finally disappeared. I had assumed that it would be with me throughout the day but a handful of aspirin and several cups of coffee later it was gone. Normally, that would have been enough to make for a great day.

But then surprise number two came. I'd decided to ask Angela out to dinner and damn if she didn't say "yes." Actually, her affirmative response was surprise number three as number two was the fact that I'd had the balls to even ask her out in the first place. Fucket Bear knew what he was doing after all.

Surprise number four was that I had a good time with Angela. We went to a place called Chanterelle out on the edge of town and we wound up having a good meal, some good conversation and some good laughs. It was surprisingly easy, and I was doubly surprised that there was no generational awkwardness to contend with during the evening. She didn't bring up pop icons, college classes or her parents, and I didn't talk about anything pre-1990. It all worked. We drank wine, talked about a few current events, and flirted like hell back and forth. It was fun. And it was just the boost I needed. Again, that would have been plenty to make for a great day.

But then came the biggest surprise of all, surprise number five. I turned and looked down at Angela lying next to me in my bed. It was probably close to three in the morning and she was sleeping soundly. She was a pretty woman, even in her sleep, and a part of me suddenly regretted taking advantage of her youth. I was, after all, twice her age. Then I suddenly flashed on Marsha and I couldn't help but smile to myself. She was twenty years older than me and she had taken advantage of me in the same way I was now taking advantage of Angela; the irony of it all was downright poetic.

Then it occurred to me that I'd had a sixty-year-old and a twenty-something year-old in the same bed with me within a week's time. A forty-year spread between the ages of my sleeping partners was impressive and I wondered if perhaps it was a Maple Grove record of some kind. It would be nice to know that my name appeared somewhere in the town's record books.

My eyes then started to get heavy and I quickly succumbed to sleep. It had been a good day.

I awoke to the sound of keys jangling. My eyes fluttered open and I saw Angela getting dressed at the foot of the bed. She heard me stirring and looked up, throwing me an awkward smile that told me she wasn't feeling good about where she was and what she'd done. I knew she would need some reassurance, so I sat up in bed, smiled, and said cheerfully, "Well, good morning there, sunshine."

"Morning," she replied with a quick nod as she continued to search for something.

"How'd you sleep?" I asked.

"Fine," she replied, still distracted by the search for her missing whatever.

"You wanna grab some breakfast?" I asked casually.

She heaved a deep sigh and momentarily stopped her search. She walked over to my side of the bed and stood in front of me, looking a lot like a kid who just got caught stealing and was trying to muster up an apology. It wasn't a face I was expecting to see. She heaved another deep sigh and then said, "Listen, you're a nice guy and all but there's something you have to know." I saw an "oh, oh" flash across my brain and then felt it crash into my stomach. "You see, yesterday wasn't a mistake," she continued. *That was sounding a little better.* "I *chose* you," she said.

I smiled. "I chose you too," I replied.

She shook her head vehemently. "No, I don't mean it like that," she said. Her eyes went down to the floor and she said, "I chose you as part of a sorority initiation thing, so I don't want you to get the wrong idea that this is going to go anywhere beyond last night." She said the words quickly, the verbal equivalent of ripping a band-aid off quickly so the pain doesn't get drawn out, and when she was done, she stood silent for a moment. I had nothing to say because I was still confused as hell. I just knew that I didn't like the direction this was headed.

"I'm pledging this sorority, see," she began again, her eyes still glued to the floor. "And they gave me the choice of having sex with an old guy or going up on stage for amateur night at The Foxy Lady down in Springfield." She shrugged as her eyes raised up from the floor and finally locked with mine. I was expecting to see sad eyes or, at the very least, apologetic eyes, but they were neither: her eyes were matter-of-fact, as if she was talking about the logic of compound interest. "I was still trying to decide what to do when I met you yesterday morning. I decided that getting naked in front of one guy would be better than getting naked in front of a whole room of strangers, so…" Her voice trailed off, giving her words time to sink in.

I was stunned and I was speechless. Here I had thought that it was me taking advantage of *her* and now I was being presented with a reality that was light years away from mine. My brain was slow to wrap itself around this new reality and I knew I probably looked like an idiot, just sitting there naked in my bed with my jaw hanging open. Before I could come up with any words to utter, Angela delivered a verbal knife to my gut. "Besides," she said with a smile. "You looked like you could use a sympathy screw."

Christ, now I was a charity case!?!? The words then suddenly came to me. "I think it's time for you to go," I said, pointing towards the door as I climbed out of bed.

"Okay, okay," she said, her hands up in surrender. "No need to get all huffy on me here. You can't tell me you didn't have a good time last night."

I looked over and saw that she was smiling the same coquettish smile that she'd used countless times the night before. Whereas the night before I had found it stimulating, I now saw it for what it was - a tool in her tool chest of manipulations - and I wanted no part of it. "No comment," I replied.

The smile left her face. "Okay, I get it," she said. "Your feelings are hurt 'cuz you thought you had seduced me and now you're finding out that it was the other way around." She shrugged. "I'm sorry about that but, really, does it matter that much who seduced who? If we both had a good time, why should it matter?"

"Trust me," I said, not even trying to hide the irritation in my voice. "It matters."

She shrugged. "If you want to make yourself miserable about this, be my guest. Most guys your age would kill to have a night like that with a woman my age."

Her words hung in the air for a few seconds, spinning around in front of my eyes so I could get a good look at them. I realized that I was once again pathetic. I was now grouped with that large and depressing category called "most men" and I didn't want to be there. I'd fought my entire life to stay out of that group and now here I was, up to my neck in a pile of "most men" who, according to the Most Men Handbook, aren't that different from the Pavlovian dog that just salivates from one feel-good moment to the next. I turned to her and said calmly, "Like I said, it's time for you to go."

"Fine," she replied, her open palm facing me in a stop sign. "Just help me find my other shoe and I'm outta here." She got down on her hands and knees to look under the bed and then uttered the words that would be the final knife in my stomach that morning. "I've got class in twenty minutes and Dr. Weaver hates it when people walk in late to her class."

I stopped in my tracks. "What did you say?" I asked. She repeated what she'd said and then I asked, "What class is it that you're rushing off to?"

"Great American Writers," she replied. "It's a tough class but Dr. Weaver does a good job of making it interesting."

Dr. Weaver. Aka Linda. Aka my ex-wife. She was Angela's teacher. *Shit!* The irony was now dripping from the ceiling.

Angela noticed my stunned look and asked, "You okay?"

"Yeah, I'm fine," I replied.

"Hey, there it is!" I heard Angela say. I turned and saw her go over and pick her shoe up from behind the chair by the door. "Don't know how the hell it got over here," she said. She put the shoe on and then said, "Well, I'm outta here. It was nice meeting you, Ben." She walked to the door and opened it. Before walking out she turned and said, "Have a great life." And then she was gone.

CHAPTER FOURTEEN

"Gosh, I don't know, Ben," Bob was saying as we sat in his office. I'd headed over to see him at The Beacon just as soon as Angela had left my motel room. "Four thousand dollars is a lot of money."

"I know it is, Bob," I admitted. "But I am in desperate need of a change of scenery right now and this loan is the only way I'd be able to get out of town for a while." After Angela left that morning, I had made a quick decision to come over and ask Bob for some money. The walls of Maple Grove were closing in on me and it was time to get out of Dodge. Fuck the tent trailer and its moldy top, I just wanted to hop on the next plane, train, bus, or mule and watch Maple Grove get smaller and smaller in my rearview mirror.

"What about the insurance money?" he asked. "That must be coming through pretty soon."

Austin T's mousy face appeared in my head and I wanted to punch it. I probably would have if it was the real thing looking at me. His words of warning, to stay in town for now, flashed across my brain but I just smiled and said a silent *Fuck you Austin T!* to his face in my head. "There's been a glitch," I replied. "So, I may not be seeing that money for a while."

Bob must have read something in my face - something that told him not to ask any more questions about the insurance check - as he said, "So what are you planning to do with the money if I agree to give you the loan?"

I shrugged. "I don't know," I said, which was the truth. "I just know that with all that's happened lately, Maple Grove is the last place I should be right now," which was also the truth. "I'd probably just head for some warmer weather for a week or two."

Bob fidgeted with a pen on his desk. "I guess what I could do is just treat it like an advance on future wages," he said. "Then just take a little out of each of your next paychecks when you come back to work."

"That's a great idea," I replied, suddenly feeling hopeful. "Who knows," I added, knowing that what I was about to say was a lie, "this trip may be just what I need to get past all of this and feel ready to climb back in the saddle here at The Beacon." There was a persistent voice whispering to me that my career at The Beacon was over; it had been talking to me ever since the fire and, though I knew it to be true, I hadn't yet admitted it to anyone, including myself.

Bob smiled. "That would be great," he said. "We all miss you around here."

I knew that was one of those try-to-make-him-feel-better lies as I could name on one finger the people who would miss me at The Beacon, and that one person was now sitting in front of me. "Yeah, I miss it here," I lied in return. "Life just doesn't feel right without coming to work each morning." Now I was really laying it on thick.

Bob nodded. "Yeah, work gives our life structure. Without work it's easy to start feeling lost and adrift."

It was true that I was feeling all those things - structureless, lost and adrift - but something told me that walking through the front door of The Beacon and sitting down at my old desk to write the same, old tired stories wouldn't be the cure for what was ailing me. Actually, The Beacon was probably a large part of the illness itself. Not trusting myself to tell any more lies without busting out laughing, I decided to get back on task. "So, what do you say about the loan?"

Bob reached into one of his desk drawers and pulled out a big checkbook. He set it down on the desk in front of him, opened it up, clicked his pen, and said, "I'm going to make this check out for three thousand bucks. If you need more down the road, just let me know and I'll see what I can do."

"Thanks, Bob," I said. "You probably just saved my life." I was surprised that the words resonated with truth in my ears. *Was I in worse shape than I thought?*

Several hours later I was on a southbound train heading for Florida. I'd decided on Miami as my destination, primarily because that was the next train out of town that was headed someplace warm. It felt strange hopping on the train with just the clothes I was wearing, without so much as a backpack in tow, but when I got past the initial strangeness, I found that I liked the feeling. I felt light. I figured I would just get everything I needed when I arrived in Miami. Shorts, tank tops and sunscreen were hard to come by in New England in December anyway, so it made sense to wait.

And wasn't this what I had in mind when I torched my house in the first place? Wasn't I looking for this feeling of being unencumbered by the stuff that normally cluttered up my life? Hopping on a train without so much as a toothbrush in hand would be a perfect way to start my new life of attachment-free living. Fuck the house. Fuck Austin T. Fuck my job. Fuck Angela and everyone like her. And fuck Maple Grove.

I then saw Kylie's face peek out from behind a wall in my brain. She looked scared. My fucket resolve quickly melted away, replaced by incredible sadness. It wasn't fair that the one thing I cared about in this entire world was now out of my reach. Linda had established a formidable perimeter around our daughter, and I had yet to find a way to scale the walls. *Fuck Linda too.*

CHAPTER FIFTEEN

Miami was hot. Beyond hot, it was sultry. My new "Miami Is For Lovers" t-shirt clung to the sweat that was running down my back. My blood had thickened against the colder New England weather and it was now struggling with trying to remove the excess heat from my body. I took a long drink from the bottle of beer in my hand. What had once been cold and refreshing, was now warm and flat.

I was sitting in a beach chair on a beach just south of Miami, looking out at the sparkling Atlantic as I worked my way through a cooler full of beer. I dumped what was left of my beer into the sand and reached into the cooler for a new one. I fished around in the ice for a bottle, found one, pulled it out, popped the top and took a sip. It was icy cold. I settled back in my chair, situated in the shade of a palm tree, and felt my body relax. This was more like it. I closed my eyes and let my mind drift.

The first image that popped into my head was of my burning house. It was strange how that image still didn't inspire any emotions in me stronger than mild fascination. It was if I thought it was somebody else's house that I was watching go up in flames and all I felt was awe at the size of the flames and the intensity of the heat.

The second image that came into my head was a smiling Austin T. He was wearing a Cheshire Cat grin and I quickly booted him out of my brain. I fired an *Asshole!* at his image as he exited.

Right behind Austin T was Linda. Hard as I tried, I couldn't muster up a good, strong hate for her. It came in flashes, but it would always just whither away. Yes, she was holding my daughter hostage. Yes, she was dating Willie the Worm. Yes, she like nobody else could make me feel small and miserable. And yes, she had quit on me and quit on our marriage. But trumping each of these reasons to hate her was one pathetic fact: I still loved her. Damn, I still loved her.

I took a deep draw from the beer bottle. It was already turning warm. I scanned the beach and saw that it was pretty much empty. Farther down, towards the hotels, I saw a lot of people in the water and on the beach but there were just a handful of seniors in my little section of sand. I had purposely chosen a more isolated stretch of beach so nobody would hassle me for having a cooler full of Coronas and so far, nobody bothered me. It felt good to be alone.

My mind then suddenly clicked into planning mode. Questions like, *So what's next?* and *What are you going to do about money?* started to tap my brain on its shoulder, demanding its attention. Hard as I tried to toss those questions out on their ear, they just wouldn't budge. It was as if they had dug their talons into my brain and they refused to leave until I gave them some satisfaction. I closed my eyes, heaved a deep sigh, and fired up my internal computer. Time to go to work.

I fed the *What's next?* question into the computer and then waited a beat or two as it worked on possible answers. It wasn't long before the possibilities started to pop up on my screen. *Move to Seattle* was the first one to show its face. I'd fantasized about moving to Seattle ever since a visit there twenty years ago. It was a city that seemingly had everything - ocean, mountains, temperate climate, good coffee - and I had fallen in love with it at first sight. Linda had thrown water on the dream, literally, by constantly reminding me how much it rained out there but now that I was Linda-less there was no reason not to pursue this possible love affair. I nudged that idea aside to see what was next in line.

Walk across the country stepped into view. It had been a dream of mine to walk coast to coast ever since I was a teenager; I have no idea where that came from, but there it was. I think the appeal to me was threefold: first, there was the sheer physical challenge of it; second, it would force me to slow down my life; and third, it would be one hell of an adventure. I could just throw my life on my back, start walking, and not stop until I hit the Pacific Ocean. I smiled. The simplicity of it all had a lot of appeal.

A thought, like a rock, then came whizzing out of the darkness and caught me between the eyes. *My frame pack, sleeping bag and all my camping gear went up in flames!* Disappointment crawled through my body. *Shit!* I wouldn't have enough money to replace all that equipment and still fund a cross-country adventure. Once again, Austin T. stood in my path; without that insurance money my choices would be severely limited. I was starting to truly hate that guy.

Mr. Practical then stepped to my mental microphone and began talking to me about returning to The Beacon. He reminded me several times about my financial situation and how I needed money to make any big moves. He also lectured me on things like health insurance and 401k plans and the like. I wasn't in any kind of mood to listen to him prattle on, so I booted him off the stage. Fuck practical.

I thought back to a conversation I'd had with Jim in The Tavern the day after the fire. We talked about having balls-out fun and punching the accelerator on life instead of constantly riding the brake. That's what I wanted to do. Figuratively, if not literally, I wanted to get out on the open road, open the throttle, and see what it felt like to have the wind in my face. And I wanted to do it before my forty plus year-old chassis started to break down. It sounded very poetic, in a Jack Kerouac kind of way, but there it was.

I drifted back to the walking across country idea. It was perfect. I couldn't let something as trivial as a lack of money get in the way of what I wanted to do. I could find ways to get the money I needed to do a trip like that; beg, borrow, or steal, there was always a way. I threw back the last of my beer and then got to my feet.

The world spun a little at first when I stood, a result of the handful of beers in my system and the heat, but after a wobbly start I got my bearings. I knew I wouldn't get to where I wanted to go by sitting on my ass in Miami drinking my money away. It was time to get serious about The Plan. It was time to take the first real steps into my new life. It was time to head back to Maple Grove.

CHAPTER SIXTEEN

There were several messages on my answering machine when I walked in the door from the train station. One of them was from Austin T. He said he wanted to see me as soon as possible. The message was a few days old, so I figured I'd better go see him right away. I threw my few belongings on a chair and headed out the door.

I had to wait for Austin T. to finish up with another client when I arrived at Brown and Brown, so I used the down time to review The Plan. I had roughly twenty-five hundred dollars left from Bob's loan, which I figured would be enough to get me a decent sleeping bag, a frame pack and then have enough left over to get me started on my adventure. I could make do without a tent, cook stove, and all the other extras that would provide comfort but weren't necessary. It would be a Spartan trip for sure, but that was part of the appeal. I would get to use my wits and my guile in ways that I hadn't done since I was a kid.

"Mr. Phelps is ready to see you now," the receptionist said, interrupting my one-man planning meeting.

I got up and headed back to Austin T's office. He stood and shook my hand, flashing me the same practiced smile that had been in my mind's eye for the past week. I hated that smile. "Good to see you again, Mr. Weaver."

"Ben," I reminded him yet again.

"Yes, Ben, of course." He motioned for me to sit and I did. "So how have you been?"

"Except for having no house, no clothes, and no money I'm just fine." I paused to let my sarcasm settle in, then added, "Oh, and I have a little sunburn on my back that's making me a little uncomfortable."

He completely stepped over my sarcasm and went for the sunburn. "A sunburn? In the winter?"

"I went to Miami for a couple of days."

"Miami? You left town without telling me?" His tone suggested that I had just been a bad boy in some way.

I ignored his tone and stayed casual. "Yeah, I did. I needed to get away from Maple Grove for a while, so I headed someplace warm. What's the problem?"

"The problem is that you are involved in an investigation and as part of that investigation we need to be able to access you at a moment's notice."

"An investigation?" I didn't like the sound of that word. "I thought we were just processing forms so I could get my settlement check."

"Before issuing any checks we must first make sure we know what happened, Mr. Weaver." We were back to Mr. Weaver. He started shuffling through papers on his desk, pretending to look for something when in fact he knew exactly where to find it. "For instance, I'm still not clear how it was that you were awakened from your sleep that night."

"I already told you that. It was the smoke alarm." I could feel a little nervous sweat forming on my forehead.

Austin T. didn't look up from his papers. "Yes, well I'm being told by the fire chief that there weren't any batteries in your upstairs smoke alarm." That was when he looked up to see how I would react to this little piece of news.

I found myself wishing that I had taken notes during our previous conversations so that I could keep track of my string of lies. I decided to try a bluff. "Maybe it was the downstairs alarm that woke me up."

He looked back down at his papers. "You said earlier that you were very drunk that night." He looked up. "How is it that a drunk man could be awakened by the sound of a distant alarm?"

"I don't know, but something woke me up that night." "And you know..." I flashed a knowing smirk even though I didn't know shit about the sound of a smoke alarm. "...those suckers are pretty damned loud." Hold strong to the lie, it was my only hope. There was, after all, no way for him to prove anything definitively either way. All he had were his doubts and his only hope was to make me crumble. Fat chance of that happening. I was like a pit bull with a bone in my mouth and there was no way in hell that I was going to let go of it. I needed that check.

"Yes, well they are certainly designed that way." I could tell that it pained him to agree with me in any way.

"What the hell is going on here?" Time to go on the offensive. "Are you guys going to pay me what you owe me or what? Christ, I've probably paid for the house three or four times over with the monthly premium checks I've been shipping your way the past twenty years. So, what's the hold up?"

Austin T. was unruffled by my little display of irritation. "As I told you before, my job is to investigate everything about this fire and only when I am fully satisfied that there are no lingering suspicions concerning its origin will I hand this to our claims department for processing."

I wonder how many times Austin T. had uttered *that* sentence in his life? Probably a few dozen at least. He had it down well. "So, you're accusing me of being an arsonist, is that it?" I made sure to hold his gaze as I said the words; any small flinch might betray the underlying truth: I *was* an arsonist.

He maintained eye contact as he said, "That's a harsh word, Mr. Weaver. Nobody is accusing anybody of anything at this point." His eyes finally went back down to his desk and I exhaled quietly. "I'm just looking at inconsistencies and asking questions, that's all."

"So, are we done for today?"

"Yes, I'm done." He then looked up and added. "But please don't leave Maple Grove again without talking to me first. Until this investigation is over, I need you to stay local."

I swallowed a wise-ass comment and just grunted my affirmation. It looked like The Plan would have to be put on hold for a while.

CHAPTER SEVENTEEN

I sipped the margarita slowly. I'd seen how quickly Rita could put me on my ass and it was still early afternoon, so I knew I'd better take it slow if I was going to make it through the day. *Fucking Austin T. Phelps.* I had a feeling that would become my mantra for the foreseeable future.

I glanced around The Tavern and saw that the place was still doing a brisk lunch business. I decided it would be smart to order some food with my drink. I got the waitress's attention and ordered a ham and cheese sandwich. Soon after the waitress walked away with my order, an unfamiliar voice asked from behind me and to my left, "Mind if I sit down?"

I turned and saw a middle-aged black man standing near my booth. "You talking to me?" I asked.

He nodded. "I am indeed."

"Do I know you?"

"No, you do not."

I looked him up and down quickly. He was probably in his mid to late fifties and he was built like a greyhound: long and lean. He had a semi-disheveled appearance - with dirty jeans and a worn and tattered coat - and the little hair he had remaining on his head was dabbled with gray. At first glance I thought, *bum.* But there was something about his eyes that steered me away from that word. Overall, he looked tired and worn, but he had an interesting glint to his eye that suggested intelligence and mischief and that was what inspired me to say, "Have a seat."

The man sat down and then extended his hand across the table. "Name is Charlie."

I shook his hand. "Ben."

"Nice to meet'cha Ben."

"Likewise." There was a short awkward silence and then I said, "So why is that you wanted to sit at my table today Charlie?"

He nodded in the direction of my margarita. "Just thought you looked like you could use a friend besides the one found in a glass."

I didn't know how to take that. On the one hand, it was a thoughtful gesture. On the other hand, he was implying that I was a drunk who may need some intervention. I decided to just give him the benefit of the doubt for now. I stifled all the defensive explanations that were standing in line on my tongue; I didn't owe a stranger any kind of explanation as to why I was sipping a margarita in the early afternoon. "Thanks," was all I said, and then I took a big gulp of Rita and motioned to the waitress for another one.

"So, how's life, Ben?" he asked.

The directness of the question took me aback. "Life is just ducky, Charlie. How's yours?"

He shrugged. "Been better, but no complaints."

"So besides helping me with my drinking problem, is there some other reason you decided to come over to my table?"

"I guess I could use a friend right now too and you looked like a good candidate to me."

"Why is that?"

"Why is what?"

"Why is it that I looked like a good candidate to you?"

He threw me a quick shrug with his head and then said, "I don't know. I guess you just seemed like an intelligent guy with a sense of humor and I like both of those qualities in a man."

I was stunned by the similarities of our thumbnail assessments of each other. "And how exactly did you determine that?"

"What?"

"That I was an intelligent, funny guy."

He smiled. "I didn't say you were funny. I just said you had a sense of humor."

I returned the smile. "Ah, a fellow verbal jouster. This could prove to be fun after all."

"I think so."

"So why is it that you're in need of a friend right now, Charlie?"

"Same reason you are. Life just ain't dealing me good cards right now and I'm having trouble staying in the game."

I had a decision to make. Should I continue to parry with this guy and just keep things light? Or should I say fuck it, head down the road with him a while, and see where it takes us? I quickly decided to go with the fuck it plan. "So, what's life been dealing you lately?"

"Same old country western bullshit. Lost my wife, lost my job, my kids don't talk to me anymore." He shrugged. "If it didn't hurt so damned much it could actually be pretty funny stuff." We both went silent and stared at the table. "How about you, Ben? What's life been throwing your way?"

I let out a wry chuckle. "Turns out that my song is the same as yours Charlie, but I just added an extra line. I lost my house too."

He whistled. "Wife get it?"

"Nope. Fire."

"Oh, that's rough. Lose everything?"

I nodded. "Just about."

He shook his head slowly. "I gotta say that there are times that I wished *my* house went up in flames."

I ignored the huge door he had just opened for me and instead just asked, "Why?"

"I just get tired of dealing with all the crap in the house. Most of it was bought by Milly anyway, so all it does is remind me what a failure I've been."

"Milly is your ex-wife?"

He nodded. "That she is. But now she's married to some plastic surgeon and living out in California with my two daughters."

"You have two daughters? What are their names?"

"Jessica and Courtney."

"It's great having daughters, isn't it?"

"Used to be. When they were younger, they were everything to me. I loved being their personal and all-powerful god when they were little girls." He heaved a deep and sorrowful sigh. "But now they're spoiled senseless and my precious little girls have transformed into snotty teenagers who only care about getting that next pair of designer jeans."

I thought about Kylie and said a silent prayer that I would never feel the need to utter words like that about her in my lifetime. "That's too bad."

"Yeah, it is. It's two more souls that have dropped out of the let's-make-the-world-a-better-place derby."

The waitress came to the table and set the ham and cheese sandwich and margarita in front of me. "You eating today, Charlie?"

"Already ate. But you go ahead."

I took a bite of the sandwich. It tasted good and I quickly realized that I was hungrier than I thought. "So, what do you do now Charlie?" I asked out of the side of my ham-and-cheese-filled mouth.

"Not much. I live off a small pension and some disability income."

I almost asked about the disability thing but decided it was too personal a question for our young relationship. "Where do you live?"

His brow crinkled quizzically. "Aren't you curious about my disability?"

I let out a small chuffing sound. "Yeah, I thought about asking about that but decided it was too personal."

He smiled. "You're right, it is. I just wanted to know if you were curious about it."

I smiled. "You're an interesting guy, Charlie."

"Likewise, Ben."

"Are you always this way with people?"

"When you get to be my age, and lived the life I've led, you get to the point of just saying screw it with all of the politeness, pretense and other bullshit."

He just opened another door for me, and I decided to step through this one. "Funny you say that Charlie. I just had a similar discussion with a friend of mine, right after my house had burned to the ground."

"Tell me about it."

I then launched into the same fuck-it-soliloquy that I had shared with Jim, just a few tables over from where we sat now, the night after the fire. I told him about the lack of fun in my life, The Party House, and how I sometimes felt like a Golden Retriever. I then told him that ever since I lost my house, I've been trying to incorporate more fuckets into my life and how I've had a mixed bag of results. I spared him the details of my one-night stands with Marsha and Angela as those were both still too embarrassing for me to talk about. I also left out my dealings with Austin T. Phelps as that just didn't seem like anyone else's business right now. Charlie sat and listened quietly to everything I said, not interrupting once with a question or comment, and when I was done, he continued to sit in silence for a couple of beats. "So, what do you think?" I finally asked.

"I think you've officially landed on Planet Fucket." He saw the "Huh?" look I threw his way and explained. "Planet Fucket. The place where you just don't give a damn about all the stuff that used to dominate your life. Jobs, careers, flossing your teeth, paying your taxes, none of it matters anymore. It all seems so pointless, so you just throw your arms up in the air and say, I'm off to Planet Fucket, where it doesn't matter what other people think about me and I get to do what I want to do."

I smiled. I liked the notion of a Planet Fucket. "So how do you know so much about this particular planet? You been there?"

He laughed. It was a deep, loud laugh that reverberated throughout the entire restaurant. If I wasn't living on Planet Fucket I might have cared about all the heads that turned and looked over at our table. "Been there?" he bellowed. "Hell, I'm the *Emperor* of Planet Fucket! I'm the fucking Lord of Fucket Manor, Captain of the Fucket Patrol, and Mayor of Fucketville all rolled into one!"

Okay, now I was starting to care a little bit that we had quickly become the primary topic of conversation in the restaurant. I suddenly thought back to when I'd done a similar thing to Jim and I now felt slightly ashamed for putting him in an awkward position that night, especially when he'd just come to offer his help. "Okay, I get the idea," I said. "You are King Fucket."

He must have sensed my discomfort as he then asked, "What's the matter, Ben? You thinking about leaving me all alone here on Planet Fucket? Aren't you the one who's spreading the Gospel of Fucket to everyone? Didn't you tell your friend in this very restaurant that he had to be able to say it before he could do it?"

My skin went cold. I had never mentioned Jim's name or the fact that we had shared a meal at this same restaurant when I'd delivered my fucket rant. *Who is this guy?* "How do you know about that?"

He smiled. It was a different smile than the ones he'd flashed at me before; this one had more of an edge to it, like he knew something that he wasn't going to tell me. "There's a lot that I know about you, Ben. I know that you've had at least one, probably two, one-night stands this past week, that you've got a new tattoo, that you've taken a trip, that you're having problems getting your settlement check, that you have a daughter and ex-wife, that…"

I put both of my hands up in a stop sign. "Whoa, wait a minute here. Just who the hell are you?"

Again, the all-knowing smile. "Have you ever seen The Wizard of Oz?" I nodded. "How about It's a Wonderful Life?" I nodded again. "Good, that will make my explanation a lot easier." He shifted slightly in his seat and then said, "I'm your Guardian Angel, Ben." Before I could react to his words - his insane, out-of-this-world-crazy words - he added, "When you said the word fucket three times in succession that night in this restaurant, you called me to you, much like Dorothy in the Wizard of Oz clicking her heels three times together and saying, there's no place like home."

I thought back to the strange sensation I'd had that night after saying the three fuckets, a sensation that I had attributed at the time to the effects of Rita. I shook off that thought and let out a wry chuckle. "So, you're saying that you're my Clarence, eh?"

He nodded. "That's right."

"So, are you still trying to get your wings too?" I decided to go along on this ride with Charlie for a while longer. He didn't seem to be dangerous and I was curious as hell as to how he knew so many details about my life.

"While it was a great movie, It's a Wonderful Life didn't accurately portray the life of a Guardian Angel. We don't need or even want wings."

"I see. So what is it that you *do* want?"

"To help you."

"Help me with what?"

"Your life."

"What if I don't want any help?"

"Oh, but you do. You've landed in this strange place called Planet Fucket and you're still feeling your way along. I can serve as your guide on Planet Fucket because I've walked its surface many, many times. I can help you avoid the land mines and at the same time lead you to the hidden treasures that you probably wouldn't find on your own."

"This is all starting to sound a little too Luke Skywalker for my tastes."

He smiled; this one warmer and less edgy than the others. "I always loved those movies. Yoda was a very wise man."

"Only he wasn't a man. He was a…" What the hell *was* he?

"He was a Jedi Knight."

"Are you a Jedi Knight too?"

"I think we all have a little Jedi Knight in us."

"Yeah, well I could sure use some of those mind meld powers right now so I could see what the hell is bouncing around in your head. So how is it that you know this stuff about me? Did the insurance agency send you to spy on me?"

"No, I told you, I'm your Guardian Angel. And that was Mr. Spock by the way."

"What are you talking about?"

"It was Mr. Spock, from Star Trek, who could do the mind meld, not the Jedi Knights."

"Well you sure watch a lot of TV up in Angelville, don't you?"

He chuckled. "I was a human, just like you, at one time too. That's the only way I could be an effective Guardian Angel."

"You walked among us, eh?"

He nodded. "And I struggled just as you are struggling now."

"So, everything you told me earlier about your two daughters and an ex-wife was a lie, is that it?"

"No, not a lie." He smiled. "The truth sometimes has different shades, that's all."

"Pretty evasive answer there, Charlie. I've found that it's the shades that get me into the most trouble."

"Well said. In this case, however, the shades are necessary. You will get the full truth, unshaded, in due time."

"So, what is it that you want from me Mr. Guardian Angel? To find God? To embrace The Force?"

"Only if you want to. For now, I just want you to meet me here every Friday for lunch."

I felt like I'd just dropped into a Twilight Zone episode. I came to The Tavern to have a drink and grab some lunch and now here I was making weekly lunch arrangements with Charlie the Guardian Angel. I swore I could hear Rod Serling's voice in the distance introducing this episode; "*Poor Ben Weaver,*" he was saying. *"He came for lunch, but little did he realize what was on the menu that day...in the Twilight Zone."* I considered Charlie's request for a moment and then heard the quiet "fucket" in my ear. "It's a date," I said. "I'll see you right here next Friday at noon."

CHAPTER EIGHTEEN

Life had gotten weird.

I was walking through town later in the day - watching all the mothers, students, shopkeepers, businessmen, and everyone else go about their days - and it hit me just how much my life had changed in the past few weeks. Just a month earlier, I was just working my job at The Beacon, thinking about the long list of Someday Things that were always bouncing around in my head, and looking forward to seeing Kylie over the holidays. Nothing out of the ordinary, but it was a life.

Now, as I walked down the street, I felt like a rock in the stream as everyone flowed by in the current around me. They all seemed to be moving with some sense of purpose and I had nothing to do and nowhere to go. A month ago, I would have welcomed this feeling: no job stress; no house stress; nothing but open-ended time staring me in the face. But the reality of my present situation was that I had nobody to share my job-less, house-less, schedule-less existence with. All my friends were working, Kylie was in school, and only crazy people like my new friend Charlie were available to play with me. I felt like a guy sitting on a deserted island with a million dollars in cash stuffed in my pockets.

I stopped at a shop window and half-mindedly scanned the contents of the window. It was Hastie's Emporium, one of those old New England general stores in which you could find anything from apples to zippers, and their display window was overflowing with various gift ideas. Some distant voice from deep in my brain reminded me that at some point I would have to find some Christmas presents for Kylie. It was a task that I'd always relished and yet now it just felt pointless and burdensome. I heaved a deep sigh and then turned away and kept walking.

The weather had turned cold, single digits cold, and I over-heard many people talking about a huge snowstorm that was coming our way. Normally that would have stirred thoughts about snow shovels, sand, and road salt, but without a driveway or sidewalk to my name I no longer had to worry about such things. I felt a chill sneak through my new winter coat and for the second time since The Fire I found myself missing my LL Bean winter coat.

As I thought about it further, there were a lot of things I was missing about my house. I missed having a familiar place to go to at the end of the day. I missed having a fridge full of beer and a pantry full of food just waiting to indulge my every gastronom-ical whim. I missed my favorite chair and being able to read the paper, watch TV or do a crossword puzzle in it with a glass of wine on the small table next to me. I missed my fireplace. I missed the privacy. And I really, truly missed my bed. I hadn't slept very well in the hotel room bed.

What the hell are you doing?!?! The words came big and loud into my head. *Your house is gone! Get over it and stop whining about it!* I couldn't tell if it was my father's voice in my head - the voice that had always told me to buck up and be a man - or if it just my own voice of reason, but it was right. It was time to end the Pity Party and move on. I pushed my ex-house off the stage, and it was soon replaced by Charlie. I replayed my lunch with him, looking for possible clues as to who he was and why he suddenly fell into my life.

I had already dismissed the theory of him being a spy for Austin T. Charlie didn't seem like the spy type and Austin T. didn't strike me as the kind of guy who would hire somebody else to do his sleuthing for him. He seemed to get off too much on going in for the kill himself.

Then I wondered if perhaps it was something that Jim had set up, to get back at me for how I treated him that night at The Tavern. That would help to explain how Charlie knew so much about what's been going on in my life. A part of me hoped that it *was* something that Jim had put together as that would indicate that my friend Jimbo - the fun-loving prankster I knew in college - was still alive and well. But as much as I wished it to be true, I had a hard time believing that Jim would arrange such a thing. He was too caught up in the responsibilities of his life, and keeping Liz happy, to waste time on something as frivolous as revenge. I checked Jim off my list of possible suspects.

I came to a section of town known as The Arbors and my attention shifted from my internal world to the external world. The Arbors was a series of streets named for various trees - Oak, Elm, Walnut, etc. - and the houses were all old Victorians from the nineteenth century, back when they took the time to build a house that would stand the test of hundreds of years of New England winters. They were all beautiful, stately houses and this time of year they all seemed to be entered into an unspoken contest of "Who-can-top-whom?" when it came to Christmas decorations. I glanced down the streets and marveled at the corridors of light and color that stretched out before me. I'd seen these streets dozens of times before during the holidays but for some reason the stunning beauty of it all was hitting me particularly hard at that moment. Perhaps it was envy, as I secretly wished that I could be sitting in one of those homes, feeling a part of the flow of family and life that coursed through each of them. Or perhaps it was as simple as just admiring the sheer spectacle of thousands and thousands of white, blue, red and green lights blinking in front of me. Whatever it was, it inspired tears to begin forming in my eyes. I was now officially and undeniably pathetic.

CHAPTER NINETEEN

"What's wrong, Dad?"

Kylie's question stirred me from my daydream. We were sitting in Hastie's Emporium, sharing a hot fudge sundae at the counter, and my thoughts had drifted to the "What next?" question that had come to dominate my mind lately. "Nothing sweetie," I responded with a forced smile. "Daddy's just thinking about what he's going to be getting his favorite daughter for Christmas."

Kylie's eyes went wide. "What is it?"

"What's what?"

"What are you going to get me for Christmas?"

"Whoa, now wait just a minute there little lady." I leaned down so I was at eye level with her on the stool. "I said I was thinking about what to get for my *favorite* daughter. What makes you think that's *you*?" I jabbed her playfully in the chest.

She giggled uncontrollably. The sound of her giggle pierced my chest and bounced around in my heart. It was probably true for most fathers, but when my little girl giggled, I could feel my knees go weak and my heart fill to bursting with incredible love. Today that love was tinged with sadness, however, as I realized that her giggling years were quickly coming to an end. I knew that I would miss those years. "Tell me," she said as she caught her breath between fits of laughter. "Tell me what you got me."

It didn't matter that I didn't have a clue as to what I would be getting her for Christmas. I could play this game forever. "I can tell you that it's bigger than a doughnut and smaller than a tree."

She giggled again. "That could be *anything*."

I noticed that she had some fudge sauce on her chin. I reached over with a napkin and started to dab it off. She thrust her chin forward to make it easier for me to clean. The trust and the intimacy of the moment hit me unexpectedly hard and I could feel tears forming in my eyes. I quickly finished and turned away from her, pretending that I needed a drink of water. "So, how's school going?" I asked, anxious to move on to new topics.

"Okay. I really like my teacher."

"What's her name again?"

"Miss Hobart."

"That's right. And what is it that you like so much about her?" I felt the tears retreating and my inner emotional state returning to baseline normal.

"She's nice. And she's pretty."

"Those are two essential ingredients for a good teacher."

"And she's smart too. William said she was a real good student when she was in college."

Hearing his name come from my daughter's mouth inspired a spurt of adrenaline to shoot into my system. I felt my pulse quicken. No matter how many times it had happened in the past, hearing Kylie say his name still upset me. But I knew better than to let her see that or make her feel bad for doing it. She was still nothing but the innocent bystander to the train wreck that was mine and Linda's marriage and I wanted to make sure she maintained that innocence. "Smart is important too," was all I said.

Kylie may have sensed my discomfort as she shifted the conversation back to Christmas. Or maybe that was simply where her greatest interest resided. "Are you coming over to the house for Christmas this year?"

"If Mom will have me."

"She will. She knows it's important to me."

It felt nice to hear her say those words. I was, and probably always would be, insecure enough in her love for me that I never grew tired of hearing her say such things. "I'm glad."

"But Dad?"

"Yeah, sweetie." I looked down and saw that her look had suddenly turned serious.

"Could you try to not freak out like you did at Thanksgiving?"

My mind did a quick rewind to Thanksgiving. I thought I had done remarkably well, all things considered, during my Thanksgiving visit. Despite William's many inane comments, despite my having to watch the small intimacies being exchanged between The Worm and the two most important females in my life, I thought I'd held it together pretty well that day. My freak out didn't come until later, when I decided to torch my house. "What do you mean? I didn't freak out at Thanksgiving."

She nodded emphatically. "Yes, you did, Dad. You freaked out at William when he was cutting the turkey."

Oh, that. Not only had William butchered the bird, showing that he was completely clueless as to how to properly carve a turkey, but he had done it with the carving knife that Linda and I had gotten as a wedding gift from my Uncle Phil. I did indeed allow my frustration to bubble out at that point, telling The Worm that he should take a remedial class in turkey carving, or some such smart-ass comment to that effect. "Okay, so I had one freak out moment. I thought that was pretty darned good, all things considered."

"*What* things considered?"

Oops. I knew better than to let weighted sidebar comments like that slip out in Kylie's presence. "Actually, it was just plain wrong what I did to him at Thanksgiving and I promise not to let that happen again at Christmas. Okay?"

Kylie smiled. It was a smile that only a child could flash — a from-the-soul, all-is-forgiven, no-hard-feelings smile. The adult version would have looked more forced and would have typically been accompanied by a "can-I -really-trust-you?" sideways glance. It was one of a thousand reasons why I preferred Kylie's company over 99.9% of the adults out there. "Thanks, Dad."

"No problem, kiddo." I reached over and rubbed her shoulder for emphasis. "Now, just to make sure I didn't get you any repeat gifts, why don't you tell me what you're asking for from Santa this year." I clicked on my mental tape recorder and waited for the possible gift ideas to flow from my daughter's mouth. I was lying of course, but it was one of those white lies that I was certain never made it into The Great Ledger that St. Peter kept. I made a mental note to ask Charlie The Guardian Angel about that one at next Friday's lunch.

"Daddy," she replied with a slight roll of her eyes. "You know that there's no such thing as Santa Claus."

I was a little taken aback by her reply. Last I knew, Kylie was still a believer in the magic of Santa Claus. Granted, she had hung in there longer than most of her peers -perhaps attributable to her only-child status, as there were no older siblings to break the sad news to her - but she had left the cookies and milk out for Santa the year before and I had loved the fact that the myth was still very much alive for her. "What do you mean?" I asked, hoping that my open-ended question would lead me to the reason behind her sudden lack of belief.

"William told me."

The three words acted like three blows to my chin. After recovering from the blows, my instinct was to start punching back. I suppressed that instinct. "What did he tell you?" I silently hoped that my voice had stayed calm and even as I asked the question. If Kylie sensed any disappointment or anger coming from me, she would run for cover.

"He told me that Santa didn't exist," she replied, oblivious to my inner emotional state. "He said that Santa Claus just represented all the things that we hoped would be a part of Christmas."

"And you believed him?"

She suddenly looked confused. "Yes."

"Well, let me just say that you shouldn't be so quick to accept everything that he tells you." I wasn't sure if she noticed that I never used The Worm's real name; I would rather chew glass than utter his name while Kylie or Linda were within earshot.

"Why?"

I struggled to find the right words, words that would place a small kernel of doubt in her mind but wouldn't make her feel like she was in the middle of a skirmish between me and The Worm. "What do *you* think about Santa?" I decided to ask, opting for a question rather than throwing out words that could be construed as anti-Worm.

She shifted around in her seat. "I don't know. I'm still trying to figure out where all those presents come from."

"What does your mother say about all this?"

"I haven't talked to her about it yet."

Wow, this was a first; I got to talk to my daughter about something before Linda knew about it. Despite my anger at The Worm I felt a surge of semi-elation. "Just so you know, *I* still believe in Santa Claus." Another white lie for St. Peter to consider.

Her eyes scrunched to suspicious slits. "No you don't."

I nodded with gusto. "Yes, I do."

She stared at me for a long time. I pretended to become re-interested in my ice cream sundae so I wouldn't have to look into her eyes with my own lying eyes. "Do you believe in flying reindeer too?" she finally asked.

I nodded again. "The whole shooting match." I set down my spoon and raised my fingers so I could count on them. "The flying reindeer," I said as I grabbed my forefinger. "The fat man in the red suit." I grabbed my middle finger. "The North Pole, the elves, the down-the-chimney thing," I rattled off, continuing to grab fingers. "You name it when it comes to Santa, and I believe in it."

Katie giggled, somewhat nervously I thought. "I think I still believe all that too, Daddy," she then said quietly, as if she didn't want anyone sitting nearby to hear her admission.

I leaned over and pulled her into a hug. "Good. That can be our little secret, sweetie," I whispered into her ear as we embraced.

CHAPTER TWENTY

I fidgeted in my chair. I was sitting in The Bean, a small coffee shop in downtown Hampton, and I was feeling restless. I had dropped Kylie at her mother's several hours earlier and I'd decided to grab a book and head to The Bean for an afternoon of leisurely reading. It was something I'd fantasized about quite often as a working stiff, but now that I had the time to do it, I was unable to relax into it. I was restless. I don't know *why* I was feeling restless, I had no place to be and nothing to do, but there was no denying that I was ready to jump out of my chair.

Perhaps it was the fact that without a full-time job to provide contrast, sitting idly didn't have as much appeal. Or perhaps my state of restlessness was attributable to my inability to stop rolling my latest visit with Kylie around in my head again and again. I still wanted to grab The Worm's neck in my hands and squeeze his throat until he turned blue. Or maybe it was my choice of books that prevented me from relaxing in my chair. I had chosen Cervantes' "Don Quixote" for my reading session — a book that had been on my must-read-someday list for many years — and I was having a hard time plowing through it. It absolutely was not in the light reading category.

Or maybe, just maybe, my fidgety state was simply the result of having consumed three cups of coffee over the last couple of hours. I set down my book and scanned the cafe. It was filled primarily with college students, many of whom were probably preparing for their upcoming final exams. It didn't take much effort for me to call up my own memories of cramming for finals in this same coffee shop over twenty years ago. Those were good days. I didn't realize it at the time, but those were perhaps the *best* years of my life. Yeah, there were papers to write, tests to take, and grades to worry about, but all those memories had faded to the background. What I remembered most was the sense of fellowship that pervaded the entire campus, especially around this time of year when everyone was focused on final exams. There was an esprit-de-corps amongst college students — a feeling that we were all in this together, suffering through unreasonable professors, excessive workloads, and impossible deadlines — and that somehow made it all tolerable. It was, unfortunately, not a feeling that carried over past the gates of the university as most workplaces failed miserably in the esprit-de-corps category. That was too bad.

I caught a glimpse of somebody approaching my table out of the corner of my eye. I turned and saw a familiar face smiling down at me. "Ben-ben? How ya doin'?"

It was Rickie Barnes. I'd known him since high school but hadn't seen him around town in years. A little voice in the back of my brain reminded me that he'd been in the state penitentiary, doing time for some drug-related charges, which would explain the recent lack of Rickie Barnes sightings. I'd played baseball with Rickie in high school and whenever I saw him, he would inevitably want to pull out that mental photo album and relive the good ol' days, even though the high school years were far from my good ol' days. "Hey there Rickie," I replied, trying to make my voice sound friendly but not too inviting. "How's it goin'?"

He shrugged. "Been better. Just got outta the joint and lookin' for work."

I silently admired his willingness to be up front with his recent struggles, though I was completely at a loss as to how to respond to what he'd just said. "I'm sorry," was the best that I could come up with.

"No worries. Somethin' will come up." A crooked smile formed. "Hey, guess who I saw yesterday."

"Who?"

"Coach Abel. He was headin' into the post office."

Coach Abel had been our high school baseball coach and he was probably close to a hundred years old by now. "Did you talk to him? How's he doing?"

Rickie lowered his head. "Nah, I didn't talk to him. I didn't want to remind him about the league championship that I cost him."

Poor Rickie. He had been our center fielder during our senior year. It was Coach Abel's last year coaching and everyone had been talking about sending him off with his first league championship. It had looked like we'd give that to him as we were playing in the championship game and had a lead going into the final inning. But then Rickie dropped a key fly ball that allowed the winning run to score and that was the ballgame. Rickie had never lived down that moment. Everyone around him quickly forgot about it but Rickie seemed to carry it with him everywhere he went, even now, more than twenty years later. A part of me wondered if his drug problem could be traced back to that day on the baseball field. I suddenly felt very sorry for Rickie Barnes.

"So, how's life been treatin' you," Rickie then asked me. I noticed him eye the chair that was sitting empty across the table from me but, selfish loser that I was, I didn't ask him to sit down. I just didn't want to play this remember-when game any longer than I had to.

I shrugged. "Life's been okay." If a bigger lie has ever been uttered, I'd be surprised. But if I'd said anything else it would have invited further conversation.

"Aren't you a writer or something?" he asked.

I nodded. "Yeah, I write for The Beacon."

He nodded a few times. Then, perhaps sensing that he'd run out of conversational topics, he said, "Well, I guess I better get going." He extended his hand and I shook it. "Great seein' ya Ben-ben. Guess I'll see ya around."

"Good seeing you, Rickie. Good luck finding a job."

"Yeah. Thanks." And with that he turned and left the cafe.

After he'd left, I silently berated myself for being such a shit. *Who was I to judge Rickie Barnes?* Christ, at least he was honest about who and what he was. I was a pathetic loser disguising myself as something more than that. Just like Rickie, I had no job. And, just like Rickie, I was a felon, the only difference being that he had been caught and I still hadn't had the official arsonist label hung around my neck. I also had a broken marriage to my name and, despite his many years in prison, I probably had fewer possessions than Rickie had at this moment in time. There was no use trying to kid myself: In the Loser Sweepstakes I would say that Rickie Barnes and I were now neck-and-neck.

I now had Rule #2 for my New Life: ***Don't be so damned quick to judge other people.***

CHAPTER TWENTY-ONE

I carried thoughts of Rickie Barnes with me throughout the rest of the day. I obsessed on the question of: What makes us into the adults that we are? Yeah, there's the whole nature-nurture thing to think about but, more to the point, I wondered what specific events did most of the shaping as we grew into adults. I decided that most of us could probably call up a handful of significant life-changing moments that, when added up, may have been responsible for 90% of the shaping of the future us. We would then pull these events out, like photos in our wallet, and hold them up to our lives from time to time to either affirm or deny who we thought we were and what we were doing with our life.

In my own life, I quickly called up four significant events. The first was when I was around ten years old. I was in a local tobacco store - back when they even had something called a tobacco store - and I was looking at comic books. Spider-Man, Daredevil, Archie, Richie Rich, I loved 'em all. The only problem was that I loved so many of them and yet the money I had in my pocket would only pay for two of them. So, I quickly made the decision that I could indeed "have it all" and, after doing a quick scan of the store to make sure nobody was looking, I stuffed every one of them, probably six comics in all, under my shirt and made my way for the door. I was just a few steps from getting away with the first crime of my short career when a large hand landed on my shoulder and a deep voice from behind me said; "Aren't you forgetting something?" I turned around slowly, my shirt bulging with the stolen goods, and there stood Mr. Antonelli, the owner of the tobacco shop. I wanted to die.

He called my parents - this was a time when everyone knew everyone else in town - and they came down to retrieve me. The sentence for my crime came down quickly and painfully from my parents. First came the physical portion of the sentence: a hard spanking on my ass with Dad's leather belt. Second came the financial punishment: no allowance for six months. And, finally, came the worst part of my sentence. It was less tangible than the other two, but it was just as real and just as painful: the sense of shame that I felt for a long time afterwards. Both of my parents were proud people and I could see that I had let them down in a big way by trying to steal something from Mr. Antonelli. They never said the words "We're ashamed of you, Ben" but they didn't have to: I felt it just as surely as if they had screamed it in my ear and then written it on my forehead.

The lesson I learned from that whole episode was that, as tempting as it was to think to the contrary, nothing came for free. There was always a price to pay. There was always a victim, sometimes seen, sometimes unseen. And there was always Mr. C to answer to, as in Mr. Conscience. That guy could be relentless. That was both my first and my last effort at shoplifting in my life and I could still call up Mr. Antonelli's stern face or my parents' disappointed looks as if the whole thing happened just yesterday.

My second life-shaping incident came in Junior High School. I was a seventh grader and I had submitted a short story of mine to a district-wide contest called, "Young Hemingway." I remember that I wasn't going to do it but my English teacher, Mrs. Prentiss, encouraged me to give it a try. It turned out that she was right, as my short story - I don't even recall what it was about - won the top prize and I was handed a big trophy and a check for $100, which was a small fortune in my 12-year-old world. I wallowed in the attention for weeks afterwards, as I received congratulations from friends, family members, teachers, and even some strangers on the street for a while, thanks to a small article next to a picture of me in the local paper. But it wasn't long before the glow wore off and I was then faced with the following question: *What are you going to do for an encore?* I soon learned that the word "potential," that everyone had used in such a complimentary way following my victory, had another side to it, and that other side had an edge to it that could do some damage when wielded indiscriminately. I felt the pressure of expectations from my teachers to "do something exceptional" and that pressure formed the seeds of my undoing as a student. Unable to perform at the level that I felt others wanted me to, I went in the other direction, away from the expectations, and by my freshman year I had become completely indifferent towards academics and successfully entrenched myself in the comfortably mediocre world of the C student. My parents hassled me about it for a while, but they eventually gave up. To this day I can't hear the word potential without cringing.

My third and fourth life-shaping events were more recent but had nonetheless shaped the current me quite significantly. The third was Kylie's birth and the fourth was my divorce from Linda. Both were powerful in their own way - one being powerful in the life-is-amazing kind of way and the other being powerful in the life sucks kind of way - and they both left their indelible mark on my soul.

My thoughts were interrupted by the sound of my cell phone ringing. I took it out of my pocket and saw that it was Austin T calling. I whispered a quick *mother fucker* and then answered the phone. "Hello?"

"Mr. Weaver. This is Austin T Phelps from Brown and Brown."

"Yeah, hello Austin. What's up?" *You're calling me to tell me that my check is waiting for me at the front desk and I can pick it up anytime, right?*

123

"I'm wondering if you could stop by my office sometime in the next couple of days."

"Why?" *Because my calendar is just so jammed up right now.*

"Uh, I'd rather talk about it when I see you in person."

Fuck came the whisper in my ear. "Austin, I have to ask you something."

"What is that?"

"Why is it that you seem to have such a Jones for me on this whole thing?"

"A what?"

"A Jones. A desire. A hankering. An out of whack need to make my life miserable."

There was a long silence on the other end. I was beginning to think that the call had been dropped when Austin replied, "So when can I expect to see you in my office?"

A complete ducking of my question. I must have hit a nerve. "I'll take a look at my schedule and get back to you." And then I hung up. *Mother fucker.*

It took me a while to calm down but when I finally did, I retrieved the mental thread from my earlier thoughts and I soon realized something. I flashed on my lone shoplifting effort from all those years ago and it dawned on me that I was doing it again. I was trying to stuff some more comic books under my shirt, attempting to get something for nothing, and all the while hoping that nobody would notice. Austin T was Mr. Antonelli in this mini-drama and his hand was resting firmly on my shoulder, just as Mr. Antonelli's had, keeping me from walking out of his store. A part of me suddenly felt ashamed; ashamed that I hadn't learned my lesson after all and now here I was repeating the same mistake more than thirty years later.

It didn't take long for my adult self to come marching into the situation, however, armed with rationalizations and justifications. My adult self told my embarrassed younger self - the one that was sitting in a mental corner feeling ashamed - that we *deserved* this settlement money from Brown and Brown. He told my younger self that we *earned* this money through all our years of hard work and our payment of thousands and thousands of dollars in insurance premiums. And, finally, he told us that we *needed* this money if we had any hopes of starting our new life.

My younger self bought into these arguments and it wasn't long before we were once again joined together as one Self, united in our desire to throttle Austin T and squeeze his skinny little neck until he gave us our settlement check. Armed with this new determination, I decided it would be a good time to go pay a visit to Austin T and see what he had on his mind.

CHAPTER TWENTY-TWO

Rule #3 for my new life: *Don't have important, life-changing conversations with people when I'm feeling pissed off.*

It didn't go so well with Austin T.

I had marched into his office, ready to do battle, and I was soon put on the defensive by the mini-Columbo. "I have a few discrepancies I need to discuss with you, Mr. Weaver," he'd said.

"Of course you do," I replied with my best obnoxious smirk planted on my face.

He didn't seem to notice, or care about, my childish smirk as he jumped right into his questions. "I believe you had said you weren't a smoker, is that correct?"

"Yep," I shot back, suddenly not feeling as cock-sure as I had been when I walked in.

He scanned his papers. "I believe you called it a filthy habit at first, and yet you then later revealed that you do indeed smoke cigars. Is that correct?"

"Yep." Time to play this straight until I saw where he was headed.

"And you also said that it was a smoke alarm that had woken you up that night?"

"Yep." I was starting to feel like I was tying my own noose and Austin T was going to toss it up and over the office rafters and hang me from it; perhaps a fitting end for a shameless arsonist.

"And yet it was determined that the upstairs smoke alarm had no batteries in it." He was looking down at the papers on his desk and he shook his head slowly. It was a shake that said, *I don't believe a word of it, you lying piece of shit, but I'll keep playing this game with you.* What he had just said was framed more as a statement than a question, so I knew to just keep my mouth shut. "Unfortunately, the downstairs smoke alarm was burned beyond the point where it could be retrieved in order to determine its functionality."

My first lucky break, I thought. "Bummer," I said, trying hard to keep the grin out of my voice.

He looked up at me, his eyes scanning me for possible clues. "Yes, it was," he agreed. His eyes then went back down to his papers. "We did however find something of interest."

Uh oh.

"It seems that there was some newspaper ash alongside the tobacco residue in the cushions of the couch." He quickly looked up and caught my eye, again looking for my reaction. "I recall you telling me that you had smoked a victory cigar of sorts that evening Mr. Weaver, to celebrate the fact that you hadn't beaten a certain man to death with a drumstick. Is that correct?"

My mind went into scramble mode, attempting to jog ahead of Austin T on this path to see where he was headed. "Yeah, that's correct," I replied.

"Did that victory cigar also involve a victory rolling up of newspapers and a victory stuffing of said newspapers into the cushions of your couch?"

His words just floated in the air in front of me for a while, swirling around and dipping and diving as if teasing and taunting me. I wanted to swat at the air and get them out of my face, but I quickly became aware of Austin T's eyes on me and I knew I had to say something. Quickly. *Best defense is a good offense,* my high school coaches used to tell me. It was time to test the veracity of those words. "What the hell are you trying to say here, Mr. Phelps?" I asked in my top-shelf indignant tone.

"I'm trying to say exactly what I had said to you during a previous visit, Mr. Weaver." There was no back-down in his tone; he wasn't going to be intimidated. *Bummer.* "Something just does not smell right about this case and my job is to figure out why. There are still far too many discrepancies in your story to allow me, in good conscience, to hand over a settlement check to you. So, until I get satisfactory answers to my questions, we are going to keep doing this." He spread his arms in front of him and I thought I detected a slight look of exasperation in his face. *Maybe I was wearing him down*, I thought.

I decided to stay on the offensive; partly because I was pissed off but partly because I didn't have very good answers to some of his questions. It was time for a grand exit. "Well that's just fucking great," I said as I bolted to my feet. "I have to put my whole life on hold because of you and your fucking petty questions." Then I did something very stupid. I bent over and ran my arm across Austin T's desk, throwing all his precious papers into the air. As they fluttered to the ground I said, "That's what I think of your questions, Mr. Phelps."

Austin T watched in horror as his papers rode the air currents to various corners of his cubicle and beyond, out into the hallway. He appeared to be in shock for a moment, but it didn't take him long to recover and the look of horror was quickly replaced by something that looked like anger, which I'm guessing might have been an actual first for Austin T. His eyes seemed to lose all emotion as he locked eyes with me and I saw in those eyes the unmistakable desire to reach down my throat, grab my heart, and then beat me over the head with it. He looked murderous.

I decided that I didn't want to stick around to see what Austin T's next move was going to be, so I turned and left his office in a semi-huff, trying as best I could to keep my indignant mojo going in the face of Austin T's Charles Manson-like glare. As I walked out of the building, I couldn't help but think that I had just destroyed any chances I'd had of ever receiving a settlement check from the Brown and Brown Insurance Company. But then a little moment of serendipity occurred that would change my odds.

I blasted out the front door - angry at both myself for my stupidity and at Austin T for too many reasons to count - and, after banging a quick left as I exited onto the sidewalk, I ran right into some poor woman who, thankfully, caught herself before falling backwards onto her butt. She quickly gathered herself and, after picking up the file folder she'd dropped on the ground, she stood in front of me, her face just a few feet from mine. It was a face that I recognized instantly and, before I could even utter my first words of apology, I heard myself saying, "Marsha?"

The two of us sat in a nearby cafe, drinking coffee and chatting, for over an hour. "How long have you worked at Brown and Brown?" I asked her at one point.

"Thirty years." There was a short pause and then she added, "Thirty long, tortuous, mundane years."

Strange as it sounded, it was good to see Marsha again. We had just shared that one crazy night together, but there was a certain something about her that made you want to be close to her; an energy, an aura, whatever you wanted to call it, I found myself smiling a lot more when I was around her. "What makes it so tortuous?"

Her face scrunched in disbelief. "Are you kidding? We're talking insurance here, Bucko. Lots of numbers, lots of papers, lots of people who actually *like* numbers and paper. It's a recipe for Hell on Earth."

I stifled the urge to blurt out Austin T's name as a fine example of a number-loving, paper-embracing resident of insurance adjuster Hell, and instead asked, "So why are you still there?"

"Two reasons," she replied quickly. She raised her index finger and said, "Money," then raised her middle finger and said, "Health insurance."

"Good reasons," I agreed, "but not good enough to make you miserable for thirty years."

She looked down at the table and mumbled, "You just don't understand." Before I could ask a follow-up question, her head came up and she asked, "So why were you in there today?" She saw my "Huh?" look and clarified with, "Brown and Brown. Why were you in there?"

My brain did a quick sorting of information, placing the innocuous details of my situation in one pile and the damning ones in another, and I then said, "I was dealing with the paperwork from a recent house fire."

"*Your* house?"

I nodded.

"Shit." Her head tilted sideways. "So why didn't this little fact come out the night we were together?"

I chuckled. "I don't recall too many life details coming out of *either* of our mouths that night."

She laughed. "Yeah, I guess you're right."

"Actually, I still don't remember too many of *any* kinds of details from that night."

"You were a little ripped that night," she agreed.

I then flashed on the fact that Marsha had said she was married. I glanced down and saw that she was now wearing a wedding ring on her left hand. She noticed my glance and said, "Yep, ol' Marsha is still married." Her eyes took on a far off look for a moment, but then she quickly snapped back and asked, "So what about you? What's your story, my friend?"

"You don't remember my name, do you?"

She opened her mouth, perhaps to attempt one last bluff, and then let out a deep breath and said, "No, I don't. I'm sorry."

I had to admit to feeling a little hurt - secretly kicking myself for blurting *her* name out so quickly, like some desperate loser - but the hurt disappeared quickly. "It's Ben."

She smiled a warm smile. "Ben. That's right, I remember now." She reached across the table with her right hand and I shook it. "I promise that from this day forward I will never forget your name again." We held hands for the briefest of moments and feeling her flesh again sent a surge of current through me. Perhaps it was just a spurt of adrenaline fueled by recognition, as our flesh had at one time shared the most intimate of moments, but there was no mistaking that it felt good. She then pulled her hand back, too soon I thought, and said, "So tell me your story, Ben."

She had emphasized my name when she said it so we both exchanged smiles before I said, "My story, huh? How much time do you have?"

"I'm a manager who everyone thinks is at some off-site meeting on the other side of town, so I have as much time as you need."

I was wallowing in the give and take that we were sharing and was happy to hear that she was in no rush to get back to work. I felt an unmistakable connection with Marsha and that connection seemed to be stitched together with threads of sexual tension that made the whole thing seem almost illicit. I was loving it. So, for the next hour we talked, we laughed, we shared, and we learned a little bit more about each other's lives. When we parted ways in front of the cafe, I gave Marsha a hug and asked, "So when can I see you again?" I had surprised myself with my forthrightness.

She then surprised me even further when she said, "How about dinner at my place this Saturday night?" Before I could even sputter out words like "husband" or "married" she added with a casual wave of her hand, "Don't worry, it'll be fine." She then pulled out one of her business cards and scribbled an address on the back. She handed it to me and said, "I'll see you at six. Don't be late."

She then turned and walked away, and I was left there standing on the sidewalk with her card in my hand and a smile on my face.

CHAPTER TWENTY-THREE

Before I knew it Friday arrived and it was time for my first lunch date with Charlie The Guardian Angel. A part of me wanted to just pretend that I'd forgotten about our little arrangement - something about Charlie made me very uneasy - but a larger part of me wanted to learn more about this guy who claimed to be other-worldly.

The Tavern was bustling with its typical lunch-time crowd when I walked in, a crowd that seemed dominated by Christmas shoppers, laden with packages, who were there to refuel before heading back out to continue their respective shopping missions. I passed by a lot of bleary-eyed, battle-worn faces as I made my way to an empty table in the far corner of the restaurant.

I sat down at the table, took off my coat, and then scanned the restaurant for any familiar faces. I saw none and then turned my attention to the menu. I'd barely read through the specials on the front of the menu when I heard a familiar voice. "Hello Ben," the voice said in a calm, friendly tone.

I looked up and saw Charlie standing at my table. "Hey there, Clarence," I replied, unable to resist another "It's A Wonderful Life" reference.

He smiled. "Mind if I join you?"

I motioned to the chair across the table from me. "That's why I'm here."

Charlie sat down, removed his tattered coat, and then just sat there and stared at me for a few beats, an almost serene smile filling his face. I finally threw him a "Well?" raise of my eyebrow and he said, "How are things?"

"Things are absolutely ducky."

"That's good to hear."

"How about you? How are things in Charlie World?"

"No complaints."

I nodded. An uncomfortable silence then filled the air and I shifted in my seat, pretending to become interested in the menu, though I'd already decided on a turkey sandwich and a cup of soup for lunch. "Do you know what you're getting?" I asked without looking up from the menu.

"I'll just have whatever you're having."

"I was looking at the liver and onions special," I lied.

"Sounds good. Make it two."

I set the menu down on the table. "Okay, look, you called this meeting today. Why exactly are we here?"

"I told you. I'm here to help you."

"But I told *you* that life is ducky, and I don't need any help."

"Then we'll just eat our lunch and talk about the weather."

There was another uncomfortable pause. "So why is it that I am the lucky recipient of all of this personal attention?"

He shrugged. "Because you need it."

I felt a small spark of anger ignite inside me. "And how the hell is it that you came to *that* conclusion?"

"Call it Angelic Intuition."

"And what's with this whole angel bullshit? Are you supposed to be on some medication that you've been forgetting to take lately?"

He shook his head, still appearing calm despite my angry outburst. "No bullshit. No medications. I am indeed your Guardian Angel."

I felt my anger subside, replaced by feelings of sympathetic superiority. This guy was obviously a little mentally unbalanced, I thought, so I should approach him much the same way I would approach someone with Down's Syndrome or a young child who just didn't know any better. "So, what is it that you do when you're not being my Guardian Angel?"

"Nothing. Being a Guardian Angel is basically a full-time job."

"Does it pay well?"

"Nope, doesn't pay a thing. The job is its own reward." His smile broadened.

"I feel like I should be offering you a medical plan or something, considering the low pay for all your work on my behalf."

His look suddenly turned serious. "Do you want to just keep making fun of me or is there something else we can talk about?"

A flash of embarrassment raced through me. "What is it that *you* want to talk about?" I asked.

"How about your lunch date with Marsha? She seems like a nice lady."

The anger came back at full throttle. "Have you been *following* me?" I shot at him, in a raised voice that turned more than a few heads in the restaurant.

Before he could answer, a young waitress came to our table. "Do you guys know what you want?" she asked in an apologetic tone that told me she knew she was interrupting something.

I glanced up at her, flashed her an "I'm sorry" cock of my head, and then said, "We'll both have the turkey sandwich with a cup of the barley soup."

"Anything to drink?"

"Two Cokes," I replied.

The waitress finished jotting down my order and then walked away. "What happened to the liver and onions?" Charlie asked with a smirk.

"Changed my mind," was my terse reply. "Of course, being the all-knowing angel that you are, you probably already knew that, right?" The sarcasm all but dripped from the corners of my mouth.

LIFE ON PLANET FUCKET

"I'm not a mind-reader," he replied. "Just an angel."

"Well, whatever you are, you're starting to creep me out."

"Just because I know a few things about you?"

"Yes, that's precisely the reason. The only way you would know anything about Marsha would be if you've been following me around and that, my friend, is creepy."

He shrugged. "There are many other ways to see things and know things beyond just simple observation."

"Like how, for instance?" I was growing weary of Charlie's verbal meandering and silently kicked myself for showing up for our lunch date.

"Don't you ever get hunches, flashes of insight, whispers of intuition?"

"Sure. But I never get flashes that tell me what my friend ate for dinner last night or how complete strangers are spending their time."

"No?"

"No."

"I'm willing to bet that you get all kinds of flashes of insight like that, but you just choose to ignore it or shake it off as a random misfiring of a brain cell."

"What makes you so sure of that?"

"Have you ever heard of limbic resonance?"

"Nope."

"Well it seems that scientists have discovered a small finger-like protrusion in our brains that acts much like a radio antenna. It receives unseen waves of information just like your cell phone or your television set."

"I have cable."

Charlie smiled. "Actually, I don't believe that you even own a television set any longer, if I remember correctly."

Oh yeah, The Fire. Another side door reminder that I no longer owned much of anything. "Okay, I get your point. So what is this limbic whatever?"

"Do you ever walk into a room filled with people and get a sense that something is wrong, before a word is even spoken?"

"Sure."

"You would say that the air is heavy in there, or something along those lines, right?"

I nodded. "Yeah, something like that."

"Well what is that? How is it that you would feel something like that?"

I shrugged. "I dunno, just a gut feeling I guess."

"What if I told you that you knew something was wrong in that room just as surely as if someone had walked up to you and said the words, *something is wrong.*"

"I'd say that you were off in Charlie Land again."

He grinned. "Charlie Land," he repeated. "I like that." He then leaned across the table, his eyes taking on a renewed intensity. "Why is it so hard to believe that you have the ability to receive the very same types of signals that your cell phone does? Is it any less amazing that you can pick up a small device, hit a few numbers, and then talk to a friend several thousand miles away as if he was sitting here next to you? Doesn't that absolutely boggle your mind at times?!?"

"I guess if I think about it like that, yeah, sure. But I don't really think about stuff like that 'cuz I just don't understand it."

"That's precisely my point." He leaned back in his chair. "There is so much that we don't understand and contained in that lack of understanding is the potential for so much growth. It's the curiosity about the unknown that pushed us to discover everything from airplanes to velcro. And in each of those cases, including airplanes and velcro, it was something in nature that inspired that original curiosity." He tapped the side of his head. "We have the original antenna in our heads but just like the prehensile tail at the base of our spines it has shrunk from lack of use over time and we've forgotten that it's there. Our ancestors knew it was there and they depended on it to gather information just as surely as we depend on our five senses to get through our lives."

"So, what's your point with all of this?" I cast a quick glance to the side to see if our waitress was approaching with our food. The sooner the food came, the sooner I could eat and then the sooner I could head for the exit.

"My point is that you must trust more in things unseen, Ben. In a word, you need more faith."

"Are you going to bring me to Jesus now?"

He shook his head. "I'm not talking about religious faith here. In many ways that type of faith can hinder more than help. I'm talking about just plain old-fashioned vanilla faith. The kind of faith that allows you to believe in things like love, friendship and forgiveness even when nothing around you is supporting those beliefs."

His words took me by surprise. He had made the quick trip from Charlie Land - a land that was easily dismissed as being outlandish - and touched down in a far different land, one that hit a little closer to home. Thankfully, our food arrived at that very moment and spared me from having to respond to his words right away. As soon as the plate hit the table, I picked up my sandwich and took a huge bite. My head stayed down for a while and I studied my sandwich as if it held some important clues to the inner workings of the universe.

Charlie broke the silence. "You're feeling uncomfortable and can't wait to finish your food and get out of here. I understand that." I lifted my head and shot him a look of surprise. He tapped the side of his head and smiled. "Limbic resonance."

"How would *you* feel?" I managed to ask through a mouthful of turkey sandwich.

He shrugged. "In my pre-angel days, I would probably feel just like you do." A Cheshire Grin snaked its way across his face. "But that's also why I was so unhappy back then. No faith."

"I have faith," I protested. I swallowed the food in my mouth. "I believe in love and all that. If I didn't, I probably would have sucked on a gun barrel a long time ago."

He nodded. "That's true. But you have a long way to go before you can say that you are truly a man of faith."

"What is it that I have to do to prove I'm a man of faith?"

There was that Cheshire Grin again. "Meet me here again next Friday."

CHAPTER TWENTY-FOUR

Some of Charlie's words stayed with me over the next twenty-four hours. Not *all* his words, just some of them. Like the ones about my lack of faith. I knew he was right, but it pained me to admit it. And I would certainly never admit it to *him*.

As I thought about it more, I realized that I hadn't always been this way, believing in the black and white world of facts over the more colorful world of faith. I thought back to my college days, when I had had been accused, on more than one occasion, of being somewhat of a hopeless romantic. I chuckled at the memory. Those two words would be at the bottom of any list of descriptors put forth by any of my current friends and associates. Hopeless *cynic* might make that list. As would the words pessimistic, unemotional, and distant. That thought made me sad. When had I changed?

It didn't take much rewinding of my life story's tape to find the likely answer: the change occurred right around the same time that my marriage had changed. Actually, to be completely fair to Linda, the changes had come *before* we started having marital problems, and, to be even fairer, perhaps even *contributed* to our problems. I seemed to recall my youthful optimism - and with it, my faith in things unseen - getting pounded out of me by the daily routine of a job I didn't want and a life I didn't choose. Coming out of college I was destined to be a famous novelist, I knew that with every ounce of my being, and as the novel-free years began piling up behind me, I slowly began to realize that life wasn't the grand adventure that I had envisioned. Life was more about paying bills and maintaining status quo than it was about exploring the depths of my soul and unlocking the secrets of the universe. That unsettling realization swirled inside of me for many years until, finally, it crystallized and became fact to me, as irreversible as my mortgage and my marriage vows.

Without being aware of it at the time, I slowly started to close myself off from the people around me - perfectly content to just hang out alone in the dark room in the corner of my soul - until one day Linda decided to give me a solid slap of awareness with the words, "I want a divorce." I really couldn't blame her for wanting out of our marriage, though I've done just that for many years. The man she was married to bore little resemblance to the man she had married. Sometimes that could be a good thing, but in our case it wasn't.

Despite my feelings of sympathy for Linda's plight - being stuck with a man who couldn't shake his dark clouds - I still resented her for taking up with The Worm so quickly. She had left no room for second chances and a tearful reconciliation when she had welcomed The Worm into her life. The door had just slammed shut and I was left on the outside looking in as the two of them put together a new life with each other and with Kylie.

Kylie. Just thinking about her brought tears to my eyes. If it were possible to love anything more than I loved my daughter I didn't know what it would be. I felt as determined as ever to keep the invisible cord intact that bound us together. I smiled. I would have to share this belief in something unseen with Charlie at our next lunch date.

A thought then shot into my head. I looked at my watch. *Damn it!* I had gotten so caught up in my daydreaming that I'd lost track of the time; I was already twenty minutes late for my dinner date over at Marsha's place. As I scrambled through an abbreviated get-ready routine - fortunately I didn't have too many clothing options to choose from - I reflected on just how strange my life had become. I was now having lunches with a self-proclaimed guardian angel and was preparing to have dinner with a married woman with whom I'd recently had a one-night stand. Life had changed quite a bit since my days of writing copy for The Beacon and driving Kylie to ballet lessons.

By the time I arrived at Marsha's doorstep I was officially forty minutes late. I had been in such a hurry to get there that it wasn't until after I knocked on her front door that I began to think about what I would say if her husband answered the door. *"Hi. I'm the guy your wife is sleeping with"* somehow didn't work for me as a viable greeting. My heart suddenly began to beat wildly. Fortunately, as was the case with most worst-case scenarios, I wasn't forced to break the glass on any emergency plans. Marsha answered the door. "Did you get lost?" was the first thing out of her mouth.

I stepped through the door, handed her a bottle of wine I had picked up on the way to her house, and simply said, "Sorry, I lost track of the time."

She didn't seem upset with my tardiness, at least that I could tell, as she ushered me into the nearby living room. I noticed that the clothes she was wearing were of the same conservative nature as what she had been wearing during our recent lunch date and her house reflected the same level of conservatism. A far cry from the Marsha I had met on that first night at The Tavern. There was matching furniture in the living room, I could see a china cabinet in the nearby dining room, and all the wall hangings and window dressings matched perfectly. With one exception. One *glaring* exception.

I walked over to the far wall of living room and stood in front of it, unsure what to say. It was painted bright lavender and clashed with everything in the room. Even my untrained, Neanderthal eye could see that. I turned to face her with a confused look on my face and just jerked my thumb in the direction of the wall, figuring that was all that needed to be said in terms of asking for an explanation.

"What?" she asked playfully. "You've got a problem with purple? Doesn't it fit in with everything else?"

"Like a wolf at a sheep convention," I replied with a smirk.

"That's my therapy wall," she said as she strode over to a nearby chair and sat down. "I paint it different colors as a way to relax." She saw my still-confused look and shrugged. "Some people knit, some people bake, I paint."

"So why this particular color?" I asked as I sat down across from her in an overstuffed leather chair.

"I liked it. I saw it in a store one day, I think it was in a display for toilet paper, and I liked it so much that I immediately went to the hardware store and found a paint in a similar color so I could paint my wall that color."

"How many times has the wall been painted?"

"Too many to count. I stopped keeping track when I reached a hundred different coats of paint."

"You've painted that same wall over a hundred times???"

"Yep." She pointed to one corner of the wall. "If you look over there you can see that it's brought that wall out a couple of inches. All those layers of paint do add up."

"I would guess so," I agreed as I looked over at the wall once again. "And does it work?"

"Does what work?"

"Does it work as therapy?"

She shrugged. "Sometimes. Other times it's just a pain in the ass but I do it anyway. Habit, I guess."

It then dawned on me that I had yet to see Mr. Marsha. "So, where's your husband?" I asked, deciding on a point-blank question rather than beating around the bush.

"You'll meet him later," she replied vaguely. "Would you like a glass of wine?"

That was a diversion if ever I'd heard one but, considering it was a subject that made me uncomfortable anyway, I was glad to change the subject. "Sure."

"Red or white?"

"Whatever you're opening is fine with me."

"Actually, I was hoping that you would open it while I got dinner on the table."

"Sounds great. Show me the way."

We both got up and headed into the kitchen in the back of the house. Still no sign of Mr. Marsha. She handed me a bottle of red wine - a Cabernet from California - and a corkscrew and then she put on an apron and positioned herself at the stove. I sat down at a nearby counter and struggled with the cork for a while before finally getting it open. She motioned in the direction of a cupboard behind me where I found a couple of wine glasses. I poured her a glass, handed it to her, and then sat back down and poured myself a glass. A very *full* glass.

Marsha noticed my glass and said, "You expecting a rough night?"

I raised my glass in her direction and replied, "Hey, it's not every night I get to meet the husband of my lover."

"Is that what you would call us? Lovers?"

I shrugged. "I'm not sure what I would call most everything in my life at this point." I flashed on Charlie, The Worm, and Austin T.

"It's just that the word "lovers" conjures an image of something more long-term, like you'd been doing it for years."

"Is there a better word for what we are?"

She thought for a moment as she stirred the pot in front of her and then finally said, "How about friends? We can just leave the sex part out of the equation for now."

It suddenly dawned on me where it was that we were having this conversation. I glanced over my shoulder and then whispered, "Are you sure we should be talking about this here?"

"Why not?" she asked casually, not even looking up from the pot. "And why are you whispering?"

My weird life just kept getting weirder. "Because your husband might hear us," I whispered.

"Oh, for heaven's sake," she said, sounding a little exasperated. She took off her apron, turned the stove down a notch, and then said, "Let's go. It's time to meet Jake."

I set my wine down on the counter and followed her out of the kitchen. We went back through the living room, into the hallway, and then up a set of stairs to the second floor. She strode into the first bedroom on the right, the door was open, and I followed. I was immediately taken aback by what I saw.

Marsha stood next to the bed, facing me, and said, "Ben meet Jake." She then looked down at the man in the bed and said, "Jake this is Ben. He's my new friend."

The man in the bed no longer resembled a living, breathing man. He looked like a corpse that had been dug up after having spent several years under ground. His eyes were sunk into his sockets, his hair was wispy and gray, and his mouth hung open as if frozen in a permanent look of awe. He couldn't have weighed more than fifty pounds. Then the smell hit me. It was the smell of death and decay. Urine mixed with feces mixed with rotting flesh. It was all I could do to not run from the room retching. Then I noticed the oddest thing. Jake the Corpse's eyes blinked. Not in an involuntary kind of way but in a seemingly deliberate way.

"Jake says it's nice to meet'cha," Marsha said matter-of-factly.

"Did he just..."

Marsha nodded. "It's the only thing left that he can control." She reached down and stroked his head lovingly. "That's how he talks to me." I thought I heard Marsha's voice crack with emotion but then she looked up and there was a smile on her face. "It's not much, but it's all we've got now."

"What's..." I had a hard time finishing my question, knowing that Jake could hear me.

"What's wrong with him?" Marsha said, finishing my question. "Don't worry that Jake can hear you." She then leaned towards me and said in a loud whisper, "He knows there's something wrong with him." She leaned back and winked at me.

"I wasn't…" I began and then thought better of it and just decided to shut up.

Seeing that I was done offering up flimsy excuses and explanations, Marsha said, "Jake has ALS, otherwise known as Lou Gehrig's disease. His body has been deteriorating slow and steady, but his mind has stayed sharp as ever." She paused for a beat, perhaps to gather herself, and then added, "It has to be the worst goddamned disease that God has ever placed on this Earth."

"How long has he been like this?"

"Like *this*?" she asked, pointing at Jake. "He's been bed-ridden the past few months. Seems like something else decides to give out every day now. It wasn't long ago that I could put him in a wheelchair and at least take him outside for a bit." She reached down and stroked his head again. "Now we're just waiting for the end."

"Why isn't he in the hospital?"

"What for? So they can fill him full of drugs and poke him with a few dozen needles?" I could hear an edge of anger in her voice. "There is nothing a hospital could do for Jake at this point." Her voice then got softer. "He said he wants to die right here at home so, by God, this is where he's going to die."

"How much longer…" I was having a hard time finishing sentences.

"Who knows. Weeks? Days? The doctors are amazed that his heart is still beating so he's on borrowed time right now."

I looked down at Jake and silently agreed that it was amazing this man-corpse was still living and breathing.

"What's that Jake?" I heard Marsha say. I then watched as Jake did a long series of blinks while Marsha watched his eyelids'

145

every movement. She then smiled and said, "Yep, this is the guy I was telling you about."

"You told him about us?" I asked, more concerned about that little fact than I was curious about how she had understood him.

"Oh yeah, I tell Jake everything."

"Everything?"

"If you're asking whether or not he knows that we slept together, the answer is yes, he does."

It would be hard to describe what I felt at that instant, but any explanation would have to begin with the words embarrassed, ashamed, and confused. It all created quite a stew of unpleasantness in my stomach. Feeling unsure of any words that would come out my mouth, I just turned and quickly made my way out of the room. I headed down the stairs and, though tempted to just head out the front door, made my way back to the kitchen and grabbed my glass of wine. I only managed to get two good gulps into my belly before Marsha came down and joined me.

"What happened to you?" she asked.

"Are you serious?" I asked, incredulous that she had even felt the need to ask such a question. "What happened to me was that I was just exposed as a charlatan to a man who is on his deathbed, that's what happened to me."

"A charlatan, eh?" she responded calmly. "Now that's another possible word to describe who and what we are."

"Why did you do that?" I asked, barely able to keep a lid on the tsunami of emotions that lay behind the words.

"Do what? Would it have been more palatable to you if you had slept with a woman who had a husband who *wasn't* on his deathbed? Were you looking forward to all the messiness of secrets and sneaking around? Did Jake's condition spoil all that for you?"

The questions were coming at me in such rapid-fire fashion that I was having a hard time sorting out my thoughts. "It's not that, it's just that…" I paused, trying to find the words. "What kind of guy delivers a punch in the gut to a guy like *that*?" I blurted out, motioning vaguely in the direction of Jake.

"I guess a guy like you," she replied calmly. She picked up the spoon and began stirring the pot on the stove.

"That's not fair!" I shot back. "I didn't know he was in that kind of condition. Christ, I didn't even know you were *married* until after the fact."

She chuckled. "I could have told you that I was the Queen of Egypt that night and you wouldn't have remembered it afterwards."

She was right. But this was no time to be giving up any ground. "What did he say when you told him about me?"

She sighed. "Listen," she began, pointing the spoon at me as she spoke. "Jake and I have an agreement and that agreement is that I should continue to live my life as I see fit." She wagged the spoon. "But no secrets." She went back to stirring the pot. "So anytime I welcome somebody else into my life, I tell him about it."

"There have been others?"

"Other whats?"

"Others," I repeated, hoping she would understand my meaning if I just said it again. She didn't. "Other guys like *me*," I added.

"Oh," she replied, drawing out the "oh" sound for emphasis. "You mean other paranoid homeless guys." She shook her head. "Nope, you are indeed a one-of-a-kind and very unique individual."

Part of me was getting angry. But another part of me was getting kind of turned on by this little game of cat and mouse. Maybe it was the wine, which I had started gulping like water. "You're a funny woman."

"I try."

"So, what's for dinner?" I asked, deciding it was time for a change of subject.

"Pasta Bolognese, garlic bread and salad."

"Mmm, sounds good. That sauce smells delicious."

"Thanks."

I noticed a slight change in her demeanor. Her playful spark had seemed to disappear suddenly. "You okay?"

She heaved a deep sigh, set the spoon down firmly and turned to face me. "For whatever it's worth, you are the first man I have invited into my house since Jake got sick. There have been no others, and this is a big deal for me." Her voice was getting louder and faster with each word. "And for another thing, I love Jake. He has been the only man in my life since high school and I can't imagine loving a man any more than I love my Jake." Tears were forming in the corners of her eyes. I knew to keep my mouth shut at this point.

"He's a good man and he doesn't deserve what he's been handed," she continued. "That's a fact. But he's been nothing but strong and courageous through this and I love him even more for that." She drew a deep breath, seemingly to try to compose herself, and then went on, her voice lower and more deliberate now. "There have been times this past year when I longed for companionship, I wanted to be held and to be treated like a woman." Her head tilted to one side and she looked at me with sad, watery eyes. "Do you know what it's like to not even be *hugged* for over a year?" I shook my head. "Well, I'll tell you, it gets awfully hard. And lonely."

"So, I talked with Jake about it and we decided that I should start to seek out some companionship, to get some of the things that he could no longer give me. It was his idea." She paused for a beat. "That was back when he could still type with his nose." The tears were now running unabated down her cheeks. She wiped her face with her apron and went back to stirring the pot. "No secrets," she whispered.

I was speechless. What was there to say to all of that? I'm sorry? Things will get better someday? Nothing I could think of was appropriate. So, we sat in silence for a while, her stirring her pot and me gulping my wine. I was hungry so I could feel the wine going right to my head. A small voice in my head was telling me to *slow down* but another, much louder voice, was saying, *fuck it…full speed ahead!* I decided to listen to the fucket voice.

"Would you mind putting the salad together for me?" she eventually asked, her calm, even voice making her sound like she hadn't a care in the world.

"Not at all," I replied, rising from my chair. My head spun as I got up and I silently hoped that the job I was about to take on didn't involve the use of any knives. "Tell me what to do."

"The vegetables are all chopped up in the fridge," she said, nodding towards the other side of the kitchen. "All you have to do it take them out, toss them in a bowl, and then throw some lettuce in there."

"I think I can handle that." Truth was, that was about *all* I could handle.

She smiled. "Glad to hear it."

I set my wineglass down and headed for the fridge. Everything was in there, just as she had said, in little plastic storage containers. I pulled everything out, found a big salad bowl on the counter, and went to work. "So, I see now why you said you needed the health insurance." I looked over at her and could see that she was confused by my comment. "In the restaurant that day, after I'd run into you outside of Brown and Brown."

An *oh yeah* look registered on her face. "Yeah, I'd be in a real world of hurt financially without it." There was a short pause and then she asked, "So how's your thing going with the house fire? You getting everything you need?"

I knew that I shouldn't get into all of it here with her now, Brown and Brown being her workplace and all, but another fucket had bubbled to the surface of my brain, nudged forward I'm sure by the alcohol in my system. "No, I'm not," I replied forcefully.

Marsha clicked off the stove and brought the hot pot over to the area where I was working. "Why not?" she asked, appearing to be sincerely concerned.

"Because of a little weasel named Austin T Phelps," I replied, not even trying to hide the contempt in my voice. I wondered for a moment if I had stepped over a line - who knows, maybe Austin T was a personal friend of hers - but her next words told me that I hadn't stepped over any invisible lines.

"Oh, you have Austin on your case, eh?" She chuckled. "He lends new meaning to words like anal and humorless, doesn't he?" She poured the sauce out of the pot and into a nearby bowl.

"And obnoxious and pain-in-the-assedness," I added.

"Hmm…if we were playing Scrabble, I might have to challenge that last word."

"But it fits," I countered. "That guy is making my life downright miserable right now and all I can think about when I see him is popping him in the nose."

"How is he doing that?" She motioned me towards the table with her head.

I brought the bowl of salad over to the table and set it down, debating whether I should get into the whole Austin T story with her. As I pulled the chair back to sit down, I had my answer; Mr. Fucket was firmly in control. "He's holding back my settlement check."

She sat down across from me. "Why is that?" She scooped some salad into a bowl and handed it to me.

I took the bowl from her and nodded my thanks. "He seems to think that there are suspicious circumstances around my house fire that are worth investigating." I took a large bite of salad to keep myself from saying anything more. I knew I wouldn't feel comfortable lying to Marsha so I wanted to avoid any territory where that would be necessary.

"And are there?"

Shit. I silently kicked myself for thinking that I could talk about this without wandering into the gray areas where truth would be my death knell. I swallowed the salad and, after taking a composing sip of wine, replied, "Not that I know of." Lie #1.

"So why do you think he's not giving you your money?"

I shrugged. "I think I just pissed him off and now it's become personal." Not really a lie, but wandering in that direction. We'll call it Lie # 1 1/2.

She chuckled. "He is indeed someone who doesn't like to be crossed."

I let out a small harrumph. "He's got a big-ass Napoleon complex if you ask me."

"You really don't care much for Austin, do you." She started filling a plate with pasta and sauce.

"I call him Rick behind his back."

"Rick?" She handed me a plate full of pasta, which I took with a smile and a nod.

"Yeah, because he reminds me of Rick Moranis from the movie, Honey I Shrunk The Kids."

Marsha laughed out loud. It was a great laugh, the kind that makes everyone who hears it smile in response. After she caught her breath she said, "You're right! I'd never thought of that before, but you are right. I'll never be able to look at him again without thinking about that and smiling."

I was suddenly feeling anxious to move on to a different topic. "So, what do you do for fun, Marsha?"

"Fun?" She laughed again, not quite as deeply as before. "I paint walls and invite strange men over for dinner, I guess."

"Am I that strange?"

She made her eyes into slits and looked me up and down. "I would say that yes, you are one strange dude, Ben."

I scooped a big bite of pasta into my mouth and then asked, "Why is that?" out of one corner of my now-full mouth.

Marsha paused for a moment and looked at me like she was considering me for the first time. She seemed to be trying to get inside me with her eyes and just when it was starting to make me feel uncomfortable, she said, "You're a man with some serious secrets, Ben. I don't know what they are, but there's something in there that you're protecting with all your might."

My feelings of discomfort returned. "Secrets?" I replied innocently. "I don't have any secrets." That lie was so huge that it took me to Lie #10 in one fell swoop.

CHAPTER TWENTY-FIVE

I took a deep breath before opening the door. It hadn't been *that* long since I'd last walked into the offices of The Beacon and yet it felt like I was walking in for the first time. I could feel my palms sweating as I pulled on the front door.

Bob had called me over the weekend and asked that I stop by on Monday morning. Seeing as I still owed the guy three thousand bucks, I didn't see that I had any choice but to comply with his request, despite my trepidation. As I thought about it, I couldn't quite manage to put my finger on the why behind my feelings. The Beacon had, after all, been a decent enough job through the years. I had always worked with decent people and Bob had been a beyond decent boss. So, what was it? All I could come up with was the analogy that I felt like a canary climbing back into his cage after having worked so hard to make his escape.

I nodded hellos to everyone as I walked through the front office area and, reluctantly, stopped occasionally to answer some questions about what I've been up to lately. "Oh, just trying to get my life back," became my pat reply, which wasn't too far from the truth. After running the gantlet, I finally made it back to Bob's office where I found him talking on the phone. He motioned for me to sit down. I closed the door behind me and sat down.

While waiting for Bob to get off the phone my eyes wandered around the room. As many times as I had been in this office, I suddenly realized that I'd never really looked around. I was usually in there to get some quick feedback on a story or approval for a purchase and never lingered long enough to notice much beyond Bob's face. There was, for instance, a picture of Bob and some other guy standing next to Carl Yastrzemski, my favorite Red Sox player as a kid. I smiled at the memory of pulling my first Carl Yastrzemski baseball card out of a wax pack when I was nine years old. The smile quickly shifted to a frown, however, when I remembered that that card, along with thousands of others that I'd collected, was now gone. Part of the big pile of ash that was my home. I continued my scan of the room.

My eyes soon settled on a strange looking artifact that could best be described as a gnome with a boner. I made a mental note to ask Bob about that one when he got off the phone. The next stop on my visual tour was a picture that caused me to catch my breath for a moment. It was a picture of me, Linda and Kylie. Kylie was maybe five years old and I recognized the picture from a summer vacation we had taken on The Cape. We all looked so damned happy. A dull ache crept into my heart and quickly spread through my entire body. It was Bob's voice that served as the safety rope that kept me from falling even farther into the dark pit of self-pity.

"So, how's it going, Ben?" he asked cheerfully.

I turned away from the picture. "Just ducky," I replied without much conviction.

"You okay?"

"No, I'm not," I replied. I pointed towards the gnome-like artifact on a nearby shelf. "I find Boner Boy to be quite disturbing. Where the hell did you get that thing?"

Bob laughed. "That's a sort of fertility good luck charm. Gail and I picked it up on our honeymoon in Fiji a zillion years ago."

I saw Bob's eyes head off to some private world for a few seconds, probably back to a time when he and Gail had sex more than twice a year. "Well, it looks like it worked for you guys, eh?"

Bob's eyes snapped back to the present. "Yeah, I guess it did at that."

"And how are Jen and Amber doing these days?"

"Fine, fine. Growing like crazy and needing their Dad less and less with each passing day."

I flashed on Kylie and the sad fact that my days as Dad-with-a-purpose were numbered. The ache returned to my gut. "You okay with that?" I asked.

"With what?"

"With not being as necessary in your daughters' lives."

Bob sighed. "I guess, speaking honestly, I'd say that no, I don't like it one bit. But I also see that it's kind of the natural order of things and I've sort of resigned myself to it." He shrugged. "The fact is, we have less in common the older they get. I just can't talk to them with any authority on things like clothes, and make-up, and boys, and..." He paused for a beat and then added, "...female issues."

"Yeah, I suppose that's true," I said half-heartedly, still not convinced that the typical separation that occurs between Dads and daughters at a certain age was inevitable. I was determined to have it be different with me and Kylie.

I looked over at Bob and saw that he was struggling with what to say next. Normally, he would ask me about Kylie or Linda, but he knew that there was a possibility of stepping into an unseen land mine. I decided to make it easy on him. "So, what's on your mind, Bob? Why did you call me in here?"

The questions put him back in his comfort zone, I could see it in his face immediately. "I just realized that it's been a while since we last saw you in here and I just wanted to touch base with you to see what the plan was."

"The plan?"

He shrugged as if it was all so self-evident. "To get you back in the saddle here at The Beacon."

Oh, *that* plan. A zillion thoughts and words shot through my head, not one of which could be shared with Bob. "I guess I don't have a plan yet," I replied, which was the truth. For once.

Bob considered that for a moment. I could tell that he too probably had his own share of unshareable thoughts bouncing around in his head. "Do you have a tentative target date yet?"

He tried to place added emphasis on the word tentative, to let me know he wasn't pressuring me at all, but I could feel the barely contained sense of urgency behind his words. "What's the problem, Bob? I'm getting the sense that some of these questions aren't really questions."

He heaved a quick sigh, as if he'd been holding his breath for a couple of minutes and was finally told that he could breathe now. He seemed to be weighing his words carefully as he said, "We're a small business here, Ben. Being down one person can put a lot of pressure on the people still here." He shrugged. "We're starting to feel your absence is all and I told everyone I'd find out when you were going to be coming back."

"Everyone?" I glanced over my shoulder, out through Bob's office window and into the main office area. I noticed a few heads quickly snap back to their computer screens as I scanned the office, pretending that they weren't watching us after all. I decided it was time to give everyone a show. I turned back to Bob, pounded his desk with both of my hands - so hard that my hands stung - and then stood up abruptly. "Well, you can tell everyone that I am *never* coming back. How's that?"

Bob went immediately into panic mode. "Now calm down, Ben," he said as he raised and lowered his arms in an attempt at getting me to sit back down. I could see him glance past me into the main office area, to see if anybody was watching and, judging from his face, I would guess that everyone was watching us now. "It was just a question," he continued, turning his full attention back to me. "There's no need to get excited."

"Actually, there's every reason to get excited, Bob." I leaned forward across his desk and fixed a glare on him. I knew even as I was doing it that Bob didn't deserve any of what I was about to give him, but that didn't stop me from making my delivery. He, and everyone watching, had to know that there was absolutely zero doubt about whether I would be returning to my job at The Beacon. "I am going through the absolute worst time of my life right now and the very last thing on my mind is worrying about whether or not my *friends*," I swept my arm towards the main office area, "at The Beacon are working too hard." I flashed on how concerned everyone had acted when I'd walked into the office a few minutes earlier and that just made me angrier. "I have done nothing but be a good employee and a good co-worker here for a whole lot of years and this is what I get in return when I'm down? What happened to support, and loyalty, and all those other things that you're supposed to get from your work *family*!?" I drew air quotes around the word family. I slammed the desk one more time for good measure. "This is bullshit!" I screamed. I then turned and walked out of Bob's office, saving my next words for after I'd opened his door, so everyone could hear them. "You can take this job and shove it up your ass for all I care." I blew past the slack jaws on my way to the front door. I opened the door and then tossed my final words over my shoulder as I walked out. "Thanks for the memories." And with that I closed the door at The Beacon for the final time.

CHAPTER TWENTY-SIX

I felt sick about how I'd treated Bob for days afterwards. I picked up the phone several times, to call him and apologize for my behavior, but each time I stopped short of making the call. I think I was afraid that he might interpret my apology as a change of mind regarding my return to The Beacon. This canary was determined to stay out of *that* cage.

As I sat sipping my morning coffee in a neighborhood coffee shop on this morning it dawned on me that I had absolutely nothing to do. Not even something to *think* about doing. I knew I wasn't going to call Bob. There were no appointments to worry about with Austin T. No dates with Marsha. No Charlie lunches. Nothing. It was a strange feeling.

There were many years, when I was working full-time, that I dreamed of having such a day. A day without direction, a day free of to-do's, a day that I could spend in whatever way struck my fancy. Now here it was and all I felt was lost. Maybe I needed to still have the taste of an *absence* of time in my mouth to enjoy the taste of a surplus of it. As it was now, my unencumbered day felt akin to having a hot fudge sundae for dessert after having just eaten a whole chocolate cake for dinner. Not quite as satisfying as it could have been under different circumstances.

I looked at my watch. Nine o'clock. I decided I would go for a walk. I paid the cashier, put on my coat, and headed outside to face my day. It was cool but not cold, the kind of day that reminds you that winter is here but doesn't punish you for it. A tap on the shoulder versus a slap in the face. I looked at my watch. Nine oh seven. It was going to be a long day.

I wandered down Main Street and it wasn't long before I had a goal to pursue. As I glanced in the various store windows, I remembered that I still had to find some Christmas gifts for Kylie. Finally, a mission. I started to pay more attention to the contents of each store window as I walked by.

As I strolled, my mind went off in all kinds of directions. I thought about Kylie and how much she enjoyed Christmas. I silently wished that would never change but I knew it would. The cold, hard adult world just couldn't accommodate the magical world of Christmas as viewed through a child's eyes. Too bad.

My mind then skipped to Marsha and our strange dinner last Saturday night. I liked Marsha. Actually, I liked her a lot. Except for the fact that she was still married, albeit to a man who had both feet firmly in the grave, there was little that I *didn't* like about her. Yes, she was a bit older than I was. Yes, she had some odd eccentricities. And yes, she had a pervasive sadness about her, but who could blame her? Then I wondered: How did she see *me*? I could see her hanging many of the same words - odd, eccentric, sad - around *my* neck. Perhaps that was part of the attraction.

Then my thoughts went to a place that never failed to make me squirm: the future. The question of *What's next?* echoed in my head. It was a question that often drifted across my mind's screen as I was falling asleep and it would inevitably keep me awake, wrestling with its answer, for hours. I had no job, little money, and no real plan in place beyond getting my check from Austin T. What was the plan after that? I had no idea. I had toyed with ideas like traveling around the country or writing a book, but those ideas were made of smoke and would just swirl around my consciousness without ever touching down and taking root. The sad fact was that I had no real inkling of the direction my life was going to take. I was still much too young to think about retirement, I had too many productive years left in me for that. And yet nothing was showing up on my mind's screen to help me decide how those final productive years should be spent.

I turned my attention back to the shop windows. I could see that distracting myself would be the order of the day. I passed a children's clothing shop and thought, for the briefest of moments, that I might try to find a cute outfit for Kylie. My more rational self stepped in quickly however and reminded me that I wouldn't have a clue as to what she might like and, more critically, what she might wear. I continued walking. The next shop that registered on my radar was a toy store. I placed it in the maybe-I'll-come-back-later category and continued walking. I looked up and saw the sign for "The Book Attic" hanging out over the sidewalk and decided that would be my first stop. Just as I was turning to open the front door of the store, two people opened the door from the inside and came bursting out onto the street, talking and laughing. It was Linda and The Worm. My initial reaction was to turn and run the other way but there was no way to avoid them. *Shit.*

Linda looked up first and I could tell she was startled to see me. "Ben," she said, more as a question than as a greeting.

I nodded as calmly and coolly as I could manage. "Linda."

The Worm thrust his hand out. "Good to see you, Ben." Always the guy to take control of a situation.

I ignored the impulse to kick him in the nuts and took his hand ever so briefly and threw him the faintest of nods. I knew he would use this moment later, when he returned home with Linda, as further evidence that I was a rude, out-of-control Neanderthal but I didn't care. "*See,*" he would say, *I tried to be nice to him but look at how he treated me!*" Then Linda would pat him on the arm and, with sympathetic eyes, say something that included the words *"for Kylie's sake"* and all would be good between them. I hated them both.

"What brings you out here today?" Linda asked sweetly, having gotten over the initial surprise.

"I'm shopping for a new life." I nodded towards the bookstore. "Think they might have one in there for me?"

She ignored my comment, nothing new there, and said, "Kylie tells me you'll be coming over on Christmas Day."

I nodded. "Yep. Wouldn't miss it for anything." I glanced at The Worm. "I can't wait to see what Santa brings for Kylie." I threw him a wink and I could see that he knew exactly where this was headed.

Not one to sit back and wait for the fight to come to him, The Worm asked, "Do you have something you want to say, Ben?"

I took another step in his direction and let my eyes fill with all the contempt that they could hold without bursting. "I have a *lot* of things I want to say to you, Worm."

Linda stepped between us. "Knock it off you two." She put her hand on my chest and pushed me backwards. "What the hell is going on here?"

"What's going on is that The Worm here decided to take it upon himself to tell *our* daughter that believing in Santa Claus is some kind of mental illness and I have a real problem with that."

Linda looked at The Worm. "Is that true?"

The Worm scrunched his face in disgust. "As usual, Mr. Loser here has twisted the facts to suit his own agenda." He looked down at Linda and the look of disgust changed to one that looked to me like arrogance, but I had to admit that the guy always looked arrogant to me. "She asked me what I thought about Santa Claus and I told her what I thought." He shrugged an arrogant shrug. "That's all."

Mr. Loser? It was good to hear that he also had a nickname for *me*. It would make The Worm fall off my tongue that much easier in the future. "She's a fucking ten-year-old, you moron," I shot back. "This isn't the time to be giving her the facts like she's one of your fucking college students."

Linda glanced around to see if any heads were turning our way. "Ben, watch your tone," she whispered.

I could feel Captain Fucket climbing into the cockpit. I didn't care if anyone was listening, or what they were thinking: all I could see was my desire to deliver a missile to the heart of The Worm. "I won't watch my tone," I snapped back. "When this arrogant bastard starts thinking that he knows what's best for *my* daughter, I've got a real problem with that."

The Worm's eyes stayed calm and in control, which just made me hate him even more. "Are you saying that you still believe in Santa, Ben?"

Everything about his question crawled under my skin like an army of ants and then started chewing on my nerve endings. His I'm-smarter-than-you-are tone, his I'm-calm-and-you-are-a-raving-maniac smugness, and even his use of my first name; it all served to raise my blood pressure to levels where I feared my temples would burst. "I'm saying that my daughter is off-limits to your Psych 101 drivel, Worm," I said through gritted teeth. I raised my index finger and jabbed it in his direction; if Linda weren't separating us the finger would have found its way to his chest. "If I hear of anything else like this again, so help me I'll come over there and wring your neck until you squeak like the little worm you are." It dawned on me at that moment that worms in fact didn't squeak, but it didn't matter, I'd made my point.

"Very poetic, Ben," he replied, still as fucking calm as ever. "Squeaking worms and all."

"Stop it you two!" Linda then shouted, pushing us even farther apart. "Save your testosterone displays for some time when I'm not around." She dropped her hand from my chest and heaved a deep sigh. "What the hell is it with you two?" She turned to me first. "Ben, I'm sorry that this situation is less than ideal for you but, damn it, it is what it is so get used to it." I knew that Linda adding a curse word or two meant that she was angry, and when she was angry, I knew to keep my mouth shut. She then turned her attention to The Worm. "And William," she said as she rubbed his arm. "You have to remember that Kylie is Ben's daughter too and respect that." Her tone was softer with him than it was with me, but it was still firm.

"But he started it," The Worm replied, pointing in my direction like some 12-year-old who had just been caught throwing rocks at a window. I could see that he hadn't yet learned the be-quiet-when-Linda-is-mad rule. I smiled to myself, knowing what was coming next.

"I don't care who started it," Linda snapped back, the earlier softness disappearing from her voice. "You're both grown men," she said, but then paused for a moment, as if trying to determine the veracity of her last words. "So you should be able to put aside your childish impulses," she continued. "If not for my sake." She paused again for a short beat and then rolled out the big guns, the magic words that could be sprinkled like fairy dust over even the most intense situations and render all else moot. "Then for Kylie's sake."

I felt my anger deflate quickly. "You're right," I uttered before I could even consider my words; saying *you're right* was certainly no way to win an argument. But she *was* right and nothing else mattered when it came to my daughter.

Linda looked at me like I'd just said *"I'm going to become a tax accountant"* or something else equally unexpected. "What did you just say?" she asked, unable to hide the surprise in her voice.

"I said that you were right." I shrugged. "'Cuz you are."

"That may be," she replied with a slight, almost tentative smile, "but I'm not sure I've ever heard you say those words before."

"It's just another one of his little ploys," The Worm interjected. "He's up to something."

Cynical asshole bastard, I thought. I took a deep calming breath and repeated a mantra in my head several times before speaking; *don't punch him in the face, don't punch him in the face...* When I was sure that I could speak without any edge to my voice, I said, "All I'm up to," *shit, those last two words came out a little snotty.* I paused to gather myself again. "All I'm up to," I repeated, free of all snotty undertones this time, "is trying to do what's best for Kylie." I shoved my hands in my pockets, not trusting myself to not make any further threatening gestures. "I guess I just want her to get to enjoy the magic of Christmas for as long as possible. She has a whole lot of years ahead of her to be a cynical, non-believing adult."

I glanced over at Linda and saw a spark - a very small spark, but a spark just the same - of the old look she used to give me when things were good between us. It was a look of admiration and although it didn't have the full wattage of past looks, I still basked in its low glow for the briefest of moments. It was The Worm's voice that pulled me from my basking. "Aren't you worried that other kids her age are going to make fun of her?" he asked, though it came across as more statement than question. "She's a little on the old side to be believing in such things."

I turned my full attention to The Worm. "And how do you know that? Is there some obscure study that was done, where they hook up little girls to a series of electrodes and ask them a series of questions about Santa, the Tooth Fairy and the Easter Bunny?" The snotty tone had returned to my voice. It was almost beyond my control. The guy grated on me too much to ignore at times. But I would keep trying. For Kylie's sake. And Linda's. I took in another calming breath and exhaled slowly. Time for a different tack. "What's your opinion on gravity?" I asked.

"What?"

"Gravity," I repeated. "Do you think it really exists?"

Worm got a knowing grin on his face. "You're not going to use the old if-you-believe-in-gravity-why-can't-you-can-believe-in-Santa argument, are you?"

"Why not? There a lot of things we believe in that we never actually see, so why not Santa Claus too?"

"Because there's no proof," The Worm stated, supremely confident in his position. "I see proof of gravity's existence every day."

I had an uneasy feeling that I was wandering into The Worm's comfort zone, building an argument based on facts and logic, and I had to find a way to throw him off his game or he would eat me up and spit me out. "Can you explain to me how cell phones work?" When it dawned on me that he probably *could* explain how cell phones worked, I quickly added, "Or limbic resonance?" I could see on his face that this last one had thrown him for a loop. *Thank you, Charlie!* Before he could gather himself enough to ask any questions, because I wasn't certain I could explain limbic resonance to anyone yet, I went in for the kill. "My point is that there are a whole lot of things in this world that we don't understand and yet that doesn't mean they don't exist. We take it on faith that they're there and sometimes that's all you have to go on." I stopped for a moment and realized I had just wandered down the same path that Charlie had taken me down last Friday. "Faith," I whispered, more to myself than to anyone else. I made a quick mental note to tell Charlie about this little exchange over our next lunch.

"What has gotten into you?" I heard Linda ask.

I looked down at her and saw the same spark of admiration mixed with a heavy dose of bewilderment. "I don't know, I replied honestly. "Maybe I'm just finally waking up to some things."

"Or maybe you're just going further over the edge," The Worm shot back.

Linda flashed him a withering look that even he couldn't miss. He lowered his eyes and shut his mouth, much like a dog would do after its owner had just tugged on its leash. A part of me felt sympathy for The Worm at that moment, knowing as I did that the domestication process had begun. He would be a well-trained husband in no time. Linda turned her attention back to me. "So, we'll plan on seeing you over at our place on Christmas morning."

I nodded. "Sounds good."

She leaned towards me ever so slightly. "And Ben," she said in a lower tone that was almost a whisper, telling me that her next words were for my ears only. "Keep up the good work." The spark of admiration grew to an unmistakable glow in her eyes.

I wasn't sure what exactly she was talking about, but it didn't matter; it was nice to be sharing a small, intimate moment with her again and I couldn't get enough of the look in her eyes. It was a look I hadn't seen for a long, long time.

She eventually broke the gaze and stepped back to The Worm's side. He had the look of a pit bull that had been muzzled but his eyes still had a trace of the old defiance that told me, *"This ain't over."* None of that mattered though; all that mattered was that Linda had been able to find it inside herself to look at me with eyes that said, *"I still love you."* Where there was love there was hope and hope was about as much as a man in my position could ask for right now. A small smile formed at the corner of my mouth. We all said our goodbyes - though whatever The Worm and I exchanged could scarcely be called a goodbye - and as I watched the two of them walk away one word hung in my mind like pre-dawn mist over a lake. *Faith.*

CHAPTER TWENTY-SEVEN

"Are you back to work yet?" my mother asked.

I had decided to pay her a visit, both to see how she was doing and, more importantly, to see if she had any great gift ideas for Kylie. We were sitting at her kitchen table, sipping coffee and munching on muffins, and her first question, of course, centered around my current level of productivity, which was nil. "Not yet," I replied, knowing that my mother wanted no part of any whiny excuses like *"I'm just not ready yet."*

She nodded, as if she could hear the words behind my words. "Is Bob okay with that?"

She'd always liked Bob. He worked way too many hours, sacrificed a lot of personal time for the sake of the business, and was honest as the day was long; all qualities that my mother held dear. "Yeah, he's fine," I lied. I had learned the valuable lesson as a child that it was best to use as few words as possible when I was lying to my mother.

Her blue eyes hadn't lost their sharpness with age and those lasers worked me up and down for several seconds before she said, "So what are you doing with yourself?"

Always the critical question with my mother. The walls of my life could be crashing down upon me and all she would care about was whether I was still doing something of value amidst the rubble. It was time to change course. "I'm trying to find the perfect gift for Kylie," I said. "Any ideas?"

Her lasers went to work again as she was obviously not pleased that I had basically ignored her question. "Give her a father she can be proud of," she then replied. "No better gift than that."

Ouch. I think the truly painful part of her comment was that there was an element of truth to it. "I'm not sure how to wrap that up and fit it under the tree," I replied, using humor, as I often did, to deflect the sharpness of her remark. I knew better than to tell her how incredibly hurtful her comment had been as she would inevitably just shrug and say, *"It's the truth."* It was as if truth trumped all else in my mother's mind, never mind that truth was subjective and her truth could maybe, possibly, not be the Universal Truth that she thought it was. I had tried many times when I was younger to get her to see that small point, but I never succeeded in finding a way to get through to her so, at this point, I was resigned to the fact that she would be this way until the day she died.

"Kids get too many gifts nowadays anyway," she added. "You'd be doing her a favor if you didn't spoil her with more gifts."

I silently chided myself for thinking that my mother would be any help with my what-to-get-Kylie question. I flashed on some of the Christmases of my childhood and I remembered how much Dad had loved the holiday. He would not only deck the halls with Christmas decorations, but he would also deck the living room, the kitchen, the porch, the yard, and the roof with every kind of decoration imaginable. We had multiple trees, wreaths, boughs of holly, wooden Santas, metal reindeer, complete with a blinking red nose on Rudolph, and lights hanging everywhere. Dad loved Christmas. And no matter how tough times were for him financially, Dad always managed to find a way to get lots of presents piled under the tree for me and my little sister Debbie. Mom was always off to the side in this picture I had in my head, cooking, cleaning, and making sure my father wasn't making too big of a mess with all his decorating efforts. She didn't seem to share his joy during this time of year. "We don't spoil Kylie," I replied. "And you know that." I let out a small chuffing sound. "If anyone is guilty of spoiling her, it would be you, Mom. You dote on her like she's a little princess."

My mother waved her hand in a way that told me that what I'd just said was a bunch of nonsense. "I never spoiled anyone in my life."

You sure didn't spoil **me,** I thought. It was time for another change of conversational direction. "So how have you been feeling Mom? Are your knees and hips still bothering you?" I knew that any discussion of my mother's health would be an incredibly short one, but it would serve as a good turn in the road, towards other topics.

"I'm fine," she relied tersely. "And why do you insist on changing the subject every couple of minutes?" She took a long sip from her coffee cup and reached for a muffin.

Uh, oh. This was the crossroads I always dreaded with my mother. A direct question was hovering in the air between us and there was no longer any way to deflect or dodge without raising her ire. But to tell the truth about what I was feeling would no doubt hurt her feelings and, worse yet, I wasn't sure if I'd be able to stop uttering truths once I'd started. I had always managed to keep my truest thoughts and feelings locked safely away from my mother, both to spare her and to also spare myself from the inevitable scorn and ridicule that she would rain down on my head if she ever got a peek at my innermost self. I decided to try playing stupid, though I knew it wouldn't work. It would at least buy me some more time to plot a strategy. "What are you talking about?"

She looked up at me, her blue lasers locked in. "You know exactly what I'm talking about."

Okay, time for Plan B. "In case you hadn't noticed, Mom," I began, choosing my words carefully before tossing them her way. "My world is a little messed up right now, so I'm a little out of sorts." Give her a partial truth, sprinkled with a little poor-me seasoning, and hope for the best.

She took a small bite of her muffin and chewed slowly, letting me hang out in the wind for a little while before responding. "All right," she finally said, "if you don't want to tell me what's going on, that's fine." She then raised a single gnarled finger and wagged it in my direction. "Just don't think you can bullshit me, Ben."

I could feel the crackle of energy arc from her eyes to mine and the wave of intense energy continued down through my body, leaving a small chill in its wake. My mother was pissed. She didn't need to say it, I just knew it. "Don't worry, Mom," I said as calmly as I could, "I would never dream of bullshitting my mother."

She held her stare for a moment longer, telling me *"I'm serious!"* and then dropped her eyes to her coffee cup. "You've got a lot of your father in you, Ben."

I didn't know if that was a good thing or a bad thing in her eyes at that moment, but I took it as a good thing because I loved my father. "Thanks, Mom," I replied.

She waved her hand as if dismissing my thank you, telling me that maybe I'd gotten her intention all wrong. "So, when do you think you might be going back to work?" Time for *her* to change the topic.

I shrugged. Still feeling the sting of her anger, I didn't want to just dismiss her question. "I guess I want to get all of this insurance stuff settled before I think about going back to work."

My mother's face scrunched up. "You still haven't gotten that check?"

I shook my head. "Nope. Still waiting."

"What's taking so long?"

"This guy who's handling my case is a total…" I paused and thought the words *dickhead, asshole*, and *mother fucker* before saying, "…jerk."

"What's his problem? Seems like a simple thing to me. A man loses his house after paying ungodly insurance premiums his entire life, that man should get a check as soon as is humanly possible." She shrugged as if the entire thing was self-evident.

"I agree. But this guy Austin T seems to think differently."

"Why?"

Uh, oh. It was an innocent enough question but once again we'd wandered into no-man's land. I didn't want to toss any more lies my mother's way, so I just shrugged and said, "I think this guy is on a power trip." True enough. "And he seems to enjoy having people like me dangling on his line." Also true. I of course left out the minor point that, in this case, he had every right to leave me dangling.

"Isn't there a supervisor or somebody you could talk to?"

I nodded. "That's going to be my next stop."

She threw me one more emphatic nod, as if to say, *Good, you do that,* and then asked, "So what are you going to do with that tent trailer in my barn?"

I tried to read the question behind my mother's question before answering. Was she testing me, to see if I really did intend to go back to work? Or was she giving me a small jab, reminding me that yet again one of my hair-brained ideas fell on its face? Or maybe she was simply asking me the question because, with the whole thing popped open like it was, it was in her way. I never knew with my mother. "I'm still planning on replacing the canvas when I get the check."

There was an unspoken *"And then?"* hanging between us but, thankfully, she would never ask that question. To her way of thinking, that would be prying and that just wasn't something she would ever do. She can ask the question about the tent trailer because it was taking up space in her barn, but to dig deeper than that initial question was off limits to her. In the days before I realized this little fact, I used to spill my guts in response to her initial questions, giving up way more information than I had to. Once I learned The Way Of My Mother in this regard, I started answering just the question, nothing more, and it made my life a whole lot easier. I focused on the muffin in my hand so I could avoid her stare. "How's Kylie?" she finally asked, once she saw that I wouldn't be biting on her unspoken question.

"She's good. Growing up faster than ever."

"Yeah, they do that."

"Any word from Debbie?" I asked. My younger sister lived in California, with her husband Joe, and I'd always thought it was no coincidence that she had chosen to make her home in a state that was as far away from Massachusetts as was possible. She and Joe had tried for many years to start a family, but they eventually just resigned themselves to a child-free marriage and were now living the lives of two-income yuppies in the San Francisco suburbs.

"They've been getting lots of rain out there. She said it's supposed to be a real wet winter this year."

"Anything else besides a weather report?"

She shrugged. "She went on and on about something going on at her work, but I honestly can't remember a word of it."

Typical Mom; hear what she wants to hear and leave behind the rest. I glanced at the clock on the wall just over my mother's shoulder and said, "Well, I'd better get going. I have to go talk some more with my friends at Brown and Brown." I took one last sip of coffee and stood up. I went over and kissed my mother on the cheek and said, "See ya later, Mom. Love you."

She threw me a dismissive wave and, as always, I was left wondering if my mother was...pissed off at me?...proud of me?...loved me? I never knew. Maybe that was the way she wanted it. *Keep him guessing and he'll keep coming back.* I gave her one last pat on her shoulder and headed out the door.

CHAPTER TWENTY-EIGHT

Before I knew it, another Friday arrived and that meant lunch with Charlie. I noticed that I didn't have nearly the trepidation that I'd had the week before as the time for my lunch date neared. I'd decided after lunch the week before that I would stop focusing on the whole Charlie The Guardian Angel thing and instead focus on Charlie The Man. He was a decent enough guy, I'd decided, and he didn't seem to mean me any harm. I would just hang out with him for an hour or so, talk about whatever comes to mind, and then go back to my life. Keep it simple.

Charlie was already seated in a booth when I arrived, so I just slid in across from him, removed my coat, and picked up a menu. "How's it goin' Charlie?" I asked in my best casual tone.

"I'm well. And you?"

"Just ducky. Have you ordered yet?"

He shook his head. "I was waiting for you."

"That was considerate of you."

He shrugged. "Not really. Just common courtesy."

"Yeah, but those so-called common things seem to get less and less common as time goes by."

"Like sense?"

"Exactly!" I replied, pointing my finger at him for emphasis. It was then that I noticed Charlie's face. I hadn't really looked at him when I sat down, but then I could see that there was an unmistakable sadness spread across his face. "You okay?" I asked, surprised by my own level of concern.

173

He forced a weak smile. "Fine. Just feeling a little under the weather today, that's all."

"Do angels get sick?"

"Guess so."

"Is it a flu bug?"

He shook his head. "It's nothing really. I'll be fine. Tell me about your week."

I looked at him hard for a beat, trying to decipher what he *wasn't* telling me, and then, unable to get a read, said, "It was a helluva week."

"What happened?"

"What? You aren't going to just *tell* me everything that happened?" I instantly felt bad for saying what I said. I could see that he was feeling beaten down and yet I still took the opportunity to challenge his angel-hood. If he truly was an angel, I just earned several demerits in my Cosmic Scorebook.

The weak smile returned to his face. "I can tell you the what's - like the dinner with Marsha, the fight with William, and the visit with your mother - but only you can tell me the whys behind each of those things." I saw the old impish spark flicker in his eyes for the briefest of moments. Even in his sickened state he managed to freak me out.

"How the hell did you know all that?" I asked reflexively, knowing full well that no real answers would be forthcoming.

He shrugged. "I keep telling you how, but you choose not to believe. Even though I'm not feeling 100% I still have my angel powers."

Thankfully, the waitress came to our table at that moment and we each placed our order, giving me more time to compose myself. *Charlie The Man..Charlie The Man...* I repeated in my head several times. After the waitress walked away with our orders I said, "So tell me a little about your pre-angel days. Where did you live? What did you do for a living?" I needed to buy some more time.

"Still trying to figure out what to make of me, eh?"

I nodded. "Yes, I am as a matter of fact."

"Okay, fair enough. I'll talk for a while if you'll return the favor when I'm done. Deal?"

"Why is it so damned important to you that I share my life with you? Isn't your own life satisfying enough?"

He let out a wry chuckle. "It's not a question of whether or not my life is satisfying. It's a matter of doing what I was meant to do, and that means helping you in any way I can."

"But why? Why me? Why don't you go help some homeless person or something?"

He smiled. "Ah, but you *are* homeless, Ben."

I returned the smile. "Fair enough. But that doesn't answer my question. Why me?"

He shrugged. "Every person who walks this Earth eventually reaches a crossroads. The road to the right is the road of Comfort, Security, and Happiness. If you choose to take that road, then the rest of your life will be spent trying to maximize the presence of all of those things in your life." He paused. "Then there's the road to the left. That road is rutted and dark and full of twists, turns and harrowing drop-offs. It's the road to your Higher Self and if you choose to take that road, then you must prepare yourself for a lifetime of Hardship, Lack, and constant Challenge." He paused again. "You can try to straddle both roads for a short while but eventually you must decide. Left or right. You can't have it both ways."

I considered his words for a moment, trying to figure out his underlying message. It didn't come to me. "So, I didn't hear an answer to my question anywhere in there. It was a great little story, but I'm still wondering, why me?"

Charlie leaned forward, the old intensity back in his eyes. "Because you are standing at that fork in the road right now, Ben. You're wondering which road to take, and my job is to help you look at the maps and eventually figure out whether you want to go left or go right."

"But *why?*" I shot back, much louder than I'd intended. "I don't remember pulling off at any rest areas to ask for directions! Who told you that I needed your help?"

He smiled. "You did."

"*I* did? When was that?!?! 'Cuz I sure missed that little moment in time!" I knew my voice was too loud, and I was starting to attract some attention from my fellow diners, but I didn't care.

Charlie, to his credit, stayed calm. "Some things happen at levels that we aren't aware of. Trust me, you asked for my help."

"And why is it that I should *trust* you? I don't even *know* you!"

"I think you both know me and trust me, Ben. You fight that reality because to admit it would mean heading down a road that involves some very tough choices. I understand that. But at some point, you are going to have to make a stand and decide, right or left. I'm here to help nudge you in the direction that you are meant to go."

"And what direction is that?"

He shrugged. "That's for you to decide."

I laughed. "Yeah, right. Should I take the Gandhi path or the Road to Caligula?" I rubbed my chin. "Let's see, if *I* were an angel which path would I try to get *my* guy to take? That's a tough one."

It's not as easy as you make it sound. Some souls just aren't ready yet for the rigors of the Road To The Higher Self. It is a very demanding road and to take it before you are ready would mean certain disaster. Likewise, to take the right turn, and pursue a life of comfort and security when you are in fact meant to be elsewhere, would be equally disastrous. In both cases the wrong choice would cause you a lifetime of inner turmoil, frustration and dissatisfaction. You would have the perpetual feeling that you were meant to be someplace else."

"So, you're saying that I could in fact be meant for Easy Street?"

"Possibly. Though I would say that burning your house to the ground may, perhaps, indicate otherwise."

"So, you're saying I should go left?"

"No, I'm not saying that at all. I'm saying it's all still up in the air and up to you to decide."

Something then dawned on me: *did he just say that I'd burned my house to the ground?* Does he know something or was he just fishing? "You're not much of an answer man, are you?" I said, trying hard to conceal my uneasiness with his earlier comment.

He smiled. "Sometimes. And sometimes not." He tilted his head. "Are you okay? My limbic center is picking up some signals of distress coming from you."

"I'm fine," I lied, perhaps saying the words a little too firmly. I composed myself quickly and added, "So what's the end game here, Charlie?" Time to dodge and deflect.

He shrugged. "No end game. Just taking it all one day at a time."

"So, saving my soul and sparing me from eternal damnation isn't on your angelic to-do list?"

Our food came to the table. The waitress placed our sandwiches in front of us and I immediately took a bite out of mine, still waiting for Charlie's response. He stared at his sandwich for a moment and then said, "You'd asked me earlier about my pre-angel life. I've already told you some of that story." I flashed on the story he'd told me at our first meeting, about an ex-wife and two daughters living in California with a plastic surgeon. "What I didn't tell you is that it was all my fault."

I waited for a few moments, expecting him to continue. When he didn't, I asked, "What was your fault?"

"The divorce. The move to California. The years of no contact with my daughters. It was all my fault."

"I'm sorry for that, Charlie, I really am. But I still don't understand what that has to do with me."

He looked at me with eyes that emanated both sadness and intensity. "It has everything to do with you. You are in danger of stumbling into the exact same pit of quicksand that I did and I'm here to help you avoid that fate." He shrugged. "That's all. I'm not after your soul, I'm not preventing you from walking through the gates to Hell if that's where you want to go. I'm just trying to help you, Ben. Can't you see that?"

It was at that moment that I knew he was telling me the truth. Call it limbic resonance or whatever, but something inside me flashed the green light and told me that Charlie was okay. Whether he was truly an angel or not didn't really matter anymore; he really was trying to help me, and I would be a fool to slap away any helping hands given my present situation. "Okay, I believe you," I said, feeling the relief that comes with uttering words such as those. "But do me a favor and lay off the angel talk from now on, okay?"

He smiled. "Okay."

We spent the remainder of our lunch date in silence, chewing on our turkey sandwiches as well as each other's words.

CHAPTER TWENTY-NINE

It was time for a change. I sat on the edge of my bed the next morning, after a fitful night filled with disturbing dreams, and decided that I needed to change something, *anything*, to help get me out of this funk I could feel myself falling into. My world had become small lately and I was beginning to feel claustrophobic. Seemed like a strange thing for a homeless, jobless guy to say, but there it was. I got up, did an abbreviated version of my morning clean-up, and headed out for coffee.

My coffee shop of choice lately had become The Bean, a small cafe just around the corner from my motel. The coffee wasn't as good as the brew at The Maple Cafe, just a couple blocks away, but that was where Angela worked, and I wasn't ready to see *her* face again. So I'd been getting my caffeine fix at The Bean. I ordered my large coffee at the counter and then took it over to a table by the window to ponder my next move.

It was still early on a Saturday morning so there wasn't a whole lot of bustle out on the street. I scanned the inside of the cafe and my eyes settled on a family seated around a nearby table. There were two young children in basketball uniforms, an older child, maybe fourteen years old, and a man and woman, probably Mom and Dad. What struck me was the dullness in each of their eyes. They were sipping hot chocolate or coffee and eating muffins and scones but there was no feeling of enjoyment or even engagement with what they were doing. Perhaps it was attributable to the early hour but there wasn't even a word of conversation between any of them. It looked like a scene from one of the *Invasion of the Body Snatchers* movies. I smiled at myself for even thinking this, but my limbic center was picking up a real sadness coming from this group. I then flashed on the final days of mine and Linda's marriage and realized that we probably looked just like that when we were out in public: nothing left to say; all feelings buried under the rubble of countless fights; and nothing left to do but pull the trigger and put a bullet into the head of our marriage. Sad.

I turned my attention away from the family and allowed my eyes to wander inward. Their first stop was the upcoming holiday. I dreaded going over to Linda and The Worm's house on Christmas Day and yet I wouldn't miss it for anything. Christmas was still so special to Kylie and I knew there wouldn't be many more of those in her future. An abrupt reminder then shot onto my mind's screen: *You still need to find her a gift, you idiot!* I still had no clue what to get her.

Next stop on my mental tour was my old house. The more time passed the more I found myself missing certain parts of my old house. More than anything else I think I missed it as an anchor for my life, a place where, no matter what else was going on, I had somewhere to go that was stable and predictable. I had often fought the routine that had become my life back then and yet that same routine now had appeal to me at times. While it wasn't any fun to mow the lawn or clean the gutters, those things had given my life a structure and a purpose that were now absent from my life.

My mind then wandered down into a dark alley that it hadn't been down before. I started to think about how I used to have such an acute sense of purpose when Kylie was younger. I was her protector, her provider, and I knew she wouldn't be able to survive without the food, shelter and care that Linda and I provided for her. It was a feeling that was both scary and empowering at the same time. I felt necessary.

But fast-forward to the present and now I found myself wondering: *Am I still necessary?* Through the long history of humankind men have always seemed to have an important role to fulfill within their own small worlds. Miss the shot at that deer and your family may starve. Screw up the crops and your family could go broke. Fail to build the house properly and it will come tumbling down in the next big storm. You stood alone between your loved ones and impending disaster. Now what do we have as a measuring stick for our worthiness? The size of our Christmas gift?

And where is the whetstone against which we hone the edges of our manhood? Where do we learn what exactly we're made of? What is the forum for us to prove ourselves? How do we show that we are necessary in some way?

The hard truth was that my daughter no longer needed me, my ex-wife definitely didn't need me, and my job was just fine without me. Where was I necessary? If I had gone up in flames with my house where would the holes be in my current life? Would there be any sense of lack or need anywhere around me? I'm sure Kylie would miss me, and be sad as hell for a while, but would her life be diminished in any way if I weren't around anymore? She would still go to school, still have lots of friends, still go on to college and a career, still get married and have kids. Life would go on.

The flip side to all of this was the question: *How would I do if I had the fates of others in my hands?* Would I do what needed to be done or would I wilt under the pressure? Did I have what it took to make life and death decisions? The fact that I torched my house to get out from under what had become a perceived burden didn't bode well for my spit-in-the-eye-of-death skills. I suddenly felt very small and insignificant.

I turned my attention back to the zombie family. They were still munching away in silence. I was hoping to make myself feel better by watching them - the fat man standing next to the *fatter* man strategy - but the truth was that I would trade places with them in a heartbeat. Yeah, they had some obvious problems, but they were all still together and that meant that there was still hope for change. I was on the outside looking in through a thick, impenetrable pane of glass and had run out of hope. I was, once again, officially pathetic.

I shot up out of my chair - so abruptly that I got a startled reaction from the zombie clan - and headed for the door. *It was time to make a change.* I had no idea what the hell that meant but it was the thought that scrolled across my brain in a perpetual loop. Once out on the street the cold air helped to slap me back into present reality. Traffic was starting to pick up a little and some nearby shops were coming to life. *It was time to make a change.* What did that mean? *It was time to make a change.* Change what??? *It was time to make a change.* I looked at my watch. Almost nine o'clock. I made a snap decision to go see the only someone I could think of who might be happy to see me.

Fortunately, Marsha was up when I knocked on her door and, thankfully, she was indeed happy to see me. Or she was just one helluva an actress. Either way, it didn't matter to me which it was, it would feel good to be with someone and away from my depressing string of thoughts. She had a paintbrush in her hands when she answered the door. "Ben? What brings you over to my neck of the woods on this Saturday morning?"

I followed her in through the open door. "Just looking for some companionship," I said. "And I thought of you."

She smiled. "That's sweet."

I shrugged. "Seems I'm a little short on friends right now."

Her smile turned into a frown. She wagged the paintbrush at me as she said, "See, now you didn't need to add that last part. You went from making me feel special to making me feel like a last resort."

"I'm sorry, Marsha. I'm feeling a little out of sorts today. Please don't take anything personally that falls out of my mouth."

The smile returned. "Feeling a little down, are we?" She threw a nod over her shoulder. "Come on and join me on my Therapy Wall."

She led me into the next room, and I could see that she had started to cover up the purple color on the big wall with what looked like a brick red color. "Going a little darker, eh?" I said.

She nodded. "Yep. It's called Passion Red and I just liked the name. Whaddaya think?"

"I like it. Both the name and the color."

She nodded towards a nearby drop cloth that had paint cans, brushes, rags, and other painting supplies strewn across it. "Grab a brush and lend me a hand."

Unable to come up with a reason not to pick up a brush, I did as I was told and was soon painting alongside Marsha. It wasn't long before I found a rhythm and I started to enjoy the act of slapping the dark red paint over the top of the purple. "Hey, I can actually see why you enjoy doing this so much," I said.

She smiled. "I'm sure there are all kinds of deep-seated psychological reasons why I do this - covering my old life so I can start fresh and all that - but the fact is that I just love the sensation of putting on a new coat of paint."

"Especially when the colors are so different," I added. "You actually get the feeling that you're doing something. I remember once when Linda had me paint a white wall white and I didn't understand why I was doing it."

"Because the original white was the wrong shade of white perhaps?"

"Yeah, that's what she said at the time, but I didn't see it. They both looked just white to me."

"That's why wives were invented. To help clueless husbands see subtle shades in the world around them."

I stopped painting and looked at her. I could see that she was smirking. "Is that what you do for Jake? Help him see the difference between white and not-as-white?"

She shrugged but continued painting. "Sometimes. Not so much anymore. If he wanted to call this wall pink right now, I wouldn't dispute it."

I didn't want to ask the next question but felt like I should. "How's Jake doing?"

"Same. No better no worse." She then lowered her brush and turned to me. "You don't have to pretend like you're interested in Jake's welfare, you know."

Her directness caught me by surprise. "I know," I said, a defensive tone creeping into my voice. "Is there a law against showing concern for another human being?

"Nope, no law," she replied matter-of-factly. "It's just that I don't want you to feel like you have to care about Jake's welfare as part of the package of having me in your life."

"Have you always been this direct with people?"

"No, not always. It may be hard for you to believe but I used to be a very shy person. Jake's sickness changed all that."

My mind returned to the thread I had been following in the coffee shop. "Do you miss the old routine?" I asked.

"The what?"

"The old routine that you and Jake had together. You know, the things that had seemed normal and almost boring at the time but now, looking back, were the things that helped to define your life."

"My, my, aren't we feeling philosophical this morning."

"A little," I agreed. I decided to be completely honest with her. "Truth is, I've been struggling with feelings of unnecessariness, if that's a word, and I was hoping that you could help me shake it."

"Unnecessariness, eh?" she repeated with a smile. "Honestly, I feel like I could use a few weeks of that sort of feeling right about now. I'm a little tired of being so damned necessary all the time."

I suddenly felt bad for even bringing the topic up. "Of course you do," I said weakly. "It was insensitive of me to even bring it up."

She slapped me on the back. "Oh, get over yourself, Ben. Stop thinking that you have to protect me from everything that comes out of your mouth. I'm a lot sturdier than you think."

I smiled. "Yeah, I can see that." My eyes then went to a spot over her shoulder. "I guess I'm still struggling with this new life of mine. No home, no job, no structure. I didn't realize just how much I relied on those things before."

She placed her hand on my shoulder, gently this time. "Have you seen someone since your house burned down?"

"Seen someone? Why?"

"It's pretty common for people to get depressed following a house fire, especially one as severe as yours. I'm surprised that Austin T didn't recommend someone to you."

I let out an involuntary scoffing sound. "All Austin T cares about is making my life as miserable as possible. I doubt he would even consider saying or doing anything that might possibly make me feel a little *better*."

"You guys still aren't getting along, eh?"

I didn't want to go down this lane with Marsha. It would involve telling more lies and I wasn't in the mood to do that to her this morning. I waved my hand dismissively. "We're fine. I'm sorry I said anything."

She considered me for a moment, probably seeing right through my lie and wondering whether to call me on it, and then said, "Yes, I do."

"You do what?" I didn't know what the hell she was talking about.

"Miss the old routine that Jake and I had together." She sighed. "I miss Saturday morning errands and Sunday morning coffee. I miss watching old movies together and going out to dinner on Friday nights. I miss fighting about money and getting the same box of chocolates every Valentine's Day. I miss it all, both good and bad."

My mind started to form my own list of things that I missed, and it was pretty similar to Marsha's. The *pre*-divorce list was anyway. The post-divorce list was shorter, but it still contained some items that made me feel a little wistful. I *really* missed sitting in my chair after work and sipping a glass of red wine. I missed my kitchen and my gas grill. I missed reading the Sunday Globe on my back porch while working my way through a pot of coffee and a couple of cinnamon buns from Patty's Bakery. I heaved my own sigh. "Yeah, I guess it's true what they say in that song about not knowing what you've got until it's gone."

"That's for damned sure."

I knew that my words had hit Marsha at a deeper level than I could even imagine - whereas my fate had been a choice, hers had been foisted upon her - so I decided it was time for a change of subject. Maybe one day I would choose to wander further into the conversational cave when I sensed discomfort, but the present-day Ben's response was always to turn and run at the first signs of unpleasantness. "So, do you have any plans for your Saturday?" I asked casually.

Once again Marsha lowered her brush and looked over at me, hard. This time she didn't hold her tongue. "Where the hell did that come from?"

"What?" I asked innocently.

"That abrupt about-face of yours. One minute we're talking about something real and the next thing I know you've made a u-turn and we're talking the weather. Why did you do that?"

Rule #4 for my new life: ***Don't even think about bullshit-ting Marsha Graves.*** "Old habit," I confessed. "I sensed that I'd made you uncomfortable, so I changed the subject."

She started shaking her head slowly. "Man, you've got it bad."

"Got what bad?"

"The I'm-responsible-for-the-rest-of-the-world syndrome. You think it's your job to make everyone around you comfortable all the time. That's quite a responsibility, Ben."

I tried to be cavalier as I said, "Yeah well someone has to do it." It fell flat.

"No, actually you don't. I know that because I tried to be that person for a whole lot of years. All I did was lose track of myself and make me and everyone around me miserable."

"Do I make you miserable?" I knew as soon as the words left my lips that I didn't mean them; I was just trying to gently push her away with my diversionary tactic, but she kept charging ahead.

"When you say stuff like that, yeah you do make me miserable." She smiled. "Not all discomfort is bad, Ben. Sometimes discomfort leads us to all kinds of good things."

"Yeah, like divorce and house fires," I mumbled.

"Hey, without your divorce you wouldn't have met *me*, right?"

I looked over at her and I suddenly felt a rush of what would best be described as a surge of love. If not love, then certainly passion. "Do we get any coffee breaks on this paint crew?" I asked, framing my words with my best bedroom eyes.

Marsha picked up on my cues immediately and threw me her own coquettish look. "I don't have any coffee brewed."

"Well maybe we can come up with our own little brew."

Without saying another word Marsha reached over, grabbed my hand, and led me into a back bedroom. It ended up being the best Saturday morning I'd had in a long, long time.

CHAPTER THIRTY

Someone had to have been leaning on Life's fast-forward button during the weeks leading up to Christmas. The days and weeks went by in a blur and before I knew what happened I was staring at Father Christmas on the doorstep and I still had nothing to put under the tree for my daughter. I started to panic.

Marsha and I had been spending more time together since our Saturday soiree and that at least partially explained the rapid passage of time. I found her to be a great companion and I always looked forward to the next time we were supposed to get together. The sex was good too. I was lying in bed with her one morning, two days before Christmas, when I freaked out on her. "What the hell am I going to do?!?!" I asked the ceiling as I lay there.

Marsha was still trying to wake up slowly so I'm sure my sudden outburst caught her by surprise. To her credit, she didn't just whack me with her pillow. "Kiss me, maybe?" she mumbled. "Or perhaps say good morning beautiful?"

"Huh?"

"You asked what the hell you're going to do and those are my best guesses."

I smiled, despite my anxiety. "I'm not sure Kylie would appreciate either one of those."

She sat up. "Oh, we're back on the what-am-I-going-to-get-for-Kylie thing again, are we? How about getting her a sane, rational father for Christmas? I know she doesn't have one of those and it's something every little girl needs."

I put on my best mock stern face. "Very funny. But not helpful." The mock stern look morphed into a very real look of anxiety. "I'm really worried. Christmas is just two days away."

"I know you're worried," she said as she rubbed my arm. "It's just that worrying about it isn't going to help. Doesn't she have a favorite hobby or something that you can help to encourage?"

Bless her heart. I knew Marsha had to be sick and tired of going down this path with me and yet she continued to hang in there and try to be helpful. I rewarded her patience and loyalty with an ugly outburst right between the eyes. "You already asked me that a thousand times and I told you a thousand times that she didn't have any hobbies." It was one of those times where I felt like shit before the last word even left my mouth. I turned to Marsha and I could see the hurt in her face. "I'm so sorry, Marsha. You didn't deserve that."

The hurt quickly disappeared and was replaced by anger. "You're damn right I didn't." She then climbed out of bed and put on her bathrobe. "And you are now officially on your own on this one." She stomped into the bathroom.

Great. Now I could add Marsha to my list of worries. I threw my legs over the edge of the bed and sat there for a moment. I said a quick prayer, asking for divine intervention regarding gift ideas for a ten-year-old girl, but soon realized that God probably had bigger fish to fry two days before his Son's birthday. My mind went off on a quick tangent, trying to envision what sort of birthday party God threw for Jesus up in heaven each year, but the tangent was interrupted by Marsha's voice coming from the bathroom. "So, what do you have planned for today?" she asked. "Other than the quest for the perfect gift."

I got up and went over to the bathroom door. She was brushing her hair in the mirror. She had thrown the bathrobe aside, so she was also completely naked. As many times as I'd seen Marsha naked over the past many weeks, I was still astounded at how comfortable she was with her own body. Linda would have rather pounded a nail into her foot than stand naked in front of both me and a mirror while brushing her hair. I smiled. "No plans. Except maybe standing here and admiring this goddess in front of me."

She stopped brushing her hair and returned my smile in the mirror. "If you think that using words like goddess will get you out of my doghouse, well let me tell you right now…" She spun around and whacked me in the chest with her hairbrush. "…that you're absolutely right." She went up on her tiptoes and kissed me on the cheek.

"I am sorry," I said.

"I know you are." She then turned and went back to her brushing. "You just can't help being an asshole sometimes."

I laughed. "Any more than you can help being a goddess."

"Exactly." She set the brush down on the counter and reached for her deodorant. "So back to my original question. Any plans today?"

"Nothing other than searching for the perfect gift."

"Don't you have your lunch with Charlie today?"

Shit. Was it Friday already? "Yeah, I guess I do. Maybe I'll just ask him if I can skip it today."

"Why? It's just an hour out of your day and you seem to get a lot out of those lunches."

She was right, of course. The last couple of Fridays with Charlie had been particularly good ones. Ever since I stopped fighting the whole angel thing, I found myself enjoying his company more. "Yeah, you're right. I guess I'll just work my shopping around it."

"So, when do I get to meet this Charlie guy? He sounds like a pretty interesting character."

"Yeah, he is that. Maybe I'll see if he wants to come over for dinner one night, how's that sound?"

"Great." She set her deodorant down. "Now if you don't mind, I have to climb on the fast track so I'm not late for work."

I kept on forgetting that the rest of the world didn't have the same jobless schedule that I did. "You have to work today?"

"It's December twenty third. Last I looked that wasn't a holiday in this country."

I smiled. "Maybe you could just call in sick today."

"So I could walk around shopping with Mr. Stressed all day? No thanks." She shooed me out of the bathroom. "Now get going so I can put my work face on. It takes some work to transform this face from plain old Marsha to Ms. Graves."

"I prefer Marsha."

"Me too. But Marsha doesn't pay the bills around here."

I wandered the downtown aimlessly for a few hours and was glad when I saw the clock approaching noon. I headed over to The Tavern a little early and was surprised to see Charlie already waiting there for me. "Aren't you the early bird today," I said cheerfully.

He returned my smile, though I noticed it was weaker than normal. "You too."

"Yeah, I'm feeling a little lost today." I sat down across from him at the table. "I'm stressing out about what to get Kylie for Christmas and I'm running out of time."

Charlie chuckled. "Yeah, I guess you are at that. Sunday ain't too far away."

"Thanks, you're a big help."

He shrugged. "It's my job." He then reached to the floor and pulled up a shopping bag that I hadn't noticed when I sat down. He placed the bag on the table in front of me and said, "Maybe you'll find this more helpful."

"What is it?"

He flashed the Cheshire Charlie smile. "Exactly what you've been looking for."

I opened the top of the bag and peeked in, hoping I'd see a check from Brown & Brown Insurance tucked in there. What I saw was a sea of silver hair. "A wig?"

"Just take it out of the bag."

I reached in, grabbed whatever it was, and pulled it out. I was soon eye to eye with a beautifully crafted doll whose eyes looked as life-like as any I'd ever seen. She had silver hair and was dressed in a shimmering white gown with veils flowing in all directions. "Wow, it's beautiful," I said as I continued to admire it from all sides.

"It's a Christmas Angel. It's one-of-a-kind and it's what you'll be giving Kylie for Christmas this Sunday."

I was flabbergasted. "I can't take this Charlie. It's obviously not something you'd find at Toys R Us and I 'm sure it holds some kind of meaning for you."

"Not anymore," he said flatly, not betraying any underlying emotions that I could detect. "And there's one more thing I need to tell you."

"What's that?"

"Her name is Angela and she has some special powers."

"Angela, eh?" I replied with a smirk. "Not very high on the originality scale there, Charlie."

"What she lacks in originality regarding her name she more than makes up for in other ways."

"Such as?"

"She has the power to grant its holder one wish."

"She does? Does that mean I get one wish right now?" I'm sure Charlie sensed the semi-mocking tone in my voice, but I couldn't help myself.

He shook his head. "Actually, no you don't. The wish has to be made within one minute of looking into her eyes for the first time."

"I waited too long, eh? Very convenient that you didn't tell me that little fact until now."

He smiled. "I didn't want you wasting a wish on something silly."

"She only has so many wishes in her, is that it?"

No, that's not it. I just don't think you're in a good frame of mind yet for making a proper wish."

"A proper wish? What's that? A wish that *you* agree with?"

"No. A wish that will actually do you some good, *that's* a proper wish."

"And you know this better than I do right now?"

He nodded. "I do."

I felt some of the old anger start to bubble in my belly. I hadn't felt any anger towards Charlie for the past many weeks but here it was again. "What exactly is an *im*proper wish if you don't mind my asking?"

"A wish that is both selfish and meant to solve a short-term problem."

"Such as?"

He shrugged. "Such as wishing for the settlement check from your recent house fire."

He was right, that would have been my wish. *How did he know that?* "And why would that be such a bad wish?"

His eyes blazed with a sudden intensity. "I think you know why."

He was freaking me out. There was no way he knew anything about how that fire started and yet I felt like that was exactly what he was referring to with his comment. Was it just my guilt working on me? Did he see something that I wasn't aware of? Is that why he's been following me around all this time? "And what if I said that I actually *didn't* know why that would be a bad wish?"

"I would say that I would be happy to tell you why, but I don't think you'd want me saying it here in the restaurant."

I leaned across the table and whispered, "Who the hell are you, Charlie? And why do you have your nose so far into my shit?"

"Haven't we covered this ground already?"

I leaned back. "Not in my mind we haven't."

A weak smile worked its way across his face. "It's two days before Christmas, Ben. Christmas is a time of magic. Why don't you just try to let that magic in and stop asking so many questions."

A million words shot across my mind's screen but all that came out of my mouth was, "Okay. For now."

"Please wish your daughter a Merry Christmas for me."

"I will." Then I remembered my earlier conversation with Marsha. "Oh, before I forget. I want to invite you over for dinner one night. Marsha wants to meet you."

He threw me a paternal smile. "While I do appreciate the offer, and as much as I would like to meet your friend Marsha, I am going to have to decline."

"Why?"

"Our deal is for Friday lunches only. No more, no less. I fear that doing any more than that would interfere with our work."

"Our *work*? What the hell does that mean?"

"I sense that you're getting angry again so let's just leave it at *not right now* for the dinner offer. Maybe after the holidays."

"Fine. I'll tell Marsha." I looked at my watch. I had no place to be, but it was a good introduction to what I was about to say; I was ready to have our lunch be over. "I gotta get going now."

Charlie nodded. "Don't forget Kylie's gift."

The reminder about the gift flushed all my anger away. Charlie had saved my ass with the Christmas Angel and I should be feeling nothing but gratitude towards him. "I won't." I reached my hand across the table. "Thanks for the gift, Charlie. You really bailed me out on this one."

He shook my hand. "Glad to do it. And don't forget to tell Kylie about the one wish before she opens it. You don't want that minute to pass without her getting to make a wish."

I stood up. "I won't forget." I put my coat on and looked over at him. "And Merry Christmas, Charlie."

He stood up and, moving more quickly than I'd seen him move before, he stepped over towards me and pulled me into a big embrace before I could react. I felt chills go through me as he squeezed me tight. It was all I could do to not start crying. Strange. "Merry Christmas, Ben," he whispered into my ear. "I hope the magic of Christmas fills your soul."

I flashed on the time my father hugged me and told me he loved me before I headed off to college many years ago. I had the same surge of emotions crackling through me. I backed away from Charlie's embrace, not wanting to start bawling like a baby in the restaurant, and said, "Thanks Charlie. I'll see you next week." I then turned and made a beeline for the door, tucking the tears back where they'd come from.

CHAPTER THIRTY-ONE

It was Saturday night, Christmas Eve, and Marsha and I were eating dinner at her dining room table. I'd been choking on a question all day and it was time to administer a Heimlich and get it out. I swallowed a bite of pasta, took a deep breath, blew it out, and then said, "So I was thinking that maybe you'd like to join me over at Linda's house tomorrow." It had come out much faster than I intended, but at least it was out.

Marsha nearly choked on whatever she was chewing. "You what?"

I shrugged casually, as if I was asking her to go to a movie that night. "I just thought it would be nice if we were together on Christmas Day. No big deal."

She let out a wry chuckle. "I would say that heading over to your ex-wife's house," she set down her fork and counted number one on her index finger, "to meet your daughter" number two, on her ring finger, "on Christmas Day" number three, on her ring finger, "actually *does* qualify as a big deal." She threw me a "do you get it *now*?" look and picked up her fork again.

I smiled. "Okay, maybe it is a big deal. But I really want you to come with me tomorrow."

"Why?"

I could see that Marsha's scanners were on at full strength, scanning me for clues hidden under my words. Knowing that, I considered my next words very carefully. "I like you, Marsha. I like you a lot. And since we've been seeing so much of each other lately, I just thought it was time to start sharing our lives a little bit more."

Her eyes continued to assess me up and down for several seconds after I'd finished talking. "Is that all?"

"What do you mean is that all? Isn't that enough?"

"Sure, it's enough. If that's all there is to it."

"What else would there be?"

"I'm just not into being that other woman who is used as a tool to make the ex-wife jealous, that's all."

I was just about to say something like, *Linda has seen me with lots of other women before,* but I checked myself. It would have been a lie and I didn't want to do that to Marsha. Instead, I asked myself that same question: *Why do I want Marsha to come with me tomorrow?* The answer I got kind of surprised me, but I shared it anyway. "The truth is that I'm scared," I said. "I'm scared that I might say something stupid and ruin Kylie's Christmas. I'm scared that I might start feeling like a loser with no life and ruin my own Christmas. I'm thinking that having you there with me will help on both of those fronts."

She smiled. "Well now, that sounds a lot like an honest answer to me."

"It is."

She assessed me some more, though her eyes were different this time: more loving, less judgmental. "Seeing as my kids and grandkids are all down at Disney World this year, there really is no reason why I couldn't go."

Shit. I'd forgotten about her kids.

"I'll call the Hospice folks and see if I can get someone to watch Jake for a while tomorrow."

Shit. I'd also forgotten about Jake. "I'm sorry, Marsha. If you feel like to have to stay here with Jake that's..."

She cut me off with her hand held up in a stop sign. "Shush, shush, shush." She lowered her hand. "Jake will be fine. He has nurses take care of him every day while I'm at work, so he's used to it."

I knew that Marsha had nurses come in to watch Jake and take care of him during the day, but I still felt bad that I'd forgotten about him with my Christmas plans. "You sure you don't want to be with him on Christmas?"

"Didn't we cover this ground already?"

"What ground?"

"The ground where I tell you that you don't have to feel responsible for Jake's situation. It is what it is, and he and I have it all figured out just fine. I'll tell you when something doesn't feel right, so you don't have to worry about trying to figure it out for me. Deal?"

There was a directness to her voice but nothing about her tone or her words said that she was angry. "Deal," I replied.

Her shoulders dropped slightly, and she took a sip of her red wine. "Truth is, I used to make a big deal out of all the holidays with Jake, decorating his room to match whatever holiday was coming up and all that. I would haul in Christmas trees, and Valentine's wallpaper, and even small fireworks for the Fourth of July." Her look turned sad. "But then I realized that all I was doing was making him more depressed. All he saw when I brought that stuff in was what he *couldn't* do with me anymore and, even though he tried to act happy and surprised, I eventually saw that it was killing him inside. So I stopped." She took another sip of wine.

"I guess I never would have thought of it that way."

"Me neither. And I didn't see it for a long time. I was too busy trying to make myself feel better to see how it was making *him* feel." Marsha's words penetrated deep into my brain and the truth behind them acted like glue, adhering themselves to several recent situations in my own life. I fell silent for several moments, rolling her words over in my mind again and again.

Her voice eventually pulled me from my thoughts. "Hey, Mr. Pensive. You still with me?"

I shook my head once, clearing my mind's screen, and was back in the present. "Yeah, I'm here. I was just thinking about your words, that's all."

"What words?"

"The ones about not being able to see through your own agenda."

"Did I say that?"

"You did. And it's something that I've been guilty of in my own life lately."

"How so?"

My first example involved my arsonist past, so I avoided that one. "With you, for one," I replied. "I can't believe I didn't think of your family responsibilities before I asked the question about coming with me tomorrow."

"No harm done there."

"I've done the same thing with Charlie too," I added. "I've been so busy staring at my own shit to see how much he's really done for me. I can't see that he's getting a single thing out of our lunches together, other than an occasional free turkey sandwich, and yet he keeps showing up every Friday. Why?"

She shrugged. "Beats me. From what you've told me though, he sounds like a pretty special guy."

I nodded. "Yeah, he is." I then made a promise to myself that I would try to be nicer to Charlie from now on and not give him such a hard time for his occasionally odd behavior.

"So, what shall we do tonight, Mr. Insightful?"

I smiled. "How about a game of Make a Wish on Santa's Lap?"

She returned my smile, hers being more coquettish than mine. "As in, I sit on your lap and you get to make a wish?"

"That sounds perfect. Is there a more appropriate way to spend Christmas Eve?"

"Not that I can think of, Mr. Claus."

CHAPTER THIRTY-TWO

I woke up excited about Christmas Day. It wasn't the excitement level of my youth, when Christmas ruled above all other days, but rather it was the adult-level excitement that emanated from an expectation of good things to come. I couldn't wait to give Kylie her gift.

The day itself was glorious. The sun was shining brightly on the snow and the sky was the deep shade of blue that could only be attained in the winter in New England, when the humidity wasn't in the air to mute it. I was ready to get the day started but Marsha seemed to be taking forever to get ready. "Come on Marsha, the day's a wastin' here," I finally said.

She was in front of the bedroom mirror, putting on one of the assorted layers of makeup. "Don't rush me, Ben. This was *your* idea to take the new girlfriend over to meet the family and I'm not going until I'm ready." She stopped applying makeup for a second and looked at me. "Besides, we can't leave until Jake's nurse gets here anyway. Do you want to go downstairs and listen for her?"

"And get out of your hair?"

"Exactly."

I grabbed the bag containing Kylie's gift from a nearby chair and headed out of the room and down the stairs. I knew Marsha was right about not rushing her but that didn't keep me from feeling impatient. I paced around the living room for a while but before I could work myself into a good lather, I heard a knock on the door. When I answered it, I saw a small, older dark-skinned woman standing there who had a warm smile on her face. "Good morning," she said. "I'm here to help with Jake." She stuck her hand out. "Name is Yancy."

I shook her hand. "Nancy?" I asked.

She laughed. "Yancy," she repeated. "With a y. As in, *why am I still standing out in the cold?*"

I apologized and ushered her into the house. "Sorry. I'm a little preoccupied right now."

She took off her coat and hung it on a nearby hook, as if she'd done it a thousand times before. "Excited to see what Santa brought you, are you?"

Yancy had an accent, but I couldn't place it. Kind of Jamaican, but not really. She was probably in her sixties, but her eyes had a brightness to them that made her appear to be years younger than that. "Actually, I'm excited to see the reaction of somebody *else* to a gift that Santa brought."

"A child?" she asked.

I nodded.

"*Your* child?"

I nodded again. "My daughter."

"How old is she?"

"Nine years old."

"Still believes in Santa's magic, does she?"

"I hope so."

"'Tis a shame when they lose that belief. Magic is a wonderful thing."

Yes, it is," I agreed.

"Do you still believe in magic…" her voice trailed off. "I'm not sure I ever got your name."

"It's Ben. And I guess I'm not sure how I really feel about magic. There are times when I wish the world *was* a magical place. But then I see so many reasons why that just couldn't be true."

Yancy chuckled. "I guess you can prove whatever it is that you want to prove in this world, eh?" I was thinking about what she'd just said when I was startled by the sound of a single clap of her hands. "Well, time for me to get to work. How's Jake doing today?"

I was suddenly embarrassed that I hadn't checked in on Jake even once since that first day that we'd been introduced many weeks ago. "Uh, he's fine, I guess." I decided to deflect a little and let my embarrassment pass. "You've taken care of Jake before?"

Yancy squinted her eyes and looked me up and down. "Who are you anyway?"

"I'm a… friend, of Marsha's," I stammered.

"How come I haven't seen you here before?"

"I come over at odd times, I guess."

She maintained her squint. "Like at night?"

I knew exactly what she was asking. And *saying*. "For the most part, yeah."

"Mmm, mmm," was all she said in reply. "Like I said, I gotta get to work." And with that she turned and walked down the hallway to Jake's room.

I stood there, feeling cheap and sordid, until the sound of Marsha's shoes on the stairs snapped me out of it. "Did I hear Yancy come in?" she asked.

"Yeah, she's with Jake," I replied, pointing down the hallway.

"What'd you think of Yancy?" she asked with a smile.

"She's quite the woman," I replied.

"Yeah, she is. She's been a godsend for me. There are times when I think that she loves Jake just as much as I do."

"It's great that she was willing to come over today," I said, trying to regain my earlier excitement.

"Yeah, it is. She said that her kids are all gone, and she doesn't celebrate Christmas anyway, so why not. She's great." I nodded. "I'm just going to go check in on them and then we can head out, okay?"

"Sounds great." A part of me felt like I should follow her down to Jake's room, just to say hi and show support, but a larger part of me wanted to avoid both the discomfort of seeing Jake and the discomfort of facing Yancy's accusing eyes. I stayed where I was.

I soon started to wonder about the day to come, wondering mostly about how Marsha would be received by everyone. Thankfully, I'd had the foresight to call Linda the night before and warn her about Marsha's joining us for Christmas Day. She'd seemed fine about it over the phone, but who knew what she really felt about it. I would soon find out. I told her to tell Kylie about it too - she was already in bed when I'd called - and Linda assured me that she would. It was Kylie's reaction that worried me the most.

"All systems are go," Marsha said as she headed down the hallway. "Let's go do Christmas at the ex's."

"You sound nervous."

"I am nervous. *Damned* nervous."

I took her hand. "If it helps at all, I'm nervous too."

"That doesn't help, but thanks for sharing."

The car ride over was quiet, each of us going through our own private nightmare scenarios, and we arrived at the house in what seemed like record time. I took a deep breath and opened the car door. Show time.

We walked up the front sidewalk hand in hand and I could feel Marsha's sweaty palms. "You okay?" I asked.

"No, but don't let that interfere with anything. I'll adapt."

I smiled at her, a real from-the-heart smile, and said, "You're really something, you know that?"

She returned the smile, though hers was more tentative than mine had been. "Thanks. But right now, all I know is that my stomach is doing somersaults."

"Mine too." I squeezed her hand. "Ready to face the music?"

"Let's go, maestro."

"In a while, crocodile." I smiled. "I guess Christmas is the day for being ten years old again, eh?"

"I feel like a ten-year-old going to the dentist to have twenty cavities filled."

Before we could take another step towards the front door it swung open and Kylie came running out. "Daddy!" she shrieked as she ran towards me. All feelings of trepidation left me instantly. I opened my arms and scooped her up.

"Hey there, beautiful," I whispered in her ear as I hugged her. "Merry Christmas."

She pulled back from the hug and said, "I thought you'd *never* get here!"

"Well here I am." I turned so that she was facing Marsha. I nodded at Marsha and said, "And this is Marsha." I then nodded at the back of Kylie's head. "And Marsha, this is my daughter, Kylie."

Marsha extended her hand. "Pleased to meet you, Kylie. Your Dad has told me a lot about you."

Kylie took Marsha's hand and shook it gently. My two lives had officially been joined. "Do you have kids too?" Kylie asked.

"I do. But they're much older than you are."

"Why aren't you with them on Christmas?" Kylie was being less shy with Marsha than I thought she'd be. Perhaps because it was Christmas or perhaps because she felt safe in my arms. Either way, it was nice to see them chatting. I noticed how good Kylie felt in my arms. I could have carried her like this all day long, smelling her hair, feeling her small, warm body against mine. I felt necessary again, if only for this moment.

"They're down in Florida with their own children today," Marsha replied with a faint twinkle in her eyes, telling me that she'd already been smitten by Kylie's charms. Who could blame her?

"At Disney World?!?" Kylie shrieked.

Marsha nodded and smiled. "Yep, they're at Disney World as we speak."

"Lucky dogs!" She then turned to me. "When are *we* going to Disney World, Dad?"

"Someday sweetie, I promise."

"I hate someday," she said with the smallest of pouts. "It's just an adult way of saying never."

I laughed out loud. "In some cases, that's true." I then turned serious and looked her in the eye. "In this case, it's not. You, Kylie Weaver, will go to Disney World before your thirteenth birthday. I promise."

"I heard that," Marsha chimed in. "He can't renege on it now."

Kylie turned back to Marsha. "What does that mean?"

"What?"

"That word, ree-nig."

Marsha smiled. "It means he can't take it back."

Kylie swiveled her head back to me. "Yeah, you can't ree-nig, Dad."

I crossed my heart with my free hand. "Cross my heart. Even if I have to carry you down there on my back, you will be on Space Mountain before you're a teenager."

I could have done this back and forth with Kylie all day long, but we were interrupted by Linda's voice. "What's going on out here?" she yelled from the doorway. She was smiling but I could tell she wasn't *really* smiling. "It's cold out here and Kylie doesn't have her coat on. Come on inside where it's warm."

I glanced at Marsha and saw that the twinkle had left her eyes. I then waved to Linda. "Okay, be right there." I then whispered in Kylie's ear. "After I go get Kylie's present out of the car."

Kylie squealed. "What'd you get me?!?"

"Every year you ask me that and every year I say the same thing. What is it?"

She turned somber. "We'll see," she mumbled.

"And what do you think my answer will be *this* year?"

"We'll see," she mumbled again.

I set her down on the sidewalk. "Why don't you run inside, and I'll see you in there in a minute."

She left my arms reluctantly. I loved that. But once on the sidewalk she gave a quick wave to Marsha and then scampered back inside. "See you inside," she shouted as she ran away.

"She's absolutely adorable," Marsha said to me when she was out of earshot.

"Yes, she is."

"I can see why that little girl is so important to you, Ben. She's a treasure."

I heaved a sigh as I watched her disappear through the front door with Linda. "Yes, she is." I went and got the bag with Kylie's gift in it out of the car and then came back to Marsha's side. "Ready?"

"Let's do it," she said with just a hint of bravado in her voice.

We strolled up the walk together - though not hand-in-hand, as I had intentionally carried the bag with the hand closest to Marsha to avoid that decision - and I knocked gently on the door that was now ajar. "Hello?"

Linda came into view out of the living room. She had a Stepford Wife smile plastered on her face as she came towards us, her right hand extended. "Hello, I'm Linda," she said sweetly.

Marsha took her hand. "Marsha. Nice to meet you. And thanks for inviting me to join you and your family today."

The great unspoken of course was that Linda did not invite Marsha at all and I started to wonder, almost immediately, if I had perhaps made a mistake by bringing Marsha. They both seemed to have their Scanning Lasers on full strength as they stood there shaking hands, looking for clues from each other as to how this day would go. I could see that my job was going to be sure that it all went well. "So, where's the man of the house?" I asked.

Linda threw me a disapproving look, no surprise there, and said, "He's upstairs getting ready. He'll be down shortly."

My comment had done its job, taking Linda's focus away from Marsha and putting it on me. Round one was a draw. "I can imagine that that Man Make-up can take a while to get on just right."

"Don't start," Linda said in her best I-mean-it voice. She then turned to Marsha, her frown quickly transforming back to the Stepford smile. "Can I take your coat, Marsha?"

"Yes, thank you." Marsha removed her coat and handed it to Linda. I tried to get a quick read on Marsha's state, but I came up blank.

"Ben?" Linda then said, turning back to me. "Can I take your coat?"

I took off my coat and placed it on top of Marsha's in Linda's arms. "Thank you." As Linda turned and headed away from us with the coats, I felt a sudden twinge of sympathy for her. Marsha was, after all, the first woman she'd seen me with since the divorce and I remembered all too clearly what that had felt like. That had been several years ago, and it was more than a little pathetic that it had taken me this long to introduce her to the wonderful world of Post-Divorce Relationships. She would be getting a crash course on this Christmas Day.

"Daddy!" Kylie's voice pulled our attention over to the living room. "Come see what Santa brought!"

I smiled. This is what I wanted the day to be about. I ushered Marsha into the living room where we saw a large Christmas tree, decorated thoroughly from top to bottom, with a bunch of wrapped presents strewn around it. Nothing had been opened yet. Good. I loved nothing more in the whole world than watching Kylie open her gifts on Christmas morning. She had never been one of those kids who just tore open gift after gift in a breathless frenzy. She had always been very slow and methodical throughout the whole process, unwrapping each gift with care, squealing with delight when she saw what it was, and then considering its contents for a long while before moving on to the next gift. It had often taken us several hours to work our way through the gifts, which had always been fine with me.

"So, what did Santa bring you?" I asked as I crouched next to her beside the tree.

She held up a package for me to consider. "What do you think *this* is?" she asked breathlessly. I gave her the you-know-what-the-answer-is look and she laughed. "We'll see," she said in a deep voice.

I nodded. "What do *you* think it is?" I asked.

She shook it gently. "I don't know." She then leaned in close to me, close enough that I could smell the sleep that still lingered on her skin, and whispered, "I hope it's an angel doll. I love angels."

I froze. My brain was having trouble registering what my ears had just heard. "What did you say?"

"I love angels."

I struggled to keep my voice even and calm. "And why do you love angels?" I glanced over my shoulder to see if Marsha had heard this exchange and I saw that she had; the surprise on her face was probably matched only by my own.

Kylie shrugged, oblivious to the impact of her words. "I don't know, I guess I just think they're pretty and magical."

"Yes, they are indeed that," I agreed. "And when did this love affair with angels start? I don't remember you mentioning this before."

"Just recently. My friend, Jenny, has an angel collection and I thought it was so cool. I want to start my own collection."

"So you don't have any angels yet?"

She shook her head. "Nope."

"Does Mommy know that you like angels now?"

She shook her head again. "Nope. I just told Santa."

"And how did you do that?"

"I whispered it to him before bed one night."

I could feel my heart racing wildly. Charlie's smiling face shot into my head and a sharp chill went down my spine. *Who the hell are you?* I asked him in my head. "I told you," he replied, much to my surprise. "I'm an angel. *Your* angel." I stood up, suddenly struck by an idea. "Could you do me a favor, Kylie?" I asked.

"Sure. What is it?"

"Could you go upstairs and get me a couple of aspirin from the medicine cabinet? I feel a little headache coming on."

"Sure." She got up and shot out of the living room and up the stairs.

I turned to Marsha and we exchanged knowing glances. "Are you thinking what I'm thinking?" I asked.

She nodded. "I think I am."

I went into the hallway and grabbed the bag that contained Kylie's gift. I brought it into the living room, pulled the gift out, and carefully removed the tag that said "Merry Christmas Kylie. Love, Dad." I then went over to a nearby coffee table and opened the drawer, hoping to find a pen. I did. I brought the pen and the gift over to Marsha and said, "You do it. She doesn't know your handwriting."

Marsha took the pen from my hand and, after giving me the warmest smile I'd ever seen in my entire life, wrote, "Merry Christmas Kylie. Love, Santa" in a large, flowing script on top of the package. It was perfect. I kissed her on the forehead and then brought the gift over to the tree, carefully placing it out of sight, behind the tree, where Kylie hopefully hadn't yet searched. I quickly returned to the couch and sat down next to Marsha, just two seconds before Linda came into the room.

"Where did Kylie rush off to?" she asked as she walked in.

"She's getting me a couple of aspirin."

"You have a headache?"

"I feel one coming on."

Linda nodded, seemingly considering if there were perhaps other words behind my words, and then, satisfied that there were not, said, "I'm sorry."

I shrugged. "It happens. Probably just the excitement of the day."

She then nodded towards the kitchen. "I'm going to go grab a couple cups of coffee for me and William. Do you guys want anything?"

"I'll have a cup of coffee," I said.

"Me too, please," Marsha chimed in.

"Two cups of coffee coming right up," Linda said and then she turned and headed for the kitchen.

"What are you going to do now about a gift from *you?*" Marsha whispered to me after Linda disappeared from the doorway.

"I don't know," I confessed. "I didn't think that far ahead."

I looked over at Marsha and she leaned in and kissed me, hard. "That was a wonderful thing you just did," she whispered, her eyes bursting with emotion.

"I don't think I really had a choice. Freaky as it sounds, I think this was Charlie's plan all along."

She smiled. "You're a good man, Ben Weaver."

I squirmed. Much as I wanted to, I didn't feel worthy of her praise. "I don't know about that," I replied honestly.

"I do," she purred in my ear.

Kylie then came bounding back into the room. "Here you go, Daddy. I brought you some water too."

I took the aspirin and glass of water from her. "Thanks sweetie." I popped the aspirin in my mouth and took a sip of water. "So, when do we start opening gifts?"

A look of exasperation swept over her face. "I don't know! Mom and William are taking *forever!*"

I still didn't like to hear his name coming from her lips. "They'll be here soon, sweetie."

As if on cue, Linda came into the living room with a tray filled with juice glasses and coffee cups. "Here we go," she said. "Hot coffee and orange juice." She set the tray down and handed me and Marsha each a cup. "Cream?" she asked Marsha.

"Please."

Before Linda could get to me with the cream pitcher, The Worm came into the room. "Hey there, everyone," he said cheerfully. "Merry Christmas."

My entire body stiffened. Even his "Merry Christmas" sounded arrogant to me. He strode over and kissed Linda on the cheek, meeting my eyes briefly as he bent over, and I swore I detected a small wink. He then extended his hand in Marsha's direction. "Hi, I'm William," he said.

I wanted to slap his hand away and scream, "*Don't touch her!*" but I resisted the impulse. Marsha took his hand and replied, "I'm Marsha. Nice to meet you."

"Likewise," he replied with a smile that he probably thought was charming. He then nodded at me and said, minus the charming smile, "Merry Christmas, Ben. Glad you could join us."

The word "us" got under my skin. Us implied that there was a "Them" and there was no doubt that he was placing me in the Them camp. As if to add an exclamation point to that notion, he went over and planted a kiss on Kylie's forehead. "Merry Christmas, kiddo," he said. I wanted Kylie to pull away, repulsed by The Worm's show of affection, but instead she just smiled up at him. I could see that it wasn't her top-drawer smile, the one she hopefully still reserved for me and only me, but it was a smile nonetheless. "Glad you could join *us*," I replied, intentionally placing added emphasis on the last word. Let the games begin.

He threw me one of his professorial, aren't-you-pathetic looks and then clapped his hands together. "Are we ready to open some gifts?"

Kylie shrieked. "Yes, we are!" She looked over at Linda and, after getting a quiet nod of approval from her, Kylie rushed over to the tree. She scanned all the gifts in front of her and then, after careful consideration, selected the first gift to be unwrapped. She brought it over by her mother, sat on the floor at her feet, and slowly began peeling off the paper. Watching how carefully she unwrapped the package caused me to swell with pride. I glanced at Marsha and she raised an eyebrow in surprise, telling me that she too was impressed by Kylie's deliberate approach to the unwrapping of her gifts.

Kylie slowly worked her way through the gifts, oohing and ahhing appropriately after each gift was unveiled. A pile formed to her left, filled with clothes, games, and various knickknacks and she would pause occasionally to scan the pile and touch a gift that was particularly coveted by her. She was beaming and her face told me that she could have done this all day long. But the number of gifts under the tree dwindled and eventually there was just one gift remaining. My gift.

She didn't see it at first, tucked as it was in back of the tree, so I had to point it out to her. "You've got one more gift, sweetie." I pointed. "Way in back."

She looked confused at first but then her eyes lit up when she finally saw the package. Marsha had done a great job of wrapping it, with shiny paper and a big bow, which further reinforced the notion that it was from Santa and not from me. My gift-wrapping skills were equal to those of a third-grader and Kylie knew it. Kylie dragged the gift out from behind the tree and exclaimed, "It's so pretty!"

I looked over at Linda and saw her and The Worm exchange confused looks. She then looked at me. "Is this gift from you, Ben?"

I shook my head. "Nope." I then looked at Kylie and said, "I'm sorry to say sweetie that I brought the wrong gift with me today. I grabbed one of Marsha's bags by mistake, with gifts to her grandkids inside, so I'm going to have to give you your gift the next time I see you. Okay?"

"Okay, Dad. No problem." She smiled at me quickly and then turned her attention back to the gift that sat in front of her. Her smile grew larger.

"Who does it say it's from, honey?" Linda asked.

Kylie read the words out loud. "Merry Christmas Kylie. Love, Santa."

Linda scowled. "Let me see," she said. She leaned forward and read the words for herself and then looked over at The Worm and shrugged.

"Can I open it now?" Kylie asked.

"Before you do," I said. "I've heard that you should make a wish before opening any gifts from Santa. His gifts often have magical powers and you never know when you might have one of those special gifts."

Kylie looked at me and her face had an "Oh, Dad!" look of exasperation, but her eyes had the look of someone who wanted to believe what I'd just told her. It was a look that I'm sure would be repeated many times over in the coming years, as she struggled to straddle the two worlds of childhood and young adulthood. I loved the look because it told me that she was still my little girl in some ways. "Where did you hear that?" she asked.

"From a friend," I replied. "A friend who knows about things like this."

She tossed me one more half-hearted look of disbelief then shot a quick glance over at The Worm. He had his arms crossed and the face of someone who was politely tolerating what was going on in front of him. I imagined a bolt of lightning crackling down through the ceiling and zapping him in the ass and that made me smile. Kylie's eyes then came back to me and I gave her a small nod.

"Okay," she said. She then closed her eyes and said, "I wish for an angel."

I suddenly felt like the bolt of lightning that I'd just imagined hitting The Worm had switched course and inadvertently zapped *me* in the ass. My head swiveled involuntarily in Marsha's direction. Her eyes looked like they were going to pop out of her head and roll across the floor. I glanced nervously at both Linda and The Worm and saw, thankfully, that neither one of them had noticed my reaction. They were focused on Kylie as she unwrapped her final gift. I looked again at Marsha and we exchanged "Holy shit!" looks of disbelief before turning our attention back to the moment of truth. This was going to be priceless.

Kylie peeled back the paper, opened the top of the box, and looked inside. Her face scrunched in confusion at what she saw, just as mine had in the restaurant when Charlie had given it to me, but that look of confusion quickly morphed into a look of delirious exhilaration when she pulled the angel out of the box. "Oh my gosh! Oh my gosh!" she shrieked. "I can't believe it! She's beautiful!" She held the doll at arm's length and then pulled it into an embrace. "I love it!"

I tried to soak in everything that was happening at once. First, there was Kylie's reaction, which was absolutely off the charts. Then there was Linda's reaction, which was absolute shock. And, finally, there was The Worm's reaction, which would best be described as confused as hell. Marsha and I shared small smiles of satisfaction amidst the chaos.

I could feel The Worm's eyes boring a hole in the side of my skull, so I looked over at him. He nodded towards Kylie and had a "Well?" look on his face, as if implying that I'd had something to do with this gift. I just shrugged in response and turned my attention back to Kylie. She was beside herself with joy. "You were right, Daddy," she gushed. "There *is* a Santa Claus and he *does* have magical powers!"

I smiled at her warmly. "Yeah, he does," I agreed. "I didn't know just how powerful he was though, until now."

CHAPTER THIRTY-THREE

It wasn't until that night that I realized I'd made a mistake. I was lying in bed when I remembered Charlie's exact words regarding the angel. *"You have to make a wish within one minute of looking into her eyes for the first time,"* he'd said. Kylie had made her wish *before* looking into the angel's eyes. And yet her wish still came true. This had all gotten a bit too Rod Serling for me.

Marsha climbed into bed and I told her about Charlie's words. "What do you make of that?" I asked her.

"It tells me that magic is everywhere," she replied. "You don't need a doll to make wishes come through."

"You sound like a Disney commercial."

She smiled. "I think Disney may actually be interested in what happened over at that house tonight."

I chuckled. "You may be right on that one. There were all the necessary elements. A little girl, a villain, some magic...all that was missing were the talking animals."

"You neglected to mention the fair princess who was in attendance."

I pulled myself up on one elbow, so I was facing her. "How could I forget *her*?" I asked with a grin. "She was the Queen of the Ball!"

She blinked her eyes shyly. "Why thank you, Sir Weavalot."

"Seriously, what did you think of the group that was assembled over there tonight?

"I think your daughter is wonderful," she said quickly.

"What about William and Linda?"

"This response took a bit longer. After weighing her words, she said, "I think both of them would flunk the Clone Test.""

"The Clone Test? What the hell is that?"

"It's actually just a one question test."

"And what's the question?"

"The question is, how well would you get along with an exact clone of yourself?"

I thought about that for a second. Interesting question. Like everyone else, I immediately applied the question to myself but then, realizing I was too tired for any self-analysis, I asked, "So why would Linda and The Worm flunk that test?"

She sighed. "I feel a little funny making a judgment like this about people who I just met, especially since one of them is your ex-wife."

"Hey, don't worry about it," I assured her. "Making snap judgments is my specialty. And trust me when I tell you that there isn't anything you could say about Linda that I would find offensive. She's my *ex*-wife for a reason. Many reasons, actually."

Marsha considered my face for a moment and then, apparently accepting that she could my words, said, "Okay, you asked for it." She then rolled over so she too was up on an elbow facing me. "William would find his clone obnoxious as hell. He would think that he was a know-it-all blowhard who never left room for anyone else's opinion."

"But that describes him to a tee."

She smiled. "Exactly. That's the beauty of the Clone Test. It exposes all those you-can-dish-it-out-but-not-take-it kinds of attitudes." Her smile grew larger. "Arrogant people detest being around other arrogant people."

"Wow, I think you're on to something here with this Clone Test."

She nodded. "It's become my personal barometer for determining who I want to spend my time with. The question gets to both who you are and how well you see yourself, two things that can make or break a human being. I have found that I like hanging out with people who could actually hang out with themselves and not go crazy."

The obvious question shot to my lips, but I didn't ask it. Yet. Instead, I asked, "So what about Linda? Why did she flunk the Clone Test?"

She looked at me sideways, her eyes asking me one last time if this was okay to do. I smiled and nodded, telling her it was fine. "Linda's score on the Clone Test wasn't as obvious," she began, perhaps in an attempt at padding what she was about to say for my benefit. "She's got a better schtick than William, less off-putting."

I raised my hand in a stop sign. "One request," I said. "Please don't use his name in my presence."

She smiled. "Okay. But I don't like your name for him."

"The Worm? Why? It's a perfectly fine name for him."

"I don't like it." She thought for a moment and then said, "How about The Professor instead?"

"I think it flatters him way too much, but that's fine if that's what you want to call him."

"Whenever I say it, you can trust that I'm imagining the most arrogant, ugly, and obnoxious professor who has ever walked this Earth."

I smiled. "Better."

"Okay, now that that's settled, back we go to Linda's Clone Test." She stopped and cocked her head. "Is it okay if I use *her* name?"

I nodded. "That one's okay."

"I have to admit that I don't understand that, because she's the one who chose The Professor over you, but that's just me. It would be *her* name that I would have a hard time uttering if I were in your shoes, not his."

Her words caught me by surprise. It didn't take me long, however, to reach the conclusion that she was right with what she'd just said. "Hmmm, I see your point. I'll have to look at that one." I nudged her arm. "But now, you have to finish your assessment."

"It's more an observation than an assessment."

"And what did you observe?"

"That Linda is a lot more controlling than she lets on. I think her clone would struggle with her over who gets to take the helm from one moment to the next. And the *real* problem would come in that neither of them would be direct about it. They would try to pull the strings from behind the curtain, a passive aggressive sort of thing. Ultimately, she would feel manipulated by her clone and resent the hell out of it. There would be a big explosion not too far down the road in their relationship." She shrugged. "I just don't see those two being very compatible."

"Wow. You are good. Do you always form these kinds of detailed assessments about people that you have just met?"

"It's a curse."

Now there was no denying the question that hung on my lips; it had to be asked. "So how did *I* do with the Clone Test?"

She smiled. "I thought that might be coming." She reached over and rubbed my shoulder. "I've given you an Incomplete grade."

"Incomplete?"

She narrowed her eyes. "I'm still deciding about you."

I knew she was lying to me, perhaps to spare my feelings, but I wasn't sure if I wanted to press it with her. Yet. "Okay, I'll let you off the hook. For now." I wagged my finger in her face. "But I want to hear about my Clone Test results before the start of the New Year. Deal?"

She stuck her hand out and I shook it. "Deal," she said. "So now can we go to sleep?"

"Not until I give you your present." My hand went down to her buttocks and I gave her a firm squeeze.

"Ooh, I think I may have an idea what this gift is."

"But you haven't unwrapped it yet."

Her hand went to my crotch. "Let's just say that I'm a good guesser."

"Are you going to make a wish before you unwrap it? I've been told that this gift has magical powers." I could feel myself responding to her hand.

"Oooh, it *is* magical!" she squealed. "It's growing right in front of my eyes, just like Jacks' magic beanstalk!"

I leaned over and kissed her. "Merry Christmas, Marsha."

"Merry Christmas, Sir Weavalot," she whispered. "And thank you for the gift that I am about to receive."

My mind then started doing an involuntary fast-forward replay of the day's activities. It had been a strange yet wonderful Christmas. I was already feeling anxious to see Charlie next Friday, so I could tell him the whole amazing story of Kylie and the angel. A voice then whispered in my ear, *"Focus."* My mind's eye returned to the business at hand and I whispered, "My pleasure, m'lady."

CHAPTER THIRTY-FOUR

Rule #5 for my new life: *The Clone Test.* That was my thought as I walked towards Brown and Brown Insurance Company the next day. I really liked Marsha's little test and the whole notion of only hanging out with people who could pass the test. I thought again about Marsha's assessments of Linda and The Worm and how right on she'd been about them both.

My mind's eye then did a 180 so it was now trained directly on me. I wondered: What would Marsha say about *me?* Would I find my clone to be obnoxious and unbearable in any way? Would we be able to be friends, or would we just fight like cats and dogs? It was a hard question to even consider, never mind answer. I came to the front door of Brown and Brown and pushed the pause button on my thoughts. It was time to tangle once again with Austin T. I took a deep breath, smiled to myself at the thought of Austin T co-existing with *his* clone, and then entered the building.

I was greeted at the front desk by a very tired-looking middle-aged woman. She appeared to be very unhappy to be there and who could blame her, seeing as it was the day after Christmas. When you added the fact that it was also a Monday morning, and she was now looking at an entire workweek in front of her, I found myself feeling somewhat sorry for her. That little bit of compassion disappeared quickly, however, just as soon as she opened her mouth.

"Yes?" she said in a way that dripped with irritation.

"I'm here to see Mr. Phelps."

"Do you have an appointment?" she asked in the same snippy tone. I felt like I was back in the principal's office at Crocker Farm Elementary School thirty years ago. This woman bore an uncanny resemblance to Mrs. Berkowicz, the cranky office secretary who always acted as if *she* was the principal of that school.

"Yes, I do," I replied calmly, trying hard not to betray my inner thoughts; *And you'd get an "F" on the Clone Test, my dear.*

"Have a seat," she said without even a hint of pleasantness.

"I'll stand," I replied, only because I felt the need to defy her in some small way.

I waited for several minutes, until Austin T finally appeared in all his asshole glory. He stuck his hand out and smiled, as if we were meeting for the very first time. "Mr. Weaver," he said. "Thank you for coming in."

I shook his hand, reluctantly. "No problem. I figure it must be pretty damned important if you had me coming in the day after Christmas."

He shifted uncomfortably and glanced over at the secretary. She had her head down and was distracted with something else. He turned back to me, looking a little relieved. "I would appreciate it if you would watch your language, Mr. Weaver," he half-whispered. "Mrs. Halpin's husband is in the hospital right now and she's feeling a bit sensitive."

I looked over at the secretary and suddenly felt ashamed. Rule #2 for my New Life: *Don't be so quick to judge other people.* Shit. I would have to try harder if I was going to have any hope of actually *implementing* these new rules in my life. "What's wrong with him?" I asked.

"Something to do with his heart, I think."

"So what the hell is she doing here?"

He frowned at my mild curse but let it slide. "She said that she wanted to work today, to take her mind off other things for a while."

I nodded and then made a snap decision. I walked away from Austin T and went over to the secretary. I stood in front of her desk and said, "I'm sorry about your husband. I hope he has a full recovery."

All the signs of irritation that had filled her face earlier suddenly melted away. Her eyes got misty and sad and she managed to croak out a "Thank you" before reaching for a tissue.

I didn't want to embarrass her, so I just smiled and walked away. Austin T looked confused. "That was nice," was all he said.

I shrugged. "Seemed like the right thing to do."

He continued to look at me for a short time and then said, "Shall we?" as he motioned towards the nearby hallway. Time to head to the Interrogation Chamber. I followed him down the now-familiar hallway, turned into his now-familiar office and sat down in the all-too-familiar Hot Seat across from him. "This is getting to be a real habit for us, isn't it," I offered.

Austin T replied with a small "hmm, hmm" sound as he pretended to scan some papers in front of him on the desk. Same old routine. I decided to go on the offensive. "So, what sorts of awful, illicit things are you going to be accusing me of today?" I asked just as calmly as could be.

That got his attention. "Mr. Weaver," he said, looking more paternal than offended. "Much as you'd like to believe otherwise, I am not the enemy. I am trying to help you get a resolution to your problem. Nothing more, nothing less."

My problem*? My only problem is* you, *my friend!* "So I'm here to pick up my check, is that it?"

He gave me the fake smile. "No, we're not quite there yet. I have just a few more blanks that have to be filled in. Please just bear with me. I promise you that I am trying to get you your settlement money just as soon as possible."

I don't believe a word you're telling me right now. "What's today's blank that has to be filled in?"

He tsk-tsked me with his eyes before turning his attention back to his papers. "It seems there is a small discrepancy in the official police report that I received the other day." He paused for effect and then said, "You told me that you had been drinking that night, correct?"

I scrambled to find that disc in my brain, the one containing all the information - mostly lies - that I had shared with Austin T about that night. "Yep," I replied, now recalling the basics of my story.

"So much in fact that you forgot to extinguish a cigar that you'd been smoking, correct?"

"Yeah, I guess so." *Where was he going?*

He flipped some pages. "And yet, when I read this police report, I don't see any mention of you being inebriated at the time." He set the pages down on the desk and looked at me. "Why is that?"

What the hell does it matter if I was drunk or not that night?!? "Well, the fact that my house was burning to the ground right in front of my eyes might have had a rather sobering effect on me, don't you think?"

"Maybe," was all he said in reply, once again twanging my nerves like a harp.

"Maybe?" I leaned forward. "How many of *your* houses have you watched burn, Austin T?"

"None, thank goodness."

"So how is it that you can presume to know anything about what I'm going through? What the hell does it matter if I was drunk that night or stone cold sober? Does that change anything at all?" I could hear my shrill voice echoing back in my ears and I took a deep breath as I sat back. I had sworn that I wouldn't do this again with Austin T and yet here I was, getting all worked up. I couldn't help myself, the guy just got under my skin.

"Again, I ask that you watch your language," he replied. "And to answer your question, the reason this all matters is because I'm trying to ferret out the truth, Mr. Weaver. And I have discovered through my many years of doing this job that if I find one lie there are many, many more lies hiding underneath that one lie."

"So, you think I'm lying to you and you're just looking to confirm that one small lie so you can start excavating even deeper for even more precious lies, is that it?"

"As always, I wouldn't use your colorful language, but essentially, yes, that's how I feel."

"Well, once again we're at an impasse, aren't we?"

"Are we?" I could see him lean forward, placing his arms across all the papers that covered his desk, perhaps to protect them from another one of my desk-clearing tantrums.

There would be no tantrum today, however. I stood up and said, "Yep, we are. You're convinced I'm a liar and I'm convinced that you're a power-hungry dickhead. I just don't see where to go from here." And with that, I turned to go. I could hear a few sputtering noises coming from behind me as I walked away but Austin T said nothing more. I strode out into the lobby area and made it a point to nod and smile at Mrs. Halpin as I walked by. "Have a nice day," I said.

She looked at me and gave me the biggest, warmest smile I'd seen in a long time. "Thanks," she replied. "You too."

CHAPTER THIRTY-FIVE

I spent the week shuttling back and forth between my motel room and Marsha's place. It wasn't something that we'd discussed openly but there seemed to be an unspoken agreement that I should keep my room for the time being even though her place was a thousand times more comfortable. I had to admit that I liked having my little room to escape to occasionally. Marsha and I had become very comfortable together in a very short period, but I still liked having a semblance of my own life somewhere, however small and pitiful that semblance may be. Besides, I still couldn't shake the notion that that was still Jake's house too and I felt like I was taking advantage of the poor guy at a time when he was no longer able to defend what was his. Despite Marsha's many assurances to the contrary, the guy had to have a problem with another man sharing a bed with his wife.

It was Thursday's mail that brought a change of perspective regarding my living arrangement.

I'd been living off the remnants of Dan's small loan and some savings since the fire, figuring that it would be enough to hold me over until my settlement check arrived. Austin T was inspiring some doubts regarding that plan, but I was still hopeful that I could wait him out with the money I had remaining. Until Thursday. Thursday's mail carried with it an abrupt wake-up call regarding what was really at stake with the tug-of-war between me and Austin T. It was my January mortgage bill.

"*Shit. Shit, shit, shit,*" was all I could think as I stood in front of my PO box looking at the bill. I stood in the post office lobby and stared down at the bill in my hand for a full minute before moving. "Shit!" I finally said out loud, so loud in fact that a young mother and her small son turned and looked at me. I lowered my head and shot out of the post office.

How the hell could I have forgotten about my mortgage payment? Easy, came the response - your house is now a pile of ash and who would think that they still had to pay a mortgage on a pile of ash?!? My shock soon turned to anger, and that anger was quickly being funneled in the direction of Austin T. I looked down at the bill one more time. The dollar amount in the lower right-hand corner would essentially drain my account. "Fucking Austin T," I muttered to the air.

"*What the hell am I going to do now?*" was the thought that followed on the heels of my angry outburst at Austin T. I had run out of options and everything now rode on that check from the insurance company. I suddenly felt very exposed and vulnerable, like my whole world hung in the balance and it could swing to any number of unpleasant extremes. Destitution. Homelessness. Strange as it sounded, it was the first time I'd felt any of these things since the fire. I had felt insulated from the normal emotions associated with the loss of my home and loss of my job, perhaps through the power of denial alone, but I was now no longer insulated. The cold, hard facts were now right up in my face and I had to figure something out. Fast.

Not knowing what else to do, I called Marsha at work. Without giving her any details over the phone I arranged to meet her for lunch. It was time to give her the whole story. Well, *most* of the story.

We met at the same place where we'd shared coffee for the first time several weeks earlier. Her face showed deep concern when she walked into the restaurant, no doubt inspired by the desperation that had probably filled my voice when we spoke on the phone. "Hey there," she said as she approached the table where I was sitting. "You okay?"

I stood up and kissed her on the cheek then we both sat down. "No, not really," I confessed. I then slid the mortgage bill across the table, so it was sitting face up in front of her.

"What's this?" she asked, squinting at the piece of paper as she pulled her reading glasses out of her purse.

"It's my January mortgage bill," I said.

She got her glasses on and picked up the bill. "Oh."

"Yeah, oh is right. As in, oh *no*."

"That's a big number," she said.

"Not so big when you're working full-time, but big as hell when there isn't any money coming in."

"Can you pay it?"

"Barely. But it wouldn't leave much left over for things like food."

She set the bill down and took off her glasses. "So, what are you going to do?"

I sighed. "That's what I want to talk to you about."

Before I could say another word, she said, "Why don't you move in with me?"

I could see in her eyes that she was being sincere with her offer. I reached across the table and rubbed her arm. "That is a really nice offer, Marsha. It means a lot to me that you would be willing to take me in like that after knowing me for such a short period of time."

"But?"

I pulled my hand back. "But there are some things you need to know about me before I can consider your offer. If you're still willing to take me in after hearing what I have to say, then I will probably accept your offer."

"Okay, now you're starting to scare me."

"To be perfectly honest, I'm starting to scare myself. So let me get this all out before I change my mind."

And then I told her. Everything. Everything, that is, *except* my decision to burn down my own house. I wasn't ready to share that bit of information with anyone just yet. But I told her about quitting my job, the loan from Dan, my one-night stand with Angela, and all my dealings with Austin T. I also told her about my messy divorce, my relationship with Kylie, and my problems with The Worm. Once I started talking, I couldn't stop. It felt good to dump everything on the table and Marsha just sat and listened the entire time, not interrupting me once. Somewhere during my monologue, she had ordered food and, though I don't remember it, I had finished the sandwich in front of me as well as my recent life story in a little over an hour's time. Once done, I sat back and raised my hands in a *"Well?"* motion. "There you have it," I said. "Unfiltered, uncensored, and in all its inglorious detail. You still want to have me as a roommate?"

She took in a deep, full breath and let it out slowly. "The short answer is, yes I do." She then tapped her watch. "The longer answer will have to wait until tonight because I have to get back to work right now." A crooked smile worked its way across her face. "Since I'm the breadwinner in this partnership now, I can't afford to get fired."

I couldn't believe my ears. "Did you not hear everything I just told you?"

She stood up and put on her coat. "Yes, I did. Every word. And, like I said, I can't get into any lengthy answers right now. My lunch hour is already going on a lunch hour and a half and I have to get back." She walked around the table and kissed me on the forehead. "This may or may not surprise you, but I already suspected most of what you just told me. It was actually a relief of sorts to finally hear you say it." She straightened up and adjusted her coat. "Except the Angela part. I probably could have done without that little detail."

I was stunned that she didn't have more of a reaction to what I'd just told her. "Yeah, the Angela thing was a mistake." I agreed. "But what about the rest of it?"

She smiled and patted me on the cheek. "Tonight. We'll talk about it tonight." She turned and walked away, throwing me a small wave over her shoulder. "See you at home."

A small smile formed at the corner of my mouth as I watched Marsha walk away. "*See you at home,*" she'd said. I never imagined how powerful, and wonderful, those four words could be.

The day passed slowly, painfully so, but the time finally arrived when I could head over to Marsha's place. When I pulled up to her house, I noticed that her car wasn't in the driveway yet. I pulled in anyway and headed up to the front door, hoping that Yancy would hear my knock. Turns out I didn't have to even knock as Yancy opened the door as I was heading up the front walk. "Well, Mr. Ben," she said with a big grin. "What brings you here during the daylight hours?" Her grin then turned to a scowl as she said, "You're not looking to put the moves on ol' Yancy, are you?"

I smiled. "As tempting as that may be, the answer is no." I went up the front steps and stood in front of her. "I'm here to see Marsha."

"She just called and said she's going to be a little late." She then stepped aside and said, "Come on in."

"Thanks."

I took off my coat and as I did, Yancy said, "I've got to go give Jake a bath. You wanna help?"

I couldn't tell if she was serious, but before I could figure out if she was or she wasn't a quick "No, thanks" shot out of my mouth.

She shrugged. "Suit yourself. Make yourself comfy, Miss Marsha should be home soon."

She started to walk away but I called to her, "Yancy!"

She stopped and turned. "Yeah?"

"Were you serious about needing my help?"

She smiled. "No, not really. I was just messin' with ya."

"Why?"

"Why was I messin' with ya?" I nodded. Her look turned more serious. "I guess I just don't want you, or anyone else, forgetting that Jake still lives here, that's all." She leaned forward and whispered conspiratorially, "He's a good man, Ben. A very good man." She then nodded twice, as if to add emphasis to her words, and then threw me a wink before heading down the hallway.

"Hey, wait up," I then said before thinking about what was about to come out of my mouth. "I want to help."

Yancy looked like I'd just told her that I wanted her to have my baby. "You sure about that?"

"No, I'm not. But let's do it anyway."

"Okay, but don't say I didn't warn you. This ain't pretty work."

"I figured that. Let's go." My words were much more confident than my thoughts as we headed down the hallway and into Jake's bedroom. The smell hit me hard.

"Not a great smell, huh?" Yancy said as she headed over to Jake's side. I didn't say a word. "Poor ol' Jake can't help it. There's a lot goin' on with this body of his right now. Ain't that right, Jake?"

I looked over at Jake and saw him wink once with his right eye.

"But we're gonna help get rid of some of that smell right now." She pulled back the covers and I saw Jake's withered body for the first time. It was not a pretty sight. He looked a lot like one of those dinosaur skeletons that you'd see in a museum, his arms shortened and pulled up to his chest in a semi-fetal position and he looked like he weighed all of fifty pounds. "You don't mind if Ben here helps me lift you to the tub, do you?"

Jake blinked twice, with both eyes this time.

Yancy nodded to me and said, "Okay, let's do it."

"What about his clothes?" I asked.

"It's easier if I take those off after he's in the tub. He's easier to carry with his clothes on. Gives you something to grip if he starts to slip away on you."

I nodded and headed over to the other side of the bed. I then reached my arms under Jake and lifted him up. He was surprisingly light. Kylie probably weighed more than he did. I could feel his bones jabbing my arms through his clothes, but it was the smell that had my full attention. It was a strange nasal stew of body odor, dried shit, stale pee, and decaying flesh. It was all I could do to not toss him back on the bed and bolt in the direction of some fresh air. But I held on and followed Yancy into the bathroom.

"Just set him down in the tub," she directed. "Nice and easy now."

I slowly lowered Jake into the tub and then pulled my arms out from under him. I could feel my fingers running across each of his ribs as my hands came out. I said a silent thanks as I stood up and my nose got farther from Jake's smell.

"Jake says thanks for the ride," Yancy then said.

"How do you know he said *that*?" I asked.

She pointed to his face. I looked over and saw him blink once, keeping his eyes closed a little longer than normal. "That one long blink is his way of saying thank you," she said. "Jake's got his own little language, don't you Jake."

He blinked once, quickly.

"Now it's showtime," Yancy said with a smile. She then started to hum the Stripper's Anthem as she reached into the tub and began pulling off Jake's shirt. I hadn't noticed this, but his shirt was split down the sides and velcro strips held it in place. All Yancy had to do was separate the velcro strips and then pull the shirt out from behind him as he sat in the tub.

"That's a pretty handy arrangement," I said.

"Yeah, I did it myself. It got too hard lifting arms and legs and whatnot, so I cut up some of his clothes and just sewed in these velcro thingies." She chuckled. "It was actually my nephew's idea. He heard me talking about my problem one day and he suggested that I just buy him some tear-away sweats, like they use in the NBA."

"Smart kid."

"Yeah, he is. He takes after his Daddy, my brother. He was a clever little kid too when he was younger," she added with a chuckle. I watched as she then pulled Jake's pants apart and removed them from the tub. Jake wasn't wearing any underwear so he was now completely naked in the tub and I couldn't help but stare at what was left of his body. He looked like someone you'd see in a picture from the Holocaust but the reality of seeing him in front of me, in his full three-dimensional glory, was a thousand times more powerful. And pathetic. And sad.

I'd seen pictures of Jake throughout the house and he looked like he was a big, strong guy at one time. In all the pictures I'd seen he had a huge smile on his face and he usually looked like he'd just been involved in something like kayaking, mountain biking, scuba diving, or some other vigorous, testosterone-fueled activity. He had been a vital, active guy not too many years ago and now here he was in front of me, looking like he would snap in half if he sneezed too hard. The fickle nature of good health and fate hit me right between the eyes. I started to think about how I would feel if I was in Jake's situation but, before I got too far down that mental road, I heard Marsha shouting.

"Hello? Hello?" she yelled as she walked down the hall in our direction.

"In here, Miss Marsha," Yancy yelled back as she checked the temperature of the water coming out of the bathtub's faucet.

Marsha came into the bathroom and looked surprised to see me standing there. "Oh, hi there, Ben. I was wondering where you were hiding."

"He was helping me with Jake," Yancy offered before I could say anything.

Marsha's head twitched slightly, as if trying to absorb something that just wasn't making sense to her. "Oh," was all she said in response, though I can imagine that she was thinking many other words.

I shrugged. "I was here anyway, and I figured she could use the help." I nodded towards Jake. "Jake didn't seem to mind."

Marsha looked down at Jake and I saw her eyes go soft. "Is that true, sweetie? Was Ben a good taxi for you?"

I looked down and saw him blink once.

"I can finish up here," Yancy then said. "You two can go ahead and do whatever it was that you were going to do."

"Thanks, Yancy," Marsha said. "Do you want to stay for dinner?"

"No, thanks. Not tonight. I'm feelin' a little tired so I think I'm just going to go home and climb into bed."

Marsha rubbed Yancy's back affectionately. "Okay. I have a check for you too, so don't leave without getting it from me."

"Will do."

Marsha looked at me and nodded her head towards the door. "Shall we?"

I started to follow her out when Yancy said, "Thanks again for your help today. Me and Jake both appreciate it."

I turned and said, "No problem. Anytime." I looked at Jake and he gave me one more prolonged blink. I smiled and said, "You're welcome."

Once out in the hallway, Marsha said to me, "You're just full of surprises, aren't you."

"What do you mean?"

We kept walking down the hall. "You come over here all these times without so much as nodding in Jake's direction and then today I come home, and I find you in there giving him a bath for goodness sake!"

I chuckled. "I wasn't actually giving him a bath. I was just helping out with the heavy lifting."

She stopped and turned, so she was facing me. Her eyes were misting over, and they were filled with the same softness that they'd had when she was looking at Jake earlier. "That was a sweet, kind thing you did. I just want you to know that."

I could feel my own tears starting to form in my eyes. I think they were inspired by both the sight of Marsha's tears as well as the residual effects of really seeing Jake, and his unimaginably terrible situation, for the very first time. I didn't know what to say so I just smiled - I'm sure it was a contorted, goofy smile - and then pulled her into a hug. We stood there in the hall, hugging, for a good long time.

CHAPTER THIRTY-SIX

It was snowing hard the next morning and I was worried that my lunch with Charlie would have to be canceled. But the snowplows came out in force during the late morning hours and the roads were somewhat passable by noon. After shoveling the driveway and cleaning off my car it was going on twelve thirty when I finally walked into The Tavern. Charlie was sitting, still with his coat on, in a booth by the window. As I approached the table, I saw that his head was down, and he almost looked like he was napping.

"Hey there, old man," I said cheerfully.

His head shot up and, after collecting himself, he turned to look at me. He was smiling but his eyes looked very tired. He had definitely been napping. "Hey Ben," he croaked. "How're you doing?"

"I'm fine," I replied as I sat down across from him. "How are *you* doing?"

"I'm good."

"You look tired."

"I've just been working too hard. Christmas is a busy time for us angels you know." He flashed me a weak smile.

I returned the smile. "Yeah, I have to admit that you earned your angel wings this Christmas with that gift you gave me."

His eyes burned brighter. "Did Kylie like it?"

"Like it?!? Oh my gosh Charlie, she was beside herself with joy. She wouldn't set that angel doll down for the rest of the day!"

I then told him about how Marsha and I had changed the tag on the gift, making it from Santa, and then about the wish she'd made before opening the gift. "What do you make of that?" I asked.

"Of what?"

"Of the fact that she made her wish before opening the gift and it still came true. I thought you said that she had to look into the doll's eyes first, before making the wish."

He shrugged. "Magic is magic. It's the believing part that's more important than any set of rules I could give you."

"I have to admit that I was more than a little freaked out when I heard her wish, knowing what I knew about what she was about to open."

A huge grin took over his face. "It was hard to deny the presence of magic at that moment, eh?"

"Yeah, it was. I don't know how you did it, but you had that entire room believing in the magic of Christmas that day." I then corrected myself by saying, "Except for The Worm. I don't think he'll ever believe in anything but his own limited intelligence until the day he dies."

"Sounds like somebody else I know."

"Hey, I'm slowing wandering over to the light side, away from the dark forces of doubt and cynicism."

He whistled lowly. "And to what do we owe this conversion? Heaven knows it hasn't been anything I've said."

"Actually, it has. Partly. And partly it's come from hanging around Marsha more lately."

"Things are going well for you two?"

I nodded. "Really well. We had a nice Christmas together and we had a great conversation last night?"

"About?"

"The Clone Test," I replied with a smile.

"Sounds like an interesting test. What is it?"

I explained the Clone Test to him. I then told him about Marsha's assessments of Linda and The Worm and how accurate she'd been. "So, my question to her has been, how would *I* do with the Clone Test? Would we get along okay, or would we be at each other's throats within an hour of meeting each other?"

"And what did she say?"

"She kept putting me off, saying that she hadn't made up her mind yet. Until last night. Last night she decided it was time to give me my assessment."

"And?"

"Some of the stuff was hard to hear, I have to admit."

"Like what?"

I took a deep breath. "She told me that I would probably end up dancing around my clone. She said that we would both be expecting to be trusted by one another, but we wouldn't be able to *give* any trust. It would be a standoff and we would ultimately feel unsatisfied with each other."

He nodded. "Good observation. Anything else?"

"Yeah." I shifted in my seat a little. "She said that we would both constantly be struggling to out-perfect each other, trying to bury our foibles and play up our successes all the time."

"So you'd be afraid to be human with each other."

"Exactly."

He nodded again. "Another good observation."

"Hey, you don't have to be so agreeable you know."

"Like I've always said, truth is truth." He smiled as he shrugged with his eyebrows.

"Yeah, I guess you're right. And, honestly, I had a hard time arguing with her after seeing how dead on she had been with her other assessments."

"So, what'd you say?"

"I didn't say a whole lot at first. I just listened to what she was telling me and kept swallowing the defensive responses that were hanging out on my tongue."

"Good boy."

I smiled. "I'm learning."

"I can see that."

"And that's eventually where she went with her assessment, to the changes that she'd seen in me lately."

"Such as?"

"Being more vulnerable, I guess. Telling her things that I normally would have kept to myself."

"Such as?"

I looked at Charlie for several beats, trying to decide if I should tell him *everything*. A voice I hadn't heard for several weeks then whispered, *"Fuck it!"* in my head and I knew the answer. I smiled. "Okay Charlie, you asked for it." I then told him the entire story, just as I had told Marsha the day before - *Was that just yesterday?!?* - plus, I added in the Big Truth, the one that had yet to be uttered, regarding my brief, but highly effective, career as an arsonist. I felt my heart's cadence increase during the telling of that last part.

The stories rolled off my tongue much easier the second time around, even the ones that I was far from proud of, and I felt less concerned about prying ears from neighboring tables than I had been the day before. When I was done, I slapped my hands on the table and said, "So there you have the full, unabridged story of Ben. The one that nobody has ever heard before except for you. What do you think?"

Charlie's eyes smiled warmly. "I think it's great that you've decided to tell me all of this but more than that I'm glad that you've decided to finally tell *yourself* all of this."

"You aren't shocked by any of this? Or disappointed?"

"About what?"

This time I did lower my voice as I said, "I'm a freakin' arsonist for crissakes."

"Oh, that." His look turned impish. "I'm not shocked by that because I already knew that. And as for disappointment, that's not something that I have any right to give you. You're on your own with that one."

"What do you mean that you already knew? How could you possibly have known about that?" I then remembered that Marsha had said essentially the same thing to me after yesterday's telling of my stories. Was I that transparent?

"I knew about all of it, from the fire to the one-night stand and everything in between, because it's my job to know those sorts of things. I wouldn't be much of an angel if I *didn't* know those things."

Here we go with the angel thing again, was my first thought. But that thought didn't stay with me very long. I could no longer ignore the fact that there was something very special about Charlie. "You know, I never got your last name, Charlie. What is it?"

"It's unimportant," he replied with a shrug.

"What is that, French?" I saw his confused look and said, "Unimportant. Is that a French last name?"

He laughed. "You've got your sense of humor back, that's good. I was worried that as soon as I said the word angel you would head for the door."

"Let's just say that I've evolved."

"And what has caused this evolution?"

I shrugged. "Lots of things. The fire. Marsha. You. It feels like my eyes are opening up after a long sleep and I'm starting to see things in a different way lately."

He nodded. "That's good to hear." His impish look returned. "So, does that mean that you believe in angels now?"

I smiled. "I don't know if my eyes have opened quite that wide yet, but let's just say that I'm more open to the possibility than I've ever been before."

"I guess we should consider that progress, eh?"

"Definitely. And speaking of progress, I'm going to be moving in with Marsha this week."

"Wow, that *is* progress. What prompted this decision?"

"Necessity. I got my January mortgage bill in the mail and freaked out. After talking with Marsha about it, we decided it made sense to move in together."

"So you're going to sponge off Marsha the Sugar Momma for a while, is that it?"

I wagged my finger at him. "Still trying to get under my skin, aren't you?"

He shrugged. "Old habits and all that."

"To be honest, Marsha and I talked about that. She was worried that it might be too soon for us to be sharing a home. But the more we talked about it last night, the more we saw how it made sense, given how much time I spend over there anyway."

"Do you love her?"

The question swirled between us, hanging in the air like a plume of cigarette smoke, as I considered my answer. *Did I love her?* It wasn't that the answer was slow in coming, it was more that I had my doubts about the answer that formed in my head. "Yes, I do" I eventually mumbled. "I do love Marsha."

Charlie smiled. "I thought so. I was just wondering if you would be able to say it."

"Honestly, I surprised myself with my answer."

"Did you tell her everything that you just told me?"

I felt a small flush of embarrassment. "Uh, most of it."

"But not the part about burning down your own house."

"No, I left that part out."

"Why?"

I shrugged. "I thought it would put her in an awkward position with her job and all."

Charlie sat silently for a few beats, probably to allow me to stew in my own juices for a while. "So when did you realize it was true?" he finally asked me.

"That what was true?"

"That you loved her."

"I think it was yesterday, after helping out with Jake."

"Her husband?"

"Yeah." I told him the story about helping Yancy lift Jake into the tub and all the associated thoughts and feelings that went with it.

"That was a nice thing to do."

"Yeah, that's what Marsha said. The thing I can't shake though is the thought that why should anyone be surprised by the fact that I did what I did? Is it because Jake is Marsha's husband? Or is it because such an unselfish gesture isn't a normal part of my MO?"

Charlie didn't answer right away. He considered my questions and then said, "What do *you* think?"

"I think that because you answered my questions with a question of your own that you think question number two is closer to the truth."

"Is that what you think?"

I nodded. "Unfortunately, yeah I guess I do. It's a hard thing to admit, but there's no denying that I've been a little self-consumed lately."

Charlie put his thumb and index finger an inch apart. "Maybe just a skosh," he said.

I smiled. "You're not going to fight me on this one, huh?"

"I've learned to choose my battles."

"And what is it that you're battling now, Charlie?"

It was a throwaway question, but it seemed to freeze him in place for a split second. "Nothing," he finally mumbled. "Not a thing."

I wagged my finger at him. "You've got a secret my little angel friend. What's going on with you?"

He smiled. "I like it when you call me that."

"What?"

"My little angel friend. I like that."

"You're changing the subject."

"No, I'm not. We were never talking about your subject so there was nothing to be changed. I just happen to want to talk about something different than what you want to talk about."

"I'm not sure I followed all that. But maybe that's your plan."

He shrugged. "Maybe."

I looked Charlie up and down. He looked much the same as he did on that first day I'd met him; old clothes, dirty coat, gray messy hair, and eyes that seemed to absorb everything in the room. But there was an unmistakable weariness to him now, a weariness that went beyond the effects of a bad night's sleep. "Where do you live, Charlie?"

"Why all these questions today?"

"It's part of my evolution. Less selfish, more aware is my motto."

"That's a good motto."

"So why won't you answer my questions?"

"Because the answers are unimportant."

"To who? To you?"

He shrugged. "To anyone. My story isn't the story that matters here, yours is."

"And who decided that?"

"Fate."

"And just how is it that you know that?"

"I just do."

"I'm sorry, you have to do better than that."

"Why?"

"Because if you don't, we're through here." I crossed my arms for added emphasis. "I want some answers, or I'm done giving *you* any more answers."

He looked at me and I thought I detected a small flash of anger in his eyes, a first for Charlie, but that disappeared quickly and was replaced by the more familiar twinkle. "You're resorting to blackmail now, eh?"

I shrugged. "Whatever works."

"Very well." He started to put on his coat. "The next time we meet I will give you whatever answers you'd like."

"Is that a promise?"

"I promise."

I reached across the table. "Shake on it." He took my hand and shook it. I noticed that his hand felt small and cold in mine. "Your hands are awfully cold, Charlie. Do you have a pair of gloves? It's pretty cold out there today."

He pulled his hand back. "My hands have always been cold. The curse of poor circulation."

"So angels have health problems too, huh? I would've thought you'd be exempt from such earthly concerns."

"Nope. It allows us to maintain the level of compassion necessary to do our work. Walk amongst them and all that."

"Hmm, I see. Is there like an Angel Handbook where I could learn about all these little factoids? The mainstream press doesn't seem to give this topic much coverage."

He tapped the side of his head. "It's all up here."

"Maybe someday you could write a book about it. It would be helpful to us mortals who have to deal with you guys on a regular basis. You could just hand it over at the first meeting and have us read it before we got started. It would save a lot of time and anguish I'll tell ya that."

He smiled. "Maybe I will someday." Then he stepped out of the booth and said, "So 'till we see each other again." I stepped out of the booth and he came over and gave me a hug. A *big* hug.

"I'll see you next Friday," I said.

He lingered in the hug for a couple of beats longer than normal and then, after stepping away, said, "Yeah, sure. Next Friday."

I felt a strange current running between us, but I didn't know what to make of it. "You need a ride anywhere today?" I'd never asked him that question before but for some reason I felt the need to ask it today, maybe just to distract me from the strange feeling in my gut.

"Nope, I'm fine. Thanks." He threw me what looked like an emotion-tinged smile and said, "Happy New Year, Ben."

I'd forgotten that New Year's eve was coming up the following night. "Happy New Year's to you too, Charlie."

"I hope it's a good year for you."

"I have a feeling it can't be any worse than this last one."

He chuckled. "Yes, that's probably true." His look turned serious. "I would venture to say that this one is going to be much, much better than the last one."

"I hope you're right."

He shoved his hands in his coat pockets. "Well, time to go." He then gave me one last small wave and walked away from me, out of the restaurant, with all my questions still trailing behind him like a string of tin cans on the back of some newlyweds' car.

CHAPTER THIRTY-SEVEN

Marsha and I decided to welcome in the New Year in low-key fashion, at home with some good food, good wine, and each other. No parties. No champagne. No countdowns. Not that we'd shown up on a bunch of party guest lists anyway, but even if we had, we would have still been committed to this more low-key approach.

My job during the day on Saturday was to go out and shop for the food and wine while Marsha did some cleaning and prep work. I was happy to get out of the house because it was one of those glorious New England days when the sun was shining brightly on the fresh layer of snow from the day before. The sky was deep blue, and I marveled at the sight of the snow-filled trees against that blue backdrop. I knew that the snow would soon melt and fall from the trees, so I wanted to enjoy the sight while it lasted.

As I drove from place to place, I thought about just how quickly my life had changed in such a short period of time. I had gone from being just another working stiff, paying his bills and living his very typical life, to being a homeless and somewhat hopeless mess, to now being a man in love, complete with a live-in girlfriend. All in the span of essentially one month. *One month!* If all my months were this full, I would probably keel over from exhaustion before too long.

I then flipped a switch in my head and changed my focus from the past to the future. What was in store for me in the year-to-come? How would the whole thing with Austin T play out?

What would I end up doing for work? Would Marsha and I still be together at this time next year? I silently prayed that the answer would be yes to the fourth question.

As I scanned the wine section, looking for just the right bottle of wine for that night, I thought about the "why?" behind my desire to have things work out with Marsha. This was a woman, after all, that I'd met in a bar and it was a relationship that began in bed, neither of which boded well for a long, happy future together. So what was it about her? Was I just desperate to be with someone, anyone, and that was blinding me to the realities of our relationship? Would I wake up one day soon and wonder, *what have I done?* Something told me that wouldn't be the case. Something told me that Marsha and I were meant to be together. Time would tell if that was a foolish notion.

I selected a bottle of Cabernet Sauvignon from Washington and headed to the register. I was standing in line when I heard a shout from behind me. "Luke?" Even though the person obviously wasn't calling to me I turned towards the voice anyway. When I turned, I saw a large man coming towards me, a huge grin splattered on his face. He looked familiar to me, but I didn't know why. "Luke!" he then said again, this time leaving no doubt that he was talking to me.

It wasn't until he was standing in front of me that I remembered where I knew him from. "Griz?" I replied hesitantly, pulling the name out of an area of my brain that was still somewhat shrouded in fog.

He pulled me into a bear hug, which I guess was appropriate given his name. "How the hell ya been, Luke?" he asked as he released me from the hug.

I decided it would be best not to correct him on my name, especially since I recalled not using my real name that day in the bar. Besides, I wasn't sure how Griz would react to being told that I'd lied to him. "Fine," I replied. "How are you?"

He slapped me on the arm. "Doin' good. Been off the whiskey for a week now." He raised the two bottles he held in his hand. "Drinkin' red wine now. Seems more civilized." He then lowered his bottles and nodded at the bottle in my hand. "I see you're thinkin' the same way."

I considered the bottle for a moment and then said, "Yeah, you just can't beat a good bottle of red."

"Gives me more of a headache if I don't watch it though," Griz then said.

I suddenly became aware of the people around me and just how loud and rough-sounding Griz was. I felt a little embarrassed. "That's the sulfites," I said. "There's a ton of them in wine."

"Sulfites, huh? Why the hell would they put those in my wine?"

"It's a preservative. It keeps the wine from turning colors and spoiling."

Griz nodded. "You're a smart fella, Luke. Are you a teacher or something?"

I shook my head. "Nope, not a teacher."

Griz grinned broadly. "That's probably a good thing, considering the tattoo you got there on yer arm. That would be a tough one to explain to the kiddies."

I looked down at my arm that was currently covered with a couple of layers of clothing. "How did you know about my tattoo?" I asked.

"I was there that night, Luke. Don't you remember? I helped you pick out the bear." His smile broadened. "The fuck it inside the tattoo was your idea though. I thought it was a nice touch myself."

I glanced sideways and saw that we were now entertaining the entire line with our conversation. I could feel my face start to flush. "I don't remember much from that night," I confessed quietly.

"Not surprisin'. You had a couple gallons of tequila in yer belly." He cocked his head. "Do you remember what the tattoo guy told you about that tattoo of yours?"

I shook my head. "Not a word."

"He told you that the grizzly he put on your arm was some Indian totem that's s'posed to give you strength and courage. Is it doin' its job?"

I thought about life since that day and I had to smile. "Yeah, I guess it has done its job," I said to myself as much as to Griz.

"That's good news 'cuz I went and got the same tattoo not too long ago." He took off his coat, rolled up his sleeve, and there on his arm was a grizzly tattoo identical to mine in every way. "I even had him put the same words on there," Griz added with a smile. "I like that whole fuck it thing."

"Yeah, it can be helpful," I agreed. I thought about telling him to be careful with those two words, about how I'd learned that they could be both helpful and hurtful, depending on the situation, but I quickly decided that it wasn't the time or the place to be waxing philosophical with Griz.

Griz lowered his sleeve and put his coat back on. "Truth is, you kind of inspired me, Luke."

"Really? How so?"

"After hearing you talk in the bar that day, and hearin' how life has been tossin' you more than yer share of bricks lately, and then seein' you flip the finger at your life like you did, with that tattoo and all…well, it just got me to thinkin'." There was a pause and I almost made the mistake of saying something, but I held my tongue. He soon continued with his thought. "It got me to thinkin' that I should get off my ass and get back in the game. So, I went and got George here." He patted his arm where he'd just shown me the tattoo. "And then I been tryin' to live up to his totem message ever since."

Another silence took hold between us for a few moments, but it was a good, reflective silence. I was suddenly completely unaware of anyone else around us. So much so, in fact, that it took the clerk behind the counter a few "Sir!" wake-up calls before I realized it was my turn to check out. I placed my wine on the counter and started to pull out my wallet but Griz caught my hand. "No you don't," he said firmly. "This one's on me."

I thought about arguing with him but then I thought better of it and just said, "Thanks Griz. I appreciate that." I could tell this was an important gesture for him and, besides, he was twice my size.

He pulled out his wallet and paid the clerk for my wine as well as his own. "No problem," he said. "It's the least I can do for the man who got my butt off that barstool."

The clerk packed up our wine and then we walked out of the store together. "So what are you doing with yourself these days, Griz?"

Once outside the door he suddenly stopped and stuck out his right hand. "Name's Dan. Dan Burns." He saw the "huh?" look I tossed his way and explained further. "Remember how I told you back in the bar how folks never use their real names in there?"

I did actually remember that part of the day, one of the few brain cells that had clung to its little piece of information. "Yeah, I do actually. It was some kind of unwritten code or something."

"Yeah, that's right." He shrugged. "So, I just thought it was time we really met each other." He stuck out his hand again. "Dan Burns is my name."

I took his large hand into mine, feeling like a five-year-old shaking his father's hand, and said, "Nice to meet you, Dan. My name's Ben Weaver."

He shook my hand hard. "Damn nice to meet you Ben." He then looked at me with a question mark on his face. "So where did Luke come from? Cool Hand Luke?"

I shook my head. "Nope. It came from Luke Skywalker."

He smiled. "A Star Wars fan, eh?"

"Yeah, Luke was my hero when I was a kid."

"So you got to be him for a day, huh?"

I let out a scoffing sound. "I'm not sure that Luke would approve of the day that I spent wearing his name."

"Oh, I don't know about that, Ben. Seems to me you were quite the Jedi Knight that day, at least in my eyes."

I smiled at the notion that my tequila and tattoo-filled binge was inspirational to someone else in any way. A new Rule for my new life quickly formed in my head. Rule #6 for My New Life: *Keep your eyes open - Inspiration can be hiding anywhere!* I liked it. "I'm glad to hear that I inspired you in some way, Dan." I chuckled. "I have to admit that I wasn't feeling very inspirational that day."

"Guess you never know how other folks are gonna see you, eh?"

"No, I guess you don't." I started walking towards my car again and Dan followed. "So, you never told me what it is that you're doing now."

"I'm helping out with this group down at the Y right now."

"What kind of group?"

"It's called Teens Rule and it's basically a way to keep kids outta trouble."

"What do you do with them?"

He shrugged. "All kinds of stuff. Today we're gonna take 'em to the Senior Center and they're gonna help prepare the free lunch that they serve there."

"Sounds like a great program."

"Yeah, it is. I figure that if I can't be with my own kids then the least that I could do is help out someone else's kids."

I then remembered Dan's story; the ex-wife, the two kids, the affair that broke up the marriage. "Remind me where your two boys live now."

A huge smile took over Dan's face. "You remembered about my boys."

I shrugged casually. "How could I forget."

He laughed. "There's a lot that gets forgotten in places like that. Alcohol and memory just don't go together very well."

"I guess that's the point, right?"

He slapped me on the back. "Yeah, it is at that. You're a bit of a philosopher, aren't you Ben."

"I guess I have my moments."

He slapped me one more time, just to make *sure* I was sufficiently bruised, and then said, "They live in Upstate New York now, with their Mom."

"And how old are they?"

"Jerry's ten and Dean's twelve now. Dean just had a birthday this week."

"They're becoming young men."

"Yeah, they are." I thought I heard a small crack in Dan's voice as he added, "They need their Dad more than ever right now."

Instinctively I reached over and placed my hand on his shoulder. "I'm sure they're doing just fine, Dan."

He heaved a deep sigh. "Yeah, Annie does a great job as their mother, I gotta give her that. It can't be easy raisin' two boys on yer own and she does better than most."

I hesitated to ask my next question but a fucket pushed it out of my mouth. "So, there's nobody else in her life right now?"

"No, thank God. She hasn't been with anyone else since we split up."

"How long has that been?"

"Goin' on three years."

"So are you still hoping that..." I stopped short of finishing my question because I suddenly realized I was wandering into areas marked None Of My Business.

Dan had gotten the gist of my question, however, as he replied, "Yeah, I guess I am hopin' that we might get back together someday. Stupid as it sounds, I never stopped lovin' Annie and I know I belong with my boys."

"That doesn't sound stupid at all," I said reassuringly, knowing from first-hand experience what he was talking about.

"So how about you, Ben?" he then asked. "How are you and your son doing?"

Yet another one of my lies from that day reared its ugly head. I didn't hesitate to correct him this time. "I actually don't have a son, Dan. I have a little girl named Kylie. She's ten years old." I shrugged and smiled. "I guess once I started telling fibs that day I didn't know how to stop."

Dan laughed. "Happens to the best of us, Ben." He placed his hand reassuringly on my shoulder. "And remember that anything you said that day was said by Luke." He patted my shoulder twice and then said, "That lyin' bastard."

His words caused me to catch my breath, unsure for the briefest of moments as to Dan's level of seriousness. But then I saw the twinkle in his eye, and I replied, "Yeah, the guy wouldn't seem to know the truth if it bit him in the ass."

We shared another laugh and then Dan said, "You really should come over to the Y one time 'n help me out with the Teens Rule kids. I think you'd like it." Before I could reply he dug into his coat pocket and pulled out a scrap of paper and a pen. He jotted something down and handed it to me. "Here's my number. Call me sometime and we'll head over there together."

I took the scrap of paper and put it in my pocket. The honest answer was that I didn't think I would ever call that number, but I opted to return to my Lyin' Luke ways and said, "I will. Thanks."

He slapped me one more time on the back, just in case I had any body parts that were still not bruised from his previous slaps, and said, "Great seein' ya, Ben. Have yerself a great New Year's."

"You too, Dan. Here's hoping the new year is better than the old one."

"I'll drink to that!" he bellowed. Then he leaned in close and whispered, "If I were still a drinkin' man that is." As he drew away, he threw me a wink.

I shifted the bag of wine to my left arm and extended my right hand. "Happy New Year, Dan."

He shook my hand, so firmly that I feared for the lives of my fingers. "Happy New Year, Ben. See ya soon, right?"

I nodded. "Right. See you next year."

We exchanged one last smile and then he turned and walked away.

Later that day, as Marsha and I stood side-by-side in the kitchen, chopping and prepping our way towards the delicious dinner we had planned for that night, I decided to tell her about my encounter with Griz, aka Dan. I had hesitated to tell her about it because that whole episode in the bar, and the tattoo that followed, wasn't one of my prouder moments. But I soon realized that I had shared worse, much worse, with Marsha so the Griz Chapter wouldn't be that big of a deal. And it wasn't.

"He sounds like an interesting guy," was her initial reply when I had finished telling the story.

"Yeah, he is that for sure," I agreed.

"So, are you going to take him up on his offer?"

"What offer?"

"The one that involved helping out at the Y."

"Oh, *that* offer." I chopped in silence for a few beats and then said, "I'm still thinking on that one."

I could feel her eyes on the side of my head, but she didn't say a word. She then went back to chopping and said, "So the story you told me about getting your tattoo in college was a complete lie, eh"

"Yes, it was. I'd like to say that it was that lyin' bastard Luke who told that fib but that was most definitely a Ben lie." I set my knife down and looked over at her. "When you asked me that question we had just gotten together and to be perfectly honest I wasn't feeling particularly proud of that moment in my life." I shrugged. "So I told a little white lie."

"Hmm," she said without stopping or looking up. "Seems to me that a lie is a lie, no matter what shade you try to give it."

"Well, I don't know about that. It seems to *me* that some lies are bigger and potentially more hurtful than others and…"

She didn't let me finish my little monologue of justification as she slammed her knife to the counter and stared me right in the face. "How about if we both make a New Year's resolution right here and now?"

"Okay."

"How about if we agree to not tell each other *any* lies in the coming year, no matter the shade? How does that sound to you?"

I smiled. "Sounds good to me."

She thrust her right hand out. "Shake on it."

I continued to smile, took her hand and shook it.

"Now kiss on it." She puckered her lips and I stepped forward and kissed her. What started as a small kiss, however, quickly morphed into an all-out tongue-fest and after a minute or so of mashing faces, she backed away. She wiped her lips once with her forearm, let out a small sigh, and then picked up her knife to resume chopping.

"What was *that* all about?" I asked, suddenly feeling quite aroused.

"That was my own lie-detector test."

"Did I pass?"

She cracked a small smile. "Head of the class."

I stepped towards her and placed my hand on the small of her back. I then nuzzled her neck and whispered, "I'd like to show the teacher what else I can do."

"Is it naughty?" she asked.

"Very."

She then set her knife down and turned so she could place both of her hands around my neck. "I have to warn you that I don't grade on a curve."

I ran my hands up and down her body. "You've got plenty of curves to go around here, Teach, and I give *your* curves an A plus."

"Oh, now you're just sucking up, so I'll give you a good grade."

"Okay, the oral part of this exam is officially over. Time for the practical portion of the test." I pulled her in close and kissed her hard. Our bodies writhed together as we struggled to get as close to each other as we possibly could. It wasn't long before we made our way to the couch in the living room and then it wasn't long after that that all our clothes made their way to the floor.

It was an hour or so later that we found ourselves back at our respective chopping stations, our hair more disheveled and our clothes more rumpled than they'd been earlier. There were also huge, immovable smiles of satisfaction etched on our faces that had not been there earlier. "That was nice," Marsha purred.

"I'll say. I can't think of a better way to close out the year."

"So, what are you thinking for this coming year?"

"What do you mean?" I asked, though I had a feeling I knew what she was asking.

She shrugged. "I mean what's in your crystal ball, what's on your radar, what's the plan, Stan. Pick your favorite cliché and run with it."

I returned the shrug. "I don't know. Pick a category and I'll give it my best shot."

"How about if we start with work."

"Undecided."

She waited for a moment, probably expecting more than one word from me, and then said, "Money."

"Definitely want some." I kept my head down, pretending to be focused on my chopping, so I wouldn't risk looking at her. I had a feeling that this conversation wasn't going to be one that would raise my stock in her eyes.

"Goals?"

"None. Other than getting Austin T to see the light."

There was another long pause before she asked, "Us?"

A broad grin took over my face. I set my knife down and then turned her, so we were face-to-face. "I may not have a lot of answers concerning my future, but I do know one thing." I took one step closer and cupped her face in my hands. "You and I are going to be together for a long, long time." I planted a kiss on her forehead. "You can take that one to the bank."

She smiled. "I'm glad to hear that." She lowered her head. "I actually don't care about all of the other stuff. I just wanted to hear you say those last words." She looked up and I could see that she was starting to cry. "It means a lot to me."

Her tears inspired tears of my own and I continued to hold her eyes even as my own vision began to blur. The Three Big Words worked their way up to my lips, but I held them there, not ready to have them see the light of day. Yet. Unable to con- jure up any other suitable words to share in that moment I elected to just pull her into a hug instead. It was electric. We stood and hugged there for what seemed like minutes, both of us rubbing and squeezing the other, wordlessly communicating the feelings we had for each other. It was nice.

When we finally separated, I could see that Marsha was still crying. She wiped her cheeks, forced a quick smile, and then went back to her chopping. Were they tears of joy? Sadness? Frustration? I had no idea. Perhaps they were coming from a source that contained a bit of all those emotions. I just knew that I couldn't ask her at that moment because that would then lead to a conversation that I wasn't ready to have. Yet.

CHAPTER THIRTY-EIGHT

The first Friday of the New Year came, and I showed up at the Tavern anxious to share some recent thoughts with Charlie. It had gotten to the point that I was now creating a little Charlie List in my head as I went about my week, jotting down conversational topics on an invisible list in a corner of my brain so I would remember to talk about them over lunch that Friday. This week had been no different and I had my invisible list, a particularly long one actually, ready to go. But there was no Charlie.

Noon came and went, and I sat there in the booth for another hour after that, nursing a cup of coffee that I had eventually ordered from the waitress who I could tell was getting impatient with me and my lack of a lunch order. I continued to plead with her to be patient but after my sixth offering of "Just another minute" I decided it was time to give up. It was after one o'clock and Charlie wouldn't be coming that day. It was his first no-show.

I handed the waitress five dollars, thanked her for her patience, and headed out the door, feeling strangely discombobulated by the curveball of a Charlie no-show. As I walked, I realized that my lunches with Charlie had become much more than an interesting diversion for me: they had become an anchor of sorts, my one bit of routine that I could cling to in what had become a very unpredictable life. No matter what else was going on in my life I could count on sitting down with Charlie every Friday at noon and processing all that was happening. He would help me to pick through the rubble of details and make some sense of it all. I always walked away from the Tavern each Friday feeling better and more centered than I did when I had walked in. Until today. Today I just felt anxious and disappointed.

I could also feel the pressure of all the unsaid words and un-expressed thoughts piled up behind the dam in my head, a dam that I had been prepared to lift at noon today. Then the question became: What do I do now? Where could I go and who could I talk to? Marsha was working, Jim was working, and there wasn't anybody else who I would even consider as a lunch companion. That thought just made me feel sadder.

Without even being aware of it I had made my way to the University and I found myself standing at the west entrance. I looked up and flashed on the many pleasant memories that were attached to this part of the campus; this was where Linda and I used to take walks together when she was first hired as a Journal-ism professor at the University. We were still very much in love back then and the walks were always charged with both the pro-fessional promise of her new job as well as the personal promise of our fairly new relationship. Kylie was still just a thought back then, an unspoken goal off in some distant future, but even the *thought* of having a child together added excitement to the edges of our marriage. Those were good times.

Without too much thought I made my way to Linda's build-ing. I was soon standing outside of the Walkowicz Building, so named because of the very large donation of some well-to-do alumnus of the Journalism Department many years ago. It was a nice building, all brick and ivy and the requisite gargoyles stand-ing watch from high on the roof, and it had always inspired thoughts of my own college years whenever I walked up to it. I stood outside in the cold air, considering both the gargoyles and my next move, for several minutes before heaving a deep sigh and electing to go inside.

The halls of the Walkowicz Building were quiet, because it was early January and thus between semesters, but also because it was Friday, and most of the professors were prone to enjoy three-day weekends this time of year. I headed towards Linda's office hoping that she wasn't one of the three-day weekend types and when I saw through the frosted glass window on her door that her light was on, I felt both a surge of relief as well as a twinge of trepidation. I stood and stared at her door for another few minutes unsure whether I should knock or just walk away. I eventually chose to knock.

"Come in, it's open," I heard her say from behind the door. I took a deep, calming breath and opened the door.

Once inside I noticed right away that she had changed her office around since I had last seen it. All the furniture was lighter, and the walls were painted a much brighter color, a vibrant shade of blue, which all served to make the office feel bigger and cheerier than I remembered it being. Linda's head was down when I walked in, so I had a few seconds to take it all in before she looked up from whatever she was doing. When she did finally look up, I saw her face transition from happy and welcoming to what could only be described as angry and disappointed when she saw that it was me standing in her office. It wasn't the face I was expecting to see. "Hi there," I managed to get out with a small wave.

"What do *you* want?" she asked, with an emphasis on the word "you" that made me feel like the words "*you fucking asshole*" were also somehow attached, unspoken, to that single word.

I shrugged casually. "Nothing really. I was just walking by and thought I'd stop in to see how you were doing." I scanned the office again, as if seeing it for the first time. "I really like the changes you made in here. The place looks great."

"Thanks," she all but spat back at me. "Anything else on your mind?"

I shook my head. "Nope." I then stepped forward one step and asked, "Anything on *your* mind?"

She appeared to get defensive as she said, "No. Why do you ask?"

"I don't know, you just seem kind of pissed off about something."

She heaved a deep prolonged sigh as she bowed her head. She paused in that position for a few beats and then when she lifted her head, she seemed to have a more resolved look on her face. "Okay, you asked so here it is." She opened a side drawer on her desk and pulled out a piece of paper. She glanced at it briefly before handing it to me with a disgusted shake of her head. "Can you explain *this* to me?"

There they were again: the unspoken words "you fucking asshole" hanging from the edges of her spoken words. I took the picture from her. When I first looked at it, I had a hard time making sense of it. The picture quality wasn't all that great and the lighting was bad but there was no denying who or what it was. It was a picture of me laying in a bed, apparently asleep, with nothing but my bare ass smiling back at the camera. It dawned on me that this was the first time in my life that I'd ever seen my own bare ass. That little fact seemed kind of odd for a man my age. I started to assess my ass – Was it too big? Too small? Too hairy? Too soft? – but before I could get very far with my assessment Linda's voice pulled me back to the moment. "Well?!?" she said. "What do you have to say for yourself?"

The truth was that I didn't have a whole lot to say because I didn't know where the picture had been taken and by whom. "Where did you get this?" I asked as calmly as I could muster, seeing that Linda was ready to go ballistic without much provocation.

"I got it from one of my fellow professors who in turn had gotten it off of one of his student's Facebook pages."

"A student? What student"

"Her name is Angela Scabelli. Ring any bells?"

The name didn't ring any bells in my head. At first. But then the name Angela bored its way deeper into my brain until it found a brain cell that I had tucked away in a corner because it contained a memory that I would have preferred to forget about, forever. Linda must have seen the light of recognition click on in my eyes as she said, "Yeah, I thought so."

"Wait a minute, you don't understand..." I began.

"Oh, I think I *do* understand," she said, with the words *you fucking asshole* screamed at me telepathically. "I understand that you are now a middle-aged man who wants to be twenty again and you think that climbing into bed with a college co-ed is an easy way to achieve that goal." She didn't even take a breath as she continued to her next thought, thus keeping me from jumping in with my own words of explanation, which was probably for the best because I didn't really *have* any words of explanation to offer her at that moment. "And I also understand that you are now a single, unmarried man who doesn't have to answer to anyone but himself so it's all really none of my business." A quick breath, and then, "But it does become my business when you do things like this, that could have a direct impact on my job as well as on our daughter." She looked at me with a slight tilt to her head. "Do you realize just how embarrassing this is for me? To have one of my fellow professors bring a picture like this to my attention?"

I wondered to myself why on earth a professor would be trolling through his students' Facebook pages in the first place and then I wondered if perhaps the nameless professor was actually The Worm. This sort of thing would be right up his alley.

"Did you know that Angela was actually a student of *mine* at one time? Is that why you did this? Was it some perverse way of getting back at me?"

I considered telling her that Angela didn't tell me that she had been a student in one of her classes until after we'd spent the night together, but then I realized, thankfully, that my best course of action at that point was to just keep my mouth shut and my tongue locked in place. *Just take your whipping and then move on*, I told myself. Lord knows I deserved every lash that she wanted to dish out. And she did go on for a while, though I had to admit that I stopped listening. She was screaming things that included words like "responsibility" and "grow up" but my eyes had drifted back to the picture that was still in my hand and I continued to contemplate my ass. I decided that, all in all, it wasn't such a bad ass for a guy my age to have.

"Do you have anything at all to say for yourself?" I then heard her ask.

I looked up from the picture and just shook my head. "Nope, not a thing."

Exasperated, she waved her arms at me dismissively and said, "I just think you should go now."

I turned to go, the picture still in my hand, but then decided to turn back to her and ask, "Actually I do have something to say. A question, actually."

"What is it?" she asked, the exasperation still in her voice.

"Who gave this to you? Was it The Worm?" Before she could answer, because I knew she wouldn't tell me the truth anyway, I said, "If it was The Worm who found this, the bigger question in my mind, if I were you, would be why the hell was he on Angela's Facebook site in the first place and what other sites does this guy visit when you're not around?" And with that I tossed the picture into a nearby waste basket and walked out the door.

CHAPTER THIRTY-NINE

The entire weekend was a black hole of nothingness for me. Marsha was busy with her own errands all weekend - the kinds of things like shopping and going to the dry cleaners that people with full-time jobs must squeeze in when they're not working – and I spent both days just hanging out and going on mental strolls. The two paths I strode down the most were the Charlie Path, wondering why he hadn't shown up on Friday and if he was all right, and the Linda Path, wondering why she still, after all these years, still had a small hold on me. It wasn't a very productive weekend.

When Monday finally came, I watched Marsha head off to work and then, sitting in her empty kitchen, I found myself sliding down a slippery mental slide that seemed headed straight for the Big D word waiting for me with its arms open wide at the bottom of the slide. Depression had always been something that I thought I could easily succumb to, given my over-analyzing nature and self-possessed orientation to the world, but I'd always managed to avoid the sharpest of its claws, opting instead for a sort of Depression-Lite from time to time, sort of like catching a small cold instead of becoming bedridden with the flu. I was a member of the Functioning Depressed Club of folks who carried on with their normal lives but always had a bank of small, dark clouds hanging on their horizon. Until now. I could feel the dark clouds rolling in closer and I knew I'd better act fast or risk being pulled into a full embrace from Big D.

I grabbed my coat and headed out the door. The blast of cold air in my face helped immediately and then the rhythmic crunch, crunch of the snow underfoot as I quickly made my way down the street helped even more. I knew I needed distraction, but the question was where to go and what to do. I knew I needed the noise and scurry of other people so I headed to a coffee shop near the University campus and found a table off in the corner, where I could see the bustle but not be in the thick of it.

As I took my first sips from my cup of coffee I thought some more about my recent near-visit from Big D. Why now? With all that I'd been through in recent years during my initial separation from Linda and then our eventual divorce, it would seem that I was now through the worst of things. But I'd noticed these dark clouds rolling in across my insides more and more in recent weeks. Why?

I watched as students, faculty, and other folks moved about purposefully in the coffee shop. There were some sitting with their laptops, focused intently on the blue screen in front of them, and others sitting in small clusters, leaning forward and discussing unknown topics with obvious zeal. I felt very separate from this swirl of activity around me, as if everyone in the world had a place to be and something to do but me. I was the lone loser adrift in a sea of doers and achievers. And then the connection was made – an obvious one in hindsight – as to why I was teetering on the brink of depression. It was all about purpose. I had none now, and a part of me craved to belong to something, anything, just to prove to myself, and others, that I belonged and had some value.

I thought about it some more and soon realized something else: I missed routine. As much as I had fought it when I was working full-time and living in the house, I now saw that routine had also been my friend in many ways. It was the routine of work that got me out of bed each morning and I missed some of the accompanying routines that went along with that: my morning coffee; the muffins that I would pick up at the Pearl Bakery most mornings; the lunches with Bob and my other co-workers; the glass of wine after work; reading the newspaper in my favorite chair. All of it disappeared with the house. I knew that I could still plug many of these things into my current life, but I also knew that it wouldn't be the same. Not even close. It was the routine of the job that had given me the base from which to enjoy these other things and without that base they would all feel empty and pointless. So much of what I did back then was re-flected back at me through the prism of work.

Going one layer deeper, I saw that there was the need to feel like I'd *earned* my small indulgences, such as muffins and wine, or they wouldn't have any value to me. It was the "hard day at the office" that made that wine taste so good and my favorite chair feel so soothing to me. Most of my old life had been structured around the theme of "Work, then recover from work" and without the work part there was no need to recover from it. All the objects of my recovery had been put in place as a kind of buffer between me and my job and now they no longer had a purpose.

As my mind turned it over a few more times, however, I saw that those things hadn't been buffers so much as they'd been *placeholders*, slipped into the gaps in my life that weren't filled by, or had even been *created* by, my job. I tried to use things like wine and muffins to fill the gaps where joy and fulfillment should have been. The trade never really worked of course but the mi-rage they created allowed me to function as if they had worked. So, when all was said and done, I just missed the *mirages* that I had created while I was working. Pathetic.

I thought some more about the mirages and outright lies that I'd manufactured for myself just so I could be a contributing citizen out in the world. There was the mirage of satisfaction and the lie of security. The mirage of love and the lie of forever. The mirage of joy and the lie of happiness. No matter which corner of my old life I shone my beam of revelation into I would find still more mirages and lies. I had built a true house of cards and now I could feel it tumbling down inside of me just as my real house had tumbled down just a couple of months earlier.

I could feel the darkness creeping in on me but some little voice inside of me said "It's okay" so I didn't fight it. Another vital role of my "Muffins and Wine Therapy" was simple distraction; keep my eyes on the indulgence and away from the darkness. But I knew that it was time to stop running and time to face the darkness, to see what it had to tell me. Some wise man had spoken about lighting candles instead of always running from, and being afraid of, the darkness. I liked that metaphor, so I struck a match, dug out a candle from one of my internal closets, and went to work.

It took a little while for my eyes to adjust to the dark but after they did the first thing I saw off in one corner of my mind was a hypocrite. He stood there, seemingly proud and erect, but everything about him screamed "phony!" It was the Me who stood around at parties, drink in hand, spouting off about religion, politics, philosophy, and any number of other topics as if he had a direct pipeline of knowledge from God Himself. This guy could argue with the best of them, and argue he did, and yet when all his empty opinions and theories rubbed up against the hard edges of Real Life, as they were now, I could see them for the worthless pile of words that they truly were. All his carefully created arguments about the nature of happiness or the definition of true spirituality were of little help to me now. It was as if Mr. Hypocrite had constructed a bridge across an internal chasm - filled with dark, raging waters below – and he stood at the edge of the bridge, a big, self-satisfied grin on his face, inviting me to try it out. But when I took my first step onto his bridge it began to crumble under my weight. It had always looked so good and strong from a distance but now, when I had to use it for something real and practical, I could see that he had built it with balsa wood instead of steel and so now I was paying the price for that bit of shoddy construction.

Looking around some more, I found another Me hiding behind a nearby large rock. I shone my light on him and he ducked out of sight behind the rock. I walked around the rock and looked down at him, crouched on the ground with his arms wrapped around himself like a scared, shivering child. This guy was truly pathetic. But I recognized him as the guy who made many of the decisions in my life. Looking at him now, and seeing who he truly was, served as a swift punch in my gut. Once again, what I thought to be true and what was *actually* true were two entirely different things. I had created the mirage of self-assuredness and confidence to get me through each day but in reality, my Ship of Life was being steered by Mr. Scared and Shivering who was now cowering at my feet. Scary. And very, very humbling.

I flashed on all the times that I had ducked behind a metaphorical rock in my life, just like Mr. S&S was now, and how I had let my fears and insecurities rule the day. Moments ranging from missed dating opportunities to missed trips to exotic locales formed a quick Collage of Regret in my head. There were far more of these moments than I had ever realized, and it soon became too embarrassing for me to continue my search.

I had seen enough. I knew now that I had a lot of work to do if I had any hope of creating a life that I could be proud of from the perspective of my future self's rocking chair. I blew out the internal candle and came back to the surface.

Still sitting in my seat in the café, but now looking through a different set of eyes, I saw people who were just like me; struggling to maintain the mirage of happiness and fulfillment in whatever ways they could. I smiled. It was now time to get to work on building that bridge of steel.

CHAPTER FORTY

I thought about telling Marsha all about my journey into the darkness when I saw her that night but then I eventually decided against it. This would be a solo journey, there was no doubt about that, and having to keep her informed of my progress and struggles along the way would just slow me down. I was on my own.

I woke up the next morning feeling anxious to get started on the creation of a New Life for myself. Actually, as I thought about it, it wouldn't be a new life that I would be seeking so much as it would be a new approach *to* life. An important distinction to make. Stop rearranging the deck furniture on the Ben Titanic and go spend some time in the engine room instead. I couldn't wait to get started.

After saying goodbye to Marsha — and hello to Yancy, who had now become Jake's full-time caregiver — I retreated to the kitchen to begin my journey. I grabbed a pad of paper and pencil from a drawer and sat down at the kitchen table, pencil poised at the ready for any nuggets of wisdom that might fall into my lap. I sat there, thinking hard, for several minutes and…nothing. My mind swirled with thoughts of everything and nothing at the same time. The thoughts were like fireflies flitting about in my head and I had a hard time grabbing any one thought for further examination. Flashes of Marsha, and Austin T, and Linda appeared briefly. Then Kylie, and Charlie, and Marsha again. I needed to focus.

I shifted in my chair and, using an old writer's trick I'd accessed many times in the past, I wrote something down on the piece of paper in front of me, just to overcome the Blank Page Syndrome. "Things I want to do with my life," I wrote in big bold letters at the top of the page and then drew two dark lines under the words. The fireflies returned. But instead of faces, this time I was seeing places. Images of Paris, Italy, and New Zealand dive-bombed in and out of view. Then came Alaska, Hawaii, and the Pacific Coast. I scribbled the word "travel" on the paper.

I pondered each of these places for a short while, realizing that many of them had been rolling around in my head since I was a child, and then turned my attention to the next wave on the horizon. The next wave of thoughts that came rolling in consisted of words like "give back" and "help" and "unselfish." I wasn't sure where these words had come from, but I wrote them all down and then wrote "Serve" in big letters on the page and drew a dark circle around the word.

I stared down at the words on the paper in front of me. Who *was* this person? Reading these words now I would have said that whoever wrote these words should join the Peace Corps or perhaps run off with the circus. But neither one of those options resonated with me so I wondered where this little exercise was going to take me. Then came the third wave. I could tell before it crashed on my mental shore that this wave was larger and packed more force than the other two. Kylie's face rode like a masthead on the crest of the wave and the only word that I could see rolling in the wave underneath her face was "legacy." I understood the meaning of this word immediately and it fell on my shoulders like an anchor. What kind of memories, and what kind of world, would I be leaving behind for my daughter? From where I sat right now the answer to that question would not be a good one.

I set the paper aside and stared out the nearby window. This whole process was going to be much harder than I thought. How does one go about putting on the brakes on his life and then charting a whole new course? And how does one go about *choosing* that new course? Saying that "anything is possible" was a great notion when I was back in college or when I was sitting at my desk back at the The Beacon, longing for a break from my mundane existence, but staring those three words in the face as I was now felt different somehow; less exhilarating and more overwhelming.

I flashed back on the time that Linda had sent me to the store in search of emergency feminine products for her and how I ended up standing in the aisle, staring at what seemed to be acres of possible choices, including dozens of brands and subsets of choices within each brand, from "absorbent" to "super absorbent," from "super thin" to "wings plus." I couldn't move for a good long time. I was frozen in place by the sheer volume of choices in front of me and had no tools for eliminating any of those choices.

And here I was again, feeling the blade at my throat from the two-edged sword called Choice. What had always been viewed as an ally was now showing me its darker side. This whole exercise was beginning to feel like more of a burden than anything else. It was as if someone had just tossed me a lead-filled lifejacket to keep me from drowning. Thanks, but no thanks. I crumpled the piece of paper in my hands and tossed it in the wastebasket as I headed out the door.

CHAPTER FORTY-ONE

Friday couldn't come soon enough for me. I needed to dump a huge load and Charlie was slated to be my dumping ground. Marsha was great in many ways but there were still parts of me that I felt it was necessary to hide from her, my chronic indecision about my life being one of those things. Someday, soon I hoped, I would be able to lay everything out in front of her without concern for any repercussions, but for now I was still feeling worried about her changing her mind and booting me to the curb. I wasn't ready to live the life of a homeless man.

I prayed that Charlie wouldn't no-show me again this week as I entered The Tavern a little before noon. Thankfully, I found him right away and an involuntary smile formed on my face as I sat down across from him in the booth. "Hey there, stranger," I said as I removed my coat.

His return smile was weak, though not from a lack of effort. "Hey there back at'cha," he all but whispered.

He looked tired and about as pale as a black man could look. "How're you doing?" I asked, not even attempting to hide the concern that I suddenly felt.

He nodded with his eyes. "Feelin' good. Sorry to miss you last week but somethin' came up."

"No problem. I'm just glad to see you here today." The smile returned to my face. "Big angel emergency last week, eh?"

"Yeah, you might say that. There's just no tellin' when someone needs an angel and I'm duty bound to answer the call every time."

"That's good because I sure need my angel today."

He leaned back and sighed. "So, what's on your mind?"

I gave him a rundown of my last two weeks. I told him about Linda and the ordeal with the Angela pictures. I talked about how I found myself missing routine and about the many mirages and lies I'd discovered in my life. And I went on at great length about the fear and trepidation I was feeling around the whole theme of "What's next?" in my life. As usual, Charlie listened to every word as if his life depended on it and when I finally sat back to take a breath, he waited a good minute before saying a word.

"Sounds like you've had a busy couple o' weeks," he eventually said.

"Yeah, it kinda worked out that way," I agreed. "That's why I was so excited to see you today.

He smiled. "The feeling is mutual."

I returned the smile and then asked, "So what do you think?"

"I think you're discovering that talking about life is easy, but the actual *living* of it is damned hard."

I nodded. "That's for sure."

"Up to this point you've been sitting in the bleachers at the school dance, pointing at the other dancers on the floor and telling anyone who would listen how you would do it differently, and maybe even laughing at them and mocking them from time to time." He cocked an eyebrow. "Am I right?"

I had just been hit between the eyes with what was called a Hard Truth. It stung, but it was a bullseye. I heaved a sigh. "Hard to admit but, yeah, you're right about me." I cracked an ironic smile. "And for whatever it's worth, you described my sixteen-year-old self to a T with that whole school dance analogy."

He reached over and patted my arm. "Don't beat yourself up over what's dead and gone, Ben. It's the here and now that's still living and breathing and *that's* where you have to keep your focus."

He was right, I knew that, and yet the regret still filled my belly. "Easier said than done," I muttered.

"Indeed it is. But guilt and regret are nothing but hungry little termites that can eat away the timbers of our soul. If you let 'em, they'll keep eating until there's nothing left. The only way to stop those guys is to get 'em under your shoe and crush the life out of 'em."

I let out a small scoffing sound. "Sounds great but, again, easier said than done."

"Anything worth doing is easier said than done, that's a fact. But if you ever want to get out on the dance floor and live a life that matters, there are some things that *have* to be done. This is one of them."

"Okay, okay…I'm a believer. How do you propose that I crush these guys?"

"You have to go home and write down every single regret you can think of, each one on a separate piece of paper. Big and small, old and new, it doesn't matter, just write 'em all down. That time you tripped little Suzy on the playground at recess in fourth grade and she skinned her knee? If you still feel any twinges about it, it matters, so write it down."

"That's gonna take a shitload of paper."

He nodded. "It will indeed. But there's no other way."

"So, what do I do with this big box full of paper once I have it filled with all of my life's little regrets?"

He threw me a grin that looked to be part Cheshire Cat. "You do to them what you did to your house."

His words swirled in the air between us for a few beats. I didn't know what to say in response because he had caught me totally off guard with his comment. I had certainly told him the truth about my house, and what I'd done, but he'd never referred to it like this before. Until now. "Uh…I don't know what to say to that, Charlie."

His smile morphed into something warmer. "I'll spell it out for you then." He pretended he was reaching into a bag and said, "First you reach in and pull out one of the pieces of paper." He fiddled with something in the air in front of him. "Then you open it up and read it out loud, making sure to say the words 'I no longer regret...' before each one." He struck an imaginary match. "Then it's time to put the little bugger under your shoe." He held the imaginary piece of paper over the imaginary flame and his eyes appeared to go off to the same imaginary place that housed the paper and flame. Without looking up he added, "It helps to say something along the lines of 'goodbye and good riddance' or a simple 'fuck you' as you watch each of 'em burn." We sat in silence for a short while, almost as if we were both watching the flame die down on the invisible piece of paper in Charlie's hand. Then he finally looked up. He raised his hands in the air in a non-verbal voila. "Simple as that."

"And what makes you think that this little method of yours is going to work?"

"This has been field-tested m'boy. Trust me, it works."

"Is this something that all of your angel clients have used?"

"Nope, you'd be the first."

"So then how can you be so sure that it will do what you say it will?"

"Let's just say that there's no experience like personal experience to prove a point."

"You did this yourself?"

He nodded. "I did."

"When?"

"Not so long ago."

"But you're an angel. Aren't you supposed to be free of such earthly burdens?"

"We are. But we still have to do the necessary work at some point before attaining this angelic state." He shrugged. "This is the method that I used. And it does work."

"Okay, okay, I'll give it a try. I'll try just about anything at this point to get out of this rut that I'm in." I sighed. "I just hope you're right."

He leaned in and his eyes were blazing with an intensity that I hadn't seen from him in a while. "The key is being honest with yourself, Ben. If you downplay or ignore certain hard-to-face truths, then this whole exercise won't do anything bust waste a lot of paper and matches." He tilted his head, but the intensity remained in his eyes. "Understood?"

"Yeah, understood."

He retreated to his original position, his face more relaxed now. "This time next week you'll be a changed man. I guarantee it."

I let out a low whistle. "Wow, an angelic guarantee. That must be worth *something*."

"It is. Trust me."

"Yeah, you keep saying that."

He smirked. "So how is that whole trust thing coming along?"

"Better. Out of necessity I've seen that I can't be the lone wolf all the time. That's made me have to trust folks in ways that I never have before."

"Good, good."

"Yeah, whatever. I'm just waiting for the easy part to come."

Charlie laughed out loud. It was the Charlie laugh that shook rafters and turned heads and it was music to my ears. "Easy comes when you die, my friend."

"I was afraid you'd say something like that."

He considered me for a moment and then said, "You talked about the word legacy earlier, and about the increased importance that word has taken on in your life. Right?"

I nodded. "Yeah, so?"

"So you are the architect of that legacy. You and you alone. Your legacy is nothing more than the life you've lived, and that life is built brick by brick each and every day that you breathe. You decide how much effort you want to put into the building of your life's structure and whether or not that structure will last very long past your final breath."

"So, I'm a bricklayer now, am I?"

"You also decide the material that you use. It could be brick or it could be feathers or anything else that you want. Your choice."

"And what if I just plain don't feel like building a house at all?"

"Then you are doomed to die a lonely man whose only legacy will be that he took up space for a while here on Earth."

"That wasn't the legacy I had in mind for myself."

"I didn't think so."

"You're my angel, can't you see what my future holds? Can't you just tell me where I'm headed and what I have to do to get there?"

He flashed the ol' paternal smile. "I think you know the answer to that question."

"Yeah, I guess I do."

"I can tell you one thing though."

"What's that?"

"I can tell you that your extended break is over and it's time for the bricklayer to get back to work. You can no longer afford to be somedaying your life away like you have. You're running out of somedays."

My heart sank and my skin went clammy. "Are you telling me that I have cancer or something?!?" I held my breath, waiting for his response.

His smile got me breathing again. "No, you don't have cancer. Though a part of you probably wishes that you *did* have cancer or some other such personal calamity. It would give you a ready-made sense of purpose in your life once again." His stare suddenly went right past me. "There's nothing like a death sentence when it comes to creating a sense of purpose and forcing you to get your life in order."

"Is this personal experience talking again?"

He broke off his stare. "Yeah, you could say that."

"A previous life of yours?"

"Yeah, something like that."

"Are all angels this vague with their responses?"

"Yep."

"Why is that?"

"We don't want you, our human clients, to expend any energy worrying about us and our problems, be they past or present."

"So as far as I'm concerned, everything is always rainbows and unicorns in the Angel Universe. Is that how it goes?"

"Yep, that's about it."

"So then who do you guys go to when you have a problem?"

He chuckled. "We don't have any problems, remember?"

"So, what was that whole bit you told me about your wife and daughters a while back? It sure sounded like there were a few problems in *that* little universe."

He sighed. "That's true, there were. But I made that exception just to gain your trust and confidence. I wanted you to see that I could indeed understand your problems because I'd lived through similar problems myself. I wasn't seeking any pity or advice from you, I just wanted you to hear my story, that's all."

I looked at him sideways. "You didn't just make all that shit up, did you?"

"No, no. I can assure you that every word I've ever shared with you is nothing but the truth." He smiled. "Angels can't lie either."

"You've got quite the code of conduct. Did someone hand you a list or something before you were granted your angel status?"

"No, there's no list or handbook. We just instinctively know what's expected of us and we do it."

"I wish my life was like that, where I just instinctively knew what to do and I did it. No deliberating, no angst, no regret. Just think it, do it, and then move on to the next thing. Clean, simple, and uncomplicated. I would like that."

He reached over and patted my arm. "Perhaps you'll get your wish at some point in the future."

"How? By becoming an angel?" I laughed. "Now that would be funny! No, that would be a travesty is what it would be. Imagine the disappointment of the poor schmuck who gets *me* as his angel!" I shook my head. "No, I'm just not angelic material."

Charlie smiled warmly. "You have more angel in you than you realize, Ben. We all do."

"That may be, but I can assure you that my angel potential is buried deeper than most. So deep in fact that it would take a few lifetimes of digging to uncover it."

He gave my arm another reassuring pat and then reached for his coat. "You've got to stop being so hard on yourself, my friend. You are no better and no worse than anyone else when it comes to your personal struggles. Remember that." He stood up and put on his coat.

I tried to hide the disappointment that I was feeling when I asked, "Time to go?"

"Yes, it's time to go." Whereas my words had been shaded with disappointment, his had a sense of foreboding and finality to them.

I stood up and asked for the final time, "You sure everything's okay?"

The big Charlie Grin exploded onto his face. "Yes, I'm sure." He opened his arms wide. "Now come give me a hug and promise me that you're going to do your homework this week."

I returned the smile. "You got it, Dad." Then I stepped into another one of Charlie's long, lingering, filled-with-warmth hugs. He pulled me in extra tight and it was the best, most intimate hug I'd ever shared with another man.

When the hug broke, and we stepped back from each other, I could see that tears had snaked their way down Charlie's cheeks. I had managed to keep my own tears at bay, though my vision had blurred at one point with the threat of coming tears. He turned his face for a moment and surreptitiously wiped his face.

Now looking more composed, he turned to me and said what would prove to be the last words I would ever hear from Charlie the Angel. "Just remember, Ben," he said with a small scowl etched on his forehead, "that both the pessimist and the optimist are always right." His scowl morphed into a smile and then he gave me an extra nod of his head for emphasis.

"I'll keep that in mind. Thanks."

He then just turned, waved, and walked out of my life. Forever.

CHAPTER FORTY-TWO

I felt silly. It was Saturday morning and Marsha was still sleeping so I'd decided to get a start on Charlie's homework assignment. I wanted to follow through on my promise but sitting there in my pajamas with a pad of paper and a pencil, trying to remember every little regret I'd experienced over my lifetime, made me feel self-indulgent and, well, silly. I had managed to jot down a few, mostly around the theme of being a lousy husband and father, but it wasn't long before I hit a roadblock. But I was focusing as best I could, and that's why I nearly shot to the ceiling when I heard a voice from behind me.

"Well, good morning there Mr. Earlybird." It was Marsha. And since I hadn't shared Charlie's idea for a homework assignment with her, I wasn't feeling too anxious to share my list of regrets with her either. I tried to slide the papers under a nearby magazine, but it was too late. "What'cha working on there?" she asked.

I considered telling her the truth but when a viable lie popped into my head, I opted for that instead. "Just jotting down some ideas on how we should spend this weekend," I replied, trying like hell to get my face to match the whimsy of my response.

She looked at me and my pieces of paper several times before saying, "Weekend plans, eh? So what'd you come up with for us?" She sat down across the table from me and placed her chin in her cupped hand awaiting my reply.

Time to tap dance. "Uh, one idea is to head into town and shop some of the after-Christmas sales."

She made a loud buzzer sound. "Nope, no more shopping for this gal. Try again."

"Another idea is to, uh, hop in the car and drive to the mountains so we can enjoy all of the winter splendor that is to be had out that way."

Another loud buzzer. "I'm not a winter fan to begin with so I don't need to see any more of it than what's right here in front of me. What else ya got?"

Then came the eureka moment. "How about just saying fuck it and heading down to New York City for the day, have a nice dinner somewhere, and then maybe even taking in a show if we can find tickets. How does that sound to you?"

No buzzer. Good sign. She looked at me a good long time and then looked at my papers again. Finally, a small smirk started to form at the corner of her mouth. "Looks like you may have a winner there, Einstein." My body relaxed. "Just one question though," she added. My body tensed again. "Why did you write all of your ideas on individual pieces of paper like that?"

Who can explain the mystery of the human brain? But there are times when it's working at peak efficiency, able to solve any problem that's placed in front of it in the blink of an eye, and you find yourself wishing that it was always this way. The answer flew into my head and then to my mouth. "Because I thought we'd just put them all into a hat and draw one out if we couldn't decide on one."

She bought it. And, as a small bonus, I also earned some oh-he's-so-cute-and-romantic points as she said, "How did you get to be so adorable?"

"Years and years of practice."

"Well, keep on practicing while I go call Yancy and see if she's available to watch Jake."

"You got it." When she'd headed out of the room, I gathered up all the pieces of paper and stuffed them into a plastic bag. This project would have to wait for another day.

It wasn't long before we were on the road to New York – Yancy had come through – and not long after that that we were walking the city streets in and around Times Square. We scored a couple of tickets from the Discount Window to see "42nd Street" and then strolled some more until we found ourselves sitting in Central Park, our feet in desperate need of a break. It was an unseasonably warm January day in the city and there were a ton of people out and about enjoying the sunny, almost-fifty-degree day. I leaned back on the bench that we'd found and let the sun beat down on my face. It was heaven. I hadn't realized until right then just how small my world had become, and it felt good to be surrounded by brand new sights and sounds.

"This is nice," Marsha murmured. I looked up and saw that she had adopted my same lean-back-and-close-your-eyes pose.

I returned to my original position and murmured a "Hm, hm," in return.

"Do you ever feel like you just want to chuck it all and run away?" she then asked.

An involuntary spasm of reaction overtook me, and I shot up to a full sitting position. "Are you serious?" I asked, unsure if I had heard her correctly.

She opened one eye but didn't sit up. "Yeah, I am. Why?"

"Why? Because what do you think I've been doing these past couple of months, that's why."

She closed her eye again and just lay in the same position, calm as can be. "Yeah, but it's not like you had a choice or anything. You just got dealt a bad hand and you're adjusting to life with that bad hand." Then came the words that knifed their way into my chest. "It's not as if you made a conscious choice to burn your house to the ground, right?"

Thankfully, her eyes remained shut so she couldn't see my reaction to her words. I considered telling her the whole story right then and there but quickly decided against it. A confession as big as that one would surely provide the death knell for a relationship as young as ours. The time would come to tell her, but that time was not now. "Yeah, that's true," I mumbled.

She bolted upright. "I'm serious."

"So am I," I replied earnestly, thinking that she was still talking about my house.

"What if I just chucked it all in the toilet and started a new life someplace else, away from all of the have-to's and responsibilities that fill up my current life?" My shoulders dropped in relief and my relief grew right along with her enthusiasm for this particular topic. She began talking faster and was all but sputtering by the end of her little soliloquy. "What do you think would happen?" she asked rhetorically. "Would the world stop spinning and would the sun stop rising? I don't think so. I think life would go on, the only difference being that Marsha Graves had stepped off the treadmill."

"You done?" I asked.

She nodded. "For now."

"So why don't you?"

"What?"

"Just chuck it all. Start over."

She lowered her head and shook it slowly from side to side. "I can't. I made a promise to Jake and I have to keep that promise."

"What promise?"

She looked up and the sun danced in her eyes that were now wet with tears. "'Till death do us part.'"

"Yeah, my wife made that same promise to me, but it appears that there is some fine print in that little promise that I wasn't aware of, an escape clause that gives you an out if things get too tough." I was surprised by the amount of bitterness that still filled my voice. Would that ever go away?

"Not in my promise. It's bullet-proof."

I smiled and rubbed her cheek. "He's a lucky man."

"No, he's not lucky at all. His luck has been about as bad as it can get and that's why I have to stay with him to the end. The man deserves something that he can count on and that doesn't just go to shit."

We sat in silence for a long time, content to just watch the steady stream of strangers walk by and ponder the many words that we had just tossed back and forth. For my part, I pondered my lack of a spine for not telling Marsha the entire truth about my house and I also pondered whether that same spine would stiffen if faced with a situation such as Marsha's. It was a bit unsettling that an answer didn't pop right into my head, but I explained it away with the notion that none of us really knew how we'd react to situations such as hers until we were face-to-face with it. Character isn't something that exists in thoughts or theory; it only exists in the three-dimensional world of action. I was living proof of that.

It was many hours later that we found ourselves sitting down to dinner in one of those only-in-New-York types of restaurants, where even a simple shrimp cocktail costs five times what you'd pay for the same shrimp in the nicest restaurant in all of Maple Grove. But I guess that's part of the experience. Besides, what did I care? Marsha had insisted on footing the bill for the entire evening, so I just kicked back and enjoyed. We had just come from "42nd Street" – the play for which we had found half-price tickets earlier in the day – and, seeing as it was now going on ten o'clock, we were both famished.

"So, what'd you think of the play?" Marsha asked me as we both scanned the menus.

"It was okay," I replied, though truth be told I had been bored to tears. Live theatre had never been my thing and when you add music to the mix you may as well just put me in the dentist's chair and begin the root canal.

"I loved the costumes," she gushed.

"Yeah, they were nice." I didn't dare look up from the menu for fear of her seeing my lying eyes.

"And the music and dancing were amazing."

"Uh huh."

"And I looooovvvveeedddd the part when they all took their clothes off and shouted, I'M FREE!!!"

I lowered my menu and threw her a "Huh?" look.

Her eyes danced with mischief. "Okay, so now I have your attention."

I smiled. "You do."

"That was pure torture for you, wasn't it? Tell me the truth."

The smile remained on my face. "It was."

"Can I tell you a secret?"

"Sure."

"I hated it too. Every minute of it." She held up her hand in a stop sign. "I know, I know, all women are supposed to love going to Broadway musicals and I am some freak of nature for admitting this to you." She lowered her hand and began shaking her head slowly. "But I just don't get it with these musicals. I keep trying to like them but they're all just so…"

"Pointless? Contrived? Boring?"

She laughed, one of her sweet, melodious laughs that was free of all self-consciousness. "Yes, all of those things."

"So why did you want to go tonight?"

She shrugged. "I guess because it's what you do when you're in New York. Visit Times Square, walk through Central Park, go to a show, and then eat an expensive dinner at a time when I would usually be curled up in bed with my book." She shrugged again. "It's like some Cosmic Imperative that you satisfy the Big Apple Checklist."

"Or else what?"

"I don't know, I never tested it before."

I glanced conspiratorially from side to side and then said, "Let's test it now."

"What? How?"

"Let's get outta here and go have some New York street food instead."

Her eyes went wide. "We can't do that, we've already been seated."

"Yeah, but we haven't eaten so much as a breadstick yet so what's the big deal?"

"I don't know…"

"C'mon, who wants to pay forty bucks for a chunk of meat that we could get for five bucks up at The Tavern?"

"It is expensive, but…"

I gave her my best Cheshire grin and said, "Sometimes you just gotta say fuck it."

She stopped fidgeting and smiled. "Okay, I'm in. How are we going to pull this off, Butch?"

I reached over and rubbed her arm. "Well Sundance, I figure that you could mosey off to the powder room and then just slip out the door. I won't be far behind."

"And what if someone sees us?"

"I'll pump 'em full o' lead."

She slapped my hand playfully. "Seriously."

"Seriously, who gives a shit? We're not committing any crimes and chances are pretty damn good that we won't be back in this place again anytime soon."

"All good points."

I looked around and saw no sign of our waiter. "So, are you ready for Phase I of the plan to be put into action?"

"Yes, sir," she said with a salute.

"Then it's showtime, soldier. Make me proud."

She glanced over her shoulder then stood up, picked up her purse, and leaned forward to whisper in my ear. "See ya on the outside, Butch." She planted a small kiss on my cheek and then, after flashing me a coquettish grin, made her way to the bathroom.

I sat there for a few beats just thinking how lucky I'd been to stumble across Marsha Graves when I was jolted to attention by a voice on my left. "Any decisions made on drinks, sir?" It was our waiter.

"Uh, my wife just went to the restroom," I stammered. "Could you stop back in another minute or two?"

"Certainly." And he was off.

My heart was pounding. I didn't know if it was because I had just been startled by the waiter or if it was because I had just called Marsha my wife. Either way, I was an idiot. I sat there and laughed at my lack of any discernible backbone before getting up and heading for the door.

I found Marsha hiding in a doorway a half a block from the restaurant. "Are we in the clear?" she asked.

"I had to put our waiter down on the way out and the cops will be here any minute, but other than that I think we're good to go."

She stepped out of the doorway and wrapped her arms around my waist. "That was absolutely exhilarating," she cooed.

"More so than the play?"

She gave me a squeeze. "A thousand times more so."

"Just imagine how we'd feel if we had actually broken a law or two along the way."

"What is it that you are proposing, Butch?"

I shrugged. "I dunno. The night is still young, and I thought maybe we could hit a bank or two before calling it a day."

"That sounds fine, but can we maybe eat something first? I'm starving."

I rubbed my belly. "Yeah, me too. This life of crime can really work up an appetite."

We walked for a short while and it wasn't long before we came upon a street vendor selling grilled sausages. The smell of cooking meat was absolute heaven to my nostrils. Without even saying a word we both stepped up to the vendor's cart and scanned his offerings. "I'll do a brat with the works," she said to the vendor. She then turned to me and asked, "How about you?"

"I'll do the same. Extra kraut if you can."

We stood there, mouths watering, as we watched the man stuff grilled peppers, onions, sauerkraut, ketchup, and mustard into each roll. He handed us our two-handed sandwiches and then, after Marsha paid him, we turned and walked away with dinner in-hand, at a fraction of what we would have paid back at Chez Fancy Pants.

The evening was as unseasonably warm as the day had been, with temperatures hovering somewhere in the upper forties, so I motioned to a nearby bench and said, "Madame?"

"Why thank you," she replied. "It's perfect."

We both sat down and before taking my first bite I raised my sandwich in front of me and, motioning towards the street scene in front of us – still bustling at that late hour -said, "Look at this view."

"How did you ever get reservations?" she asked in her best mock-serious tone. "This place must be booked most of the time."

I nodded and then took a big bite from my sandwich. It was delicious. "It is," I mumbled through my mouthful of food. "But I have connections."

"Lucky me," she said before taking her first bite. Other than an occasional moan or "Mm, mm" noise, those would be our last words for the next ten minutes. We both focused on our respective sandwiches and savored each bite as they slowly disappeared.

"I think that was the best meal I've had in a long, long time," she finally said after her last bite had been chewed and swallowed.

I wadded up my empty wrapper and soiled napkin. "I agree. My belly is feeling very happy right now."

"I just may have to add that to my Big Apple Checklist from now on."

"What? Ducking out of a fancy schmancy restaurant and then munching a hot dog on a bench in mid-January?"

"Exactly."

I smiled at her and she smiled back. Her smile wasn't just any smile however; it was the smile I had seen at The Tavern on the first night we'd met and the smile I'd seen on several occasions since that night. It was the kind of smile that made me think of high school and first love; the kind that says, *"I'm all yours, do what you want with me."* I reached over and rubbed her leg. "What say we head back to the room and work off some of this sandwich?"

"Sounds like a plan, Butch. Lead the way."

CHAPTER FORTY-THREE

The glow from our trip lasted for several days after our return from the city. It had been just what I'd needed – a break from the glum realities of my present life – and it was a testament to Marsha and her unique charms that she had helped to keep my dark clouds at bay for so long following our return. But now she was back at work and I was back to being just another homeless, jobless, and purposeless loser. What now?

It dawned on me that I hadn't heard from Austin T for a while and I contemplated giving him a call. On the one hand, the "no news is good news" part of me thought that perhaps Austin T was running out of ammo and he was just putting off giving me a call out of some pathetic sense of professional pride. On the other hand – and this was the hand that had held the most sway up until now – Austin T could just be gathering more bullets to load into his gun, and I would be wise to steer clear of him for as long as possible. It was a tough choice, because I still really needed that settlement money, but my chicken-ass self ultimately won out – again – and I decided to just let that sleeping dog lie without any poking and prodding from me.

So, what now?

My lack of purpose was now morphing into acute feelings of boredom and I was clueless as to how to change that. Once again, I came face-to-face with the realization that the very routine that I had put a match to a couple of months ago – the job, the house, the responsibilities – had been my friend in many ways as well as my enemy, ways that were visible to me only in hindsight. Without that structure I was floundering in a sea of amorphous sludge that threatened to drown me if I didn't build myself a boat. Fast.

Then a little voice tapped me on the shoulder and whispered, "Maybe it's time to go back to work." The idea that had had zero appeal to me several weeks ago now, suddenly, seemed brilliant. I grabbed the phone and dialed The Beacon.

Someone picked it up on the third ring and said, in the staccato monotone that is the signature of every newspaper around the world, "Hello. Beacon. What can I do for you?"

"Hi," I replied casually. "Who is this?"

There was a short pause and then the voice on the other end said, slowly and quizzically this time, "This is Edna. Who's this?"

Edna the receptionist. Nice woman, though a bit slow at times. She had come to The Beacon following her husband's death many years ago, looking for a way to make some money as well as to get out of the memory-filled house. I could relate. "Hi Edna. It's Ben Weaver. How are you doing?"

Her voice brightened slightly. "Oh, hi there, Ben. How are things?"

"Fine, just fine," I lied. "Hey, I need to talk to Bob. Is he around?"

"Yeah, he's in his office. Just a second." I waited for the clicking sound that signified I was now on hold, but it didn't come. There was a short silence and then Edna came back on the line and asked, "How's it going with the house thing, Ben? Has that all been settled yet?"

While I appreciated Edna's concern, I also hated having to answer questions like this one. So, I did what I always did: I lied. "Almost there, Edna. Thanks for asking."

"That's great, Ben. Glad to hear it. "Just a sec, I'll get Bob for you."

"Thanks Edna." Then I heard the clicking sound and I was on hold. I took a deep breath and rehearsed the spiel that I was about to deliver to Bob. I hadn't thought it through completely but the rough outline I had constructed in my head included words like "I miss the hubbub" and "I feel ready to get back to work again." Keep it simple. It was a good minute before I heard the clicking sound again and Bob's voice came on the line. "Hello? Ben?"

Keep it calm and casual, I told myself. "Yeah, hey there, Bob. "How's it goin'?"

A deep sigh. "Oh, you know. Every day's a race to the finish line. Not much changes here. How are you doing?"

"Just great." I waited a beat and then added, "Well, maybe not all that great. I miss working, Bob, and I'm thinking that maybe it's time for me to climb back in the saddle over at The Beacon."

Silence. Long, dead silence. "Uh," I finally heard him say. "I don't know what to say to that, Ben."

My heart rate quickened. "What do you mean you don't know what to say?"

More silence. "You've been away so long, and I hadn't heard from you. And the way you left here last time, I thought…" His voice trailed off, but I knew exactly where it was headed. My heart sank.

"You filled my position?" I asked as calmly as I could muster, though I'm sure my voice betrayed my inner anxiety.

"I had no choice, Ben. You know how crazy things are here even when we're at full staff. Being down one reporter put too much stress on everyone else, so I decided to pull the trigger on hiring someone to fill your position. I'm sorry."

"Who'd you hire?" was all I could think to ask.

"Josh Stark."

"Josh Stark? The same Josh who worked in circulation?"

"Yeah, same guy. He'd been bugging me for a long time about a reporter's job, so I decided to give him a chance back around the first of the year."

"But he's just a kid," I all but screamed into the phone.

"So were you at one time, Ben. He's worked hard and he deserved the shot."

I didn't know what to say. A lot of things ran through my head, but even in my upset state I knew they wouldn't be productive, so I just said, "So I guess that's it."

"Don't sound so fatalistic here, Ben. I'm sure something will open down the road, and I'll of course give you priority for any position that comes up. I promise. It's just that I hadn't heard from you and…"

I cut him off. "Yeah, you already said that. No hard feelings here, Bob. You take care of yourself." And then I hung up. The door on my career at The Beacon had officially slammed shut.

It took over an hour for my anger to dissipate but it eventually did – after a long walk and a lot of choice words directed at nobody in particular – and after I had finally calmed down, I could see Bob's point. I had indeed left his office in a huff the last time we'd spoke, and I had indeed told him I was through at The Beacon. What was he supposed to do? Hold my job open forever? I couldn't blame him. Much as I wanted a scapegoat at whom I could focus my wrath, Bob Collins wasn't to blame for my predicament. I was.

Knowing now that a Plan B would be called for – and having no Plan B in mind – I decided to take out the hammer and smash the glass on The Emergency Plan, the one that had been hanging out in an outpost of my brain for several weeks. I pulled out my wallet, picked through the various small pieces of paper that always seemed to accumulate there, and found the scrap of paper I was searching for. I picked up the phone, took a deep breath, and dialed the number that was scratched on the paper.

The scene in front of me was madness unleashed. I stood in the lobby of the YMCA and there were teenagers running around everywhere, screaming and laughing with the abandon that only teens possessed, as if nobody's needs or comfort mattered more than their own. I shuddered to think that Kylie would soon be transforming into one of these.

A voice startled me from behind. "Hey mister," the voice asked. I turned and saw a short, pimply-faced boy looking up at me. "You gotta nickel?"

He seemed to ask his question in a way that was both presumptuous and rude. It got under my skin and, before even checking my pockets, I heard myself saying "no" in a way that implied an "*and leave me alone*" tacked on to the end of it. I don't know if he got the hidden message imbedded in my tone or not, but without another word he ran off to join his pack.

I then saw a huge mountain of a man making his way through the wild throng. He was looking right at me and he had a huge grin spread across his face. He seemed to be completely oblivious to the craziness that surrounded him, and it wasn't long before he was standing in front of me, his hand extended. "Good to see you, Luke."

I shook his large hand. "You too, Griz."

"I wuz kinda surprised to get your call." His smile broadened. "But it was a good surprise."

I threw him an ironic smirk. "Yeah, I kinda surprised myself." There were many, many more words lined up behind that simple statement, but I decided to keep them to myself.

He jerked his thumb over his shoulder. "So whaddaya think of this place?"

I scanned the chaos once again. "Seems lively."

He laughed his loud Griz laugh. "Yeah, I got 'em doing a treasure hunt right now." He leaned in closer and whispered, "To work off some of that teenage energy, ya know?" He then leaned back and threw me a conspiratorial wink. "They don't listen to nothin' when their tanks are full. I just gotta get 'em wore down a bit before tryin' to do anythin' else with 'em." He then thumped me on the shoulder. "And don't be surprised if some of 'em stop by and ask you for somethin'."

"Yeah, one of them just stopped and asked me for a nickel."

"Did'ja help him out?"

I suddenly felt guilty and small. "Uh, I tried," I lied, "but I couldn't find a nickel."

He waved his hand in a don't-worry-about-it kind of way. "No big deal. For them, it's the lookin' that's more fun than the findin'."

I looked again at the scene around me. "Yeah, they seem to be having a good time."

"So, what is it that I can do for ya, Luke?" he then asked me.

You can give me a sense of purpose, I thought. "I don't know exactly…" I replied, unsure of what was going to come out of my mouth. "I guess I'm just looking for something to do with my life while I sit in limbo with the insurance company." I surprised myself with my honesty; that was *exactly* what I was looking for right now.

"They still givin' ya a hard time?"

I nodded. "Yep. Harder than ever. I'm not sure I'll ever see that money."

"Why are they bein' such shits about this? Seems to me that a man's house burns down he should be seein' a check pretty damn quick."

Uh, oh. Time to go back to being Ben the Prevaricator. "I agree, they are being shits about this. And I don't know why they decided to make me the target of their shit-headedness." I shrugged. "Just lucky, I guess."

Griz slapped me on my back and I resisted the impulse to say "Ow." I did, however, run my tongue over my teeth, feeling as if the impact from Griz's slap may have dislodged a few fillings. "Good for you, Luke. Don't let those assholes get ya down!"

I wasn't sure what he meant because, truth was, those assholes – at least one in particular – *had* gotten me down. To the point that I was now standing in the middle of teen chaos looking for a helping hand from a former alcoholic. "I won't," I muttered.

"So yer lookin' fer somethin' to do, huh?"

I nodded. "Yes, I am."

He rubbed his chin for a moment and then said, "Well, I could use a little help here a few days a week." His hand dropped. "Can't pay ya much though, Luke."

"That's okay. It's not about the money," I lied, though only partially.

He clapped his hands together. "Great! Griz and Luke together again." He smiled big. "Somethin' tells me that you and me are gonna make a great team, Luke."

I couldn't help but return his smile; it was too big and sincere to ignore. I agree, Griz. I think we're going to make beautiful music together."

He laughed. "I don't know about that, but I do know that we're gonna knock some teenage skulls together and get 'em to learn some things whether they want to or not."

"That sounds like a plan. When can I start?"

"How 'bout right now?"

My heart rate accelerated, and my brain screamed "*No!*"but my mouth said, "Sounds good."

When I finally saw Marsha that evening her first words to me were, "What happened to you?!?" I guess I looked a little frazzled.

"Teenagers happened to me," I replied as I took my coat off and tossed it on a nearby table, not even bothering to deal with the closet. I was too tired to do anything but pour a glass of wine and find the nearest chair.

She chuckled. "You finally called your friend Griz, eh?"

"I did." I walked past her and found an opened bottle of wine on the counter. I grabbed a glass out of the cupboard, gave myself a full pour that would make any sommelier scream in protest, and then made my way to what had become my new favorite chair.

"And?" I heard Marsha ask from behind me as I headed for the living room.

I plopped myself down in the chair with a loud "Ahhhhh…" I then took a large sip of wine, let it work its way down my throat, and only after taking a second sip did I reply, "And it was the hardest and longest day of work I can remember having in a long, long time."

She sat across from me, on the couch, and let out a small chuckle. "That tough, huh."

"Teenagers are an entirely different breed of human. They don't think, breathe, or behave like anything I've ever seen before."

She fell back in the couch and threw me a wide grin. "Not much experience with this age group I take it."

"Zilch. I'd always just steered clear of teenagers because I found them consistently loud, obnoxious, and disrespectful."

"That's all part of their job description. It's their job to get under our skin and make us want to choke the life out of them."

Remembering that Marsha had raised her own kids into adulthood, I asked, "Even with your own?"

She laughed. "*Especially* with your own. I loved my kids, both of them, but when they were teenagers, I wanted to do things to them that I never would have guessed I was even capable of thinking."

I took a huge gulp from my glass. "So, what did you do?"

"I eventually realized that I couldn't take anything personally that they said or did at that age. They weren't themselves, their bodies had been hijacked by the gallons of hormones that were being dumped into their systems and my job was to just love them and support them until they got control back of their internal steering wheels." She shrugged. "That realization made things a whole lot easier." She smiled. "Not perfect and not always tranquil, but easier."

"I'll keep that in mind. It's just that when they're in your face, all you want to do is get them *out* of your face, using any means possible."

"I hear you, Ben. And I can feel your pain, truly I can." She came forward on the couch and leaned towards me. "But if you remember nothing else, remember that no matter how obnoxious they may be at times, they're all just struggling, insecure kids underneath it all. They may act like they're invincible know-it-alls but they're not. They are ultra-sensitive to everything being said and done around them so be careful on both counts."

"I'll keep that in mind too. Did your kids eventually snap out of it?"

She slid back on the couch. "Yes, they did, thank God. They're both wonderful adults and I often wonder how that happened."

"Why?"

"There were times that I thought I'd lost them forever, that they were destined to be rotten adults just like they were being rotten teenagers."

"When did the turnaround come?" I was now asking questions with Kylie in mind more than the monsters at the Y. Having seen what awaited me in a few years I wanted to be as prepared as possible for that day when she went through the metamorphosis into teenagerhood. I was certain that some, maybe even most, of the kids I worked with today had at one time been sweet and obedient children just like my Kylie. I took another gulp of wine.

"My kids were different in so many ways but they both seemed to emerge from the Dark Tunnel Of Teen-ness at around the same age. I got my wonderful kids back towards the end of their high school years."

"No scars?"

"On me or them?" she shot back with a laugh.

"Both."

"I can't speak to the state of their insides, but on the outside they both seemed to be scar-free."

"And you?"

She sighed. "I have to admit that it took a few years for some of my battle scars to heal." Her look became distant. "They can say some things at that age that really sting. It's like they know your soft spots – you know, your weaknesses - and they don't hesitate to go right for them when they need to."

"Nice. I can't wait."

Her eyes met mine and she had a maternal smile on her face. "Hey, not every kid goes through this. Your Kylie is a sweetheart and she may just waltz on through the teen years without a hitch."

I scoffed. "That's probably what you thought about your own kids."

"Honestly, I didn't have any clue what to expect from my kids. I didn't have a mother or anyone else around to warn me about what was to come so they caught me completely by surprise when they started to act up."

"That must have been tough."

"Yeah, it was. Especially given that Jake was just starting to show the first signs of his disease back then." Her face went somber. "It was not a good time for me."

I reached over and rubbed her leg. "You seem to have come through it all pretty well, Marsha. That's a real credit to you."

She forced a smile through suddenly misty eyes. "Thanks for saying that. There are times when I think I've been nothing but a miserable failure at everything I've done in my life."

"How can you say that?" I continued to rub her leg. "You have your two great kids, a bunch of grandkids, a nice house and career…you've got a lot to be proud of." I reached over and rubbed the side of her cheek with the back of my hand. "Unlike your homeless, jobless, and aimless boyfriend."

We exchanged smiles. "That's true," she replied. "Thanks for reminding me of yet another potentially huge mistake I've made in my life." She grabbed my hand and gave it a hard squeeze. "Seriously Ben, you've been a Godsend for me. Thanks for that."

"For what? For allowing you to take me in like some stray dog and giving me a place to lay my head down each night? It should me thanking *you*, you silly woman."

"I guess we both have things to be thankful for then, eh?"

"If you say so. Personally, I think you're getting the short end of this deal."

It was her turn to rub my cheek. "Time will tell. For now, you have to stop calling yourself homeless and jobless; you have both now."

I had managed, for a short while, to forget about my trail by fire at the Y that day but now the memories came flooding back. I felt my body stiffen. "Yeah, I guess I do," I muttered before taking one big final gulp of wine.

CHAPTER FORTY-FOUR

Two weeks passed and I managed to get through them without killing a single kid. That was no small victory. To my surprise, by the end of the second week I had begun to look forward to heading off to the Y each afternoon. I had grown accustomed to the noise level as well as the constant swirl of teen energy and that had allowed me to settle in and start enjoying the kids.

I got to know many of the kids, but after two weeks I had picked some favorites. The kid I favored above all others was the very same short, pimply-faced kid who had tried to bum a nickel off me on that very first day. His name was Cody and there was something about him that made me want to put my arm around him and help usher him into adulthood. I couldn't explain it, but there it was. I found myself always keeping at least one eye cast in his direction no matter what was going on. If it appeared that he was getting hassled by some of the bigger boys, I would wander over in his direction in hopes that my presence would help to diffuse the situation. If I saw him sitting alone in a corner, I would sidle over, pretending to look elsewhere, and wait to see if he would call out to me; I had learned – thanks to some early advice from Griz – to not force myself on any of the kids. "Let 'em come to ya," he had said. "These kids can smell a phony like you and me smell dogshit," he said in his own, unique Griz-like way.

It was around the start of my second week that Cody had called out to me from his seat in a corner. I turned, pretended that I hadn't seen him there, and then walked over to him. "Hey Cody, how you doing?" I asked casually.

"Okay," he replied with a shrug.

"What'cha doing over here by yourself?"

Another shrug. "Just chillin'"

I pointed to a nearby chair. "Mind if I join you?"

Yet another shrug.

I sat down and looked out towards the non-stop madness. "I don't know how I survived all of this," I murmured as I shook my head slowly.

"Survived what?"

I waved my hand at the madness. "This. Being a teenager."

He lowered his head. "I wish I didn't have to be one," he mumbled. "I wanna be your age so I wouldn't have to go to school anymore. I could just hang out, play video games, and nobody would bug me."

I chuckled. "Unfortunately, being an adult isn't all video games and potato chips. We've still got out own sets of problems. Different ones than yours for sure, but problems just the same."

"Like what?"

"Like paying bills, and putting up with stupid bosses, and dealing with relationships that don't work out. Stuff like that."

"Gee, I can't wait."

I reached over and patted him on the shoulder. "I'm not saying this to bum you out," I said reassuringly. *Bum you out?* I thought to myself. *I* never *say bum you out.* It was yet another one of my efforts – some good, some bad – to Speak Teen. "I'm telling you this just so you can see that there's not going to be some magic age when all of your problems just disappear. You've just got to enjoy the age you're at right now, with all its ups and downs, because, believe it or not, there's going to come a day when you're going to be looking back on this time of your life as The Good Ol' Days."

"You don't."

"I don't what?"

"See this age as being the good ol' days."

I quickly remembered my crack about surviving the teen years. "I said that I couldn't believe that I survived being your age, I didn't say that I didn't *enjoy* those years." Truth be told, I didn't enjoy those years, but I figured I could make my point by playing a little game of semantics with Cody.

"Did you?"

Uh, oh. "Did I what?" I asked, trying to buy more time.

"Enjoy being a teenager."

I decided quickly that a white lie was called for in this situation. Telling Cody the truth – that being a teenager was the most painful, miserable, and soul-scarring thing I'd ever gone through in my life – would just add yet another brick to the poor boy's load. "There were good things and bad things about it," I finally replied, feeling good about my half-truth. "But overall I would say that it was a real fun and exciting time." Now *that* was a pure, unadulterated, 100% lie. But a good one, given Cody's state.

"What was so fun about it?" he then asked, his tone laced with disbelief.

Uh, oh. "I guess it was just a time when I wasn't a small kid anymore, so I could do things that I couldn't have done before that."

"Like what?"

Fortunately, my brain kept pace with his questions. It was hard to maintain a conversation built on lies. "Like staying up later. Like hanging out with my friends. Like watching better movies. Like making my own money so I could buy stuff that I wanted. Things like that."

His head went down again. "That doesn't sound so fun and exciting to me," he mumbled.

I shifted in my seat, so I was facing him. "Why don't you just tell me what's up with you right now, Cody, and I'll see if I can help you out."

We sat there in silence for a while, me wondering if I had been too direct with him, and him probably wondering if he could trust me with whatever it was that was bothering him. He finally spoke, haltingly at first. "It's my Mom," he murmured. I leaned in closer so I could hear whatever it was that he was about to say. "She's never home."

I waited a few beats and then asked, "Why is that?"

He fiddled with a loose string on his pants for a while and then said, "She works all the time."

Another pause, and then, "Why does she work so much?"

Bingo. His fiddling got more frantic for a few seconds and then the floodgates opened. "She says it's 'cuz she has to pay the bills, but I think it's 'cuz she doesn't want to be around the house and think about Dad. She always told me how much I looked like him and now that he's gone, I think seeing my face just makes her feel bad."

"Where's your Dad, Cody?"

"He got blown up over in Iraq," he replied without hesitation.

"I'm sorry."

He shrugged. "It was really hard for a while but now I'm kinda forgetting about him." He went back to fiddling with the string. "I wish my Mom would do that too."

"Do you have any brothers and sisters?"

He shook his head, which was still lowered so I couldn't see his face. "It's just me and my Mom."

I put my hand on his shoulder. "That does make it tougher."

I thought I sensed him leaning into my hand a bit, as if he wanted to draw closer to this little bit of physical contact, but then he abruptly pulled away and shot out of his chair. "I gotta go now," he mumbled as he ran off.

I sat there for a moment, wondering if I'd said or done something wrong, but then I looked down at the carpet below where he'd been sitting, and I had my answer. There was a small, dark, and still wet circle on the carpet. Cody had been crying.

Besides Cody, the other thing that dominated my thoughts during this two-week period was the question of: "Where's Charlie?" I had shown up for our next Friday lunch date, anxious to show off my first paycheck from the Y with him, but ended up eating alone and leaving after an hour and a half. The same thing happened the following Friday too. I was officially worried.

I asked around about him at The Tavern, hoping that one of the waitresses knew something about him, but nobody knew anything. I had to admit to feeling a little embarrassed about asking complete strangers about a man with whom I had shared so many lunch dates. As much time as we had shared together, I still knew so little about Charlie's life.

Perhaps, I thought, he *was* the mysterious angel that he claimed to be after all and, with his mission now accomplished here on Earth, he ascended to Angel Heaven to live out his eternity. Even *thinking* those last words made me shudder; was I finally losing it? And, besides, how could any self-respecting angel think for even a moment that their mission was accomplished when it came to my life? I was still a wreck and one small paycheck from the Y didn't change a whole lot.

But those were all selfish thoughts; more than anything else I felt concern for my friend Charlie. Where could he be? The answer to that question wouldn't come for another week.

CHAPTER FORTY-FIVE

"Oh my gosh, what am I going to do?" was the question that started one Tuesday morning. Marsha had just hung up the phone and, as it turned out, had just gotten word from Yancy that she couldn't make it to watch Jake that day. A close relative had dropped dead the night before and she would be busy dealing with that sad fact for the next few days. After calling the hospice care agency, to see if she could get a last-minute fill-in for Yancy, she hung up with yet another "Oh my gosh, what am I going to do?" They told her they were booked solid and they wouldn't be able to help her for the foreseeable future.

The answer crossed my lips before I'd even thought it through. "I'll watch him," I said.

Marsha turned to me, her look saying that she didn't believe what she'd just heard. "You'll what?"

I had to admit that the words came tougher the second time around as I'd had a few seconds to think about the ramifications of my raised hand. "I'll watch him," I repeated.

She stood there staring at me, obviously trying to read into what I'd just said to see if there were any hidden messages that she was supposed to be receiving. There were none, and she eventually saw that as she said, "You know I wouldn't be letting you do this unless I was absolutely positively stuck, and I had no other options."

"I know."

"It's just that I have some really important meetings today and it's too late to change things around and…"

I stepped towards her, grabbed her shoulders and looked her square in the eye. "Marsha, I know. Don't worry about it. I got it."

Her desperate look quickly morphed into the most loving smile I think I'd ever seen in my entire life. "Thank you," she whispered.

Her look was so powerful that tears formed in the corners of my eyes. "No problem."

She leaned in and kissed me gently on the cheek. "Yes, it is a problem. I know that and that's why I'm feeling incredible love for you right now."

"Yeah, I can see that."

She then glanced at her watch and said, "Oh my gosh, I have to go."

"That's your third oh my gosh this morning. I think it might be a new record."

She smiled. "It has been quite the oh-my-gosh morning." She walked over and grabbed her coat from the hook by the door. As she put it on, she said, "There's a list of instructions for Jake's daily care in the drawer next to his bed. It should tell you everything you need to know but if you have any questions just call me."

"Got it."

She finished buttoning her coat and then came over to me, grabbed my shirt collar, and pulled me in close. "And you can count on receiving the best thank you present of your life when I get home tonight. I promise you that."

We exchanged a short, yet passion-filled, kiss. "I can hardly wait," I then said as she turned to go.

She put her thumb to her ear and her pinky to her mouth, as if using an invisible phone, and said, "Call me. With anything." And with that she was gone.

I stood in the hallway thinking, *What the hell have I done?* for several seconds after the door closed. I'd had zero experience with anything even remotely resembling home health care and yet, here I was, alone with a man who could do nothing more than blink his eyes. What if he had a seizure? What if his heart suddenly stopped? What if I screw up and he dies on my watch? Marsha would never forgive me. Panic settled into my belly. It didn't take me long to realize, however, that there was no way out of this now – I had willingly taken on the job – so I took a deep breath, exhaled slowly, and then made my way back to Jake's bedroom.

As I walked into the bedroom I was hit, as always, with the same smell of death and decay that always filled Jake's room. I suppressed my gag reflex and instead pinned my best cheerful, life-is-good, smile on my face. "Hey there, Jake. How's it goin' today? Looks like you're stuck with…" My voice trailed off as I looked down and noticed that Jake wasn't even awake. Tremendous relief swept through me. Maybe he would just sleep the whole day away and thus relieve me of any real care-giving responsibilities. I sent out a silent prayer request, a rarity for me, asking for a quiet, uneventful day.

Seeing that Jake was sound asleep I decided to go grab a book to help pass the time. I went out to the living room, picked through the shelves of books, and eventually decided upon an old Michener book, *Chesapeake,* to be my companion for the day. I headed back to the bedroom, not having been gone for more than five minutes, and was assaulted by a new, stronger, odor as I entered the room. *Shit,* I thought. *He pissed himself.*

I quickly made my way to his bedside and as I drew closer my nose told me that my initial assessment had been correct. The strong smell of fresh urine was unmistakable and, when combined with the stew of stale odors already hanging in the room, caused me to belch a small bit of bile into my mouth. I very nearly expelled the entire contents of my stomach onto Jake but, thankfully, I managed to take a few calming breaths and keep my breakfast where it was.

I pulled back the covers and saw that the damage wasn't as bad as I thought it was going to be. He was wearing a large diaper and the diaper had managed to catch most of Jack's pee. There was a small yellow circle on the sheet next to his leg where the diaper had leaked a little but that was it. Not so bad. I quickly scanned the room, saw a box of diapers on a nearby shelf, and went over to get one from the box. On the way back to the bed I noticed that Jake's eyes were now open. His expression hadn't changed a bit – his mouth still hung open and his face remained frozen in place – but his eyes were now tracking me across the room. "Hey there, Jake," I said with a smile. "How ya doin' this morning?"

Like an idiot, I paused for a moment awaiting a response but then, realizing none would be forthcoming, I continued with what I had been doing. I came back to his bedside and started to undo his diaper. Feeling the need to explain what I was doing, I said, "I'm sorry about this Jake, but I'm the guy who has to do this for you today." I glanced up at his face and saw that he was blinking his eyes. Not knowing what that meant, I went back to what I'd been doing.

I had gotten the front of the diaper unfastened and then rolled him over onto his left side so I could get the diaper out from under him. I was standing on his right side so that meant pushing him away from me so that his backside was now facing me. He was extremely easy to move as he weighed no more than a child and I found myself fixating on the fact that this man lying in front of me used to weigh more than I did. I had just slid the last of the diaper out from under him when it happened.

My right hand was underneath his left hip, giving me added leverage for maneuvering him, and I used my left hand to yank out the diaper. Once it was free, I tossed the diaper into a nearby bucket and then turned my attention back to Jake. My eyes returned to his backside just in time to watch as a yellowish-brown ooze came cascading out of his ass and began covering my arm that was still wedged between his left hip and the bed. It was a waterfall of shit and I just stood there, frozen in disbelief, as the viscous flow worked its way down my arm. It was then that my breakfast decided to come up and spray itself all over Jake and the bed. I stood there and hurled uncontrollably for as long as it took to empty my stomach.

When the convulsing stopped, I yanked my hand out from under him and then continued retching as the yellowish-brown ooze dripped from my arm. It was a total blitzkrieg of smells, sights, and sounds that assaulted my senses in a way that they'd never been assaulted before. I couldn't stop retching as I made my way to the bathroom and quickly turned on the shower, not even stopping to worry about where I was splattering the vile ooze coming off my hands and arm. I didn't wait for the water to warm up as I stuck my arm into the stream. The ooze began streaming off my arm and into the tub and I puked one more time, the vomit joining the ooze in the tub basin to create a thick, chunky stew of smelly, swirling stew. I retched again but brought up nothing but air. My stomach was officially empty.

I went down to my knees and just sat there on the bathroom floor, panting and sweating as if I'd just returned from a ten-mile run. I felt exhausted. I couldn't get myself to move for several minutes.

I don't know how long it was exactly that I sat there, but it eventually occurred to me that I'd left Jake covered in piss, shit, and puke in the other room. Every cell in body was screaming "Don't go back in that room!" and yet I knew what I had to do. I wiped my mouth one more time, reached over and turned off the water in the tub, and slowly got to my feet. My knees were weak, and my legs wobbled, but I managed to stay upright. I went over to the bathroom mirror and splashed some cool water on my face. I also found a tube of toothpaste and swished some of its mint-infused relief around in my mouth. I then heaved one last deep sigh and turned towards the bathroom door. It was time to face the inevitable.

The scene in front of me as I walked into the bedroom was both nauseating and pathetic. Jake hadn't budged an inch the entire time I'd been gone, which meant that he'd been lying there in a sickening blend of bodily emissions – both mine and his – helpless to do anything but endure it. I wondered if his sense of smell was still alive. If so, the sad and pathetic factor just shot through the roof.

Without thinking about it, because thinking would be my demise in this case, I went over to the other side of the bed so I could see Jake's face. His eyes were open, and he was blinking furiously but I just ignored all that and said, "It's time to get you cleaned up, Jake." I then put my arms underneath him, pulled him over to the edge of the bed, and lifted him up just as I'd done once before when helping Yancy. Jake was light as Kylie and the whole project would have been a breeze except for the strong aromas emanating from his soiled body. I tried to shut out the smells and get him to the bathroom as quickly as I could.

I managed to get him into the tub without any further episodes and, once he was safely in, I turned on the water and began the process of sponging him off. He was still blinking away, obviously trying to communicate with me, but I didn't have the time or patience to make the attempt at understanding him. I just wanted to get him cleaned up and back in his bed as soon as possible. I turned my head away from his face and watched as the chunks of vomit streamed off his body and down to the drain, where a significant pile of chunks had piled up. I looked around the bathroom, saw a small hand towel hanging on a hook, and got up to grab it. "Be right back," I mumbled to Jake.

I got up and went over to get the towel. When I turned back to the tub, I felt like I saw Jake for the first time that day. Up to that point he had been nothing more than an inanimate task that had to be performed; there had been nothing unique and human about him. Until now. Looking down at him in the tub, his limbs shriveled and contorted, I saw a man who had lost his manhood, a human being who had lost his humanity. The sight of him lying naked and helpless in the tub shot through me like a jolt of electricity, lighting up each of my senses and emotions along the way. It was both touching and unsettling all at once. I shook it off and continued with my mission.

I reached down into the tub with the towel, using it as a glove, and scooped a handful of chunks from around the drain. The tub started to drain right away. I left the water running and turned on the shower so it could rain down on Jake and continue the rinsing process. He closed his eyes and I knelt back down next to him to lather him up. I scrubbed him from head to toe and back again, wanting to get every crevice clean.

Finally feeling satisfied that I'd done as good a job as I could, I turned off the shower and dried him off. The process was slow, because Jake could provide no help at all, but I eventually had him dried and ready for clothes. Clothes. I realized that I had no idea where to find a clean set of clothes for him. "Be right back," I mumbled again.

I got up and headed into the bedroom, looking around for the most likely hiding places for Jake's clothes. The cacophony of strong odors still filling the room nearly threw me backwards onto my butt, but I took a couple of deep breaths and plowed forward. I noticed that the room had been stripped of most of its furniture in order to make room for a series of machines. I saw that one of the machines had an oxygen tank attached to it, which made its purpose obvious, but I had no clue what the rest of them would be used for; I said a silent prayer that I wouldn't have to *learn* their purpose at any point during the day. I started opening drawers in the small dresser next to the bed and ended up coming across a large file folder that was labeled JAKE'S INSTRUCTIONS. It was then that I remembered Marsha's final words to me about finding everything I needed to know in the dresser drawer.

Feeling foolish, I opened the file and scanned the top page of instructions. Right at the top of the page, in bold letters, was the warning: "DON'T CHANGE JAKE'S MORNING DIAPER UNTIL AFTER HE HAS RELIEVED HIS BOWELS!" Now I *really* felt like an idiot. I scanned the rest of the page and got a general idea of Jake's daily routine. It was going to be a long day. I also learned what each of the machines was for and surmised that it would be 50/50 as to whether I would have to use any of them during the day.

Picking through the file I came across a sheet that caught my eye. I pulled it out and saw that it was a cheat sheet for Morse Code. I looked at the series of dots and dashes that represented all the letters of the alphabet and it was just a few seconds before the light went off in my head. I smiled to myself and then, remembering that Jake was still sitting naked in the tub, I set the file folder down and resumed my search for his dry clothes.

I quickly found a full set of clothes folded and stacked in a bottom drawer; I pulled them out and made my way back into the bathroom. Jake was just as I had left him – no surprise there – so I knelt next to the tub and began the process of dressing him. "I think I just discovered the key to speaking Jakese," I said to him as I wrapped his shirt around him. As I fastened his shirt closed in front, I saw that he was blinking away again. "Whoa, not yet," I said. "Wait until we get back into the bedroom so I can have my little dictionary with me." It didn't take long to get him fully dressed, thanks to Yancy's velcro fasteners, and when I was done, I said, "Okay, give me a sec." I then got up and went back into the bedroom to assess the damage.

The room was still filled with the strong stench of poop, puke, and pee and, not wanting to start vomiting again, I made the decision to strap on the mask hanging on the nearby oxygen tank. I then turned the valve at the top of the tank and felt instant relief as the pure, odorless oxygen filled my lungs. It was a much-needed respite from the foul air that surrounded me, and I suddenly felt re-energized. I walked over to the bed, carrying the oxygen tank with me, and looked down at the puddles of un-mentionable goop scattered all over the sheets and blankets. I shook my head at the sight and then muttered "This has gotta go" under my breath.

I then folded all the bed covers in onto themselves so that the goop, and Jake's soiled clothes, ended up being contained at the bottom of one large sack. Knowing I wouldn't be able to carry the large sack as well as my new best friend, the oxygen tank, I took off the mask and set it aside. Then, being careful not to let anything leak out the edges, I hoisted up the sack of bed-ding and carried it out the bedroom door, into the hallway, through the kitchen, and into the backyard, where I promptly stuffed the entire bundle into the large garbage can I found situ-ated next to the house. I then heaved a deep sigh; step one was complete.

Back in the bedroom I noticed that the air had already im-proved significantly now that the piles of goop were gone. I also noticed that Jake's bed had a rubber cover sheet on it which I blessed up and down, knowing that I no longer had to worry about disinfecting his entire bed. I went back into the bathroom, gave a quick nod and smile to Jake sitting in the tub, and grabbed a towel. I wet the towel in the sink and then went back into the bedroom to wipe down the rubber sheets, clean up stray spills, and then remake his bed. The entire clean-up process, from ini-tial accident to the final tossing of the soiled towel into the garbage can, took close to an hour and by the time I got back to Jake in the tub I was feeling frazzled and on edge. *What the hell did I get myself into?* kept on running through my head.

"Okay Jake, here we go," I said as I knelt next to the tub. I picked him up and, ignoring his face and those constantly blink-ing eyes, I carried him back to his bed. I set him down on the clean sheet, pulled the covers up and over him, and then plunked myself down in the chair next to the bed. I was exhausted.

I just sat there with my eyes closed for a minute or two and then, feeling slightly more composed, I opened my eyes and glanced down at Jake. He was looking straight at me and it was then that I looked into Jake's eyes for the first time. Every other time I'd looked at him I had seen his broken, shriveled body first and his eyes were just a small part of that larger picture. This time it was different. This time I saw his eyes first and the broken body was a small, almost insignificant piece hovering in the background. I saw that there was a person behind those eyes and that person had something to say to me.

I reached to my left and picked up the file folder that contained all of Jake's instructions. "Just a second, Jake. Let me grab my dictionary." I leafed through the papers in the folder and quickly found what I was looking for: the cheat sheet for Morse Code. I also found a pen and small notebook in the drawer and so, with the cheat sheet in my lap and pen poised, I said, "Okay Jake, fire away."

I thought I detected a small twinkle in his eyes before he started blinking away. It didn't take me long to see the patterns – short blinks for dots, long blinks for dashes, and a closed-eye pause for the end of a word – and I was soon scribbling letters on the pad. Dot, dot, dot…S. Dash, dash, dash…O. Dot, dash, dot…R. Dot, dash, dot…R. I saw where this was headed, and I felt a small lump form in my throat. "Dash, dot, dash, dash…Y. I set the pad down. "Jake, you don't have to apologize to me for anything. That was nothing more than an accident, that's all. It should be me apologizing to *you* for blowing chunks all over you."

He began blinking again and I scrambled to get my sheet and pen back in position. Dot, dot, dot…S. Dash…T. Dot, dot, dash…U. Dash, dot…N. Dash, dot, dash…K. I chuckled. "Yeah, I'll second that." I looked at him sideways. "So, you can still smell, eh?" He gave me one long blink, which I recalled from before meant "yes." "So your mind and all of your senses work but not much else, is that it?" Another long blink. "Then I *really* owe you an apology. That whole scene was *not* pretty."

He blinked out his response: "Seen worse."

I let out an involuntary snort. "Yeah, I guess you probably have." I thought for a moment and then asked, "Do you have a lot of pain?"

"All the time."

"Is there something I can do to help you with that?"

"Not now. Maybe later."

And so it went for the rest of the day; Jake blinking away instructions and me serving as his arms and legs. I never had to refer to the instruction folder again and *Chesapeake* just sat on a nearby shelf, right where I'd left it when I'd first come back into the room that morning.

CHAPTER FORTY-SIX

Marsha seemed taken aback when I told her that I could watch over Jake for as long as it took Yancy to return from her funeral – turned out that an aunt had passed away down in North Carolina – and it took her a while to warm up to the idea. She was in a tough spot, we both knew it, but that didn't prevent her from saying, "I could just call in sick, you know."

"I know," I replied that day. "But why waste sick days when you don't have to? I can just call Griz and tell him I won't be able to help him out at the Y for a few days. He'll understand."

She considered me for a long, long time and then asked, "What is it with you two? When I came home that first night, I thought I'd find a broken man, ready to bolt through the front door just as soon as I walked through it."

I had decided that there was no need to share mine and Jake's big mess with Marsha – ever – so as far as she was concerned, we'd had a nice tranquil, uneventful day together. "We're part of the same club, that's all."

"Oh? And what club is that?"

I smiled. "It's the we-love-Marsha-Graves club. Jake's the president and I'm his VP. It's amazing what can be accomplished when you're united around a great cause like that."

That one got her. Tears snaked their way down her cheeks as she said, "How the hell did I get so damned lucky?"

I shrugged. "Clean living, I guess."

She laughed. "No, that is most definitely *not* it. But I won't tempt the Fates any more than necessary, so I'll just leave it at being thankful for my good fortune."

"Fair enough. And I'll do the same." We exchanged warm smiles, which led to an even warmer kiss, which finally led to a smoking hot embrace, which inspired me to want to take it all one step further.

As always, she saw right through me and whispered "later" in my ear. She pulled out of the embrace, a coquettish grin on her face, and said, "Work beckons my dear, but I look forward to a continuation of these proceedings upon my return."

"Count on it."

Her coquettish grin morphed into a tearful, crooked half-smile as she reached over and rubbed my cheek. "Thank you, Ben. For everything."

"What you continue to fail to realize is that all of these thank yous should be flowing the *other* way. It's *you* who are saving *my* ass through all of this."

She lowered her hand and reached for her coat. "I don't see it that way. But I guess there's room for both of us to be grateful, eh?"

"Yep, I guess there is indeed."

She finished putting on her coat and then said, "So I'll see you tonight."

"Count on it."

We settled into a routine for the next few days: me taking care of Jake and Marsha showering me with a seemingly endless stream of gratitude. The time with Jake passed quickly each day and the time with Marsha was unbelievably wonderful each night. It was a good week.

I also learned some more about Jake over the course of those few days. I got better with the Morse Code, to the point that I rarely had to glance at the cheat sheet, so our communication became smoother and more effortless. There were also no more accidents like we'd had on the first day and that made life a whole lot better for both of us.

One of the tidbits that Jake shared with me nearly knocked me over backwards. I had just finished changing his diaper and had sat down in the chair next to his bed when I saw him blinking away. I grabbed the always-close-at-hand notepad and pencil and before long I was looking down at the following sentence, spelled out in Jake's usual shorthand: "Glad Marsha found u." I was blown away.

I was speechless for a good ten seconds but then I eventually managed to get out, "Thanks Jake. I'm glad to hear that you feel that way."

He blinked his response. "Lots of losers before u."

I laughed. "To tell you the truth, I'm not so sure I don't qualify for that same loser label."

"U don't."

"There's a lot that you don't know about me, Jake."

"Know enuff."

"Did you know that I don't have a job or a home right now?"

"Yep."

I was confused. "How do you know all that?"

"Marsha told me."

I chuckled. "You guys really do tell each other everything, don't you."

"Everything."

"Did she tell you about my ex-wife and daughter?"

"Yep."

"And my empty bank account?"

"Yep."

"And how about my multiple murder convictions and my place on the FBI's Most Wanted list?"

"Ha ha."

It was interactions like these that caused my focus to slowly shift away from Jake-the-broken-body and focus instead on Jake-the-trapped-person. At first, I was totally surprised by the thoughts and insights that were coming forth from this shriveled man who looked like he should be in a casket instead of a bed. It didn't seem possible that there could be a fully-functioning mind contained inside the decaying body that I saw in front of me. But there was indeed a mind there, a very sharp one I found out, and it wasn't long before I saw that first and his physical features a distant second.

By Day Two we were attempting crossword puzzles together. It was embarrassing to admit, but he was better at them than I was. "Four-letter word for Russian king that begins with a t," I would say.

"T...S...A...R," he would then blink out for me.

We became a pretty good team.

It was at the end of Day Four, a Thursday, when he tossed the hand grenade in my lap. We had just heard from Yancy and we now knew that she would be returning to her duties as Jake's primary caregiver the following morning, Friday. I gave Jake the news, figuring it would make him happy, but instead he blinked out, "B...U...M...M...E...R"

"Why is that a bummer, Jake? I thought you liked Yancy."

"Do. Like u better."

I smiled. "I find that hard to believe. Why would you prefer me over Yancy?"

"U got penis too."

That one made me laugh out loud. "That I do, but I don't see how that makes me any better or worse than Yancy."

"Does for me."

"Fair enough." I shifted the pencil to my left hand and reached down to touch his shoulder. "You've got me and my penis here for one more day. How would you like to spend it?"

He started blinking right away and I scrambled to get my pencil and paper back into position. "Let's go for bike ride," he said.

I smiled. "Good one. You got any other options to choose from?"

"Favor."

"Sure, what is it?"

I wrote out his response, but it took me a few beats for what I'd written to sink in completely. At first, I thought he was joking. "Another good one," I said. "You're quite the joker today."

"Not joking," he responded.

The smile ran from my face along with all the blood in it. "Jake, what the hell are you saying?"

"Its time."

"That's not for you or me to decide."

"Is too."

"Jake..." I stammered, "that isn't something that you can ask of somebody else."

"Can't do myself."

I didn't know what to say. I looked down at the piece of paper in my hand and read the words on it one more time: "Put me to sleep forever." I shook my head slowly from side to side and then crumpled the paper in my hands and tossed into a nearby wastebasket. We didn't talk about his request again for the rest of that day.

CHAPTER FORTY-SEVEN

Friday came and that meant another date with Charlie. I was anxious to talk with him about my week with Jake, especially the little favor request he made of me, and so I found myself saying a series of silent prayers as I made my way to The Tavern. "Please let him be there," I mumbled to The Keeper Of The Universe. "C'mon Charlie, I need you today," I said in my head. "Please, please, please," I was saying under my breath as I walked into the restaurant.

I took off my coat and made my way over to what had become our usual table and saw two women sitting in the booth. No Charlie. I scanned the rest of the restaurant, looking for Charlie's unique, unmistakable face. No Charlie. I even wandered into a back room of The Tavern, typically closed off except for large celebrations and special occasions, but still no Charlie. I felt my insides deflate.

I headed back into the main part of the restaurant, thinking I'd make one more pass through to see if I missed him the first time, and when I'd made it about halfway through, I saw someone stand up out of the corner of my eye. Hoping it was Charlie, I turned quickly. Just as quickly, I saw that it was a middle-aged woman who had stood up; definitely not Charlie. Before I could look away and resume my search, however, I noticed that the middle-aged woman was looking at me. She had a strange look on her face, as if she knew me from somewhere and was trying to pull up a name. After giving me a quick once-over, she took a few tentative steps in my direction.

"Ben?" she asked when she had gotten close enough.

I took a step closer to her. I saw that she was a woman who was probably five to ten years younger than Marsha but who looked to be five to ten years older. She reminded me a bit of my Aunt Lillian who had the two-edged genetic gift of looking the same today, at age sixty-four, as she had at the age of thirty-four. "Yeah," I replied. "Do I know you?"

She stuck her hand out. "No, you don't. My name is Lilly and I'm here on behalf of Charlie."

I smiled to myself when I heard her name, but the smile fell away when I heard her say Charlie's name. "Is he okay?" was the question that automatically fell from my mouth.

Lilly shifted her feet. Bad sign. "Uh, I'm not sure what to say to that," she stammered. "I'm a neighbor of his and he asked me to bring this to you today." She reached into her coat pocket, pulled out an envelope, and handed it to me.

I took the envelope and then re-asked my question. "Is he okay?"

Lilly's mouth opened and closed several times before she finally said, "Look, Charlie told me all about you and what he's been doing with you each week." She looked at a point somewhere beyond my left shoulder. "He's a good man who has had a rough life so don't judge him too harshly, okay?"

"Is he dead?" I then asked, deciding to give voice to the huge elephant of a question that had been filling my brain.

I could see her start to shake ever so subtly and her eyes came back to mine. "Yes, he is," was all she said.

I nodded, unsure what to say next.

Her response hung in the air between us for several beats as we both considered what her words meant to each of us. For me it meant the death of a friend, one of the few I had in the world, and the birth of what would now be an unsolvable mystery: who *was* Charlie? It was then that I remembered the envelope that I now held in my hand. I raised it to eye level and considered its weight and thickness; would all the answers that I sought be contained in this envelope?

"He wrote that the day he died," I heard Lilly say.

I lowered the envelope. "And what day would that be?"

"The day before yesterday."

I could see her eyes start to glaze over. "Were you there?"

She nodded. "Yes, I was." She paused for a moment and then added, "I was the only one there."

"I'm sorry," was all that I could think to say. "I wish I'd known."

She shook her head. "You weren't supposed to know. That's the way he wanted it."

I took one step closer to her. "Why? Why didn't Charlie want me to know that he was sick and about to die? Why didn't he want me to know that he had a neighbor and a life? Why did he want to die alone?" The questions just kept tumbling from my mouth. They would have continued to tumble if Lilly hadn't raised her hand in a stop sign.

"I've said too much already," she muttered. She then pointed at the envelope. "Everything that Charlie wanted you to know will be contained in that letter." She then pulled a pen from her pocket and reached for the envelope. "May I?" I handed her the envelope. She scribbled something on the outside of the envelope and handed it back to me. "I gave you my phone number. If you have any more questions after you've read Charlie's letter you can call me."

I looked down at the number and then back to Lilly. I stifled the million other questions that were pushing at my lips and simply said, "Thank you."

We stood there for an awkward moment and then Lilly stuck her hand out. "It was nice to meet you," she said.

I took her hand in mine and shook it gently. "Likewise. And thank you for bringing this to me." I raised the envelope and shook it a few times in her direction.

"No problem. Charlie was a good guy and I was glad to do it for him. I hope you find the answers that you're after in there."

I let out an involuntary scoffing sound. "I doubt I'll find *all* of the answers that I'm after, but hopefully there will be a few."

She smiled. "Like I said before, go easy on him."

I nodded. "I will. He's been nothing but a friend to me and I'm just thankful for the little bit of time that we had together."

Her smile broadened and she started nodding slowly. "Me too."

It was obvious that there was nothing left to say so we both did the awkward shuffle thing, mumbled some goodbyes, and it wasn't long after that that I was sitting in a booth, alone, tearing open the envelope to see what Charlie had to say to me from his deathbed.

The first thing I noticed when I pulled the pages from the envelope was that the entire letter was written in longhand, in a beautifully flowing script. It dawned on me that it was probably Lilly's handwriting and that she had most likely taken dictation from Charlie as he lay there dying. The first tears formed in my eyes. I took a deep breath and began reading.

Dear Ben, it began. *If you're reading this, it means that I'm now gone and you're probably reading this in our favorite booth at The Tavern. I'm sorry I couldn't join you for lunch today.* The tears thickened in my eyes.

I want to tell you that I truly enjoyed our Fridays together. They were the highlight of each week for me. I didn't have many things to look forward to in my life during these past many years and this was something that I truly looked forward to. Thank you for that. A single tear snaked its way down my cheek.

I can imagine that you have a few questions about me right now - seeing as angels aren't supposed to die (insert smile here) - and I want to answer as many of them as I can for you. First, as you have already surmised, I am not an angel. Far from it. I am a man, just like you, who has more regrets than joys and who, in his final moments, wanted to snatch a few victories from the gap-ing jaws of Defeat when it came to my life. In the interest of brevity, I will just say that my life was just as I had described to you during our first meeting. Ex-wife…two estranged daugh-ters…blah, blah, blah. It's a story that could be told a million times over in this country. I get bored just telling it so I will spare you any more poor-me details. And, really, it doesn't matter be-cause the only important part of my entire story is that I fucked up. Big time.

I set the letter down and flashed on my own life story. I re-alized that I too was bored with all its details. The nugget contained in all of it was that I missed my daughter. That was it. The rest was just irrelevant noise. I tucked that thought away for future consideration and continued reading.

It's because of this – the fact that I fucked up – that your conversation with your friend, about saying more fuck-its and what not, caught my ear one night at The Tavern. I was sitting at the next table over from you that night and I heard everything that you had to say about your life, your regrets, your house fire, etc. It was then that I first thought about how each of us could use a guardian angel at times like that, to tell us what to do and how to climb out of these holes that we dig for ourselves. It was later in the evening, after you'd left with Marsha, that I decided that I would become your guardian angel, Ben; to give me some-thing worthwhile to do with my time and to perhaps add some bits of redemption to what had been a fairly wasted life up to that point. I'm sorry for deceiving you, but I didn't see any other way. I can only hope that the deceit provided some benefits to you and that you can forgive an old man for indulging in this little bit of fantasy. Trust me when I tell you that my intentions were nothing but honorable.

I set the letter down again and ruminated on the one word that would always stand next to Charlie's name in my head: faith. I smiled at the memory of those conversations, and the verbal wrestling matches that he had engaged in with me over that one word, and I said a quick, silent thank you to him in my head. I then went back to the letter.

I knew that I didn't have long to live as I sat in The Tavern that night. I had been thinking about just ending it all sooner rather than later when you and your friend walked into my life. So, in many ways, you were my angel, Ben. It was you who convinced me that I still had a reason to live. That reason was this: I wanted to help you to avoid stepping into that same deep, dark hole that I had stepped into many years earlier. I saw your future unfolding before you as if I were watching a slow-motion replay of my own life – the bitterness, the endless self-pity, the inevitable and bone-chilling loneliness – and I wanted to figure out a way to push you onto a new course, away from the black hole that would swallow your life just as surely as it had swallowed mine. I thought that if I could save one life from unnecessary pain that perhaps it would ease my own pain in some way. Silly, I know.

I thought about his words; was I bitter and lonely? Being honest, I had certainly been feeling those things – and then some – but it seemed like they were on the ebb, not impacting my life like they had been. Was that because of Charlie? Or Marsha? Or Griz? Or maybe a combination of all of them? Who knows. What I did know was that Charlie had gotten the whole take-my-life-back thing rolling with his no-bullshit take on me and my life during our once-a-week chat sessions. I said another silent thank you to him for that.

And now it's time to reveal the secret behind my angelic, all-knowing nature: I followed you. I became your unseen shadow for the better part of most days, for as long as my health allowed, and then I would use a second Angel Tool to fill in the rest: I guessed. (insert laugh here)

I could hear a loud Charlie Laugh echoing in my ears and it made me smile.

It didn't take me long to get a feel for your life, Ben, and to see the parallels between what you were doing and what I had done many years earlier. You were piling up experiences between you and your pain to serve as a sort of buffer. Women, alcohol, tattoos…you name it, and I had done it too at one time or another. But after a while I realized that these things would never fill in the hole that existed in my heart; I was using smoke as a patch and that smoke would swirl away soon after each experience. By the time I realized that, and realized what it was that I really craved, it was too late: my wife and daughters had moved on and I was officially on the outside looking in.

I flashed on Kylie's face and the tears returned to my eyes.

Don't make that same mistake, Ben. Please. If you remember nothing else that we talked about, please remember this: your daughter is worth fighting for. Don't lose yours like I lost mine. She still loves and adores you. Pull that in and keep it close. Always.

And the last word that I want to leave you with is one of our favorites (insert smile here): Faith. I've watched you become better friends with this word over the course of our visits and I hope that you can maintain that relationship long after I'm gone. You have a good heart Ben Weaver and with just a little bit of faith you can create a life worth living. Trust me.

Take good care of yourself Ben and I will see you on the other side.

> *Your Semi-Angelic Friend,*
> *Charlie*

I set the letter down on the table and let out a deep sigh. A tornado of thoughts and emotions swirled through my brain but the one that kept coming into focus was: he's gone. Charlie was out of my life forever. The thin layer of mist re-formed in my eyes.

The second thing that came into focus was Rule #7 For My New Life: *Enjoy the special people in your life while you can – you never know when they might be taken away from you.* I repeated this new rule in my head several times before folding up the letter, tucking it into my pocket, and walking out of The Tavern.

CHAPTER FORTY-EIGHT

"What do you mean he's been asking for me?" It was Monday morning and I happened to run into Yancy in the front hallway as I was leaving, and she was coming in.

She took off her coat and hung it on a nearby hook. "Just what I told you," she said. "He wants to know when you're going to come take care of him again." She stepped towards me, and her face was serious but her eyes had a mischievous twinkle to them. "I know you're unemployed and all," she said, "but you best not be trying to take my job here."

We shared a quick laugh and then I said, "You don't have to worry about *that* ever happening."

"So what should I tell him?"

I considered it for a moment and then, remembering the sudden hole that had appeared in my schedule – meager as it was – a few days earlier, I replied, "Tell him Fridays. I'll take care of him on Fridays from now on. Does that work for you, Yancy?"

"Sure, no problem. I can always use a regular day off." She nodded emphatically. "Fridays it is then. I'll tell him today."

And that's how my Fridays with Charlie abruptly changed into Fridays with Jake.

The week passed quickly and before I knew it, I woke up to the one-week anniversary of Charlie's death; or, more accurately, the one-week anniversary of my *knowledge* of Charlie's death. It was also the day that I was to begin my new weekly arrangement with Jake.

"I still can't believe that it's come to this," Marsha mumbled as she applied her eye make-up that morning.

"Come to what?"

"That the two of you have you have become such good chums."

"I wouldn't say that Jake and I are chums just yet."

She set down whatever beauty tool it was that she'd had in her hand and looked over at me. "What would you say that you are then?"

I thought about it and then the word "friends" popped out of my mouth.

"What's the difference?"

I shrugged. "I dunno. "Chums are just more…chummy." I realized that what I'd just said sounded stupid, so I quickly added, "To me, it implies a history together and a certain comfort level with each other. Friends just means that you know each other and like each other. That sounds more like me and Jake."

She nodded as she considered my words. "Sure, I get it. Friends it is. We'll save chums for farther down the road."

I smiled and then stepped over to her so I could kiss her neck. "You and I, however," I whispered in her ear, "are about as chummy as they come."

She let out a girlish giggle. "Stop it, that tickles."

I could tell by her tone that she didn't want me to stop at all, but I did. Stepping back, I said, "So how's my buddy Austin T doing these days?"

She went back to her beautifying regimen, moving down to the lips now. "Same as ever. There's only one Austin T Phelps and I don't think he'll be any different twenty years from now than he is today."

"Amen to that. What's his story anyway? What makes Austin T such an Austin T?"

"I don't know a whole lot about him. I know that he's married and that he and his wife go to church a lot." She shrugged. "I've always just put Austin into the category of someone who hasn't gotten punched in the gut by life very often, so he still has the luxury of dividing everything into two categories, one black and one white. He's never been much of one for considering the many wonderful shades of gray that exist out here in the real world."

I laughed. "That is for *damn* sure. I don't think he could spell gray if you spotted him the g-r-a."

"I honestly believe that he would stop talking to me completely if he ever got wind of our little arrangement here."

"Why?"

"Why? Why would a rigid, ultra-religious man have a problem with a married woman shacking up with another man under the same roof as her dying husband?" She put her finger to her chin. "Hmmm. How many of the Ten Commandments am I breaking here?"

I chuckled. "Yeah, I guess this is about as gray as it gets, huh?"

"Gee, do you think?" There was a short silence and then she asked, "So have you two figured something out yet?"

Her question caused a sudden and noticeable shift in the tone that filled the room. We both knew that she already had the answer to that question, seeing as she could access my file any time she wanted to, but I also knew that this was her way of asking "How are things going for you?" That wasn't something that she could find in a file anywhere within the offices of the Brown and Brown Insurance Company. "It's kind of at a standstill right now. I haven't heard anything from him in a while and I don't know what that means."

She didn't stop applying lip liner – another amazing feat of female dexterity – as she said, "Do you want me to look into it for you?"

It seemed like a simple, innocuous question but it was the first time that Marsha had ever offered to intervene on my behalf with Austin T. Before I could even think it through completely, I replied, "Nah. I'll take care of it myself."

"No problem. Just let me know if you ever change your mind. There is no expiration date on my offer."

"Thanks. I will."

She stepped back from the mirror to assess her handiwork. "So, what do you and Jake have planned for today?" she asked without taking her eyes off her own image in the mirror.

"Oh, the usual. A quick 5-mile jog, then it's off to do some skiing, and I thought we'd finish up with a little ballroom danc-ing down at the Senior Center."

I watched as she stopped primping and just froze in place, her eyes still looking at the now-motionless woman in the mirror. At first, I thought that my little joke had hurt her feelings but then she murmured, "You know, it wasn't too long ago that that might be a fairly typical day for Jake. The guy was an absolute physical fitness nut."

I just stood there for a while, looking and feeling dumb, and then decided to go and hug her. "I'm sorry," I cooed into her ear.

She hugged me, hard, and then said, "No need to be sorry. I'm way past that." We stepped out of the embrace and she looked up into my eyes. "It's just funny how quickly things can go from being a day-to-day reality to being the punchline of a joke."

"I'm sorry," I began, "I shouldn't have…"

She put her finger to my lips. "No, there's no need to apol-ogize. Really. Jake's condition is a fact right now and there's no point in ducking or dodging those facts. It's just that…I don't know…I can't believe how fast everything moves sometimes."

Charlie's face then popped into my head and that got my head nodding. "Yeah, that's for sure." I then smiled and said, "Remind me to tell you about Rule #7 tonight."

She gave me a funny look and then cast a glance at the clock by the bed. "Okay, I will, but I gotta get going right now." She went up on her toes and kissed me on the cheek. "You two have a great time jogging, skiing, and whatever else it is that you'll be doing today."

"Will do."

I walked her down the stairs, said another quick goodbye at the door, and then headed to the back of the house to see my friend, Jake.

The first thing that I noticed when I walked into the room was that the air was clear. No smell. That was a good start to the day. Hey there, Jake," I said cheerfully. "How goes the battle?"

I walked around the bed so that I could see his face. He was awake. "Morning," he blinked out to me; at least that's what I *think* he said to me. I was a little rusty with the Morse Code, but I caught enough of it to surmise that that was what he was trying to say.

"And a good morning right back at'cha," I replied. "How are you feeling this morning?" I picked up the nearby pad and pencil and prepared to translate.

"Not feeling much."

I thought about his reply for a moment and then realized that he was making another of his many jokes. "Ha, ha," I replied. "Good one."

"Thnx."

"So now that the floor show is over are you ready to get started on our morning routine?"

He blinked a yes.

"Great, here we go." I first changed his diaper, which was soiled, and then I disconnected all the tubes and wires that were always hooked to his body and carried him into the bathroom. Once there, I set him into the tub, removed all his clothes except the waterproof diaper, and started running his bath water. "Time to clean you up, my friend," I mumbled as I fussed with the water temperature.

Once I had the temperature just where I wanted it, I sat back and waited for the tub to fill. I glanced at Jake's face and noticed that he was blinking so I said, "I think I missed part of that, could you start over?"

He blinked out, "Thnx for coming."

"No problem. Glad to do it. You're stuck with me every Friday from this point onward, so the lesson here is to be careful what you ask for."

"Glad."

"Yeah, I am too," I replied, feeling my throat clench up ever so slightly as I uttered those four words.

CHAPTER FORTY-NINE

The weeks shot by. Before I knew it, I was looking down at bright crocus blossoms popping through the ground in Marsha's front yard. Spring was coming. It had been a long, exhausting, life-changing winter and I was ready for the change of seasons to possibly help usher in a change of life for me.

It was a Saturday afternoon in March, and I was heading off to pick up Kylie for a lunch date that we had arranged. I was feeling excited to see her. It seemed as if she grew about a foot in both height and maturity each time I saw her, and I was curious to see what sorts of changes awaited me this time. Ever since Charlie's death I had tried to see her at least once a week and, thus far, I had been moderately successful. She and I still enjoyed the hell out of each other's company, and I said a silent prayer after every visit that that would never change.

As I walked to Linda's house, I took in all the early signs of spring: the sap buckets hanging from the maple trees; the small buds on the bushes; and the bright green leaves reaching out of the ground, telling everyone that the tulip and daffodil bulbs were awakening from their winter slumber. The air was filled with the smell of fresh mud and the sun shone brightly, though the air still had a crisp, wintry bite to it that made wearing a light jacket necessary. My heart was light and my steps were quick as I made my way over to the east side of town where Linda and Kylie lived.

It didn't take me long, however, to shift my focus from the external world to my own internal world. My mind wandered aimlessly for a while, but it wasn't long before it settled in on Charlie and the small service for him that I'd attended a few weeks earlier. It had been a sad service, and not just because it was a reminder of his recent death. The truly sad part for me had been seeing his real *life* for the first time; where he lived, how he lived, and how many people shared that life with him. If Maple Grove had a slum, then Charlie had lived in it. He'd lived on the edge of the old industrial section of town, down on the south side, and the building he'd lived in was way past its prime, more suitable for rats and cockroaches than anything else. Lilly, the woman who had given me Charlie's letter at The Tavern, had arranged for the service and decided to hold it at her place, just upstairs from Charlie's place. She was the building manager and she'd offered to give me a tour of Charlie's place when I'd arrived for the service that day since nobody else had arrived yet.

"How long has he lived here?" I'd asked as she struggled to unlock his front door.

"Five years," she'd replied as she finally succeeded in getting the door to open. She clicked on a light as I walked in.

Charlie's home had been just two rooms in a large, old house that Lilly told me was owned by a guy who had moved to North Carolina long ago. She was paid a small sum to live in the building and watch over the house and its tenants for him. I looked at the moldy walls, peeling paint, and decrepit furniture and asked, "Does this guy ever put any money back *into* this place?"

"Nah. Not worth it to him."

"How long have *you* lived here, Lilly?"

She shrugged. "Too long."

It was hard to imagine a man of Charlie's age and angelic stature living in such filth. "Was he happy here?"

Lilly had paused before answering. "As happy as can be expected," was what she'd eventually said. It dawned on me at the time that those were perhaps the same words that an observer would use to describe me and *my* life.

If Charlie's rundown apartment had been sad, the situation reached depressing when we finally made our way upstairs to Lilly's place. The place itself was light years ahead of Charlie's when it came to the paint and décor, but the truly depressing part came when I saw just how many people showed up at Charlie's service: there were a grand total of four people, including me and Lilly. The other two mourners were also residents of the building, one being an older woman who looked as if she was a part-time bag lady and the other being a middle-aged man who appeared to hear voices that weren't audible to the rest of us. That was it. That was the circle of humanity that gathered around Charlie's memory to pay its respects. Like I said, depressing.

The words that floated in my head that day – as they were now, during my walk to see Kylie – were words that Charlie had written himself in his final Angelic Epistle to me. I couldn't recall his exact words, but the gist of his message had been: "Don't make the same mistakes I did and end up like me." I pulled those words in close and vowed to never forget them.

As I strolled, the rhythm of my strides induced a quasi-hypnotic trance in me; the thread of thought in my head broke loose from memories of Charlie and wafted in my cranial breeze for a short while before attaching itself to Jake. We'd had many good Fridays together, sharing stories and doing crosswords together, but this past Friday he had re-introduced a question that I'd hoped had been a one-time deal. "Will u help me die?" he'd blinked out to me towards the end of our last day together. As I'd done before, I waved off the question with some version of "you can't ask me to do something like that" and then pretended to not see him as he continued to blink out his response. I felt bad for ignoring him, but I had zero interest in going down that path with him. It was already bad enough that I was an arsonist, I had no desire to add murderer to my criminal resume.

I reached Linda's door just as the Jake thread was struggling to break loose, which was excellent timing; the less I had to think about Jake's request, the better. Unfortunately, The Worm answered my knock and he got to bear the brunt of my just-arrived sour mood. "My, my look who's here," I said through my best fake smile. "My favorite professor and wife-stealer. How's it hangin' today, Willie?"

His look said it all: anger, contempt, and arrogance all rolled into one package. "Just great, Loser. As always, it's great to see you."

I stepped past him and into the house, not wanting to give him the satisfaction of getting to invite me in. "Likewise. Kylie around?"

I heard a small scoffing sound come out of his mouth from behind me. Was he mocking me? "No, she's off in search of a real father. She should be back anytime."

Without taking the time to consider my next move, I spun around and put myself right up in The Worm's face. I jabbed my finger just inches from his eyeball and hissed, "Don't fuck with me, Worm. I'm a desperate man and I have a whole lot less to lose than you do." I gave him one last finger jab for punctuation and said, "Remember that."

Something in my face must have registered with him because when I stepped back, I could see that the look in his eyes had changed. Gone was the above-it-all arrogance, replaced with what looked like genuine fear. Perhaps realizing that I'd just seen something that he didn't want me to see, he recovered quickly and pulled the thin blanket of arrogance back over his eyes. "A heathen to the end," he muttered. And then, "I'll go see if Kylie is ready."

After he'd walked away, I was surprised to find that I didn't feel more elated at having just drawn blood from The Worm with my sharp verbal sword. It wasn't too long ago that I would have been dancing the jig in honor of my little victory but all I felt was empty. And a little ashamed. What was *that* all about?

I didn't have a whole lot of time to consider the question as Kylie came bounding down the stairs and the sound of her voice was like a huge wave on my internal shore, effectively washing away everything except my thoughts of her. "Daddy!" she screamed in the voice that always told me that she was still my little girl. I loved that voice.

I bent over and welcomed her into my arms. As I scooped her up and hugged her as tightly as I could without crushing the breath out of her, I felt small puddles of tears forming in the corners of my eyes. Not wanting The Worm to see my tears, I turned so I was facing the wall. "Hey sweetie," I whispered in her ear. "How's my little princess?"

"Good," she screamed into my ear as I continued to hug her. "Where are you taking me today?"

I pulled her back so I could look into her face. It was a beautiful face. How the hell did I ever help to produce a child as beautiful as this? Was there some freak recessive gene floating around inside of me that decided to finally make itself known and visible through this amazing child? Ah, questions that will never have an answer; I tended to specialize in those. "I thought we'd go out for pancakes today, so we can get some of that yummy maple syrup that they've been making." I smiled to myself at my use of the word "yummy" – a word that I would never, ever use except in the company of my daughter.

"Yay!" came the scream in reply, telling me that I had made a good choice.

Linda must have heard all the commotion because it was soon after Kylie's last shriek that she appeared. "What's all the ruckus out here?" she asked, though the small smile at the corner of her mouth told me that she really didn't care to know; there was a part of her that loved the fact that Kylie and I still got along so well.

"Daddy's taking me out for pancakes at the Sugar Shack!"

"My, my, my, that does sound good. Maybe we should come along," she then added while simultaneously tossing me a wink.

I glanced over to see if The Worm had caught the wink, but he was preoccupied with something on a nearby table; probably still nursing his bruised ego from earlier. A part of me wished he'd seen the small bit of surreptitious communication between me and Linda, to show him that I still had a small foothold in this household, but once again it didn't seem to matter as much as it had before. Strange. I turned my attention back to Linda. "Yeah, sure, why don't you do that. We could all sit around the table and share our favorite Easter Bunny stories, since Easter is coming soon." It was a small dig at The Worm, for his Santa Claus comments a few months earlier, and I noticed that this one got his attention. Sure, it didn't feel as good as it once did, but it still felt pretty damned good to get under The Worm's skin.

He turned away from whatever it was he was doing at the table and opened his mouth to deliver his retort, but before he could utter a word, Kylie shot back, "Daddy, you know there's no such thing as an Easter Bunny."

The Worm and I locked eyes and I could see that he was wrestling with whether he should deliver the message that waited on his tongue. He then dropped his eyes, shook his head, and turned to head out of the room. Round two goes to Ben The Loser. "Oh yeah," I muttered in reply to Kylie. "I forgot."

Linda had noticed the silent arm-wrestling match between me and The Worm as she said, "William, where are you going?"

"Going to get some air," he muttered as he continued to walk away. "Finding it hard to breathe in here."

Linda threw me a withering glance and I just shrugged my reply. I thought I detected a tiny smirk forming, however, as she turned her attention to Kylie. "Do you have your jacket?"

"Not yet. I'll go get it." I set her down and she ran off to find her jacket.

"So how are things?" I asked after Kylie was out of earshot.

"Just fine. As long as you're not around." I could tell that she meant that in a good-natured way, so I just ignored it. "How are you doing, Ben?"

I shrugged. "Except for the fact that a good friend just died and another one has two feet in the grave, everything is hunky dory."

She was reaching for me, and opening her mouth to say something, when Kylie came bursting back into the room. "Ready!" she said excitedly.

Judging from the softness in her eyes, the words that Linda was about to say were going to be nice ones. But, if they were, they were going to have to wait for another day because she shifted her attention back to Kylie and said, "Do you have your hat and mittens too?"

Kylie slapped her jacket pockets. "Yep."

"Did you put your warm socks on?"

"Yep."

"And how about your blanket, first aid kit, and flare gun?" I interjected. "Did you pack those too?"

Linda flashed me the exact same look that she used to flash me whenever I mocked her tendency to over-mother Kylie – it was a look that had equal parts amusement, exasperation, and, dare I say it, love, contained within it. A warm wind blew through my insides. It was a small, wonderful taste of The Way Things Used To Be. "That's enough out of you, Mr. Wise Guy," she retorted unconvincingly.

"Just trying to help," I threw back, tossing in the old, mischievous Ben twinkle in my eyes for good measure. I couldn't remember the last time I'd tossed that look Linda's way.

She noticed it, I could tell, because she got the same old look of mock exasperation on her face. We were officially flirting.

Kylie broke the spell with a shriek of, "Let's go, Daddy!"

We both fumbled with goodbyes, as if we were high school kids after a first date, and then Kylie and I headed off to the Sugar Shack. We ended up having our usual wonderful time together – filled with lots of father-daughter laughter and bonding – but there was a persistent question that buzzed around my head the entire time that day: *"What the hell just happened back there?!?!"*

CHAPTER FIFTY

The thing with Linda continued to bother me for several days afterwards. The most bothersome part of the whole thing was that it reignited some hopes and dreams that I thought had died long ago. Thoughts like "*maybe we could get back together someday*" and questions like "*does she still love me?*" danced in my head as I went about each day.

Marsha must have noticed my distractedness as she said to me one day, "Are you okay?"

Knowing that I couldn't share any part of what I was thinking with her – it would crush her – I said, "Just thinking about some things." It wasn't the whole truth, but it wasn't a lie either. I wanted to believe that I was done lying to Marsha Graves.

But the thoughts and questions persisted. It was a time when I really could have used a lunch date with Charlie to help me sort things out. I tried to imagine what he would tell me in this situation, but it wasn't the same. I finally decided to give Jim a call and see if he could help me find some answers.

I hadn't seen Jim since just after the fire back in November – when I'd gone on my fucket rant after a few too many margaritas – and I was more than a little surprised that he agreed to have lunch with me without first making me beg for his forgiveness. I had been pretty rough on him that night. But it must be true what they say about time healing all wounds because when we met at The Tavern that day, he greeted me with a warm hug and a big smile. "Long time, no see," he said to me as we sat down. "I thought you'd joined the Peace Corps or something."

I flashed on the long, twisting road that I'd traveled since I'd last seen Jim and all I could do was smile: a whole lot of life had been packed into the past many months. "Nope. Just living life," was all I could think of to say in reply.

"How did things end up with your house?"

"Still yet to be determined."

"You're kidding me," he said, sounding truly surprised. "You still haven't gotten a check for that? What's the hold-up?"

I shrugged. "Don't know." I thought about Austin T and the whole insurance mess and for some reason it didn't raise my blood pressure like it once had. Jim's question should have ignited a whole barrage of profanity-laced comments from me about Austin T and his irritating, control-freak ways but nothing bubbled up. It just didn't seem to matter as much to me. Very strange.

Jim considered me for a moment and then asked, "And you're okay with that?"

"Not really. But I have no control over it so I'm just putting it on a back burner and whatever happens, happens." Hearing my words bounce back at me, I sounded like some New Age geek and I wondered: *Where the hell did that come from?*

Jim must have thought the exact same thing because he said, "Are you sure that you're Ben Weaver? Because you're starting to sound a lot like some guy who should be taking yoga classes and driving a Volvo."

I laughed. "Yeah, I guess I do at that. Just chalk it up to the newer, calmer Ben."

"I didn't know that such a guy existed."

"He didn't until just recently. And he's still getting his bearings so don't be surprised if he still loses it occasionally and the *old* Ben shows up."

He let out a scoffing sound. "Don't worry. I'm more than used to *that* Ben's behavior."

I didn't know what he'd meant by his comment, but it made me think back to some of the things I'd said to him the last time we were together. "Hey, that reminds me. Before we go any further, I just wanted to apologize for what I said and how I acted the last time I saw you. I was a real jerk that night and you didn't deserve any of it."

There was a short pause before Jim said, "Wow, an apology too. Are you sure the pod people haven't gotten to you?"

I was a little stung by his comment, implying that the Ben he knew never apologized for anything, but I didn't show it because, well, I deserved it. "Yeah, I'm sure."

He raised his hand in a stop sign. "Wait a minute, that was uncalled for." He lowered his hand. "You were trying to apologize, and I threw you a zinger. Sorry about that. Your apology is accepted."

I'd forgotten what a genuinely good guy Jim was; I think I'd gotten into the habit of seeing his shortcomings first and stopped seeing all the good stuff hiding behind those foibles. "Fair enough," I said with a nod.

"And besides," he then added as his eyes lowered so that he was looking at his hands resting on the table. "A lot of what you said that night was true." He looked up again and a rueful smile was etched across his face. "Cruel, but true."

"To be honest, I don't remember everything I said that night. I do remember being hard on you though and there's never a good reason for doing that to a friend."

He shrugged. "Yeah, well I guess that's what friends are for sometimes. You get to knock them around a little bit and they still come back for more."

I reached over and patted his arm. "Don't worry. There won't be any knocking around going on here today." I took my hand back and added, "Unless of course you want to throw a few verbal punches *my* way."

"Nah, I'm done." He shifted around in his seat a little and then asked, "So what is it that's on your mind? I have to admit that I was a little surprised when I got your call after all these months, so I figured it was something big going on with you."

I heaved a deep sigh. "How long do you have today?"

"I can stay as long as I need to. I told work that I had some stuff that had to get done outside the office today so let 'er rip."

I took in another deep breath and then proceeded to unload my burden. I told him about Charlie and his recent death. I told him about Marsha and our budding relationship. I told him about Jake and his outrageous request. I told him about Griz, and Cody, and the kids at Teens Rule. And I told him about the last time I'd seen Linda and how her behavior had left me feeling confused. The entire unburdening process probably took the better part of an hour, during which time sandwiches and drinks had also been ordered, delivered, and consumed. It felt amazingly good to get it all out.

Jim hadn't said much during my telling of the various stories and he didn't say a whole lot immediately after I was finished either. He just continued to munch on his french fries and utter an occasional "hmmm" sound for a minute or two. Finally, though, he wiped the french fry grease from his fingers, then interlocked his fingers in front of his face and said, "You've been a busy, busy boy, haven't you?"

I threw him a nod. "Yeah, you might say that."

"I guess I'm finding it hard to believe that you've packed all of this into the last few months. You must be exhausted."

I chuckled. "Yeah, a little bit I guess. But don't forget that I'm still basically unemployed so all of this shit has become my full-time job."

"Well if that's the case, you should ask your boss for a raise 'cuz you're doing the work of ten men right now."

A grin worked its way across my face. "A raise would really come in handy right about now. Any idea who I'd talk to about that?"

He shook his head. "Nope, sorry. Something tells me that the CEO of the Universe is a pretty busy guy right now so he probably wouldn't agree to meet with you to hear your grievance."

This was the Jimbo I loved: funny, playful, and irreverent. I gave myself a small, silent pat on the back for making the decision to call him. "Wow, it's tough being the little guy."

"Yeah, well, get used to it my friend. Living the life of a little guy is a tough, thankless job."

A little voice in my head told me to ask the next question: "Are you okay, Jim?"

A quick, pithy answer didn't tumble from his lips and that told me a lot. Before answering me, he looked up at the ceiling, then over at the far wall, and then he heaved a huge sigh. After all that, he finally said, "Yeah, I'm fine. Besides, this lunch date isn't about me, it's about you. So, where were we?"

"We were at the part where you stop bullshitting me and tell me what's on your mind. We just spent the past hour on me and that's long enough." I leaned forward with concern in my eyes. "So, what's up with you?"

Another sigh. "I don't know." He paused. "I just can't seem to get a handle on it." Another pause. "It's as if life was going in fast-forward all around me and I was just standing still in the middle of it all." Yet another, though longer, pause. "I'm just feeling so..." He didn't finish the thought, perhaps because he felt that uttering the word would make it more real somehow. I knew all about *that* little game.

I decided to help him out with the last word. "Unhappy?"

He looked up and I could see that his eyes had taken on a profoundly sad veneer. "Yeah, unhappy."

"Any idea where that's coming from?"

He shook his head. "To be honest, it kinda started soon after our last time together. I couldn't stop thinking about your golden retriever comment."

"I'm so sorry. I…" He wouldn't let me finish.

"No apologies necessary, Ben. Trust me when I tell you that all you did was tell me something that I already knew. I'd been feeling like my life was one long list of compromises even before our dinner that night and then when you went off on your little diatribe about feeling like a well-trained dog and the need to say more fuckets in our lives, well…" He just shrugged as his voice trailed off, knowing that there was no need to say anything more.

"So, what's come of all this soul-searching?" I smiled inside, realizing that the tables had officially turned, and I was now the therapist and Jim was lying on *my* couch. It felt good to be in the new role; I was tired of hearing my *own* story.

"It's like you said that night, I've lost my sense of fun and adventure. I don't even recognize myself sometimes. I feel like I'm nothing more than an extension of Liz and the kids."

I chuckled. "I can see where that would be easy to do with Liz; she's a pretty strong woman."

"Look, I know you've never really cared for Liz, and I get that. But it's not her fault that I lost my balls somewhere along the way. To be honest, I *handed* them to her, and I only have myself to blame for that."

Wow. I wasn't sure I'd ever heard Jim being this honest about his relationship with Liz. I looked over at his hangdog face and I couldn't muster anything but compassion for the guy. He was basically sitting at the exact same crossroads I had been at many years earlier, the only difference being that he was still married. He still had a chance to change things. He could still create a different future for himself, one that included a wife and kids. Charlie's words shot into my head: *Don't make the same mistakes I did and end up like me.* It was time for me to slip into the Guardian Angel role. I leaned forward and made sure I had his eyes locked in on mine before I said a word. "Listen to me, Jimbo," I began, trying to pull up every ounce of sincerity I could muster and then push it out my eyeballs so Jim could see that I meant what I was about to say with every bit of my being. "Your family is worth fighting for, don't ever forget that. Once you turn your back on them, there's no going back." I reached over and grabbed his forearm for added emphasis. "Trust me on this one."

"Yeah, I know, but..."

I slammed the table. Hard. It definitely got his attention, as well as the attention of every other person in the immediate vicinity of our table. "No buts about it, Jimbo," I said firmly, ignoring the stares of the surrounding strangers. "This is too important to attach any buts to." I got up out of my seat and leaned over so far that our noses were nearly touching. "You... must... fight... for... your... family." I sat back down. "Everything else is just bullshit and lies." I wagged my finger at him. "Remember that."

He started to say something, thought better of it, and then said, "Okay. I get it."

I stared at him for a good long while and then, satisfied that my point had been made, I said, "Okay, now that that's been settled, we can start wading into the pool of bullshit and lies that's making your life so miserable." I leaned back in my chair. "Dr. Ben is in the house. Time to tell him what's on your mind."

"But we didn't come here today to talk about me and my problems," he replied. "What about you and your stuff? It sounds like you and Linda..."

I wouldn't let him finish. I waved my hand dismissively and said, "My time is up. This is your time. To tell you the truth, I am sick to death of my stories. You'd be doing me a huge favor by changing the channel for a while and letting me hear somebody *else's* story for a change." I clapped my hands together. "So let's dive in. Dr. Ben is a busy man and his hourly rate is off the charts, so you don't want to be wasting any valuable minutes."

CHAPTER FIFTY-ONE

The Linda thing bugged me for another whole week. I just didn't know where to put it in my mental storage shed. On the one hand, it was both affirming and ego-inflating to have my ex-wife flirting with me again. On the other hand – the *bigger* hand in this case – I wanted the whole thing to just go away. I had just begun to put together a new life, one that didn't include Linda, and I didn't want to jeopardize that new life. I was to the point that I could say that I loved Marsha, I really did, and three was a crowd when it came to the love game.

As I thought about it some more the question came up: Did I still love Linda? My immediate answer had always been a resounding "Yes!" but now I was wondering if that had just become a habit and underneath that habit was a different answer, the *real* answer. I knew that we had loved each other at one time in the past and I knew that I loved how the two of us had produced a child as wonderful as Kylie, but did I still love her? I didn't have a definitive answer to that question yet but the fact that I was even asking it told me a lot. I tucked it away for further study.

Foremost on my mind for this day was a field trip that I had agreed to chaperone for Teens Rule. I hadn't been back to the Y for weeks, and then Griz had called me to see if I could help with this trip he had organized to the Basketball Hall of Fame down in Springfield. "We miss your ass around here," he had said on the phone in his inimitable Griz way. "And besides, we got twenty kids signed up fer this thing and I can't watch 'em all myself."

I quickly agreed to help, mostly out of a sense of guilt from having shirked my Teens Rule duties for so long, but after hanging up I asked myself, "What did you just do?" The thought of being responsible for the whereabouts and actions of twenty squirrelly teenage boys in a strange place, away from the safe confines of the YMCA, was a bit daunting. But it was too late for any second-guessing: I had agreed to help and Griz needed me.

When I got to the Y that morning most of the boys had already arrived and they were out of control. They were running around, screaming, wrestling with each other, and swinging backpacks at whatever moved. In the center of it all was Griz, just standing there sipping on his coffee with a calm serenity that belonged on the face of a man who was watching a sunrise or staring out at the ocean, not standing in the middle of a teenage tornado. He saw me and waved. I picked my way through the gauntlet of whirling backpacks and flying teens and made my way, unscathed, to his side. "Hey there, Luke," he said jovially. "Glad you could make it."

I wanted to say "Me too" but couldn't quite get the words out just yet. "You've got quite a group here," was what came out of my mouth.

He scanned the chaos and chuckled. "Yeah, it's quite a collection, that's fer sure. Seems like all the acrokids signed up fer this trip."

"Acrokids?"

"I heard that somewhere and I liked it." He leaned in and whispered, "It means all the kids with acronyms next to their names. ADD, ADHD, PDS." He winked. "You know, the wild ones."

"What's PDS? I haven't heard of that one before."

"That's 'cuz it's a Griz original. Stands fer Pretty Damned Sly. I save that one fer the real special ones." Another wink.

It was then that I spotted Cody. He was standing on the edge of a cluster of kids, pretending that he was a part of the group when, in reality, I knew that he wasn't. I yelled his name and, when he looked over at me, I threw him a smile and a wave. He ignored me. He pretended he didn't see me and turned his attention back to the group of boys. "What the…" I muttered.

Griz must have heard me because he said, "Looks like you've got someone pissed off at you."

"Yeah, it does," I agreed. "But I don't know how that could be. I haven't been around enough lately to do anything to him."

"That might be part of the problem. I don't know fer sure but from what I've seen and heard, that boy Cody has some real issues around the theme of folks leavin' him behind."

I flashed on Cody's story and realized that Griz was probably dead on with his assessment. "Yeah, you may be right on that one," I replied softly, suddenly feeling like a jerk.

"And besides," he added, perhaps thinking that I hadn't been humbled enough, "don't ferget what I told you on yer first day on the job." He saw my look of confusion and said, "Let 'em come to you." He nodded in Cody's direction. "An adult yellin' to a kid that age is like slappin' a big ol' sign on his back that says *I'm uncool* to all of his buddies."

"I guess I'm a little out of practice."

He slapped me on the back. "Don't worry. You'll get the hang of it again. You've just been outta the saddle a little too long."

His comments swirled in the air between us for a while and I knew he wanted me to say that I would be coming back to Teens Rule on a more regular basis, but I wasn't ready to make that promise just yet. I felt like there were still some things that I had to sort out before I could make any commitments like that. So, all I said was, "Yeah, I guess you're right," and left it at that.

I pretended to watch a group of kids wrestling in front of us, but I could see out of the corner of my eye that Griz was looking at me, hard. I knew he wanted to just ask me point blank if I was coming back to work with him at the Y but, bless his heart, he just swallowed the question and instead he simply asked, "So how are things?"

I shrugged. "A little confusing right now." I didn't want to get into the whole Linda thing with him, so I added, "But nothing that won't work itself out with a little time." I turned to face him. "How about you? Any more word from Annie and the boys?" Classic deflection.

He grinned. "I just spoke with Dean and Jerry the other day as a matter of fact. They're both doin' great and we're talkin' about a possible visit sometime this summer."

"That's great, Griz!" I returned the slap on the back. "You must be thrilled."

His grin broadened. "I am. I haven't seen my boys for a long time." I thought I detected a small quaver in his voice as he added, "Too long."

The bus driver then came over, probably offering a welcome emotional respite for Griz, and said, "Bus is ready to go. You can load 'em up any time you want."

Griz quickly returned to his role of Teen Rustler and shouted, "Okay gang, let's load 'em up."

The boys didn't exactly snap to attention and then march in formation at the sound of Griz's voice, but they did slowly make their way to the bus with occasional side trips to chase a friend or throw a rock. What was it about boys and rocks? I too recalled not being able to walk by a stray rock when I was their age without kicking it, juggling it, or throwing it at something. It was some sort of male imperative that we were unable to resist. I smiled at the memories.

I waited until everyone else was on the bus before climbing on. It was a small bus, one of those half-buses built for groups like ours, and once on the bus I looked around for an available seat. Griz was already sitting with a kid so I looked further down the aisle. There was no way I was going to head to the very back of the bus, where the very worst of the acrokids had taken up residence, so I glanced at the middle aisles. I quickly spotted an empty seat about halfway down the aisle, right next to Cody. I hesitated for a moment and then, after whispering a quick "fucket" to myself, headed for the empty seat.

I sat down next to him and he immediately turned his head towards the window. I took in a deep breath and said, "Look, I know you're upset with me and I want you to know that I think you have every right to be." No response. "I'm sorry that I haven't been coming around lately but I've been busy with some other things and, well…"

He turned abruptly so that he was facing me and the look on his face could only be described as pure hate. "I don't care if I ever see you again," he screamed in his high, squeaky voice, though it hardly caused a dent in the din that filled the bus. Then, after tossing me one more venom-filled look, he turned back to the window.

I did a quick scan of the bus and saw that nobody else was really paying attention to the drama that was playing out in our seat. That was good. I waited a few beats, to allow Cody to settle down a little bit, and then said, "I know you don't mean that, that you're just pissed off at me because I did exactly what every other adult in your life has done to you." I paused for a bit, both to see if my words were having any impact and to kick myself for sounding like some Dr. Phil wannabe. His body language seemed less agitated and I took that as a good sign. The next words came out of my mouth before my Internal Editor got his hands on them. "I want you to know that I'm going to be coming around the Y more often from now on. I promise." When my Internal Editor heard what I had just said he was pissed: I had just delivered a promise that I had hesitated to make with Griz just a few minutes earlier. What was I thinking? But it was too late now; the promise had been made and now I had no choice but to follow through on it.

Cody provided no visible sign that he'd heard what I just said but I knew that he heard me. For him, the final proof could only come with time. The poor kid had probably been given so many empty promises in his short life that "I'll believe it when I see it" had most likely become his personal mantra. My job now was to make sure he saw what had just been promised. I felt my muscles tighten ever so slightly.

CHAPTER FIFTY-TWO

Time continued to whiz by at an alarming rate. April came and went and before I knew it the calendar was being flipped over to May. I'd managed to keep my promise to Cody and showed up at Teens Rule at least four afternoons a week for the entire month following the field trip. It was tough on some days, but I did it. I'd established enough of a track record of consistency that he started to trust me again and we quickly became real pals. It felt good. I'd even had him over to the house a couple of times and he and Marsha hit it off immediately. Life was finding a good rhythm and I welcomed the respite from the drama that had become my life. It was on the first Friday of May that the respite ended abruptly, and my life took one more huge turn.

It was a gorgeous Friday; one of those rare spring treats that Mother Nature tosses at New Englanders, with bright blue skies, a thermometer hovering around seventy degrees, and zero humidity. A perfect day that folks from California wouldn't bat an eye at but which weather-battered New Englanders give thanks for because they know it won't last. It was my day to watch Jake, which was fine, but I knew that it would kill me to watch a day such as this one just come and go through Jake's bedroom window. So, I came up with an idea.

It took some planning for several days before, but hearing the weather guys talk about the Friday-to-come, and how gorgeous it was going to be, convinced me that all the effort would be worth it. With everything finally in place, I walked into Jake's bedroom that Friday morning and said, "You ready?"

He blinked the sleep from his eyes and then said, "For what?"

"For an adventure," I replied as I began his morning routine.

I kept one eye on his face so I could see what he was saying as I changed his diaper and cleaned him up. "What do u have in mind?" he blinked out.

"We're going to get out and enjoy this beautiful day together."

"How?"

I smiled. "You'll see." I finished changing his diaper and then went over to the dresser to search for clothes. "And you're going to wear real clothes for a change, my friend. No tear-away pajamas today." I reached into the drawer and pulled out a long-sleeved polo shirt. I held it up so he could see it from the bed. "Nice, huh?"

"Studly," he blinked.

I laughed. "Studly's good." I grabbed a pair of sweatpants from another drawer and went back to the bed. I surveyed all the tubes and wires attached to his body and heaved a deep sigh. "Okay Jake, here's the deal. For us to have this adventure I'm going to have to take all this stuff off you and leave it off for a few hours. Is that okay with you?"

"U bet," he replied quickly.

I still wasn't sure what each of the tubes and wires was for, but what I did know was that each of them served a purpose in the overall goal of keeping Jake alive. One machine helped him to breathe whenever he struggled with that and another one delivered an electrical shock to his heart if it ever decided to stop. Those were the important ones. I had yet to see either machine in action during my Fridays with him and it was that lack of firsthand experience that gave me the confidence to do what I was about to do. I slowly disconnected each tube and wire from his body, making careful mental notes on how to reconnect each of them when we returned, and it wasn't long before he was completely free of all connections. "There," I said as I stood back to look him over. "Jake unplugged."

"Ha, ha," he blinked.

"Now for the final touch," I said as I picked up the shirt and sweatpants. I stripped him down and then struggled for a while to get him into his new clothes. I saw very quickly why Yancy had opted for the tear-away versions as it was very difficult to manipulate all his lifeless limbs into the various sleeves and pant legs. Finally, my mission was accomplished, and I stepped back with a flourish and said, "Voila!"

"How do I look?" he asked.

"I'll show you." I went off into mine and Marsha's bedroom, grabbed her mirror, and then returned to his bedside. I propped him up against the headboard and put my hand on his chest so he wouldn't fall, then held up the mirror with my other hand so he could see himself. "Whaddaya think?"

"Studly as hell," he blinked.

"That's for damned sure," I replied with a chuckle. I then lowered the mirror and, making sure his head didn't flop forward, lowered him back down to a reclining position in the bed. "Give me a sec, okay?" He blinked a "yes" and I buzzed around the room one last time, throwing whatever items I thought might come in handy into a backpack. Satisfied that I had everything I'd need, I went back to his side and said, "Ready?"

"Not sure what for but ready."

I reached under his body and scooped him up like a new bride. "Then let's go," I said. I turned and headed out of the bedroom, down the hall, through the kitchen, and out the back door. Jake felt like he'd gotten even lighter since the last time I'd lifted him up, if that was even possible, and I had no problem negotiating all the obstacles and doors with him in my arms.

Once outside, I headed for the driveway and, once there, turned Jake so he could see what was waiting for us there. "Ta da!" I said triumphantly. I looked down at his face and saw that a single tear was snaking its way down his cheek. He didn't say anything; he just sat there and stared as more tears joined the stream that snaked its way down his face and off his chin.

"Okay," I finally said, "I don't want to have to go back and change you out of wet clothes so let's get this party started." Truth was, I didn't want to start crying myself. I carried him over to where the bike was sitting in the driveway and lowered Jake into the special seat that had been built into the front of the bike. I'd never seen anything like it before but when I told the guy at the bike shop what I wanted to do he had steered me towards a guy named Chris who built customized bikes for all kinds of things. As it turned out, my request wasn't all that special, and he had a bike on hand that was perfect for me and Jake.

"I get people in here all the time who want to do this kind of thing," he'd told me when I walked into his small shop that day. "That's why I started this business in the first place. I had a nephew who was battling leukemia a few years back and I knew how much he'd loved his bike, so I wanted to get him out one last time. There was nothing available that would allow me to do that, so I went to work on finding an answer." He looked down at the bike that I would eventually rent and patted the handlebars. "It took me two weeks to build the prototype for this, but I got it done in time to take Billy out a few times before he gave up the fight."

I didn't know what to say so I said nothing; one small plus to getting older: knowing when to keep your mouth shut. After adequate time had passed to honor Billy's memory, I said, "I know Jake is going to love the hell out of this."

Then Chris caught me totally off guard when he looked up from the bike, a quizzical look on his face, and said, "Jake? That wouldn't be Jake Graves, would it?"

Stunned, I replied, "Actually, yeah it is Jake Graves. You know him?"

A smile cracked across his face. "We used to be riding buddies. That guy was a freakin' genius on a mountain bike." A far-off look took over his face. "He used to take on trails that nobody else would even *think* about tackling. I used to think he had a death wish or something, but then I saw that the guy was just fearless." He nodded a few times and then added, "And talented as hell."

"Yeah, so I've been told."

His eyes came back to mine. "I'd heard that he was sick, but I didn't know he was *that* sick. I hadn't seen him up on the trails for a while, but I'd just assumed that he'd eventually kick whatever he had and I'd see him up there again, bombing down some hill."

"I don't think he's gonna be able to kick this one."

"That's too bad."

"Yeah, it is."

"What'd you say your name was again?"

"Ben. Ben Weaver."

He reached out his hand and I shook it. "Well Ben, a friend of Jake's is a friend of mine." We continued shaking hands in that silent moment of bonding that men go through and then he added, "Tell him Chris says hi, would you?"

"I sure will."

He chuckled as he let go of my hand. "Actually, you'd better tell him that it's Red Man who said hi or he won't know who it is you're talking about." He saw my confused look and said, "Jake had a nickname for everybody. He took one look at my red hair and red bike when we first met, and I was Red Man to him from that day onward."

"Red Man it is then."

He clapped his hands together. "So how is it that I can help you with this project of yours, Ben?" We then spent the next couple of hours rigging up the bike and its attached rumble seat with belts, straps, and other gear so that Jake could ride with me securely, and comfortably, during our upcoming outing.

Once I had Jake in his seat, I began the process of lashing, cinching, and securing the dozen or so straps across his legs, torso and head; knowing that Jake had zero muscle control, I told Chris that I wanted to be sure that every one of Jake's body parts was accounted for and secured. "Red Man says hi by the way," I said as I cinched the forehead strap into place.

"Good guy," he blinked in reply.

"He tells me that you were quite the daredevil on your bike."

"Was."

"He also said that he thought you had a death wish. Is that true?"

No reply. I had said it as a throwaway line, just to make conversation, but his lack of a response gave my gut a small nudge. "Did you hear me?" I asked.

"I herd u."

I stepped back and looked him in the eye. "What do you have to say to that?"

"Didn't then. Do now."

I knew where this was headed and decided to change the subject. "So, what do you think of this contraption that Chris rigged up for you?"

"Nice. Who Chris?"

I smiled. "Oops, I mean Red Man. He told me that you wouldn't know who Chris was."

"Where r we going?"

I continued strapping him in. "We're going to go on a long ride and see where the fates take us."

"Like it out here."

"How long has it been since you've been outside, Jake?"

"Months. Year. Not sure."

My heart sank. The grim reality of Jake's recent past hit me in the face like a wrecking ball. For a guy like Jake, who thrived on being physical in the outdoors, it must have been the worst kind of torture when he first became sentenced to a life in bed. "That's a long time," was all I could think to murmur in response.

"Smells good out here."

I suddenly became aware of the cacophony of scents that filled my nostrils, the most overwhelming of which was the scent of fresh, sweet lilac, a sure sign of spring in New England. "Yes, it does," I agreed.

"Smells alive. Not used to that."

I flashed on the stale, heavy air – saturated with an amalgamation of unpleasant odors - that typically filled Jake's room and I nodded my agreement. "Yeah, I can see why you say that, Wild Man." I smiled at my use of the nickname that Chris had told me belonged to Jake at one time.

"Used to like that name."

"Red Man says you wore it well."

I finished securing the last strap and then stepped back to check it all out one last time. He looked like something you'd see in a Frankenstein movie – strapped to the chair before the jolt of electricity was delivered – the only difference being that Jake looked very un-monsterlike, his body so withered that he would have a hard time scaring anything larger than a mouse. I gave him the thumbs up. "Looks good. You ready to roll?"

"Let's go."

I suddenly remembered one last piece of business. I stepped towards Jake and gave him my very best I-mean-business look. "You have to promise me just one thing before we take off."

"What."

"Marsha knows absolutely nothing about any of this and we have to keep it that way, okay?"

"K."

"She would flip out big time if she knew that I took you off your machines like this."

"U r right. Secret is safe."

I smiled a conspiratorial smile. "Then let the guy adventure begin." Not waiting to see if he said anything in response, I walked over to the side of the bike, climbed onto the seat, kicked up the kickstand, and shoved off.

It took a while to get the hang of it – the added weight in the front of the bike creating unique balance issues – but it wasn't long before I got it all figured out and we were cruising down the street at a pretty good clip. A part of me wished that I could see Jake's face as we whizzed down the street but then I remembered that I wouldn't be able to see much anyway, seeing as none of his facial muscles worked, so I was content to just be the driver and leave Jake alone with his thoughts for a while.

I chose all quiet, low-traffic streets and snaked my way towards the University and a public park that I knew abutted its south end. The park was filled with cherry blossoms, daffodils, and forsythia this time of year and I wanted to share that visual feast with Jake. It took us about a half hour, but we arrived at the park unscathed and I steered the bike towards a small glade surrounded by cherry trees at the far end of the park. The park was quiet this time of the day so, except for a smattering of students sitting on benches reading their books, we had the place pretty much to ourselves. Every person that we did pass, however, couldn't resist staring at our little two-person caravan as it went by. I had to admit that we looked unique, and I would have stared at us too.

Once at the glade, I dismounted the bike and walked it the last dozen or so steps from the sidewalk to a nearby bench. I positioned the bike so Jake could feel the sunshine on his face, as well as see the display of bright pink blossoms against the backdrop of a drop-dead-gorgeous, impossibly blue sky. It was stunning to me so I could only imagine what it was to Jake. Satisfied that he was well-situated, I sat down on the bench in front of him and asked, "So, what do you think?" I waved my arms around as if I had created this amazing painting that stretched in front of him.

"Butiful," was his one-word reply.

"Yeah, I agree. I've always liked this place, especially this time of year."

"Thanks for sharing."

"No problem. What did you think of the ride here?"

"Culdnt stop smiling," he blinked out. Then, as an apparent after-thought, he added, "Inside."

I chuckled. "I'm glad you enjoyed it."

Then - as if through an unspoken agreement that words would no longer be adequate - we just sat there for a long while, taking everything in and processing it all in our own, private way. It was another person's voice that broke our reverie.

"Ben?" the voice asked from behind me. I knew who the owner of the voice was before I even turned around. "Is that you?" the voice asked.

I turned on the bench and saw Linda walking in our direction. My heart rate went from zero to sixty in a split second. I stood up and greeted her with a quick hug. "Hey there, Linda," I said as casually as I could. "What brings you to this neck of the woods?"

She stepped back out of the embrace. "I was going to ask you the very same question," she replied as she stole a few quick glances over my shoulder at Jake sitting behind me. "I was between classes and thought I'd go for a short walk so I could enjoy part of this day."

I stepped aside so she could get a good look at him and said, "And I just wanted to bring Jake here, so he could see the cherry blossoms." I walked over to Jake's side, placed my hand on his shoulder, and said, "Linda, meet Jake. Jake, this is Linda. My ex-wife."

She stepped forward and nodded down at Jake. "Nice to meet you, Jake," she said with a smile. It was a good smile, one that wasn't manufactured, and I could feel my insides stir at the sight of that smile.

I then looked down at Jake and waited until he was done blinking out his response before turning my attention back to Linda. "He says that it's nice to meet you too."

She looked baffled. "How did you…"

"Morse Code," I replied. "Jake here has Lou Gehrig's Disease and the only thing left that he can control are his eyelids. So that's how he communicates."

I could see that she had a million questions swirling through her head but the one that eventually popped out of her mouth was, "And how do you know Jake?"

It was my turn to have a million things run through my mind but the response that I settled on was, "We're friends. I take care of him on Fridays." Simple, true, and not so vague as to invite further inquiry. I said a silent prayer that she wouldn't dig any deeper with more questions.

She opened her mouth slightly several times, as if getting ready to speak, but she ultimately just nodded, telling me that she wouldn't be asking any more Jake questions. That was good. "It's funny that I found you here," she then said, "because I was going to call you."

"Oh yeah? About what?" I went back over to the bench and motioned for her to sit down, which she did. I sat down next to her.

Her eyes went to the ground. "I wanted to apologize for how I acted the last time we were together. It was…inappropriate."

I felt a little uneasy having this discussion in front of Jake, but I went ahead anyway; I would explain everything to him later. "How so?" I asked innocently, though I knew exactly what she was talking about.

She looked up at me and threw me an ironic smile. She was on to me. "You know exactly what I mean, Ben."

"Are you talking about the fact that we were actually being civil to one another for a change? Or that we may be getting to the point where we can say that we like each other again? Is that what you're talking about?"

"No, no, all that is good, and I'm glad for it." Her eyes went to the sky. "It's just that it felt like maybe we were both trying to rekindle something that shouldn't be rekindled, that's all."

Now I was feeling uncomfortable having Jake within ear-shot. But I was also feeling a little pissed off at what Linda had just said and my anger won out over my embarrassment. "And what makes you so sure that what we were feeling was such a bad thing? Maybe there are some things that happen for a reason."

"And maybe there are some things that we do just because they feel good at the time, but they aren't the best things for us in the long run." She reached over and placed her hand on my arm. "I'm glad that you don't seem to be as angry at me as you once were, Ben, believe me I am. But I don't want your lack of anger to be interpreted as anything more than what it is."

I looked over at her, my eyes blazing. "Hey, there were two people standing there that day."

She took her hand away. "Yes, that's true, there was. And what I've had to realize is that I will always love you and what we had together at one time. The fact that we have a daughter to-gether means that we will always be connected in some way, but I don't want that connection to cloud what we know to be true."

"Which is what exactly?"

She heaved a deep sigh. "That you and I just don't belong together. We tried it and we failed. The best thing for us to do now is keep our eyes forward, on these new lives that we've cre-ated for ourselves."

She was right with everything she said, I knew that. But hear-ing her say it hurt, deeply, because I think I secretly wanted it to be *me* saying those words. But instead of voicing my agreement I gave in to the hurt and said, "Hey, it wasn't me who failed. You were the one that decided to call it quits." They were old, tired words that I'd said in one form or another a thousand times before, but this time they felt different as they came out; they didn't pro-vide any sense of satisfaction or relief and they actually tasted a little bitter in my mouth. It was as if I was a former smoker taking a drag on his first cigarette in ten years and my body, unaccus-tomed to the harsh chemicals that I was inhaling, had a violent reaction to its old friends, wanting to expel the poisons rather than embrace them.

Linda shook her head and started to stand but I grabbed her arm and pulled her back to the bench. "Wait," I said. "I'm sorry I said that. It was completely uncalled for and I was way out of line." I took a deep breath and continued before she could say anything. "Truth is, I was thinking the exact same things about us." I then looked at the ground, ashamed at what I was about to say. "It just bruised my ego a little to hear you say it, that's all."

Her hand came to rest on my arm again. "Thanks for saying that, Ben. I appreciate it." She then punched me playfully and I looked up to see her smiling. "And why the hell did you learn this apologizing thing so late in life?"

I shrugged. "Slow learner." I hesitated for a moment, unsure if I wanted to do what I was thinking about doing, but then whispered a silent "*fucket*" in my head and said, "There're a few other things I wanted to tell you too."

"What's that?"

I nodded in Jake's direction. "Jake here is actually Marsha's husband."

"The Marsha who you brought to our house for Christmas?"

I nodded. "Same Marsha." I let her take in that piece of news for a few seconds and then said, "And I love her."

"You love Marsha?"

I nodded. "I do. And what I've realized just recently is that I don't want to do anything to jeopardize that love. That's why our little flirting episode the last time I saw you threw me for such a loop. It stirred up doubts that I didn't want to have."

"I'm sorry for that. I…"

"No, no more apologies. I think we both had to go through an episode like that in order to get here, where we are now."

"Which is?"

"Which is a point where we know for certain that what you and I had together is over, for good." I shook my head slowly.

"I've had one eye on the past for so long that I missed out on a lot of good stuff going on right in front of me. I don't want to do that anymore."

She rubbed my arm. I'm glad to hear that. You deserve better than that."

"I don't know about the deserving it part, but I sure like how it feels. It's a whole lot better than feeling pissed off and depressed all the time."

"I'll bet." She then looked down at her watch and said, "Shit!" She bolted to her feet and said, "I'm sorry Ben, but I'm already late for my next class. Can we continue this conversation some other time?"

"Sure, no problem."

She flashed me a sweet, sincere smile and then kissed me on the cheek. "This was a great talk. I'm glad we bumped into each other."

"Me too."

She tossed a "nice to meet you" at Jake and then took off at a half-jog down the sidewalk. I looked over at Jake and saw that he was still blinking out a "goodbye" to her back.

I then turned and watched her disappear into the distance, rehashing our conversation in my mind as I stood there. Once she was out of sight, I sat back down on the bench and said to Jake, "Quite the show, eh?"

"Fun to watch," he replied.

"Yeah, I'll bet."

"U both still luv each other."

"Yeah, we do."

"That good."

I smiled. "Yeah, I guess it is."

"Same with Marsha."

"What's the same with Marsha?"

"She still luv me."

I felt a tingling sensation in my cheeks, signaling approaching tears. "Yeah Jake, she still loves you a whole lot."

"That good."

I nodded. "Yeah, that is good. We are very lucky men, Jake," I then said, not stopping to think about how my words would make Jake feel, he who can't do anything more than bat his eyelid. Thankfully, he didn't seem to notice or take offense.

"She luv u too," he blinked out.

"Who? Marsha?"

"Yes."

I was surprised just how *un*-squirmy his comment made me feel, probably due to the trip I'd just taken down the Truth Path with Linda. "Yeah, I think you're right. I *hope* you're right. 'Cuz I sure love the heck out of her."

"She lucky. You good man."

The tingling sensation returned. "Thanks Jake. That means a lot to me coming from you. More than you can imagine."

"Welcome. Mean it."

"Yeah, I know you do." A thought then popped into my head and I said, "Jake, you have to promise me something."

"Won't tell Marsha about this."

I chuckled. "Yeah, exactly. I hate keeping secrets from her, but I don't want her worrying about anything getting rekindled with Linda. It ain't gonna happen, we know that now, so all this stuff would just hurt her unnecessarily. Agreed?"

"Agreed."

I nodded for emphasis. "Good."

"Favor from u."

Without thinking I said, "Sure, what is it."

"Let me die."

The three words served as a punch in the gut. All the good, warm feelings that had been stockpiling inside of me got pushed out of my body along with my breath. "Jake, we've covered this before, and…" I saw him start to blink so I stopped talking.

"Please listen to me."

I exhaled slowly. "Okay, I'll listen. Go ahead."

It took him several minutes to blink out the following little speech but what it lacked in length and structure it more than made up for in sheer power. "No life for me back there," he began. "Just a burden. Ready to go. Butiful day today. Good day to die." He paused for a moment and then added, "Please."

I just sat there, unsure of what to say. On the one hand, everything he said made sense and I would probably feel the exact same way if I was inside his body. I flashed on the life he had back in his bedroom, and it didn't take a genius to see that it was no life at all. Diapers, tubes, and lying motionless in the same bed, looking at the same four walls, every minute of every day was no way for a man to spend the last days of his life. I knew that.

But on the other hand, what he was asking of me was impossible; I could no more kill Jake than kill myself. And even if I *did* somehow muster the courage to grant this crazy wish of his, what the hell kind of future would that create for me and Marsha?!? Sure, I have a few small secrets that I've kept from her, but this…this dwarfed anything else that I could come up with on the whole I've-got-a-secret front. "*Gee Marsha,*" I could imagine me saying, "*I don't quite know how to tell you this but, well, the truth is…I killed your husband.*" Bam. Right between the eyes. Then there would be the look of total shock on her face that would soon be replaced by total contempt as she reached for the phone and called the police. No thanks.

"Jake, I get why you're asking this of me, I really do, but…truth is, I just don't have the guts to do it. I'm not a killer."

"Don't have to be."

"I don't have to be what?"

"Killer."

"But you just asked me…"

"To let me die. That all."

"But how are you going to die if I don't kill you?"

"Kill myself."

"If that's true, then why did you ask me?"

"Need u to promise to let me do it."

"What do you mean?"

"Not call for help. Just let me die."

The bigger question in my head was wondering how the hell a guy with zero control over his body was planning on killing himself – would he blink himself to death? – but the question that came out was more selfishly motivated. "What will I tell Marsha when she finds out that your dead body was picked up at a park that's miles from our house? I don't think she's going to believe that you *walked* here."

"Bring me home after dead."

I'm sure my voice went up a few octaves as I replied, "Bring you home? Just toss your dead body on the bike and haul you home? Pedal your carcass through town as if nothing was wrong? Is that your plan?"

"Yes. Look same as before."

I looked at him strapped into the bike, every appendage cinched in tight, and I realized that he was right: nobody would notice anything different. "But what would I tell Marsha…" I half-muttered to myself.

"That I died. She be releeved."

I thought to myself that Jake must be getting tired, or overly excited, because he was usually a very careful speller. Sure, he took shortcuts sometimes, but I always had the sense that any spelling mistakes were intentional on his part. Not this time. I didn't have the advantage of any body language to read, I just had my gut to give me clues, and my gut was telling me that Jake was feeling agitated. "Okay Jake, let me get all of this straight. You want me to just sit here while you kill yourself – using god knows what method – and then you want me to pedal you home, put you back into your bed, hook you up to all of those machines, and then call 911 to tell them that you stopped breathing. Is that about it?"

"Yes. Xacly."

Another mistake. The man was probably getting pretty wound up inside with all this talk about ending his life. "Jake, I don't know…"

"Plez."

Plez. I rolled the misspelled word around in my head for a while, trying to imagine the power and emotion that stood behind it, until a much larger, even more powerful word, stormed into my head and shoved it aside. "Fucket," I heard in my head. "Fucket," echoed again, much louder this time. "FUCKET!!!" reverberated in my ear a third time, so loud that I thought for sure Jake must have heard it. I looked over at him and saw that he was just sitting there, eyelid quiet, waiting for my answer. I took a deep breath, held it, and then blew it out slowly. "Okay," I finally said. "I'll do it."

CHAPTER FIFTY-THREE

The hospital was unbridled chaos. I sat in the Emergency Room waiting area and watched as it filled up with one wounded, bloodied body after another. "It's the warm weather," a nurse had said to me when I commented on the packed room. "We always get a crowd on these early spring days. People are so excited to be out hiking, biking, grilling, motorcycling, and the like that they forget themselves and do some pretty stupid things." She then flashed me a wry smile and said, "Spring Fever is a very real thing for doctors and nurses."

I settled in a chair between a kid with a broken arm and an older man with a pretty mashed up face. "Motorcycle," he said to me through a semi-toothless grin when he caught me glancing over at his face.

"How long have you been waiting here?" I asked.

He shrugged. "Couple hours. Probably be a couple more before I see a doc." He nodded towards the packed room. "They got their hands full here today and I just ain't banged up enough to go to the front of the line."

"You look pretty bad to me."

"Been worse before." He pointed up at his face. "These are just bumps and scrapes. I'll be fine." He smiled at me again and I returned the smile before turning my eyes and thoughts inward.

I settled back in my chair and replayed the past couple of crazy hours across my mind's screen. I was still finding the whole thing pretty damned surreal. First there was Jake back in the park, literally willing himself to die after I'd agreed to his plan. I couldn't believe how quickly he'd done it. From the time I said yes to the time that he failed to respond to my nudges couldn't have been more than a couple of minutes. *"He must have really wanted to leave,"* I remembered thinking.

Then the reality of what I'd just done hit me. Hard. That's when the tears came. I cried over his lifeless body for quite a while, as much for Jake's death as for the certain death of my relationship with Marsha. *"What the hell did I just do?"* played on a constant loop in my head as I wept, wanting more than anything else to rewind the clock and deliver another emphatic "NO!" to Jake's request.

But the reality of my situation soon settled in and so, finally accepting that Jake was gone, I got started on the plan that Jake and I had agreed on. I pedaled his dead body home, being careful to take side streets and see as few people as possible. Once home, I took the bike around to the back of the house, glanced around for any prying eyes, and then carried him into the house. I felt the huge ball of paranoia growing in my belly at that point.

It took me a long time to remember how to reconnect each of the tubes and wires that I'd pulled from his body that morning, my anxiety and growing paranoia only adding to my confusion. When I finally thought I had it right, I stepped back from the bed, took in one final calming breath and then took my cell phone out of my pocket. "Okay, Jake," I'd said out loud. "Showtime."

I thought I sounded convincingly frantic when I spoke with the 911 operator - perhaps attributable to the practice I'd gotten with my prior performance following my house fire - and the paramedics arrived at the house just a few minutes after I hung up. All my earlier concerns about the placement of Jake's tubes and wires were washed away when I watched the paramedics seemingly rip every one of them from his body in order to make room for their life-saving efforts. They tried everything –

paddles, needles, compressions – but I knew that it would all be in vain; there was no way that Jake would agree to come back to that body. He was finally free of his decaying, malfunctioning physical prison and I said a silent prayer that he was happy in his new home, wherever that was.

The paramedics eventually got Jake's body onto a gurney and, with an artificial respirator huffing away into his face, they carted him off to the waiting ambulance. It wasn't until I was on my way to the hospital, following behind the speeding ambulance, that I remembered a very important piece of the plan: call Marsha. I cursed myself many times over as I pulled out my cell phone again and dialed her work number. Thankfully, my call was forwarded to a receptionist who told me that Marsha was in a meeting. I told the receptionist that this was important and that she was to tell Marsha to call Ben as soon as possible. It wasn't until after I'd hung up that I thought about what I was going to say to Marsha and, more importantly, *how* I would say it. I couldn't stop sweating as I drove to the hospital.

It wasn't until I was at the hospital, and talking with a nurse, that Marsha called me back. "Ben?" she all but screamed into phone when I picked up. "What is it? What's wrong? Is Jake okay?" The three questions came out as one sentence because she never took a breath. She knew something was up; like every other woman I'd ever met, she had this sixth sense that told her when something about the world around her wasn't quite right. This female quality had always amazed me.

I took a deep breath before responding. "It's Jake," I began. "He stopped breathing, and…" That's all I managed to get out.

"Where are you now?" she blurted out.

"At the hospital. I…"

"I'll be right there," was all I heard before the connection went dead.

I paced nervously in the waiting room prior to her arrival and it wasn't long before she came bursting through the door. I had prepared an entire speech to give to her about what had happened, but she didn't give me a chance to deliver it. "Where is he?" was all she said when she strode in, her face a black-streaked mess of running mascara. She had been crying. A lot.

I wanted to hug her and comfort her but, despite her tear-streaked face, she didn't seem to want to be comforted. Her eyes were all business. So I simply pointed to a nearby swinging door and said, "They took him back there." I opened my mouth to say something else – something stupid probably – but she was gone before I could get it out. That was just as well.

She strode purposefully over to the nurse's station, said something to the nurse on duty, and then she disappeared through a door. And that was the last I'd seen of her. So here I sat, between the broken arm and the mashed-up face, waiting to deliver all the words that I'd had several hours to rehearse; words that would hopefully convince Marsha that I was sorry, for everything. I was sorry that Jake was dead. I was sorry that I hadn't called her sooner. I was sorry that I'd agreed to Jake's plan. And, most of all, I was sorry that I might have screwed up our relationship, the best thing that had happened to me in a long, long time.

I sat and stewed in my unsaid words for another couple of hours and watched as one-by-one the broken arms and mashed up bodies had their names called and they each disappeared through the same door that Marsha had walked through earlier. When it got to the point that I was seriously thinking about just saying "fucket" and walking out the door, Marsha appeared in front of me. I don't know where she'd come from – certainly not through the door that I'd been watching like a sentry for the past couple of hours – but she stood there in front of me and simply said, "Hi."

I looked up and saw that even though she had washed her face, and scrubbed off all the black streaks, she still looked like she'd been put through the wringer. Her eyes were red and swollen, her cheeks were blotchy, and her entire face looked tired and drawn. Despite all of that, however, hers was the face that I wanted to see more than anything else in the world and she looked beautiful to me. "Hi," I replied as I stood up. "How are you doing?"

"Been better," she said sadly. I could see more tears forming in her eyes. "I could really use a hug," she then said.

Without another thought I reached out and pulled her into a full embrace. She squeezed me in tight and that was when the tears started to fall from my eyes. The tears that fell were made up of equal parts guilt, relief, and love, but that didn't matter; all that mattered was that I was holding the woman I loved in my arms. "I'm sorry," I muttered repeatedly as we stood there hugging and crying. She had no idea that the "sorry" that I kept repeating in her ear was for far more than the pain that she was feeling and that if she actually *knew* all that I was sorry for, she would probably break the embrace – and my arm – in a heartbeat. But she didn't know, not yet, and for that I was extremely grateful.

She didn't say a word, but I could feel that she was crying too. I wanted to stand there in that embrace forever, partly because it felt so good but mostly because I knew that to break the embrace meant finally having to explain what had happened with Jake, and I wasn't in any kind of hurry to do *that*. So we stood there like that in the middle of the emergency room for a long, long time.

Eventually, however, the tears ran out and, after one last squeeze, we stepped out of the embrace. "Whew," she said as she wiped her face. "I'm exhausted." I didn't say anything as she continued to blot her face with her sleeve. "I must look pretty damned scary right now," she added.

I flashed her a warm smile, all eyes and no teeth. "You look great," I assured her.

"Thanks for the lie but I know better." She then stopped fussing over her face and looked up at me. "How are *you* doing? This has been quite a day for you too."

Uh, oh. Time to face the music. "I'm fine," I lied. "I…" I was struggling to find my next words when she raised her hand in a stop sign, effectively stopping me in my verbal tracks.

"Before you say another word, I want to tell you a little story." She lowered her hand and motioned to the empty chairs behind us. We both sat down and then she continued, "I had an interesting conversation with the doctor." She shifted around in her seat a little, in an apparent attempt to get more comfortable, but I wondered: *Does she know something? Is she just trying to make me sweat a little?*

Once settled, she said, "He was trying to explain to me what happened with Jake when he mentioned that the paramedics had noticed something was wrong with how Jake's defib machine was hooked up. Two of the leads were reversed." *Shit*, I thought. *They did notice after all. Shit, shit, shit.* I braced myself for the upcoming accusation as the future-that-would-never-be with Marsha flashed in front of me. It seemed like she waited days before delivering this next sentence but, ultimately, the long wait was worth it because it ended up being the sentence that would forever more be known as "The Best Sentence I'd Ever Heard." She reached over and placed her hand on my leg before saying, "I don't know what happened in Jake's bedroom today, Ben, but I want you to know that I don't *want* to know. Ever. It doesn't matter."

I didn't realize I'd been holding my breath until I relaxed a little and let out a huge exhale. I was tempted to say something, but I realized that anything I would say would come out sounding guilty, so I just sat there and rubbed her hand. I watched as her face changed from being somewhat calm and in control to being contorted and full of profound sadness. Tears once again filled her eyes and then streamed down her cheeks. "I've never told anyone this before, but Jake asked me to help him kill himself." I felt a jolt of electricity zip up my spine. She then looked over at me with her sad eyes and added, "Many times."

I held her gaze even though every part of me wanted to look away from her and hide my guilt-filled eyes from her. But to do that would be telling her something that she had just said she didn't want to know, and this was not a time for me to be selfish, I knew that. So, I set my jaw and reached up to wipe the tears from her cheek. "The first time he asked me," she continued, "was when he finally lost control of both of his arms. He'd lost control of his legs first, but he'd adjusted to that okay." She let out a small chuffing sound. "He'd even gone out and bought one of those bikes that you pedal with your arms. He loved that bike." She smiled and shook her head. "His goal was to get strong enough to pedal that thing across the country, as a fund-raiser for ALS research." We sat in silence for a while, rolling that vision of Jake slowly making his way across the United States around in our heads. After hearing what Red Man had to say about him, I would've given him good odds on finishing that trip if his body had held up.

"But it wasn't too long before he started to lose control of his arms," she continued, her smile now gone. "And having no arms was torture for Jake. That's when he started to give up." Another silence, this one much heavier than the last one. "He told me that if he couldn't use his bike, couldn't hug me, and couldn't even wipe his own ass, then there was no reason to live anymore." Her voice lowered to a whisper as she said, "That's when he started asking me to help him end it all."

Her eyes went to some far-off place as she said, "He had all kinds of ideas on how to do it. Poison. Smothering. At one point he even asked me to go get one of his guns and do it that way." Her head rolled slowly from side to side and the tears flowed faster. Her voice was barely audible now, but I heard her mutter, "But I couldn't do it. I couldn't do it." Her eyes then returned to mine and I could see the depth of her grief; they were the saddest eyes I'd ever seen. My own eyes welled up in response. "That isn't something that a husband should ask of his wife," she said, her voice stronger now. "I knew it was what he wanted, but how could I…" She didn't finish the sentence, there was no need to, as her tears escalated into all-out, shoulders-heaving, sobs. I slid closer to her and pulled her into a sideways embrace. She continued to mumble, "I couldn't do it…I couldn't do it" in broken, sob-wracked syllables as she cried into my chest.

The sobs eventually subsided but she stayed in the same position, her face buried in my chest. She took in a few calming breaths, exhaling slowly after each one, and then said, "So that's why I told you that I don't care what happened today." My body tensed and I hoped that she didn't feel it. I was glad that her eyes were still embedded in my chest. "Because all that matters is that Jake finally got what he wanted." She paused before adding in a whisper, "He's earned that."

And that marked the end of any discussion around the theme of "What Happened To Jake?" All of the details about our bike ride to the park, his death wish, the discussion of The Plan, the nerve-wracking ride home with his dead body, the 911 call, and all the rest of it just got gathered up, tossed into a large mental suitcase, and then placed in a corner of my brain's attic, never to be opened again. And that was fine with me.

CHAPTER FIFTY-FOUR

Jake's funeral was an entirely different affair compared to the service I'd attended for Charlie a few weeks earlier. The church where the service was held was packed to overflowing and the words that were shared that day painted a picture of a man whose life had been well spent. I thought on more than one occasion that I hoped that my own service would be this well-attended and filled with as many kind words. A large part of me doubted if that would be the case which cast a small, dark cloud over my thoughts throughout the service.

The dark cloud grew larger when, about halfway through the service, I saw Linda sneak in and sit down in the back of the church. My first thought when I saw her was: *"How did she hear about this?"* My second thought was: *"Good for her for coming."* And my third thought – the one that filled my head for the remainder of the service – was: *"Shit. The park. I can't let Marsha know that Linda met Jake in the park!"* Because that would lead to questions about what the hell Jake was doing at the park that day and that would in turn lead to the possibility that the Suitcase of Truth would have to get dragged out of the attic and opened. I felt my heart rate quicken and my palms started to drip with sweat.

Thankfully, I had told Marsha at home that morning that this was a day for her and her kids and that I would hang back and let them mourn without worrying about me. So, I was sitting a few rows back from Marsha, who was in the front row sandwiched between her daughters, and that allowed me to sweat and fret in my own little world. I decided that I would make a beeline to the back of the church just as soon as the service ended and let Linda know to keep our encounter in the park to herself in front of Marsha.

The service ended and, since I was sitting at the end of a row, I got into the aisle quickly. I made my way to the back of the church, going slowly enough as to not attract any attention, and would have made it to Linda in no time if not for an unplanned detour. "Hey, Ben," I heard somebody hiss at me from one of the pews.

I turned and saw Red Man standing a few people in and he was making his way towards me. I had no choice but to stop and wait for him, my eyes glancing furtively in Linda's direction. I could see that she was still seated and chatting with an older woman seated next to her. Good. I turned back to Red Man who was now free of the pews. "Hey Chris," I said.

We shook hands solemnly and then he said, "I didn't get a chance to talk to you when you brought the bike back and I was just wondering how the day went for you and Jake. Did the bike work out okay?"

I knew that Marsha was still up in the front of the church, but the Paranoid Ben still turned to make sure she wasn't within earshot. Satisfied that the coast was clear, I said to Chris, "It worked perfectly, Chris. Thanks again for your help that day. It meant the world to Jake to be able to get out on a bike one last time."

Chris smiled broadly. "Man, that's so good to hear. When I first heard about Jake's passing, I was worried that it might have happened before you guys had the chance to do your thing." He nodded a few times and then added, "I'm glad to hear that the Wild Man got to be in the saddle one last time."

Paranoid Ben then stepped back into the Captain's Chair as I said, "Hey Chris, can I ask a favor of you?"

"Sure. What is it?"

I leaned in conspiratorially and whispered, "Could we please keep the whole bike thing to ourselves?" I could see that he was confused by my request so I added, "We didn't tell Marsha about it and, well, let's just say that she may not have approved of our little adventure."

Understanding made its way across his face. "Ah, I get it. A little impromptu guy adventure, eh?"

I smiled. "Exactly."

He returned my smile. "That makes the whole thing even better. Jake would have done the exact same thing."

"I think you're right."

He winked. "No problem. Happy to keep that one locked away."

The web of conspiracy widened. Now I had to convince one more person to take the vow of silence. "It was great to see you again, Chris." I reached out and shook his hand while jerking my left thumb over my shoulder. "I have to go talk to someone else in the back of the church before she leaves."

"Great seeing you too," he replied with a smile. "I hope to see you again down at the shop." He then squeezed my hand extra hard and added in a whisper, "And don't worry. Your secret is safe with me."

"Thanks. And I will try to make it by the shop again, I promise." We swapped guy-looks that said the deal was sealed and then I turned to resume my search for Linda.

The aisles had filled up with people during my short conversation with Chris and I could no longer see Linda anywhere. *Shit.* I "excused me" my way through the crowd and it wasn't long before I was standing in the foyer of the church, looking from side to side for any sign of Linda but there was none. *Shit.* Then a scary thought hit me: What if she decided to go to the *front* of the church to offer her condolences to Marsha?" Panicked, I turned and re-entered the main part of the church. My eyes went to the front rows and I saw that Marsha and her daughters were still standing there talking with a growing circle of people. No sign of Linda. Relief swept through my body.

I went back out to the foyer and, still not seeing Linda, I went out the door to see if she had made her way outside. Knowing Linda, I felt confident that she wouldn't have left without having first offered her condolences to Marsha, so she had to be somewhere. As I walked out the door, I felt a small twinge of guilt that I was running around trying to cover my own ass while Marsha mourned her dead husband, but I quickly justified my actions under the heading of: "This Is For Marsha." My only goal was to maintain the silence that she had requested so, in truth, my actions were entirely selfless. That was of course total bullshit, but it helped to propel me forward.

Stepping outside I was hit right away with ultra-bright sunshine. It was a huge contrast to the dimly lit church, so it took my eyes a few seconds to adjust. Once they did, I saw Linda standing on the front sidewalk talking with…Chris. "What the hell?" I said out loud, though nobody was close enough to hear me. Why would those two be talking? Does she know Chris? The whole thing was getting too damned weird. I took a deep breath and headed down the steps towards the two of them.

Chris saw me first and said with a smile, "Well hello again."

Linda turned to see who he was talking to and she too smiled when she saw me. "Hey Ben." She stepped towards me and gave me a hug. "How are you doing?"

"I'm doing okay," I lied. "Funerals are never what I would call happy occasions."

"No, they're not," she agreed.

Then the questions started to stack up at my lips and it was all I could do to let them out just one at a time. "What are you doing here, Linda?" I asked as casually as I could.

She shrugged. "I saw the death notice in the paper and just thought I'd stop by to support you and Marsha." She shrugged again. "That's all."

I nodded. "Well, that was nice of you," I said, though it was all I could do to not just spit out my next question. I waited a beat or two – long enough to not sound frantic – and then asked, while wagging my index finger between Chris and Linda, "Do you two know each other?"

She looked at Chris then looked back at me. "I was going to ask you the very same question." She nodded at Chris. "Chris here owns the bike shop where William and I always take out bikes." She smiled. "He sold us Kylie's first bike without training wheels." Yet another harsh reminder of the pieces of my daughter's life that The Worm was stealing from me. But that didn't seem to matter, not today anyway, so I shoved that thought aside as she added, "So how do *you* know Chris?"

I did a quick assessment of the situation and decided that full disclosure would be the best option at this point. "Chris is the one who designed the bike that you saw at the park the other day, the one with Jake in it." I glanced over my shoulder, to appease Paranoid Ben, and then looked at Chris who appeared to be confused by my disclosure which, I had to admit, would have confused me too after what I'd just said to him a few minutes earlier inside the church. "Look," I said in a lowered voice, "I don't know when Marsha is going to come walking out of that church so I'm just going to cut to the chase." I threw a glance at Linda and saw that her brow was now furrowed, telling me that she was very interested in what I was about to say. I nodded at Chris and said, "As I just told Chris inside, Marsha doesn't know anything about my little bike adventure with Jake and I'd like to keep it that way. Right now, you two are the only ones who know about it so I'd appreciate it if we could keep this secret right here in this small circle. Whaddaya say?"

The furrows deepened in Linda's forehead for a moment and then they suddenly disappeared. "Sure, no problem," she said. "I can do that."

"I already took my blood oath on this one," Chris chimed in.

I heaved a sigh. "Thanks, you guys. I appreciate it."

"Just one question," Chris then added. "How is it that *you* two know each other?"

Linda and I looked at each other and shared a smile. "Oh, we go way back," I replied.

"Ben is my ex," Linda said.

"Your ex?" he said, seeming genuinely surprised. "Wow, you guys don't seem like a divorced couple. I usually sense tension and weirdness when I'm around divorced couples, but you guys seem so…friendly."

Linda and I shared a look – it was a good look, filled with sweetness and kindness – and then I said, "Yeah, we are friends. It took a while, but we're good friends now." Linda threw me a small, barely perceptible, nod which told me that she agreed. It was a great moment.

"Good for you guys," Chris said, breaking the moment. "I hope that if I ever get divorced that I can be around my ex like this."

I turned my attention to Chris. "My advice to you is, don't ever get divorced. Trust me on that one."

It was at that moment that Marsha walked up. I hadn't seen her coming and her voice caught me by surprise. "There you are," she said from behind me. "I thought that maybe you decided to leave me at the altar."

I turned, wondering how much, if any, of our conversation she'd heard. I opened my arms and she stepped into my embrace, the warmth of the hug telling me that all was good. When she stepped out of the hug I said, "How are you doing?"

"Fine." She jerked a thumb over her shoulder. "I left Nickie and Sarah to deal with all of the aunts back in the church." She nodded towards Chris and Linda. "This looks like quite the party."

Linda was the first to step forward and hug Marsha. "I'm sorry for your loss Marsha," she said as they embraced. I had to admit that it warmed my heart to see the two of them hugging; my two lives were officially meshing together.

Chris then stepped forward and gave her an awkward hug. "I'm sorry too," he said. "Jake was a great guy."

"Yes, yes he was," Marsha concurred. Her face then scrunched a little as she said to Chris, "Do we know each other?"

Chris's face reddened slightly. "Oh, I'm sorry. My name is Chris. I, uh, used to bike with Jake."

Marsha smiled warmly. "You wouldn't be Red Man, would you?"

"Yeah, that's me," he replied with a hint of pride.

"Jake used to talk about you a lot. He enjoyed your rides together."

A broad grin took over his face. "Likewise. Wild Man was pretty amazing on a bike."

"Wild Man?"

The smile dropped from his face. "Uh, yeah." Chris glanced at me, then glanced at Marsha, and back to me again. He was obviously nervous – like he'd revealed something that was supposed to be kept locked away – and all I could think was: *Be cool. Don't make her suspicious.* I decided that it was time to step in.

"Seems that Jake was quite the daredevil on his bike," I interjected casually. "Chris here was telling us some of the stories from Jake's earlier days."

Marsha heaved a deep sigh, which thankfully masked the equally deep sigh that Chris had heaved simultaneously; he was glad to be off the hook. "I always told him that he was going to die on that bike of his," she said, completely unaware of how much her words impacted the three people standing in front of her. We didn't dare look at each other but I could feel their invisible eyes on my face. What Chris and Linda *didn't* know was just *how* accurate Marsha's words had been. I choked down a small gulp. "I don't know what it was with him," she continued, "but he seemed to be happiest when he was looking Death in the face and then thumbing his nose at Him." She shook her head. "I guess Mr. Death always gets the last word in, eh?"

Nobody said anything for a few beats. I eventually broke the silence when I said, "Yeah, that bastard doesn't make too many exceptions, that's for sure."

"It's funny though," Marsha replied, "but there would have been something very poetic about Jake dying on his bike rather than on his back in a bed." She paused for a moment, as if she wanted her words to jab at me a little while longer, and then added, "He would have liked that."

A thundering herd of questions and comments quickly formed in my head and I had to rein them in like wild horses: *Does she know how he died? How did she figure it out? Is she mad about it? Happy about it? Or was that just an off-handed remark?* It took every ounce of strength that I had to not just start blurting everything out and telling her the whole story. But I didn't. I just waited until the last of the internal wild horses was under control and then said, "It's a shame that we don't get to make that choice, about how and when we die." It was when my words bounced back at me, and I actually *heard* them, that I smiled; the gift that I had given Jake was that he got to make that choice. He had died at a time, and in a place, that felt right to him. He didn't have to lay there and just wait for Mr. Death to come around in His own sweet time; he got to lower the final curtain when he knew he'd run out of reasons to hang around on stage, on his own terms in his own way. I suddenly felt proud to have been a part of that process with Jake. It was then that I formulated Rule #8 For My New Life in my head: ***There is no shame in asking for help.***

CHAPTER FIFTY-FIVE

The following weekend arrived, and I woke up on Saturday morning to an empty bed; Marsha was gone, which was unusual for her on Saturday mornings, one of her few mornings to sleep in. I listened for the shower or any other sounds of activity but heard nothing. I got up, went through my morning routine, threw on some clothes and headed out to the kitchen. I followed my nose towards the irresistible aroma of brewing coffee that was wafting through the house.

Once in the kitchen I saw the mess that we'd left from the night before, when we'd started prepping for the dinner we'd be hosting Saturday night. Both of Marsha's daughters would be coming over, along with their husbands and children, and she wanted to make it extra special which meant two full days of preparation. I poured a cup of coffee from the half-full pot and made my way out to the dining room. That's where I found Marsha.

She had her old sweats on, and she was halfway through the re-painting process on her Therapy Wall. The new color was a bold shade of blue. "Nice color," I said as I walked in.

She stopped painting and looked over at me with a warm smile on her face. "Good morning."

"Good morning right back at'cha." I went over and planted a kiss on the cleanest of her two cheeks.

"You sleep okay?"

I took a sip from my cup. "Better than you did it seems."

She sighed. "Yeah, I got up pretty early this morning. Too many things running through my mind." She nodded at the wall. "So, I decided to get up and do this one last time."

"What color is that?"

"It's called Cobalt Blue. It was Jake's favorite color."

"I like it."

She smiled. "That's good to hear because we're going to be living with this one for a long, long time."

"Need some help?"

"Always." The smile on her face morphed into one that exuded huge quantities of warmth and love and I felt my knees weaken at the sight of it.

I tried to return the smile, but I had a feeling that mine didn't have quite the same wattage as hers did; it was something that I would need to work on. I set my cup down and grabbed a paintbrush. "Well then move over." I gave her a playful hip check and she slid over a step.

"So, are you excited about hosting my clan tonight?"

"Actually, yeah I am. I like Nickie and Sarah." That was the truth. I'd only been around them a handful of times but each time I saw them I became increasingly impressed with what nice young women they were. The first encounter had been a little rough, as I felt like they were trying to size me up and figure out my intentions for their mother. But every visit after that had been smooth and pleasant. I'd never known what to attribute their welcoming ways to – I wasn't sure I would do the same if I was in their situation – but I was thankful that they'd never taken their father's situation out on me.

"They like you too." She then let out a small laugh. "Of course, a lot of that is thanks to Jake."

"What do you mean?"

"Do you remember that first time they came over to the house and met you?"

"Yeah, I do. I was nervous as hell."

"Do you remember how cool they were towards you?"

"Yeah, how could I forget."

"Well, Jake sensed the same thing when they went back to see him that day and he told them to knock it off. He told them that you were a good guy and that you made me happy and that was all that should matter to them." I glanced over and saw that tears were running down her cheeks as she painted, causing the paint that was smeared on her one cheek to run down her face.

"That was nice of him," I said as I felt my own throat start to tighten up.

"Yeah," she whispered, "it was."

We continued to paint the wall, eyes forward, in silence.

My mind then started spinning with a kaleidoscope of images of people and events that had made up my past six months. The journey had been a wild one and the day with Jake in the park seemed like a perfect fit with the rest of my crazy life. Standing there, painting the wall with Marsha, I felt a sudden desire to get off the roller coaster and climb into the swan boats with Marsha so I could cruise through the more tranquil Tunnel of Love from that day onward. I craved peace and tranquility. I wanted a life that had more routine than hand grenades. To get there meant first shedding some baggage, I knew that. So, without much thought or inner debate, I blurted out something that had been locked away in a thick, steel safe for the past six months. I surprised myself with how quickly the words tumbled out. "I burned down my house," I said quietly without stopping the movement of my paintbrush or turning to face Marsha. The whole sentence came out smooth and easy, as if I was telling her that I had to go to the store or do some laundry. It was *after* the words came out that my heart started to pump furiously as I waited for her response.

Thankfully, she didn't make me stew in the silence for too long. "I know," she said just as calmly and quietly. Her head didn't turn, and she kept right on painting as she added, "I've known that from the beginning."

That response got me to drop my paintbrush. "You *knew?*" I replied incredulously. "How the hell did you know *that?*"

She kept on painting, never missing a beat. "Austin T told me his suspicions when he first started on your case." She shrugged. "Austin T may be an asshole but he's also a pretty damned good investigator. I believed him."

I didn't know what to say. So, I did what I normally did in these situations and sputtered on about several different things simultaneously. "But if you knew…" I began. "But what about…" I said in follow-up. And then came the grand finale, my one complete sentence. "Wait a minute," I said. "Are you saying that you trusted Austin T over me?" As it turns out, the answer to that question mattered most of all to me.

This is where she finally set her brush down and looked at me. "Listen Ben, everything about your behavior back then said "I'm guilty" so yeah, I trusted Austin T's instincts in this situation. As it turned out, both his and my instincts were correct." She let those words sink in for a while and then continued. "I didn't care that you burned your house down Ben. I still don't. What I do care about is what I told you many months ago and that is that I don't ever want you to lie to me." She bowed her head. "Lies can torch a relationship just as quickly as you torched your house." Her comparison worked perfectly as I felt spurts of guilt and regret spraying my insides.

"I don't know what to say," I replied, which was the truth. But that didn't stop me from trying. "I'm sorry that I lied to you," I began tentatively. "But I didn't see that I had any choice because of where you worked. I didn't want to put you in an awkward position with your job and I didn't want you to have to choose between me and your job."

"So why are you telling me now?" she asked quietly.

I thought about my answer to this question very carefully because I knew that the next words out of my mouth would decide the course of my life from that moment onward. Finally, feeling confident that I'd found the right words, I said, "Because I love you, Marsha. I love you and I want to spend the rest of my life with you. I feel like my life is beginning again right now and I don't want any secrets getting between me and this new life." I heaved a deep sigh and then continued. "I'm tired. I'm tired of fighting, I'm tired of lying, and I'm tired of everything being so damned hard." I reached up and placed my hand on her shoulder, rubbing it gently. "I'm ready for easy. And I want this new, easier life to be right by your side. Always."

She looked at me and considered my face for a few moments – her eyes betraying nothing about what she was feeling – and then a small smile started forming at the corner of her mouth. "Good answer," she muttered.

Relief coursed through me. I stepped closer to her and put my hands on her hips. "It's easy when it's the truth."

She wagged a finger at me and flashed me a look of mock anger. "Remember that."

I smiled. "I will. Don't you worry about that."

"One more question for you."

"Shoot."

"Did you mean what you said to Chris at the church, about not ever getting divorced?"

The question caught me by surprise. She had heard part of that conversation after all. I could have bought myself a little more time by playing stupid about what exactly she was asking, but I knew exactly what she was asking, and it was no time to be playing stupid. "Yeah, I did."

"Does that mean that you wish that you'd never divorced Linda?"

Marsha wasn't dancing around her feelings and I owed it to her to not dance around mine. The Truth Fest continued. "Yeah, I wish that Linda and I had never gotten to the point that divorce felt like our only option. I say that for a lot of reasons but more than anything else I wish that for Kylie. She deserved better from me." My eyes left Marsha's and went to the wall behind her. I could feel tears starting to nudge at my ducts. "I know without a doubt that I'm a zillion times better than The Worm in the father department, even with all my faults, and it kills me to think about him having such a large impact on my little girl's life." I'd never said those words so honestly and straight-forwardly before and it felt good to say them without all the accompanying anger, sarcasm, and other stuff that usually hung on them, all of which just served to mask the one truth that was hiding behind it all: I missed being around my daughter. Big time.

I let out a small exhale and my eyes returned to Marsha's. I could see that small patches of hurt and doubt had started to infect her eyes. "But," I then said emphatically, "the fact remains that I *am* divorced and for the first time since the split I can honestly say that I'm okay with that." I mustered up all the emotion I could and sent it out through my eyes to Marsha's eyes; it was important that she saw, and felt, what I was about to say next. "Linda and I are done. The last shovelful of dirt has been tossed on the grave where our relationship is buried. There was a time not too long ago when I couldn't have said those words, but a lot has happened recently that has gotten me to see that truth." I reached up, grabbed Marsha's shoulders, and squeezed them tight. "You are the only woman who matters to me now, Marsha. I know that without even a fraction of a doubt." I then said the two words that a few weeks ago could have never left my mouth with any kind of conviction, but that now came marching out like two pillars of stone, standing at attention between the two of us just as soon as they were uttered. "Trust me."

Her eyes quickly softened, and the same small smirk formed at one corner of her mouth. "Another good answer. You're on a roll."

I shrugged. "Like I said, it's easy when all you're doing is telling the truth."

She nodded emphatically as another unspoken "*remember that*" floated in the air above her head. "So, what's next for us?" she then asked.

I nodded at the wall. "First we finish up Jake's wall."

"And then?"

"We have a wonderful dinner with everyone tonight."

"And then?"

I felt my jaw set. "And then I tie up one last loose end." **Fuck the past,** I thought. **It's dead and gone.** I smiled as I picked up my paintbrush, knowing that Rule #9 For My New Life had just been created.

CHAPTER FIFTY-SIX

I drove in with Marsha to the Brown and Brown Insurance Company first thing Monday morning. I had stewed about the "What next?" question throughout the entire weekend and had, ultimately, settled in on a decision that centered on what would become Rule #10 For My New Life: *The easy way isn't always the best way.* The Rules were coming fast and furious now. The thread for this lesson wove all the way back to the moment that I decided to burn my house down and it was only now that all the ramifications for that decision were coming into focus for me. The new clarity that I was experiencing was thanks to a lot of people – Charlie, Griz, Jake, Marsha, and many others – and today was my day to honor their efforts; it was time to get my life back.

"You sure you don't want me to be in that meeting with you?" I heard Marsha ask me from the driver's seat.

I looked out the car window and saw that we'd arrived at our destination. I turned to her and forced a smile. "Yeah, I'm sure. Thanks though."

"I know Austin T better than you do and it might help to have me there."

I reached over and patted her leg. "You're right, it would be a big help, and it would make things a whole lot easier for me, I'm sure." I threw her an ironic grin. "But I've decided that the easy way isn't always the best way to do things. I need to do this myself."

She rubbed my hand. "Okay. You're the boss."

We climbed out of the car and walked into the front lobby together, hand in hand. It felt good to be telling the world that we were together as a couple. I noticed the secretary at the front desk – I'd forgotten her name – glance down at our hands as we walked in. "Good morning Mrs. Graves," she said as we approached the desk.

"Good morning Mrs. Halpin," Marsha replied. She then nodded in my direction. "Mr. Weaver here would like to talk with Mr. Phelps. Is he available?"

"Uh, I'm not sure. Let me check." She then picked up the phone and, once she had a connection, turned her back to us in an attempt at having a semi-private conversation with, I assumed, Austin T.

I glanced over at Marsha and she threw me a wink. I smiled at her and then leaned in to whisper, "What's with all the Mr. and Mrs. stuff? It makes me nervous."

She glanced over at Mrs. Halpin to make sure she was still preoccupied with her phone conversation, which she was, and then whispered back, "It's Mrs. Halpin. She has always insisted on maintaining that level of formality."

"Is she the boss?"

"No, but would you want to stand up to her and tell her anything different?"

I recalled my earlier interactions with Mrs. Halpin and then said, "No."

Marsha nodded and smiled. "Exactly."

We heard the phone click back into the receiver and we snapped back to attention. "Mr. Phelps says that he can see you shortly," Mrs. Halpin said formally. "If you have a seat, I will let you know when he's available." She waved her hand in the direction of the chairs on the other side of the lobby.

"Thank you," I replied. Marsha and I turned to walk towards the chairs but then I remembered something and turned back to Mrs. Halpin. "One last thing," I said.

"Yes?"

"I was just wondering how your husband was doing these days. Is he feeling better?"

She looked at me suspiciously at first but then her eyes registered sudden recognition and they softened. "Oh yes, I remember you now," she said almost semi-sweetly. "He's doing much better now. Thank you for asking." I detected a small twinkle in her eye and the faintest of smiles forming as she said her thank you to me.

"Glad to hear it," I replied with a warm smile. I then turned to head over to waiting area.

"What the heck was that all about?" Marsha whispered to me as we walked.

"Oh, just the fruits of an earlier lesson learned."

She just nodded, taking my vague answer at face value, and then said, "Well, it's time for this girl to get to work."

I turned and pulled her in close. I could see a small flash of trepidation run through her eyes and then she cast a quick sideways glance, perhaps to see who was watching us. But when her eyes came back to mine, they had a more determined set to them, and I knew that she had just used my magic word to wash away all her little fears and hesitations: *fucket*. I smiled at the thought of her using that word. "You okay?" I asked.

"Just great," she replied, and I believed her.

"Hope you have a great day."

"Same to you. Good luck in there with Austin T. Don't let him steamroll you."

"I won't." I hadn't yet told Marsha what it was that I wanted to talk to Austin T about; I thought it better that way. If she knew what I was about to tell him she wouldn't be worried about him steamrolling me. I smiled. "I'm steamroller-proof today."

She looked at me sideways, trying to read my face, but saw nothing so she simply said. "Call me when you're done in there, okay?"

I nodded. "I will." I then leaned in and planted a small kiss on her lips. "And thanks."

"For what? You wouldn't let me do anything."

"For understanding. And for supporting me even though you don't have a clue about what I'm about to do."

She gave me another sideways glance, this one accompanied by a suspicious smile. "And just what is it that you're about to do?"

I reached up and rubbed her cheek. "You'll know soon enough."

She glanced at her watch. "Okay, Mr. Vague and Mysterious, I really do have to go now." She stepped in, gave me a quick hug, and then turned to go. "Don't forget," she then said as she raised an invisible phone up to her ear.

"I won't," I promised.

After Marsha walked away, I sat down in one of the lobby chairs and got comfortable, figuring that Austin T would probably leave me out here to stew for a while. I picked up a magazine off the nearby table and pretended to read it. While I mindlessly flipped through the pages, I thought back on the weekend that had just passed. It had been an eventful one, in a good way, and all the events of the weekend had served to nudge me in the direction that I was currently headed.

More than anything else, it felt good to have the air completely clear between me and Marsha. Telling her about my arsonist past on Saturday had released a huge pocket of pressure that'd been messing up my insides – more than even I'd realized – and it allowed a burst of sunlight to come in through a newly opened window and shine down on our fledgling relationship. I felt hopeful about our future together.

The arson confession had also inspired me to search my internal attic for any other hidden boxes that I should bring out and open in front of her and I found a few, though none were as large as the ones that I'd already opened. The only box that remained tucked away at the end of the weekend was the box labeled "Jake." But that was a box that I felt good about leaving closed, because Marsha's wishes had been very clear on this one and, truth be told, I think she knew *exactly* what had happened with Jake, but she just didn't want to hear the words. Yet. Something told me that the Jake box would be getting opened at some point down the road, however, probably over a glass of wine and after enough time had passed that she could bear to hear the truth without all the guilt and sorrow adding extra weight to it. But for now, I was more than happy to keep those words from her and maintain the secret. It was the least I could do for her after all that she'd done for me.

The other part of the weekend that had provided a nudge for me was the dinner party with Marsha's clan. It had been a nice gathering, filled with lots of good food and good conversation, but it was a perfectly innocent question over dessert that had gotten my internal wheels turning. I had been sitting next to Marsha and her daughter, Nickie, during dinner but when we went into the living room for dessert, I ended up sitting next to Gene, Nickie's husband. That evening was the first time I'd met Gene and he seemed like a nice enough guy – young, earnest, and obviously deeply in love with his wife – and a guy who seemed to be genuinely interested in the people around him. A rare trait. It was this quality that probably inspired him to ask me the following question: "So Ben," he said jovially, "what is it that you do for a living?"

The next few moments went by in slow motion. The first thing I noticed was that Marsha and Nickie stopped serving dessert from the tray on a nearby coffee table and they both, in perfect unison, turned their heads in my direction with their mouths hanging open in slight shock. The next thing I noticed was all the air getting sucked out of the room. After that came the looks that were quickly exchanged between Gene, Marsha, and Nickie, looks that told me that poor Gene hadn't gotten the internal memo about not asking certain questions of the poor unemployed homeless guy. This realization – that I'd been talked about behind my back in that way – made me feel suddenly self-conscious. And embarrassed.

Knowing I had to say something in response to Gene's question, however, I shook off the feelings of embarrassment and replied, "I'm between jobs right now. I was a reporter for the Tribune for many years."

Under normal circumstances, Gene would have probably asked me several follow-up questions – about what type of reporter I'd been, what were some of my more memorable stories, why did I leave the newspaper, and the like – but after realizing that he had inadvertently stumbled into an unmarked mine field, all he could do was slowly back out of the situation as quickly, and carefully, as he could. "Uh, do you guys need any help over there?" he asked Nickie and Marsha.

"Yeah," Nickie replied quickly and oh-so-sweetly, "could you get us some more coffee cups from the kitchen, honey?"

Gene had sprung from his chair like a man set free from Death Row.

I'd glanced over at Marsha after he left but she pretended to be preoccupied with the dessert tray. It wasn't until later that night, in bed, that I got to ask my question. "What was that all about earlier tonight?" I asked her as we both adjusted the bed covers to our liking.

"What was what about?"

"The whole thing with Gene. The poor guy got both barrels from you guys and I want to know why."

"Oh, that." She finished adjusting the covers and then let out a small sigh. "I had just told Nickie and Sarah that your employment situation was a sensitive topic for you right now, that's all."

"You didn't."

"I did. Why? What's wrong with saying that? It's true."

"First of all, no it's not true. And secondly, nobody likes to have people talking about them behind their back. It makes me feel like some pitiful charity case who can't take care of himself."

"Sorry."

"Are you embarrassed by me, Marsha?"

That one got her attention. She turned her body, so she was facing me full on and said, "No, of course not. What would make you ask a question like that?"

I shrugged. "Just the fact that you felt the need to cover for me with your family. It makes me wonder if you're embarrassed by the truth about me."

This was when Marsha's tone had changed, going from soft and supportive to more forceful and matter-of-fact. "Listen, Ben. If anyone is embarrassed by your situation, it's you. You walk around with this apologetic air around you and you dodge and duck questions like a boxer ducks punches. So, if you're looking for people who aren't proud of who you are and what you're doing you should just go look in the mirror first."

Her words had caught me by surprise and if I were indeed a boxer, she would have scored a knockout. I was speechless for a while, secretly hoping that she might take back some of her words, but she didn't. All I could get out at that moment was, "Wow."

"I'm sorry if what I just said hurt you, Ben, but it's true. If you think about it, you'll see that I'm right." She then bent over, kissed me on the cheek, and then rolled over, turned off her light and went to sleep. And that was that.

And think about it I did; for several hours that night, laying there in the dark, and then all day on Sunday. And after all that thought I ended up coming to two conclusions: one, Marsha was right; and two, it was time to do something about it.

It was realization number two that had me sitting here in the lobby of Brown & Brown Insurance on this Monday morning, waiting to talk with Austin T.

He made me wait about a half hour before he finally came out to get me. "Mr. Weaver," he said in his best so-glad-to-see-you tone as he walked up to me. He extended his right hand in my direction and added, "To what do I owe the pleasure of this visit?"

Okay, now he was going a little over the top. Everything about him reeked of bullshit but I wasn't there to call him on it. Today's mission was different than that of prior visits; today there would be no harsh words, no verbal sparring, and no angry exits. Today was my day to take control of this situation that had been a sliver under my fingernail since the day I'd first met Austin T. I stood up and took his hand. "Thanks for seeing me on such short notice," I replied, ignoring all his fake pleasantries.

"No problem. Should we go back to a conference room?"

I noticed that he didn't offer up his office for our meeting, probably attributable to his fear that I might have another desk-clearing fit of rage and scatter his precious papers all over the place. I allowed myself a small private smile at the memory of that day. It had felt good, for sure, but there wouldn't be a repeat performance today. I brought my focus back to the present. "Sure, that sounds good."

He turned and started walking towards the back offices and I followed behind. As we passed the front desk Mrs. Halpin and I exchanged small smiles and nods, telling me that we were now friends. One small victory from my time spent at Brown & Brown. We made our way into a small conference room just down the hall and Austin T closed the door behind us. After we both got settled into a chair he leaned across the table, fingers folded just so, and asked, "So what brings you in here today?"

I noticed that his tone had changed ever-so-slightly; gone was the I'm-your-best-friend joviality and in its place was a tone that was more professionally curt. His eyes betrayed his obvious dislike, and mistrust, of me and now that we were alone in the room, he could let his true feelings shine through. That was good; it would make my task that much easier. I shifted in my seat and then said, "I've come here to withdraw the claim on my house." Simple, clear and right to the point.

Austin T's face went through a series of different expressions. He started with confusion, looking as if he wasn't sure his ears had heard my words clearly. Then, realizing that he had indeed heard what I'd just said, he appeared to look a little hurt or disappointed. I wasn't sure what that was all about until a few seconds later. That look disappeared quickly, however, and was replaced with a look of steely-jawed determination and anger. That was the look that he settled on as he said, "You can't do that."

Now it was my turn to be confused. And, yeah, a little bit pissed off. "Excuse me?" I replied, trying with all my strength to keep Ben The Smart Ass out of this discussion. He was pulling at his leash, wanting to jump into the fray and go for Austin T's throat. But I kept him in check. For now.

"You can't withdraw your claim because there's a strong potential that a crime was committed in relation to the burning down of your house."

He said all the words in a Joe Friday just-the-facts-ma'am staccato, as if he was reading me my rights, and I could feel the raw anger bubbling up inside me. I took a calming breath and said, "A crime? If there were any crime committed, and you had facts to back up that claim, we both know that I wouldn't be sitting here right now. So, spare me the bullshit and just get me the paperwork to withdraw my claim." I had to admit that the swear word had felt good coming off my tongue; it was a small, delicious bone that I'd tossed to Ben The Smart Ass and it made him happy as hell.

We sat there in a small-scale macho stare-down for a while and then I noticed the look of disappointment slowly return to Austin T's face. It was then that it hit me: he was disappointed that he wouldn't get to continue the hunt. He was being forced to lower his gun and allow the wounded buck – which would be me in this case – to run back into the woods and there wasn't a damned thing he could do about it. He was powerless to continue the pursuit, to apply the eventual death blow, and that went against everything he believed in. It was then that a small smile began to form in my gut; Ben The Smart Ass was pissing his pants at the thought that we had officially turned the tables on Austin T and that we would get to be the sliver under *his* fingernail for a while. I tried to keep the smile in my gut from moving up to my face.

He eventually dropped his eyes and, without saying another word, got up and left the room. I could tell by the way that he had thrown his chair back, and then slammed the door, that he was not a happy man. The smile crept up my throat and slowly worked its way across my face. It felt good to be in control.

As I sat there, I realized that there was a part of me that had been holding out a small, irrational hope that my conversation with Austin T would have gone differently. It was the part of me that still liked to take the easy way out and that part of me had been hoping to hear Austin T say something along the lines of, "But I was just getting ready to cut you a check!" in response to my request to withdraw my claim. Silly, I know. But that part of me – the part that had hatched the whole torch-my-house plan in the first place – was now, thankfully, out of the driver's seat and he'd been replaced by a self who knew that a large settlement check from Brown & Brown Insurance Company would not solve all my life's problems. As a matter of fact, this new self who was at the helm of my life's ship knew that all that money, if it had come to me without a hitch many months ago, would have surely created more problems for me than it would have solved. There would have been no Charlie, no Griz, and certainly no Marsha. The smile broadened across my face. *The easy way is not always the best way.*

Austin T came storming back into the room, his disappointment having obviously morphed back into anger, and he tossed a piece of paper onto the table in front of me. "Sign this," he said curtly.

I looked down at the paper and then back up at him as he hadn't bothered to sit down again. "Do you happen to have a pen?" I asked as sweetly as I could.

With a loud huff and a roll of his eyes he reached into his shirt pocket and pulled out a pen. "Here," he said with as much contempt as he could possibly squeeze into that one word.

"Thank you," I said with a smile as I took the pen. I looked at the pen and saw that it was engraved with his name and the words "Top Broker 2004" on the side. I pointed at the words and nodded my approval but all he gave me in return was a muffled "hmph" sound. I scanned the short document, saw that it would do exactly what I wanted it to do, and then signed it at the bottom. I then set the pen on top of the paper and stood up.

What I did next was something that I would have never predicted in a kajillion years, especially if you had asked me a couple of months ago, but I knew that it had to be done. I extended my hand to Austin T and said, "I just want to say thank you." He suddenly looked like he had just gotten a bullet to the forehead as his jaw dropped and his eyes went wide with shock. "I know that we didn't get along at times," I then added, which may be the biggest understatement that's ever passed from my lips, "but I want you to know that I don't blame you for anything that's happened and I don't hold any ill will towards you for holding back my check." I stopped and thought for a moment, then added, "As a matter of fact, believe it or not you helped me in more ways than you'll ever know, and more than a settlement check ever possibly could have. Your delaying of the check bought me some time to realize some things that I wouldn't have seen on my own." I waggled my extended hand to get his attention and said, "So I just want to shake your hand before I go and say thanks."

The shock never left his face as he raised his right hand in an almost zombie-like fashion and shook my hand. He didn't say a word.

I looked him in the eye, shook his hand one more time, and said, "Thanks. For everything." I waited for him to say something, but no words were forthcoming, so I dropped his hand and walked out of the room. Austin T was now where I'd wanted him to be for a long, long time: in my rearview mirror. The Austin T Phelps chapter had officially ended, and I couldn't wait to get started on a life without him in it.

CHAPTER FIFTY-SEVEN

Marsha was a little pissed that I'd taken such a huge step without first consulting her, but after I explained the reasoning behind my decision to cut all ties with Austin T and the house she understood. "You're certainly not one to let any moss grow under your feet, are you?" she'd said after a lengthy conversation on the topic.

I chuckled at that observation because it wasn't too long ago that I was King of the Moss Growers; as a matter of fact, it was those very same moss-growing skills that contributed to my divorce from Linda. She'd called me a "cynical creature of routine" at one point towards the end of our marriage, when the gloves had come off and we weren't hesitating to say anything at all to each other, no matter how hurtful the words might have been. Those words had stung at the time – though I of course didn't let *her* know that – but all they did now was make me smile. She'd been right about me then and Marsha was also right about me now. "No, not any more," I'd responded to Marsha's observation. "And that's why I have one more thing that I have to do."

It was a couple of days later when I found myself walking up the front sidewalk to Linda's house. I hadn't called ahead to let anyone know that I was coming because I didn't want to have any expectations buzzing around my visit; I wanted it to be a complete surprise. I knocked on the door and, judging from The Worm's face when he answered my knock, he was indeed surprised. "Good morning," I said cheerfully.

His look of surprise quickly became one of apprehension as he replied, "What the hell are *you* doing here?"

Stay cool, Ben. I shrugged and put on my best casual tone as I replied, "Just decided to stop by for an impromptu visit."

His look hardened. "Well Linda's at work and Kylie's at school so you're out of luck today."

Perfect. I knew that would be the case and I also thought I'd remembered Linda telling me one time that The Worm didn't have any classes on Wednesdays, which meant that there would be a good chance that he'd be home this morning. Alone. "Actually, I'm not here to see them today. I'm here to see you, William."

I don't know if it was the fact that I was standing on his doorstep claiming that I was there to see him and only him, or if it was my use of his proper first name, but the look of surprise returned to The Worm's face. "What…why…" he sputtered at first. But then he gathered himself and said, "What is it that you want from me?"

I noticed the dark cloud of suspicion covering his face, as if he was trying to figure out what exactly I was up to and perhaps stay one step ahead of me. His efforts, though understandable, would be futile because there was no way in hell he would be able to anticipate what was about to come his way. "I'm here to say that I'm sorry," I said as clearly as I could so there would be no mistaking my words.

"You're…what?"

I had figured that it would take a couple of attempts for my words to sink in; there had, after all, been many years of insults, mistrust, and anger built up between us and it can take a while to dig through a pile of shit that deep. "I'm sorry," I repeated. "For everything. For all the insults I've tossed your way, for all my snide remarks, and all my lousy behavior. I'm sorry for all of it."

He looked from side to side as if he was expecting somebody else to jump out of the bushes. "Is this some kind of joke?"

I shook my head. "Nope, no joke. I'm dead serious, William."

"Could you stop using my real name? It's making me nervous."

I smiled. "Sorry about that. None of the other names I've used in the past seem to fit anymore and that's the only other name that I know to use."

He returned the smile, though it was a tentative one. "How about using Bill instead. That will send fewer chills up my spine."

I nodded. "Bill it is then. From this day onward."

His body language changed slightly as he stood there in the doorway, opening up more and showing less mistrust. "What's up with you, Ben?"

The fact that he used my first name told me that he was thawing a bit. That was good. I shrugged. "I just realized that it was time." I paused for a beat before continuing, "Time for us to put all of the shit behind us, time for us to stop beating up on each other, and time for us to realize that we both have the same goal."

"Which is?"

"To love Kylie and Linda the best way we know how."

He smiled and nodded. "A good goal. And one that I agree with."

"Good. That's step one." I saw his eyebrow rise slightly, telling me that he was curious about steps two, three, and beyond, so I continued. "The next step is for me to tell you the truth."

"About what?"

"About why I've always given you so much shit and why I've always hated your guts." These last words got his attention and I could see some of the apprehension creeping back into his eyes so I plowed ahead before he could duck back into his protective shell. But first I took a deep breath and let it out slowly; these

411

next words were going to be the hardest ones to say. "Truth is, I was pissed off at Linda all these years and you got to be the punching bag for that anger. I was pissed at her for choosing to end our marriage and I was pissed at her for deciding that without getting my input first." I drew another deep breath. "And I want you to know that I forgive you for sleeping with my wife while we were still married."

Those last words buzzed between us for a while, like a swarm of angry hornets, and I could see that Bill's first impulse was going to be to start swatting at the hornets and attempt to shoo them away. This truth – that Linda and Bill had slept together before she and I had officially separated – had never been uttered between any of us so I'm sure it was more than a little shocking to him to have it thrown in his face like this. They had probably worked out their own version of the truth regarding the initial days of their partnership – a version that didn't include words like "cheating" and "adultery" – so they could go on feeling good about themselves and their relationship. But truth was truth, and the undeniable truth was that Linda was still living under our roof, as a wife and mother, when she decided to take that first step through the doorway marked Life Without Ben. That was a fact, and it wasn't until this moment, standing there with William, that I verbalized that. It felt good, kind of like the good that you feel when you stick a needle into a puss-filled boil; it hurts more than a little bit, but the overwhelming feeling is one of relief because all of that built up pressure was being released from behind the boil.

Bill didn't say anything for a long time, which was actually just fine with me, because his silence was actually an acknowledgment of the truth that I'd just tossed at him; if I had said these same words a few months ago we would have probably been clanging verbal swords now, each of us trying to find an opening to deliver the death blow. His silence marked progress. Feeling emboldened, I plunged forward with what I saw as the next important step in our move towards a more harmonious relationship. "I'll take your silence as a thank you," I began, being sure to smile in a way that assured him I wasn't trying to be flip or sarcastic. Seeing that I still had his attention, I said, "The next important step for us Bill is to talk about Kylie." I could feel the tingling in my cheeks as I said her name. *Hold it together, Ben*, I said to myself; I didn't want to start bawling in front of The Worm.

I'd never talked directly to The Worm about my daughter, always feeling like to do so would somehow legitimize his connection with her and that was the absolute last thing I ever wanted to do. He had always been nothing more than an intruder in Kylie's life – a temporary one at that, in my mind – and to discuss her with him in any way would give him a measure of power that I wasn't ready to give up to him. I was her father and should therefore be *the* man in her life up until the day that I handed her over to her husband on her wedding day. There wasn't any room for a third person in the father-daughter relationship that I'd forged in my head and there certainly wasn't any room for the man who had slept with my wife and who'd contributed to the destruction of my marriage. That was how I'd always felt, and I felt nothing but justified for feeling that way. Until now.

I could see now that no matter how angry I got, and no matter how justified I felt for my anger, the fact would remain that I was no longer the only man in Kylie's life – I wasn't even living with her anymore for crissakes – and the best that I could hope for was to try to make the situation as easy as possible for Kylie. It was time to stop thinking about me and my own bitter feelings and instead try to focus on the impact that all the fighting and anger was having on the young, innocent victim who was sitting quietly on the sidelines. The tingling feeling returned to my cheeks. I took in a slow, deep breath, held it for a few seconds, and then blew it out slowly. This was going to be hard.

"What about Kylie?" I heard The Worm ask me.

Slow and steady, Ben. "Kylie is *the* most important person in my life, Bill," I began. "And because she's that important to me, I am always thinking about her happiness and well-being."

"Me too," he interjected. "I…"

That's as far as I let him go before cutting him off with an upraised hand. "Please don't say anything just yet." I lowered my hand. "I need to get this all out before I have any second thoughts or before I do something stupid like punching you in the nose." That shut him up. I took another deep breath and continued. "Ever since you came into my family's life, I've viewed you as an arrogant prick who wasn't worthy of the love and affection of my wife and daughter." I shrugged. "That's the truth." I watched as The Worm opened his mouth to say something, then think better of it and swallow whatever words he'd had on his tongue. I had to hand it to him: this had to be pure torture for him and yet he was just taking it on the chin without a complaint, and without slamming the door in my face. Good for him.

"Because I saw you as an unworthy prick," I continued, "I saw it as my duty to protect Kylie from you and your prickiness." I flashed a small internal smile at my new word. I raised my hand again. "Please don't take offense to any of this, Bill. I know it's hard to hear right now, but trust me when I tell you that all of this has to come out so I can get to the better stuff that's hiding behind it." He nodded his assent, though I could tell by the set of his eyes and jaw that it was a grudging assent. I lowered my hand and returned the nod before continuing. "You gotta understand what it feels like to be the father in this situation." My vision suddenly went blurry. *Shit, don't cry!* Then an old friend came swooping in and with the power of his one magic word he let me know that it was okay to show The Worm the full depth and breadth of what I was feeling. *Fucket,* I whispered into my internal ear. So, I kept talking, no longer worried about keeping my emotions in check. "She's my little girl, Bill." This brought more tears. "She's the reason I get out of bed every morning, and she's the last thing I think about every night before I close my eyes." I took a deep breath. "I've fucked up everything else in my life so far and I don't want to fuck this up too. I want to be a good father to Kylie, in every way, and that means protecting her from unnecessary pain and anguish whenever I can. I can't shield her from everything, but I sure as hell am going to take the bullets for her whenever I can."

I took one small step closer to The Worm; I had to make sure he understood, fully, the depth and breadth of my next words. "I need you to hear this next part, Bill." I shook my head violently, surprising even myself with the levels of emotion that were bubbling out of me. "Make no mistake about it, I am not a violent man by nature, but I can, and will, do *whatever* it takes to protect my daughter." I paused to allow the possibilities of "whatever" to infiltrate his brain and then, channeling all of my emotion through my eyes and into his, I said, "You'd better take good care of her, Bill. I mean that. For better or worse, you're another father figure to my little girl" – those words were like a knife to my gut, but I knew they had to be said – "and that means knowing that everything you say, and everything you do, is going to impact her in some way." I raised my index finger and wagged it at him. "Always remember that."

He nodded solemnly. "I will," he croaked.

I could tell that I had his full attention. Good. "If we don't have any problems in that area then we probably won't have any problems, Bill. What happens between you and Linda is none of my business and how you live your lives is up to you. All I care about is Kylie at this point; you do right by her, and you'll be doing right by me." I shrugged. "Simple as that."

I could see his face relax a little bit. "Understood."

He seemed to get it, so I decided that it was time for a little levity. "Are you sure you're up to life with a teenage girl?" I asked with a wry smile.

He must not have seen my smile because his look stayed fairly somber when he replied, "I don't know. I'll do my best." I half-expected a "sir" to tumble out of his mouth as he looked like a scared soldier addressing his commanding officer.

I slapped him on the back. "You can relax now, Bill. The heart-to-heart is over. I think you understand what I was trying to say, right?"

He heard the silent *"at ease, soldier"* and his shoulders dropped; I thought I could actually hear his ass un-puckering. "Yeah, I get it," he said, trying to get the old swagger back into his voice, but he failed miserably; fear still shaded the edges of his words.

"Good. Now we can all just be one big, happy extended family from this day onward."

"If you say so," he mumbled. The realization of just how intimidated, and afraid, he'd been seemed to be settling in to his gut and he didn't seem to like how it was feeling.

The Worm was a proud man, despite his jello-like spine, and I could see this whole episode making him angry if he dwelled on it for too long. Not wanting that to happen – and thus losing all the ground that we'd just gained – I said, "Look Bill, I know I'm not the easiest guy in the world to get along with sometimes." I smiled. "It's a character flaw that I'm working on." A small harrumph of agreement fell out of his mouth. "Part of that work that I'm doing involves being more honest with the people around me." I nodded in his direction. "And you're one of those people." *Okay, time to kick off the training wheels,* I thought. "Linda picked you over me," I blurted out. "She picked you over me," I then repeated, quieter this time. *Focus.* I ignored the echo in my ears of the words I'd just spoken – words that I'd never uttered before – and said, "I say that to you now because it's important to remember that I didn't *choose* any of this, Bill. It was all chosen *for* me and I've been forced to play catch-up with all the choices that were being made around me. Well, I'm just now catching up on some of the bigger things that have happened and that can only make life easier for everyone." I smiled. "I know I'm a little slow on the uptake, and a little thick in the head, but I finally got there." *A little self-deprecating humor should help soothe some of his wounds,* I thought.

My words seemed to help as the hurt and anger drained from his eyes and he said, "Yeah, you are."

My smile broadened, hopefully telling him that the coast was now clear. It was now time to change the subject. "So, any big plans today?"

He shook his head. "Nope. Just have to do some work out here in the yard to get the garden beds in shape."

I cringed. I thought back on all the years of back-breaking work I'd put into this yard, to get it just the way I wanted it, and how I was then forced to hand it off to someone who didn't care about it or know shit about any of it. I swallowed my feelings and asked, "So how are the rose bushes doing around in back?"

He shrugged. "They seem to be doing okay. Linda had me prune the hell out of them last fall."

I nodded. "Yeah, you gotta do that with roses." I swallowed again and then added, "Try spreading some bone meal around them this spring. It encourages the bushes to produce more flowers."

"Thanks for the tip. I'll give it a try." He then inadvertently asked the very same question that had placed poor Gene in Nickie and Marsha's doghouse a few nights earlier. "So, what are you doing for work these days, Ben?"

It was meant as a casual, throwaway question and I was surprised to discover that I took it that way; if The Worm had asked me that same question a couple of months earlier, I would have been all over him. I was also surprised by the words that came out of my mouth and just how calmly they were said. "I'm working at the Y," I replied without hesitation, "helping out with a group called Teens Rule."

He nodded as he considered what he'd just heard. And then, bless his heart, he simply asked, "Do you enjoy it?"

The final surprise came as I replied, "Yeah, I do." And I meant it.

We stood there and shuffled our feet uncomfortably for a few minutes, struggling to find suitable topics for small talk, but then, realizing that this new relationship of ours was much too young to support small talk, I raised my hand and said, "Well, Bill, it's time to say goodbye. Thanks for listening."

He took my hand and shook it gently. "So long, Ben. Thanks for coming by."

I looked him square in the eye, flashed him a warm smile, and gave his hand one more squeeze. Between men, the handshake said everything that needed to be said. No words were necessary. From this day onward Bill and I would be starting the next, hopefully more civil, phase of our relationship.

I headed down the steps, threw him one more wave over my shoulder, and then began my walk back home as I heard the door shut behind me. As I walked, I was struck by just how light I felt; it was as if my entire chest had been filled with helium and it was all I could do to keep my feet on the ground. I knew that I'd been holding in a lot of bitterness and anger towards The Worm but, judging from the current lightness of my being, it had been a helluva lot more than even I had realized. It felt good to have dumped the load. It was then, while walking home, that I formulated my final Rule For My New Life. This was a biggie and so I gave it a big name: *"Charlie's King Fucket Rule."* It would be the one that would give me the final push necessary to begin this New Life that I'd been talking and dreaming about all these years since the divorce. It was both simple and obvious in so many ways and yet it had proven to be elusive as hell, thanks to both my pride and my stubbornness. Only now did I see it for what it was: a necessary step towards reclaiming my life. I felt a breeze of relief waft through my insides as I saw how fortunate I was to have realized all of this while there was still time to do something about it. I looked up to the sky and whispered a quiet "Thank you, Charlie." I owed the man my life. I continued walking, and even started whistling a mindless tune, as I contemplated Charlie's "*King Fucket Rule*":

Forgiveness is the biggest Fucket of all.

Amen.